FORGED IN BLOOD
FORGED
BOOK ONE

KITT FIONA

Copyright © 2025 Crystal Ying
All rights reserved.
The characters and events portrayed in this book are fictitious. Any similarity to real people, living or dead, is coincidental and not intended by the author.
No part of this book may be reproduced, stored in a retrieval system, or transmitted in any means, electronic, mechanical, photocopying, recording, or otherwise, without the express written permission of the author.
ISBN: 979-8-9943656-0-1
Ebook ISBN: 979-8-9943656-1-8
KDP ISBN: 979-8-9943656-2-5

Cover design by: Markee Books
Printed in the United States of America

 Formatted with Vellum

*For the survivors, the fighters.
For those who endured what never should've happened.
You're not broken. You're not alone. You are worthy.*

TRIGGER WARNINGS

This story includes content that may be potentially triggering. If any of the following is triggering for you, please do not read this book. Reader discretion is advised.

Triggers: Abuse, child abuse, domestic violence, drugs, rape, humiliation, grief and loss, murder, crime, guns, knives, daggers, trauma, violence, animal dissection (in a biology lab)

CONTENTS

Prologue	1
1 Just Another Day	3
2 Eighteen	12
3 Grace	20
4 Ashthorne	30
5 Lucian	43
6 First Taste	53
7 Ashthorne Hall	61
8 Fight Or Flight	73
9 Truth Of The Heir	81
10 Blackmoore Academy	89
11 Blackmoore Four	100
12 Assholes	112
13 Survive	122
14 Welcome	135
15 Recon	140
16 Sablehall	146
17 Pressure	158
18 Rage	162
19 Ghost	164
20 All For One	174
21 One For All	187
22 New Hair, Who This?	197
23 A Kiss To Remember	207
24 Boys, Boys, Boys	218
25 First Steps	227
26 Halloween	236
27 Cry Me A River	244
28 Aftermath	256
29 Free	264
30 The Cage	270
31 Fighter	279

32 War	291
33 The Crucible	302
34 Finally	312
35 The One Who Listens	321
36 The Cold Prince	326
37 Ready Or Not	328
38 Here We Go	334
39 Forged In Blood	343
Forged in Betrayal - Coming in 2026	353
Acknowledgments	355
About the Author	357

PROLOGUE

The kitchen smelled like strawberries and batter. That's the first thing I remember — the way the air clung to my skin, warm and sweet, like something magic. My feet stuck to the floor with every step, pulling up little popping sounds as I chased the sunbeams across the linoleum. The radio was playing something old and full of horns, fuzzy and skipping every few seconds like it was trying to remember how the song went.

Mama sang along anyway, off-key and loud. She held a wooden spoon like a microphone and danced around the kitchen like it was a stage. Dada watched her from the stove, smiling and tapping his foot to the beat.

"Gracie, how many waffles would you like?" Dada asked.

"Five, please!" I held up my hand to show him. "Like me!"

He nodded, turning back to the stove. "Exactly right, my smart girl. Five waffles coming right up!"

"Watch out!" Mama said as she spun past me in her socks, arms flung wide as if she could fly. "Crazy woman on the loose!"

"You'd better catch her before she flies away, Gracie!" Dada warned.

I giggled and threw up my arms to block her, laughing when she scooped me up instead and spun me around. The light blue walls blurred with the white cabinets. I felt like we were spinning through the sky.

"Faster, Mama!"

"If I go any faster, we'll both take off," she said, eyes shining.

Her laughter bounced off the walls. I remember thinking it was the prettiest sound in the world. Prettier than music. Prettier than birds singing outside the window. Better than anything that came from cartoons. It sounded like something that would never stop. She smelled like vanilla lotion and cinnamon, and a little like the cigarette she'd left in the sink, forgotten.

"You girls relax. I'll bring the food out shortly." Dada continued to hum to the radio.

I pressed my face to Mama's shoulder as she carried me to the couch and flopped down with a dramatic sigh.

"I'm pooped!" she announced. "We are never cooking again!"

"But Mama, we weren't cooking. Dada was!"

"Excuse me?" She gasped. "You talking back to me, little missy? Oh, I'm going to get you!" She tickled my sides.

I shrieked and laughed until I could barely breathe. She kissed my hair and pulled me close. I grinned and snuggled closer.

Her arms wrapped around me, warm and familiar. She always held tight. Like she didn't want to let go, even when she had to.

"Isobel, I have a secret," she whispered into my ear.

"What is it, Mama?" I whispered back.

"You are my absolute favorite person in the whole wide world." She smiled down at me.

"You told me that yesterday." I giggled.

"Well," she said, brushing a strand of hair from my forehead, "it's still true today, and will remain true forever."

"I love you, Mama."

"I love you, my sweet Isobel."

1 JUST ANOTHER DAY

"You stupid fucking bitch!" his voice travels down the hallway. A glass breaks, a chair gets knocked over, a dull thud, then back to the tense silence.

I sigh as the warmth of the dream melts away like cotton candy on my tongue. My chest aches whenever I dream of that time with Mama. I remember her words, even though I didn't fully understand them. How the sunlight hit her face, how it caught in her hair, and how I thought she looked like a glowing angel.

I thought the world would always be that small. Just us, a messy kitchen, and music we could dance to. I didn't know people could break. That sometimes they disappear without ever leaving. That love can curdle and laughter can fade like smoke. Sometimes, when I close my eyes, I go back to that moment. To her heartbeat under my cheek.

To the last time she felt like home.

As I sit up slowly, the worn spring mattress creaks beneath me. When my feet hit the floor, the cold zips up my leg and goosebumps erupt in their wake. My shoulder throbs, and my shirt is stuck to my back. I can't help but wince as I slowly peel the shirt away from the cuts.

The air smells stale and sour with mildew. Early morning light leaks through the duct tape and grime that cover the window, casting the room in that ugly yellow light. The walls are yellow too, but not the nice kind like sunshine or buttercream. It's the kind of yellow that looks like it used to be white, before water and nicotine stains ate through it.

I stand slowly, my body aching. Some of it old, some of it new, some pains will never go away. Most of which I don't want to think about. I lift my shirt and look in the cracked mirror that sits against the wall. The bruise on my ribs is turning green around the edges. There's a darker purple one across my stomach, with faint finger marks along my arm.

What little clothes I have are stored on broken hangers in the closet, if you can even call it that. Different hoodies and shirts from the lost and found, a couple were stolen. Two pairs of jeans, and a pair of forgotten sweatpants I swiped from a bench in the locker room. One pair of jeans fits for the most part, but I can't button up since the button is gone, and the other I've been wearing for two weeks straight. Nothing matches. None of it is really mine.

I grab a t-shirt and a black hoodie, sniffing it before pulling it on. I pull on the same jeans because I don't really have much of a choice.

"Celia!" his voice booms throughout the small house. "What the fuck is this?"

I can't hear Mama's reply, but a few seconds later, a door slams.

"Did you just slam my fucking door?" Heavy footsteps pound down the hall like drumbeats in my ears, warning me of the inevitable danger.

I grab my backpack and slip out of the window before the footsteps get too close.

The walk to school takes twenty minutes. I cut through the gas station and through an alley full of broken glass from a busted window.

By the time I make it to school, I'm still thirty minutes early. I make my way to the girls' bathroom on the far side where no one goes. The last sink, farthest from the door, doesn't squeal the entire time the water is on. I rinse my face with ice-cold water. Brush my teeth with a dollar-store toothbrush, bristles fried from use, and a travel toothpaste that is just about out.

The door creaks open, and I don't have to turn to look.

"You look like hell."

I glance up to meet her eyes in the mirror. "Good morning to you too, Maeve."

Maeve hops up on the counter beside me. She's wearing different colored socks, a hoodie that she is swimming in, and her blonde curls have been shoved underneath a beanie that has a faded middle finger patch on it. Her eyeliner is smudged like she went to sleep with it on. Probably did. She digs through her bag and holds out a roll of mints.

"Picked these up for you, just in case you get tired of that off-brand cinnamon flavor."

I pocket them with a silent nod of thanks.

"Your eye is a little puffy," she says with a shrug. "Just say the word, I'll key his car."

Rummaging through my busted backpack, I dig out the dollar-store concealer I managed to steal and begin patting the concealer gently over the bruising on my jaw.

"I'm fine."

Maeve rolls her eyes like always.

I fish out the plastic comb, missing a couple of teeth, out of my bag and start trying to detangle the birds' nest on my head. The light flickers overhead like fluorescent hell, but still better than home. I quickly give up trying to tame my ash brown hair and pull it back into a messy bun.

"Did you do the history assignment?" she asks, digging through her hoodie pocket for a stick of gum, ripping it in half, and handing me one side.

I pop it in my mouth. "Didn't get the chance."

She pulls hers out and hands it to me. I copy it as quickly as possible. Half of me expects a teacher to come in and bust me, but the other half knows no one will. They never do.

Maeve and I have been friends for years. Most kids didn't want to hang out with the kid who wore the same dirty clothes for weeks at a time. Maeve offered me her juice box one day at lunch, and we've been like sisters ever since.

Maeve fidgets with the string on her hoodie and chews her gum as I copy the homework. This is what friendship looks like when you're surviving. A half-used assignment. A mint. A place to brush your teeth without being touched.

"You know you can always stay at mine, right? My mom already said it's fine. I have blankets and pillows to make a cot for you in my room, or you can sleep on the couch."

Maeve says this at least once a week without fail. I love her and her mom for being there for me, but I never take them up on it.

"I can't," I mumble, handing her back her assignment.

"You can," her voice is sharp, "you just won't."

"She needs me."

Maeve scoffs, "She needs rehab, and your stepdad needs a one-way ticket to a shallow grave."

I flinch at her words.

"Sorry," she mutters, "you know I just hate seeing you like this."

"I know."

The silence stretches, loaded with all the things we know the other will say.

"She was better before," I whisper. "Before him."

Maeve's eyes soften as she nods. I sling my backpack over my shoulder just as the bell rings

"Well, no matter what happens, you know I've got you."

I smile back at her and squeeze her arm.

"If you change your mind, though, just come. No questions, no explanations needed. I'll leave my window unlocked." She nudges me gently.

I nod. I won't go, and she knows it.

AT LUNCH, Maeve hands me the extra sandwich her mom always makes for me. Peanut butter and jelly, a little squished, wrapped in wax paper.

"Tell her thanks," I mumble, taking a bite.

Maeve shrugs. "She already knows."

I take my time eating only half, drinking water from the bottle I always refill at the water fountain. I wrap back up the other half and stash it in my hoodie pocket for dinner.

After the last bell, I head to the gym, and Maeve meets me outside. The locker room is always empty this time of day, and, if I time it right, I can shower before any of the girls come back. Maeve keeps a look out for me, pretending to scroll on her phone and bobbing slightly to the music playing in one ear.

I shower fast. The water is barely warm, and I use cheap soap that leaves my skin feeling dry. I inhale sharply as the water and suds run down my back, the cuts burning into me. Mumbling a curse, I push through the pain.

When I come out dressed, hair still dripping, Maeve tosses me my hoodie.

"Eight minutes," she says, "new record."

"Thanks." I smirk, pulling the hoodie back over me and tying my hair back.

"You know I'd pay good money to see you fight someone for being in here."

I giggle. "We don't have any money."

"True."

We head out together, wet hair clinging to my neck and making my hoodie damp. No matter what I do, I always feel like there's a thin layer of grime on my skin.

The sun's low by the time we leave campus, long shadows casting their marks over the cracked sidewalk. Everything has a hazy film like weak tea. My boots scuff the pavement as we walk, our shoulders brushing sometimes.

"So," Maeve drags the word out. "You're turning eighteen next week."

I make a noise that's not quite a groan but not really a response, either.

"I was thinking," Maeve continues undeterred, "we could do something fun. Maybe go to an arcade, sneak into a movie, break into the pool again."

"We never even got in the pool." I smile at the memory.

"No, but I nearly broke my ankle hopping the fence, so I think it still counts."

I sigh, "I wish I could, but –"

"You can." She bumps her shoulder against mine. "School will be out, you'll be free for the weekend, you could sleep over. Come on, Iz, we'll wear dumb clothes and pretend we're not from this shithole for a night."

"I can't, because my birthday is on Friday." My voice is quieter now, "You know how he gets when he gets paid."

Her mouth flattens into a tight line. "Right."

We walk in silence for a bit.

"Let's go to the mall during the day. I just need to make sure I'm back before him," I concede.

"I'll take that. I just don't want you spending your birthday alone."

The farther we walk, the uglier the houses get. The grass gets patchier and changes colors. I tug my sleeves down over my hands, shoving them in my hoodie pocket.

"If I showed up with a baseball bat, would you let me swing it?"

"Depends on who you aim it at." I chuckle when she shoots me a look.

"You know exactly who," she deadpans.

Truth is, I hate my birthday. It's never been about cake or candles or making wishes. It's just another night I hope to survive unscathed.

"Maybe next year." I sigh.

"Just saying, my window is always unlocked."

I nod as we head to the park between our houses. It has a rusted jungle gym, and the swings creak like they're haunted. The smeared graffiti on the slide says, *'Suck it, Kevin.'*

Maeve climbs up on the picnic table and stretches out, arms behind her head. I sit on the bench below her, my legs curled up. The air smells like grass and cigarette ash. Somewhere in the distance, a dog barks and a train blares its horn. It's peaceful.

"You ever think about what you want to do?"

I shrug. "Not really."

"Liar."

"I'm serious."

Maeve turns, her face thoughtful. "You ever think about leaving? Doing something bigger?"

"I try not to think about that. College costs money, so do cars, so does rent, and food, and breathing." I huff.

Maeve sits up, frowning at me. "Okay, but just like...pretend. Pretend none of that matters. What would you want to do?"

I bite the inside of my cheek as I think.

"I dunno, I'd just want a place where the door locks and have somewhere warm to sleep. Maybe get a dog." I shrug.

Maeve hums. "I'd visit you and bring you snacks. I'd also make sure the dog loved me more."

"He'd hate you on sight." I poke her.

"Yeah, right." We laugh.

She's quiet for a few seconds. "I think I'd want to open a little shop or something. Maybe a bookstore. With cute, mismatched vintage chairs and coffee. Maybe I'll get a cat and name him something punny."

"I could see that for you." I smile.

The sun's dipping behind the trees now, bleeding orange and red like the sky is on fire. I don't want to leave this moment. This bench, with this girl, and dreams of the future. Maeve nudges my foot.

"Gotta get going?"

"Yeah."

"Text me so I know you're good."

"I will."

My house sits like it's slumping under its own weight. The paint is peeling, the porch light is busted, and the screen door sits crooked. One of the front windows is cracked.

There's no car in the driveway. The porch groans under my feet. I steady myself at the door, taking a deep breath. The handle's sticky when I turn it.

The TV is on, too loud and too low, voices murmuring. The air smells like cigarettes, sweat, and cheap beer. I close the door softly behind me, and out of habit, I shrink my shoulders, tuck my head, and make my way through the house. I know exactly where to step to avoid any creaks. Past the TV, past the half-eaten microwave dinner on the arm of the couch, the overflowing ashtray and bottles that litter the floor.

Mama's in the corner of the room, half on the floor, half off the couch. One arm draped limply over the cushion, eyes closed. Her thin dull hair stuck to her cheek.

I peek in the kitchen to check for him. He's not here. The tightness in my chest eases.

There's a stain and a smear of something on her shirt. Her lips are pale and cracked, her breathing shallow.

"Mama," I nudge her. "Mama."

No answer.

I press two fingers to the base of her neck. Her pulse is weak, but it's there. Her chest rises shakily. I breathe out some relief.

She reeks of sweat, vomit, and the sour tang of alcohol. There's a crusted stain on the floor beside her, old bile. I pick her up off of the ground and drag her back onto the couch, positioning her on her side so she can't choke.

I gather the empty bottles and containers around the room, stacking them into a plastic bag I found under the sink. I empty the ashtray and throw out a broken mug. I grab a blanket and fold it over her.

No one will really care, but it gives me something to do. I can't even really remember the last time I had a conversation with my Mama.

I'm crouched on the floor, trying to clean the crusted bile when I hear the door slamming against the wall. I hear his keys jingle, a muttered curse, then his boots walking down the hall.

I freeze, wishing I could just vanish. I stay quiet, hoping if I'm small enough, he won't see me. The TV is still murmuring in the background.

"Celia!" he shouts, and as he turns the corner, his dark eyes land on me. I'm not sure what he sees.

"She threw up, I was just cleaning it up."

"Hmph."

I don't dare respond.

He walks past me, brushing my shoulder, and it takes everything in me not to flinch or move away. He leans over to stare at her, his dark, greasy hair falling over his eyes.

"Useless." He sneers, turning to me.

He grabs my chin, and his fingers dig into the bruises I've covered. I flinch without meaning to.

"Don't pull away from me, daughter." He spits the last word in my face.

I freeze, keeping my face blank and neutral.

"You clean up?"

"Yes, sir."

"Good girl." He says it like it should be a compliment. All it does is make my stomach turn.

"Go to your room, keep your goddamn mouth shut. If I hear even that floor creaking, you'll wish you were never born."

"Yes, sir." I turn and amble out of the room. I don't run. Running makes noise. I make it to my room and close the door, the click sounding behind me.

I sit down on my mattress. The frayed material from it never having had a sheet on it tickles my hands. The springs creak as I sit. I freeze again. I don't even breathe as I strain to listen for any noise.

I peel off my hoodie and change into a shirt to sleep in. It used to belong to my mama before she stopped caring about laundry. It still smells faintly like her before everything. Or maybe it's all in my head.

I lie back and tuck my knees to my chest. Outside, someone revs an engine too loudly, a dog barking. Then silence again.

I text Maeve.

> Me: All quiet.

> Maeve: Leaving the light on, just in case.

I want to believe there is a version where I take her up on that, but I know this one isn't it.

2 EIGHTEEN

*I*f I don't set any expectations, I can't be disappointed.

This birthday really doesn't mean anything, just one year closer to freedom.

The mall is still waking up by the time I arrive. I sit at one of the empty tables in the food court, watching stores unlock their gates one by one. As more families and kids enter, trying to escape the increasing heat, the noise around me grows. Kids crying, teenagers laughing, and an old man shouting at the pretzel vendor.

Maeve shows up with a giant iced coffee for us to share and a *'Happy Birthday'* balloon tied to her backpack.

"Cute."

She slides into the seat across from me, pouring half of her coffee into the second cup and sliding it over.

"You're eighteen now, got to celebrate somehow."

I take a long sip of the heavenly drink. It's rare when we get to have anything that tastes this good.

"Ready to be a menace?"

"I've always been a menace."

She snorts, "True."

We wander in and out of the stores like we have all the time in the world. We try on clothes we can't afford, sunglasses we'll never buy, and spray over-priced perfume on each other's sleeves, pretending we belong here. Just two teenagers, killing time.

Maeve and I stop at the photobooth. She pulls me inside and shoves a crumpled dollar into it.

"I look like a raccoon." I glare at the screen, wiping under my eyes. "And a bird's made a nest in my hair."

"You look great, like we survived the apocalypse. It's a vibe."

We make stupid faces, tongues out, middle fingers up, one blurry shot of us laughing so hard I can't remember what set it off. When the strips slide out, she hands a copy to me.

"Happy birthday, Iz." She smiles.

"Thanks." I tuck the photo into my pocket. I don't have much, but I have her. Honestly, I'm not sure where I'd be otherwise.

We grab a greasy side of fries and sit by the window, watching as people come and go. We laugh as we create stories for people, voicing their outrageous thoughts.

Maeve pulls a small box out of her backpack and places it in front of me. It's wrapped in Christmas paper.

"Happy Christmas." She grins.

"You didn't have to get me a present, Maeve." I blink at her.

"Yes, I do. You're my sister."

I tear off the wrapping paper and open the box. Inside is a cheap silver ring shaped like a snake, coiled once, with tiny black stones for eyes.

"It's perfect."

"We match, see?" She holds up her hand, showing me the same ring on her finger. "Twin threats."

"I love it." I slide it on.

Maeve and I sit and chat a while longer, and the sun begins to dip. We both know I need to leave soon.

"Text me when you get in." Maeve pulls me in for a hug, squeezing me gently.

"Always."

∼

ON THE WALK HOME, I let my mind wander for once. As a birthday gift to myself. Normally, I try not to let myself imagine a future, because to want something like that feels impossible most days. Hope is a fickle thing like that — deadly dangerous.

I'll get a job, find my own place, sleep in a real bed, eat real food, and lock the door. I'll buy my own clothes and have my own belongings.

No more stolen hoodies, no more school showers, no more bruises hidden under concealer.

I picture a beat-up couch with a blanket. A dog. I'd be able to watch TV, listen to music, and just exist.

My chest aches with how badly I want that to be my reality. I hold onto that dream for a little while longer. That version of me who's normal, who can celebrate her birthday. Who has clean sheets and a quiet house.

I tuck it all away like a photograph back into a box and push it into the back of my mind. The streetlights flicker on and reality crashes back in. The sun is disappearing behind heavy clouds, and everything darkens. It's ominous. The familiar heaviness settles in my chest.

My house comes into view, no car in the driveway. I breathe out a sigh of relief that he isn't home yet. Maybe I'll have time to take a quick shower, find something to eat.

I push open the front door as quietly as I can. The air inside rolls over me like a wave—cigarettes, sweat, and something sharp under it, like sour vodka and old meat.

The TV is on, a show flickering blue and white across the walls. One of the cushions is on the floor, along with a handful of beer bottles.

He's in the recliner, feet up, his face half in shadow. An empty bottle of vodka rests on the coffee table. I feel his dark eyes on me the second the door clicks shut.

"Where have you been?"

I keep my head down and don't dare to move or breathe. His recliner creaks as he stands, crossing the room to me. He sniffs the air, a slow, deliberate inhale.

"I asked you, where have you been?" His voice slithers under my skin.

"I was at the mall with a friend." I stare at my feet.

"With a boy?" His putrid breath fills my nostrils.

"No, sir."

"Then why are you wearing perfume?"

My heart drops. "People were spraying stuff at the mall," I say a bit too quickly. "They always hand out samples."

He laughs; it's a mean and ugly sound. I want to cover my ears.

"That fancy perfume, huh? Smellin' like some little rich bitch."

I don't respond. I barely even breathe. It's too late, though, and I know it.

"Why were you at the mall?"

"It's my eighteenth birthday."

He snorts. "Eighteen, huh? Think you're a grown woman now? Think you can go strutting around? Doing whatever you want?"

Silence is safer, but even silence can't save you when he's made up his mind.

"You know what they say about little rich bitches?" He steps closer to me.

The glint in his eyes makes me want to run.

"Answer me." His rough hand closes around my neck and pulls me against him. His greasy brown hair falling forward.

"N-No, sir." I can't help the stutter.

But that just cost me. Every muscle in my body tenses, preparing for the blows, the beating I'll have to endure. My heart beats so hard I think it's trying to escape from my chest.

If only I were so lucky.

His smile, slow and dark, spreads over his face. He lowers his face to mine. "Little rich bitches are good little girls for their daddies."

He drags me into the living room, throwing me on the floor. I fall back on my hands, the carpet rough against my palms. I look over at my mom, lying on the couch with a needle in her arm. Her eyes are glazed over like glass windows, and no one's home.

I look up at him as he rubs his hand over the bulge in his jeans.

"Are *you* going to be a good little girl for your daddy?" He chuckles as he curls his fingers in my hair and draws me up onto my knees, my scalp burning in protest.

"C'mon now," he whispers as he undoes his pants, "make Mama proud." He glances at the couch.

My mom still hasn't moved. I'm not even sure she's breathing. I watch as she blinks slowly. He pulls himself out as he keeps his grip on my hair. Hot tears roll down my cheeks.

"Please, don't do this," I whimper.

"Beg again." He sneers.

I shake my head, clenching my jaw.

This can't be happening.

"Open your mouth and take it. Or else Mommy gets a beating."

My mind races. There's no way out. I'm stuck. I can't let him hurt her.

My lips part slightly and he shoves himself between my lips. Pushing to the back of my throat, and I gag. He groans. My hands tremble as I try to push against his thighs, but his hips jerk me closer, his grip on my hair tightening even more.

"You bite and you die."

I cry out, and he pushes himself deeper. Even with my eyes shut I can still see the flickering lights of the TV, canned laughter to a sitcom I will never know. He continues thrusting into my mouth as I struggle to breathe through my tears.

He finally pulls out and shoves me back. I try to crawl away, but he pulls my legs back to him.

I kick him with my other leg, but that angers him.

"You stupid little cunt!" He flips me over, backhanding me so hard black spots dance in my vision.

He takes advantage, grabbing the front of my jeans and ripping them down my legs. I cry out from the burn and snap back into myself.

Fight.

I swing my fists, trying to push him off me so I can run. I can't let him do this to me. I refuse.

He smashes the empty vodka glass against my head, and it breaks. It doesn't register as pain at first—just shock. A brutal jolt that rattles through my skull. My eyes vibrate in their sockets.

Shhk.

Then the sound of his belt buckle jingling.

He brings the belt down, my forearms sting trying to cover my face.

The loud crack continues to steal the air from my lungs. I can't tell if the cracks are his belt or thunder. I squirm, trying to buck him off me, but he uses his body to press down on me, his knee digging into me. Then he punches me. Pain explodes against my ribs, then my side. He flips me over onto my stomach. I can barely hear the words he's yelling into my ear as I sob into the carpet. He grinds himself into my ass.

As he pulls me up by my hood, I choke and splutter, clawing at my neck.

"You ain't gonna be nothin' but this, Isobel. No one will want you. There's only me now." He throws me down and punches my side again, and all the fight leaves my body.

He wrenches my hips up and shoves them against his groin. He rips my underwear, his fingers dig into my hips, hard enough I already know that it's going to bruise. There's no ceremony, no warning, he forces himself inside me, the pain bright and sharp. He groans and the tears come faster.

He moves his hand under my shirt and grabs my breast so hard I cry out again.

The TV is still laughing, my face mashed against the rug. Salt from my tears and the metallic tang of blood swirl in my mouth. I retch but nothing comes up. He hisses through his teeth, every thrust shoving me harder into the floor.

He yanks my hair and pulls me against him. "You smell good." His voice is in my ear while he squeezes my chest again, and I sob.

"This is all you're good for. No one is ever going to want you." He grunts. "Even your daddy didn't want you."

I count the seconds until there's nothing left to count.

He uses my body to get himself off, then his impossible weight finally lifts off me. Wetness runs down my legs.

He wipes himself off in my hair. The sound of his pants zipper. Everything hurts. I'm floating above my body. Sounds are muffled. I just want the ground to open up and swallow me whole. To find comfort in the darkness. To be nothing.

He grabs me, and I scramble to get my feet under me, but my jeans are still around my ankles. He drags me down the hall to my room.

He yanks open the door and tosses me inside like he's throwing out a bag of trash.

"There's a part of you that wants this," he says with terrifying serenity, a sick smile crawling over his face. "Don't worry. Pretty soon you'll be begging for it." He scans the threadbare room, then slams the door shut.

I lean against my mattress. I can't breathe too deeply or else there's a sharp pain.

My hand fumbles for my phone, but the pocket is empty. It must've slipped out.

Fuck.

I claw at my jeans, every movement sending sharp, electric pain through me.

The laughter from the TV is gone, but I can still hear it in my head.

She was there, high out of her mind.

Didn't save me. If anything, she just watched.

That almost hurts more than what he did.

Almost.

The part of me that used to braid her hair and cuddle on the couch with her, the one who danced in the kitchen, still thought she would come back to me someday, she'd say she was sorry, and we'd leave.

But she won't, not after this. She's already gone, just left her body behind.

Now I have to leave mine too. I stayed for her, but I won't stay for this. The little girl inside me curls up and dies right here in this room.

3 GRACE

The air takes my breath. The swirling wind bites through my thin shirt. I slowly climb out of my window, being mindful of each ache in my body.

The rain hits my skin like shards of glass. The sky is wide open, water soaking through everything.

I need to get away. To find help. Anything to escape from this hellhole.

From *him*.

I need to get to Maeve's.

I stagger, my vision spins and tilts.

I stumble down the road, using the parked cars to keep from swaying. My body rocks like I'm on a boat in a storm, everything pitching. My surroundings blur into one long smear of light and noise.

My eyes pulse. Sounds are louder now. The hiss of tires on wet pavement. The echo of my own ragged breathing. My limbs feel heavy. My skin too tight.

Everything hurts.

Then —

A flash of light.

A blaring horn.
Tires screeching.
Darkness.
Another bright light. I think my body is moving.
A mixture of faded voices around me. The voices multiply and overlap.
"She's bleeding."
"Possible abdominal trauma."
I'm underwater, the words blur. The voices fading farther and farther.
There's a soft light, it's warm and inviting. I'm so tired.
"She's crashing! Get a crash cart now!"
Then blissful nothingness.

THE RHYTHMIC BEEPING is strangely comforting. There's a weight in my stomach, it's not painful, just pressure. Like something heavy is resting there, stitched into me.

Slowly, my vision comes into focus — soft lights, clean sheets.

My throat is dry, and my tongue is stuck to the roof of my mouth. My head pounds. There's an IV in my arm, a pulse monitor beside me.

Hospital.

I don't remember deciding to stay alive, but... here I am.

A figure moves in my periphery. I turn my head. A woman in her late thirties, maybe, lab coat, tired eyes. She stands up.

"You're awake." Her voice is gentle. "You gave us a scare."

I try to speak, but nothing comes out. She pours a cup of water and helps me sit up just enough to sip.

"What happened?" I croak.

"You wandered out into the street and collapsed. Luckily, the driver was able to stop and didn't hit you. He brought you to the hospital."

I blink.

"You had internal bleeding from a laceration on your liver. We operated to fix it. You also had a deep cut on the back of your head, we sewed that up as well, and you have a concussion. You were very lucky."

I don't feel lucky. I feel like someone scooped out all my insides, and now I'm just an empty carton of ice cream someone discarded in the trash.

"Can you tell me your name?" She walks to the table at the end of my bed, flipping open my chart.

"Is—" I clear my throat. "Isobel Mason."

"Date of birth?"

"June 27th."

"How old did you turn yesterday?"

"Eighteen."

I see the change in her eyes, from sadness to empathy. The pieces are clicking into place.

"Is there anyone I can call for you?"

Only one name comes to mind. *Fuck, that's depressing.*

"Yes, please. My best friend, Maeve."

"Alright, write her number down, I'll call her." She hands me a notepad and a pen. I scribble down her number and hand it back.

"While you were unconscious…" She pauses and folds her hands in front of her. "We ran full imaging. Scans. X-rays."

I nod, barely.

She doesn't look away. Her voice stays calm. "Isobel…there are signs of long-term physical abuse. Multiple old fractures. Ribs, wrist, cheekbone. Several healed improperly. Scarring consistent with burns and deep cuts. Severe tissue bruising over time."

Each word feels like another layer being peeled away. Someone is finally looking at the damage. She's not asking. She's not guessing. She knows, the proof shown all over my films.

"None of this is new. And none of it is your fault."

I stare at her hands resting on the table. She doesn't rush me. I can't bring myself to meet her eyes, not wanting to see the pity in them.

CLANG.

I jump, the beeping accelerating.

"Hey, it's okay. You're okay." She crosses over to me and reaches out to soothe me.

I flinch.

She immediately lifts her hands.

"It was just a tray, you're okay. Take a slow, deep breath for me."

I turn to see a nurse picking up different packages off the floor and putting them on a metal tray.

The beeping starts to slow. I close my eyes and focus on breathing.

"That's it." She continues quietly, "The police have been notified. They'll want to speak with you when you're ready. But right now, you're safe. No one can hurt you."

Safe.

I don't know how to operate inside this body. Don't know how to live in the skin they stitched shut. She watches me a moment longer, then reaches into her coat pocket and pulls out a small badge clipped to her ID.

"I'm Dr. Ramirez. I'm the trauma surgeon on call tonight, and I'll be overseeing your care while you're here."

I nod again, just barely. It feels like I'm watching this happen to someone else.

"There's something else we need to talk about," she says, her voice quiet but clear.

She shifts slightly, putting her hands in the pockets of her white coat.

"When you arrived, you had injuries that suggested recent sexual trauma. We treated what we could, but we haven't performed a forensic exam."

The words sound like another language. I hear them, but I can't understand them. Not fully, at least.

"You don't have to decide right now," she adds. "But the sooner we do it, the more evidence we can preserve. It's completely your choice. No one will force you. We'll support you either way."

I stare at her. She's not looking away. Not awkward. Not pitying. Just present.

"Okay, let's do it."

"All right," she says. "We'll have a nurse come in shortly. Someone who is trained specifically for this. She'll walk you through every step."

Dr. Ramirez walks to the open door of my room and leans out, calling a name. I feel dirty and I want to shower. But I've seen the shows, I won't be able to until this is over.

There's a soft knock, and Dr. Ramirez steps aside to let in a woman wearing light blue scrubs, a warm cardigan wrapped around her shoulders. Mid-40s, calm eyes. Clipboard in one hand, a wheeled cart in the other.

"Isobel," Dr. Ramirez says, "this is Nurse Lang. She's a certified SANE, which stands for Sexual Assault Nurse Examiner. She's here to walk you through the next part, if you're ready."

I sit up a little straighter. My voice is barely a whisper. "Okay."

Dr. Ramirez nods at us and leaves, shutting the door behind her. Nurse Lang gives a small, reassuring smile.

"Hi, Isobel. I'm really sorry you're going through this. But I want you to know, I'm here for you. Everything we do tonight is in your control, all right?"

I nod. She rolls the cart over slowly and sets her clipboard down.

"I'll explain everything before we begin. You can stop at any time. You can skip any step. You don't even have to answer my questions if you don't want to. This exam is here to collect evidence, but only if you consent."

My hands twist the blanket in my lap.

"I want to do it," I murmur. "Just... I want to get this over with."

She nods once, understanding. "I understand. If for any reason, you need a break, just let me know and we'll stop immediately."

She pulls on gloves, her movements calm, practiced.

"What happened to my clothes?"

"They were bagged as evidence."

"There was a photo strip in my back pocket. Can I get that back?"

"I will make a note for them to take a look and get that back for you, okay?"

I nod, and Nurse Lang scribbles on her clipboard.

"First, I'll ask you a few questions, just basic medical history, and anything you remember about what happened. I know it's hard. You don't have to go into detail unless you want to."

I nod again.

"Then we'll begin the exam. That will include collecting samples, swabs, photographs of injuries if you consent, and a physical exam. I'll narrate every step before I do it and ask before I touch you."

"Will it hurt?" I'm not sure she heard me.

But her face fills with compassion.

"Some parts might be uncomfortable. But we'll go slowly, and you can ask me to stop at any time. You're safe here."

There's something in the way she says it that makes it almost feel true. Not just words. A promise.

She moves around the bed, prepping supplies, her presence is warm and comfortable. No rush. No drama. Just a woman who believes in me and knows what to do. I let myself exhale. Nurse Lang sits beside the bed, clipboard balanced on her knee.

"We'll start with the questions. If you don't know the answer or don't want to say, just tell me. Okay?"

I nod.

She keeps her voice soft. "Do you know the name of the person who assaulted you?"

"Daniel Mercer." His name tastes like rot in my mouth.

"Relationship to you?"

I hesitate. "Stepfather."

She doesn't blink. No surprise. No pity. Just a quiet, "Thank you."

More questions follow: recent showers, the last time I used the bathroom, and how long I was in the rain. I answer what I can. She never pushes.

"I'll start with a few photographs of visible injuries, only if you consent. Then I'll examine you, check for tears or bruising, and collect samples."

I nod. "It's okay."

She pulls a warm sheet up over me. "I'll make sure you're covered the whole time. I'll walk you through everything. Just breathe with me."

The camera clicks softly.

My arms. My thighs. My ribs. My back. The fading yellow of old bruises layered under the new.

She pauses at one point, gently lifting the collar of my gown to reveal a hand-shaped bruise.

"This one's fresh," she says, voice like silk. "I'm documenting the shape, don't move, you're doing great."

The exam itself is slow, clinical. I flinch at parts. Bite the inside of my cheek. But she doesn't let it get away from me.

"You're safe," she repeats, again and again. "You're doing exactly what you need to do." Her voice pulls me back when I start to feel like I'm floating away from my body.

I'm shaking by the end. Silent tears streaming down my cheeks. But I did it. It's done. She covers me back up, snaps off her gloves, and looks me in the eye.

"You did something incredibly hard tonight, Isobel. I'm proud of you."

The words don't sink in. Not yet. But I hold onto them anyway. Nurse Lang is just finishing packing up the kit when there's a knock at the door. She looks over.

Dr. Ramirez steps in, followed by a man in a plain suit and a badge clipped to his belt. Early 40s. Not the kind of cop who wants to scare you, at least not today.

"Isobel," Dr. Ramirez gestures to the man beside her, "this is Detective Harlan. He's here to take your statement, only if you're ready."

I nod.

Nurse Lang exchanges a few words with Dr. Ramirez and Detective Harlan. Their voices low and quiet. Then she rolls her cart out with a silent nod. Dr Ramirez closes the door behind her, then stands against the wall. Detective Harlan walks over and positions himself at the foot of my bed, opening a small notebook on the table.

"I know you've been through something awful tonight, Isobel," he says, voice even and slow. "And I'm not here to push you. But I want to ask a few questions while the details are still fresh. Just what you know. What you remember."

"Oh, I'm sure I'm not going to forget this night any time soon." I know the sarcasm won't do anything but I can't help it.

He glances at Dr. Ramirez, then back at me. "We're trying to get a clearer picture of your situation."

I swallow hard.

"He's not my real dad," I say. My voice is hoarse. "Daniel. He's just been around since I was five. My mom—" I stop. I don't know what to say about her. About what she didn't do.

"Okay." He nods. "And do you know your mother's full name?"

"Celia Mercer," I whisper. "But she used to go by Mason before she got married. "

He scribbles something down, the sound of his pen scratching the paper comforting me somehow.

"Is your biological father in the picture?"

The fuzzy memory of him making waffles that morning flashes in my mind.

I shake my head. "My mom has never told me who he was. Always said he was gone."

"Gone?" Detective Harlan raises an eyebrow.

"She didn't clarify...but from what little I can remember of him, it doesn't seem like him to just leave. And I think I would've remembered if he died."

The soft look in his eyes as he watched my mom, when he looked at me.

What happened?

My mind starts to race, trying to think back.

"I remember we left and then met with Daniel. Could he have done something to my dad?" If my eyes get any wider, they're going to fall out and roll across the floor.

Detective Harlan nods. "It's possible. Especially with Daniel's violent history."

"Is there any way you can find him?"

"If Daniel did do something, he could be missing. We can try to take your DNA to get a familial match in the Missing Persons Database."

"Yes. Please, can we do that?"

"Of course, I'll have an officer come by with a saliva kit shortly." Detective Harlan closes his notebook, folding his hands over it. "Isobel, I need you to understand this is a long shot. But I promise I'll do my best to find him for you. I'll put a rush on it in the lab."

"Thank you." I force a smile.

What's one more swab?

"Of course." He opens his notebook again, steadying his pen. "Can you take me through what happened to you?"

The door swings open with such a rush it hits the wall.

"Isobel!"

I flip the blanket off my head and turn. Maeve barrels toward me, her hair wild, eyes glassy with panic. She stops next to my bed, mouth agape, as her eyes travel over me.

"Oh my..." she whispers. Her hand trembles as she brings it up to her mouth. "Iz..." Her eyes well.

I reach for her, fists clinging to her sleeves and pull her to me. Maeve wraps her arms around me before I can say a word. Her arms tighten as if she lets go I'll disintegrate into dust and float away on the wind.

"Isobel, honey, are you alright?" Maeve's mom rushes in, setting her purse down in the seat next to my bed.

"Hi, Brenda, I'm okay." I melt into her as she wraps her arms around me.

"When they called, Maeve and I..." She pulls back, her eyes soft and warm as she runs a hand down the side of my face. "I'm so sorry, honey."

I shake my head, taking a shaky breath. "No, please don't apologize. There's nothing you need to be sorry for."

Brenda takes a seat as Maeve gets comfortable on the bed.

"What happened?" Maeve takes my hand.

I take a deep breath and give them the highlights of the night. I watch as Brenda's face pales, while Maeve's fills with anger.

"You're coming to stay with us when you're discharged. I'm not taking no for an answer." Maeve's eyes bore into me. "That fucking asshole! I can't believe he touched you! What a sick perv!"

"Language, Maeve," Brenda scolds, but there's no weight behind it.

Maeve rolls her eyes. "Whatever, Mom. You know it's true. I hope they lock him up and throw the key somewhere in the ocean."

I chuckle. "You and me both."

4 ASHTHORNE

My legs dangle off my car seat. The world outside is a blur of headlights and streetlamps. The radio hums out soft melodies. Mama is whispering to herself.

"Don't look behind us." Her knuckles are white on the wheel.

We've been driving for what feels like forever. The car smells like coffee, smoke, and cherry lip gloss.

"Are we there yet?"

Her gaze meets mine in the mirror, her eyes wild and tired.

"Not yet, baby. Soon. Take a nap, then by the time you wake up, we'll be there."

"Okay, Mama."

The next time I wake up, I'm on a bed. Mama is pacing the room, looking out of the blinds. The motel room is cold and smells.

"What's wrong, Mama?" I sit up, rubbing the sleep from my eyes.

She jumps, turning quickly. She crosses over and drops onto the bed.

"Nothing." She holds my face and pets my hair. "Nothing at all, Isobel. We're just... going on vacation."

"Will Dada be going on vacation with us?" I rub my eyes.

I don't understand the look on her face.

"No, baby, he won't."

"Why not?"

"We're getting away from monsters." She lays me back down.

I think she means the kind of monsters that live under the bed. I nod and believe her.

There's a knock on the door and she jumps.

"Who's that, Mama?" I sit up.

"Mama's friend." She gives me a small smile.

She opens the door, and a man fills the frame. It's not Dada.

He has dark slicked-back hair, dark eyes.

I don't like him.

Mama and the man talk as he steps inside, but I can't hear them.

I want Dada.

He hands Mama a little baggie and she quickly grabs it. The man walks over and crouches beside the bed. He just stares, and it makes me feel bad.

"Who are you?"

His smile is small. It doesn't look real.

"I'm Daniel. I'm going to be your new daddy."

THE ROOM IS TOO bright and too clean. Silence rings in my ears. Anger and frustration bubbles in my chest.

It's been a few days since Detective Harlan was here. Every day, more and more memories seem to unlock.

How could I just let her take me away from my dad? All the while, she was leading me further into the monster's den. I didn't know then that sometimes monsters hid in plain sight.

I try to search my mind for memories of my dad, but it's like they're buried under layers and layers of lies that Mama placed there.

She said she was keeping me safe.

That he was gone.

What could have been so bad about the man who made waffles and hummed along to the radio?

What did Daniel do to him?

Before my thoughts can continue to spiral, Maeve and Brenda walk in. Maeve plops down a pink box of pastries on the table while Brenda holds a tray of drinks.

"Morning, Iz!" Maeve chirps, handing me a donut.

"Morning. Thank you, guys, you really didn't have to bring anything."

"Oh please." Maeve takes her usual seat by my feet with a donut of her own. "You deserve this sugary treat after all the hospital food."

I shrug my shoulders, taking a bite.

"How are you feeling?" Brenda snags a fritter for herself before taking a seat.

"Better. Definitely ready to get out of here as soon as they let me."

"I understand. Well, it shouldn't be that much longer." Brenda smiles as she hands me a drink.

A knock sounds at the door. Detective Harlan stands in the doorway. My stomach flips.

"Hi, Isobel, you're looking much better than when I last saw you."

"It's the donut." I grin while holding it up.

He chuckles as he comes in.

"Please help yourself, detective." Brenda gestures to the box.

"Thank you." He nods and smiles.

"Did you find him?" I put my donut down. The tension in my stomach grows with every passing second.

Detective Harlan's eyes scan over me.

"Well?" Maeve moves to sit next to me, taking my hand. "Put us out of our misery."

"We did find him."

The words echo in my mind as Maeve and Brenda speak, but I can't process any other words. *They found him. My dad.* That thought causes something else to shift. The hope that starts to bloom quickly burns like acid.

What if he's worse? What if he's just another monster in better clothes? I grew up in a house where the monsters weren't under the bed. They walked through the front door like they owned the place.

"Isobel?" Detective Harlan's voice cuts through the river of thoughts.

"Huh?" I look up around me.

"Are you alright?" His forehead crinkles.

Maeve squeezes my hand, and I nod.

"Yes, sorry, I was just… processing." I clear my throat. "So, I was right, he was missing?"

"Not exactly."

My brows furrow.

"So, when we ran your DNA through the Missing Persons Database, we got back a match, but it was for you."

My chest tightens. I can't breathe. "I-I'm sorry…did you say *I* was in the database?"

He nods. "Your DNA matched a child reported missing nearly thirteen years ago. Your name was listed then as Isobel Grace Ashthorne."

I stare at him.

"I don't— That's not—" I shake my head. "That doesn't make sense."

"We double-checked. The report was filed by Lucian Ashthorne, your biological father. There's been an open case ever since. Your mother vanished with you when you were five years old."

The pit in my stomach becomes a chasm.

She took me away.

Away from my dad.

Took me and told me he was the one who was gone.

"Has he been contacted?" Brenda asks.

"Yes, we contacted him and he's on his way here. We didn't disclose what happened to you, just that you were in the hospital."

"What if she doesn't want to see him?" Maeve asks.

"Then that is her choice, but with her father's position, we needed to contact him immediately."

"His position?" I tilt my head.

"Yes." He clears his throat, adjusting the collar of his shirt. "He said he'd be here within the few hours. He's flying in from California."

My thoughts swirl. He's alive. He's coming from California. He was looking for me.

"Thank you, detective." Brenda stands, walking over and placing a hand on my shoulder. "We really appreciate you putting a rush on this."

"Of course. It's my pleasure. I have an update about your case if you're ready to hear it."

My mouth dries at the thought of him. "Hit me with it."

"Daniel and your mother were both arrested. Daniel for rape and aggravated assault, Celia for possession. We've been trying to offer her a plea for her cooperation and testimony against Daniel."

"Let me guess, she's not." Maeve looks at me.

Detective Harlan shakes his head. "She won't take the deal. He was denied bail. The DA is doing what he can to try to negotiate a deal, so you won't have to testify. It'll take some time though."

My head bobs as he talks, each word makes something in my chest lift.

"Your mom was granted bail of $2,500 but no one's come forward to pay that, so she'll be held until trial. Additionally, from what I've heard, she's been detoxing, so it's probably for the best she stays inside."

"Finally," Maeve mutters.

"Will I be able to visit?"

He shakes his head. "No, the jail doesn't allow visits, but if there's a number you'd like her to call you on I can pass that along."

My heart drops. I don't even know what I'd say to her. Or what she'd say to me. "Thank you, for the updates. And finding my dad." The word feels foreign in my mouth.

"Of course." Detective Harlan fishes a card out of his pocket and places it on my table. "If you have any questions or need anything at all, please give me a call anytime."

"Thank you." Brenda gestures. "I'll walk you out."

"Get better, Isobel. We'll be in touch."

I give him a small grin. He takes a donut out of the box with a napkin and follows Brenda out.

Maeve exhales heavily. "Well, that was... a lot."

"No kidding." I stare blankly into my lap.

"You have a dad."

"Thanks, Captain Obvious." I roll my eyes.

"How do you feel about it?" She nudges me with her shoulder.

It's my turn to take a deep breath, forcing the air out through my lips. "There's a lot of feelings but I feel like they're all fighting for the spotlight. I'm shocked. Angry at my mom, for taking me away from him. I'm scared and worried because what if the memory I have of him is just another lie?"

Maeve chews on her lower lip.

"I understand, but we can't go down the 'what if' path because it's just going to lead us in circles. So, feel all your feelings, and just take it a step at a time."

Isobel Grace Ashthorne.

Grace is delicate, soft, and I'm not sure I've ever been either.

THE NURSE PEEKS IN. "Isobel, your father is here to see you."

The nurse lingers in the doorway. "He's just outside," she lowers her voice. "Should I let him in?"

The sheets suddenly feel too heavy. Like they're trying to pin me down. I glance at Maeve, then back to the nurse.

"Can I just... have a minute?"

The nurse nods, and the door clicks shut. Maeve keeps one hand still wrapped tightly in mine. I'm not sure what I'm feeling. Hope? Dread?

"I'm scared," I admit.

"You have every right to be." Maeve squeezes my hand. "You got this. I'll be here with you. "

"What if he's like him?" I murmur. "What if he's worse?"

"From what you told me, I don't think he will be. Either way, you don't have to trust him, just meet him and feel out the situation. No matter what, I've got your back."

The knock comes again. I flinch.

Maeve gives me a look. I know if I shake my head, she'll run up against that door and barricade it until I give her the okay.

I dip my chin. There's no use in avoiding the inevitable. The door creaks open.

Lucian Ashthorne steps into the room.

I sit up a little straighter, my heart pounding so loud I wonder if he can hear it from across the room. He's tall, wearing a sharp suit, and a long black coat. His black hair is neat and styled back, with streaks of silver at the temples and through the sides. His eyes match the storm blue in mine. Or I guess, mine are like his. He stands there staring in disbelief.

"Gracie." His voice silences every thought.

My eyes fill with tears. "Dad," I whisper.

His face breaks open. Pain, loss, and love. He takes a careful step closer, then another. He stops a foot away from the bed, pulling off his black gloves slowly.

"I—I can't believe it's you," he breathes out. "I've imagined this moment so many times, but... never like this."

Maeve shifts on the edge of the bed, protective. Her eyes flicker from him to me. Lucian notices, nods to her.

"Can I hug you? It's alright if you're not comfortable."

Another memory flashes across my mind. My scraped knee, he kissed my tears away, cleaned my cut, and held me until I felt better.

"Yes." My voice is small.

He takes the last few steps and his arms wrap around me.

It's a foreign feeling at first. His scent fills my nose, and its familiar. Comforting. A tear slips down my cheek. This feeling, this love, comfort, was ripped away from me. My body slowly relaxes in his hold.

He pulls back, brushing his thumb across my cheek, brushing my tears away.

"You're so grown up," he whispers then shakes his head. "I've missed you so much."

He pulls me back into his arms, and I let him. Out of the corner of my eye, I catch Maeve wiping at her face.

He lets me go but his hands linger on my arms for a bit longer. Then moves the chair closer to the bed.

"Happy late eighteenth birthday." His smile is small.

My fingers twitch underneath the blanket. My chest flutters.

"Thanks."

Lucian nods once, his jaw tight. "I never wanted this to be how I found you. In a hospital bed. Hurt." He pauses, clenching his jaw and taking a slow breath. "You've been through things no child should ever endure. And I know I can't change that. But I can promise you this, Gracie... I need you to hear this and believe me when I say I will do everything in my power to protect you."

I want to believe him. God, I want to. But I've heard promises before. From people who were supposed to love me. Still, something in his eyes makes my heart skip, not fear this time, but hope.

Recognition. Like he's known me all along. Like I've known him.

There's something about how he says the words, like this isn't a father making an empty promise, it's a man with means and power.

I blink fast, throat closing again. He doesn't say 'I'm sorry'. He doesn't say 'You're safe now' like some empty comfort. He tells me the only thing I want and need to hear.

"Why didn't you keep looking for me?" It comes out accusatory.

He freezes for a second then his shoulders drop. "Oh, Gracie, I did. I hired private investigators and they couldn't find what happened to you. And the news... people eventually move on. But I promise you I never moved on. I prayed every day that I'd find you."

I look at him, his shoulders relaxed, his face open and the sincerity in his eyes is easy to see.

"Why do you keep calling her 'Gracie'?" Maeve is staring a hole into his head.

He smiles at her and then turns to me. "We named you after my mom. She died when I was twenty. She was an amazing woman. When you were little, I was the only one you allowed to call you Gracie."

My chest warms.

"I'm not here to take anything from you." He holds up his hands. "Not your name. Not your friends. Not your life. If you want me to call you Isobel instead, I can."

"No, it's okay. I like Gracie, but only you." I smile.

A smile creeps across his face as if those words make him the happiest man in the world.

"Gracie it is then."

There's a beat of silence.

"Mama never really talked about you."

Lucian's jaw flexes.

"She never said your name. Not once. Just... looked over her shoulder all the time. I remember now she said we were going on vacation."

I pause, fingers twisting in the sheets. "I asked when I was little. Where you were? She just told me to drop it. Said you were dangerous. That we had to keep moving."

I can see the tension in every line of his body.

"She said that we had to hide. But I didn't know from who," I add.

His voice is low. Controlled. "She told me that she was taking you out for the day. A trip to the park. She never came back."

That doesn't fit. Doesn't track. But... it explains the fear. The silence. The weight in my mother's eyes whenever I asked where I came from.

"Why?" I whisper. "Why would she run if you weren't hurting her?"

Lucian doesn't speak for a moment. "She was in trouble. She didn't trust me enough to let me help." His voice tightens. "Or maybe she didn't want to be saved. I don't know. I've asked myself that question a thousand times."

A breath catches in my throat.

"She took you to punish me," he says, quieter now. "And I let that punishment change me. But I never stopped searching. Never stopped hoping."

I hold his gaze, swallowing roughly.

"I thought Daniel hurt you."

He scoffs. "He couldn't hurt me, so he did the only thing he could think of. He took you. I just... I wanted you to be safe. I wanted to be your father. It got harder as time passed. Not knowing what you looked like, what kind of person you were growing up to be."

The ache in my chest blooms again. Not pain. Not quite hope, either. Just the sharp, aching shape of something I've never had. The reality that an entirely different life was taken from me.

"What happens now?" I ask, my voice barely louder than a breath.

Lucian's expression doesn't shift, but something in his posture eases.

"You're eighteen now, so what you do next... that's something only you can decide. I want you to come with me, Gracie. But I won't force you."

"You're giving me a choice?" I blink.

His chin dips. "You've had too many choices taken from you. That ends here. I want to give you the world. But if you're happy here, that's all I can count on."

I don't know what to say. There are so many feelings tangled up inside me: anger, relief, disbelief.

"But... I don't know you." I pull at my finger. "I don't know anything about you."

"You don't have to," Lucian replies. "Not yet. You don't owe me anything. But I'm offering you a home with me, a fresh start."

Maeve's hand tightens in mine. Lucian glances between us.

"If she wants to come visit," he adds, "or stay for a while... That can be arranged."

Maeve raises her eyebrows at me like, *Okay, maybe he's not the worst.*

I don't smile. But a quiet type of hope starts. Lucian waits. He doesn't press, doesn't try to fill the space with reassurances. That alone makes the uncertainty in me ease.

But still, I can't say yes. Not yet.

"I... I think I need time." I pause, the whir of the air conditioning filling the space. "To think. To figure out what I want to do."

His expression doesn't falter. If anything, it softens.

"Of course," he says. "You don't have to decide anything right away. You've already survived more than anyone ever should. I want you to take your time."

I watch him stand, expecting him to leave. But he doesn't move toward the door yet.

Lucian reaches into his coat and pulls out a small black box — sleek, matte, understated. He opens it and sets it on the tray beside my bed.

A phone.

Not just a phone — the latest model. Thin. Polished. The kind of thing kids at school would kill for. The kind of thing people like me could never even dream of touching. Brand new.

"I had it activated," he says with a nod. "It's yours. Fully encrypted. Private. Only your doctor and I have the number. If you want to reach me, for any reason, you can. Or don't. That choice is yours too."

I stare at it. I've used phones with prepaid minutes. This one is pristine. I don't think I've ever had anything new in my life.

"Thank you." I tear my eyes away from the device.

"I'll let you get some rest. I can only imagine this has been quite the day for you." He straightens his coat. "I'll be staying nearby at the Ritz. Just a few blocks from here. Room is under Ashthorne, if you need it."

Lucian starts toward the door again, but before he steps out, he glances back one more time.

"I meant what I said, you don't have to be alone anymore, you have me. I'd like to come back tomorrow and get to know each other. How does that sound?"

"Sounds good." I grin.

He returns the smile, nodding to us both.

Then he's gone. Giving me the choice to decide which path I want to take.

The door clicks shut behind him, and for a moment, it's just me and Maeve. The silence stretches out.

"You look just like him, except your hair is like your mom's color."

"Really?"

"Yeah."

We fall into silence again. Maeve's still holding my hand, but her eyes flick toward the tray.

"You gonna touch it?" she asks.

I look at the phone like it might bite me. It's sleek and too nice. I'm not worthy of touching it.

"I don't know," I admit.

Maeve shifts closer and reaches for it, popping it out of the box.

"Damn," she mutters, turning it over in her hand. "This is the one with the face recognition. These are nice."

She hands it to me, screen still dark. I hesitate, then press the side button. It lights up. Clean, minimal home screen. Only a few apps. The background is plain. There's one contact in the favorites list. Lucian Ashthorne. I add Maeve's number from memory and save her in my favorites.

"I think he means it," Maeve says after a moment. "About giving you a choice."

I nod, thumbing the smooth edge of the phone.

"But what kind of choice is it, really?" I speak my thoughts. "Go with the rich guy I don't know, or... what? Stay here and be nobody?"

She watches me for a beat, then says, "You don't have to love him, Iz. But maybe... just maybe... you get to have something different now. Something better. Like the futures we talked about. As much as I want you here with me, I want you to have everything. If he can give you that, then you should get the hell out of here."

I just stare down at the glowing screen, my thumb hovering over the icon that could call him back with a single tap. Freedom looks like a lot of things. Right now, it looks like a phone I didn't ask for... and maybe a future I might actually get to choose. I set the phone down on the tray, still in disbelief. Maeve's watching me, quiet. Waiting.

"I used to dream," I say, almost without meaning to.

She tilts her head. "Yeah?"

I nod, eyes on the wall.

"When I was little... I used to dream that my dad who made waffles would find me and take me away. He'd see the bruises and save me and Mama."

I laugh, but it's not really a laugh. More like something breaking in half.

"But even when someone finally did say something, I just bounced around in the system. Daniel and my mom would always convince them to let me come home."

Maeve's hand finds mine again, no words needed. Just warmth.

"And I started thinking... maybe I wasn't worth saving."

I finally look at her. "But you never treated me like I was nothing. You made me realize that I could be more."

Maeve's throat works like she's trying not to cry. "You've just been surrounded by people who didn't deserve you."

I blink hard. "Do you think I'll ever stop feeling like I'm still in that house?"

"I think so," Maeve gives me a small smile. "Maybe not right away. But you will."

Her eyes fill with unshed tears. "Someday you'll stop expecting the floor to collapse from out under your feet."

I close my eyes and press my forehead to her shoulder. Just for a second.

"Thanks for not leaving."

"Never," she says, fierce and sure. "You're stuck with me forever. Ride or die."

5 LUCIAN

My eyes snap open, throat tight, pulse pounding in my ears. I stare up at the ceiling and rest my hand on my chest. I pull air slowly through my nose then out my mouth. My pulse steadies and quiets.

Morning light filters through the hospital blinds. I turn and spot Maeve curled up in the chair beside my bed, a blanket covering her.

I turn my head and spot the phone, sitting innocuously on the table. I stare at it. My nerves hum under my skin.

I chew on my lower lip then reach over and grab it. Before I can think too much about it, I'm typing in his name. The results load fast.

>Lucian Ashthorne
>CEO of Ashthorne Global Security, Major shareholder in
>> multiple tech and logistics companies.

There's a photo of him in a suit, clean cut, jaw set like stone, shaking hands with an older man. Another in a black jacket, standing beside a tactical vehicle.

I scroll further. There's an old article — *Man Offers $1 Million Reward* *for Missing Daughter.* The photo of me is so young I barely recognize myself. I'm smiling from ear to ear, no shadows to be seen. My hair is shiny and neat.

It's such a stark contrast to school photos I remember taking and seeing the proofs of. I rarely smiled, always circles under my eyes, my hair barely tamed.

They list the date I vanished. My name. My age. The comments flooded with theories, thoughts, and prayers.

He never stopped. He really did look for me.

I sit with that for a minute, then glance towards the door. I'm ready, at least more than I was.

Maeve groans and stretches in the chair, giving me a sleepy smile.

"Whatcha doing?"

"I was Googling him."

"Ooh. Stalker time, huh? Find anything good?"

I shrug. "I saw news reports about me going missing, more about his company and things, but nothing gossip worthy."

"Hm, shame." She yawns, bundling her blanket around her before climbing onto my bed.

We spend some time chatting. About nothing and everything. My mind keeps trying to wander off and I have to ground myself in the moment.

We're laughing at a show when there's a soft, measured knock.

Maeve glances at me. I nod once, and she rises to open the door.

Lucian steps in quietly. He's dressed in the same dark coat, though his shirt is different today, crisp, collar unbuttoned. Like he didn't sleep but still wanted to look composed.

His eyes land on me first.

Maeve gives me a quick look — *you good?* — and I nod again. She slips out.

"Hey."

"Hey," he echoes, voice warm but cautious. He stays near the door. "You sure you're up for this?"

"Yeah," I say. My voice feels a little steadier now. "Sit?"

He crosses the room to the chair Maeve left behind and lowers himself, elbows resting on his knees. Like he's unsure how to bridge the gap.

"Are you alright?"

"I think so." I hesitate, then glance toward the tray table where the phone rests. "I Googled you."

His mouth quirks. "I figured."

"There's a lot about you out there. Security company, military, reward money. You've got... quite the reputation."

Lucian nods. "Most of it's true."

"But none of it's *you*." I meet his eyes. "I don't want the press version. I want the one real you. My... dad."

Something shifts behind his eyes, a flicker of emotion that sharpens his eyes, then smooths away.

He nods once. Slow. "Alright."

My hands fidget in my lap. "So... tell me something. Not about your job. Just... who you are. When you're not being CEO Ashthorne."

He leans back, humming and looking up at the ceiling. "I hate loud parties. I like to cook, but I don't know how to make that many things. I don't sleep much. I drink black coffee, usually too much of it."

He pauses, then adds, "I still keep the drawing you made of a pirate ship. Crayons and finger paint. It's in my office."

"Seriously?"

He nods. "It's a terrible drawing."

A startled laugh breaks out of me. "How old was I?"

"You were four." He smiles, tilting his head. "You labeled the cannonballs. 'Booms.'"

A giggle bubbles out. Lucian watches me like he's memorizing this moment.

"You can ask me anything," he says. "And if I don't know the answer yet, I'll find it. For you."

I look at him. Really look.

"I don't remember much. Just flashes. A warm place. A laugh. The sound of someone humming off-key."

Lucian doesn't interrupt. He just waits.

"The main memory I remember was you making waffles in the morning and mom singing along to the radio."

Lucian smiles. "I'd make waffles every Sunday. It was a tradition my parents had with me that I wanted to continue."

I smile. "You said your mom died; is your dad still alive?"

Lucian shakes his head, letting out a heavy exhale. "No, they both died in a car accident."

"I'm sorry." My brows furrow.

"It's alright, it happened a long time ago."

We're both silent for a moment.

"What was it like before? When we were… us. All together."

His expression changes, softens with something that might be grief, or longing. Or both.

"You were always awake before the sun," he says after a moment. "Used to crawl into bed with me just to watch the light come through the blinds. You had this little stuffed bear, mangy thing. You named it Monster."

"Sounds about right."

"You were loud when you were happy, and quiet when something was wrong. You always knew when something was wrong."

He shifts in the chair. "You hated wearing shoes. You ran barefoot down every hallway, every park path."

"I still do," I murmur. "Well, I would if the paths weren't covered with broken glass and needles."

Lucian's smile dims.

"What about her?" I ask. "What was she like… before?"

He's quiet for a long time. "She was bright," he says after a long pause. "Fun. Reckless, sometimes. But she loved you. I never doubted that."

"But she left."

His eyes meet mine. "She ran."

Right. It's something I'll need to get used to.

"She didn't even take any of your things," he adds. "No records. Just you."

I swallow hard, my throat thick.

"I used to think maybe you didn't want me," I whisper. "That maybe I wasn't enough to come back for."

Lucian's voice is rough when he says, "That was never true. You're my daughter. You were the only thing I ever wanted back."

I sit with his words, letting them settle like dust in my chest.

Then I look at him, at the man with the iron-straight posture and the weariness buried in his eyes. The stranger who isn't quite a stranger anymore.

"What about now?" I ask. "What's your life like?"

Lucian tilts his head a little, raises his eyebrows. "Now?"

"Yeah. After me. Without me."

He exhales slowly, leaning back in the chair. "I live in Ashthorne Hall. The place is too big and too cold, but it keeps the city out. It's been in the Ashthorne family for generations."

"Do you live alone?"

There's a pause. He doesn't flinch. But he does lower his eyes. "No," he says. "Not anymore."

I go very still.

"I did. For a long time. After you disappeared, it was hard to stay in that house. Too many memories. Too much silence." He flexes his hand on the armrest.

"A few years went by. I kept working. Kept searching. That's all it was. And then, there was a contractual agreement I needed to meet to keep my position."

"So, you got married... for business?" Lucian was a powerful man, a CEO. "I'm guessing a contractual agreement came into play to keep some sort of image up for your company."

Lucian gave a dry, almost-smile. "Yes. In part. It wasn't some grand love story. Adrienne and I. She understood the arrangement. She'd lost her husband years before. I'd lost you. It made sense on paper."

He paused, looking down at his hands briefly, before looking back up to meet my eyes.

"She has a daughter. Dakota. She's your age. She was 9 when we got married."

He must see the flicker in my expression because he rushes in with, "She's not a replacement. I need you to hear me when I say that. No one could ever replace you, Gracie."

I nod, letting it sink in, the shape of this new life he tried to build in the ruins of the one he lost.

"Does she know about me?" I ask after a beat.

"She does. I told her I was coming to see you last night."

"And how did that go?" I bite the inside of my cheek.

"She was excited." Lucian's gaze softens. "She's always known about you. Dakota used to ask about you, even when we didn't have any answers."

"What's she like?" The question escapes before I can stop it.

"She's strong-willed. Ambitious. A little dramatic. She's a dancer, so that comes with the territory. But she's kind, bubbly. I think..." He hesitates. "I think you'll like her."

I blink, not sure what to do with that — this girl, my age, a stranger who's known my name for years. I don't know how to feel about any of this — this entire *family* I never knew about, this version of Lucian who seems steadier than the ghost I imagined for years.

I'm not mad. Not exactly. I just suddenly feel... behind. Like they've all lived a hundred lives while I was trying to survive just one.

"She's had everything," I whisper.

"Not true, she went through hardships of her own, losing her father at a young age," Lucian says.

That surprises me. So much that I actually look at him again.

"She'll want to meet you," he adds, quieter now. "It might not be perfect. But I'd like you to have that choice."

Choice. There's that word again. I sit with that word. Let it expand in my chest.

"I don't know if I'm ready to meet her," I say.

"I'd be surprised if you were."

We sit there in a silence that feels like a beginning.

When Maeve returns, Lucian and I have settled into a comfortable conversation. We cover the lighter topics and just take the time to get to know each other. Lucian orders us lunch and it's a hundred times better than the hospital food.

When Brenda comes after work, she brings us all dinner and Lucian helps her set out the food containers and portion them onto paper plates.

"I feel like today has been quite the eye opener," Maeve whispers.

"Definitely. He's how I remember him for the most part. Obviously most of the details are new, but his smile and his laugh. He's how I remember him, just a bit older."

"I'm glad. I was prepared to fight him if he even looked at you wrong."

We giggle together.

Lucian looks over at us. "Ready to eat, girls?"

Knock, knock.

The door opens and a nurse walks in holding a clipboard.

"Wow, it smells amazing in here!" Her smile is warm as she saunters in. "I'm so jealous."

"It's from this little Chinese restaurant down the street," Brenda says.

"Oh, yes, I love that place!" The nurse sets a clipboard down on the tray next to my bed. "I bring good news. You'll be discharged tomorrow."

"So soon?" Lucian's brow is furrowed.

The nurse nods. "Yes, Isobel's been here for about a week and she's healing nicely. There's no bleeding, no signs of infection, and the doctors are pleased with her liver function."

"I feel fine, promise." I look at Lucian and the lines on his forehead smooth out.

"You will be fatigued for a few days, so take it slow. No heavy lifting for at least a week." She taps a pen on the clipboard. "Read through everything and don't hesitate to ask any questions. Sign at the bottom and then you'll be discharged in the morning."

"Thank you." I smile.

"My pleasure. I'll get out of y'all's hair now and let you enjoy that delicious dinner." She gives us one last smile before shutting the door behind her.

"That's great news, honey." Brenda breaks the silence.

Maeve and I exchange a look. *But where am I going to go?*

Lucian clears his throat. "I have an idea I want to run past everyone, and you can let me know what you think."

We all nod.

"We haven't had much time to get to know each other exactly, and I'm not trying to push you for an answer. But maybe you can spend the next week at the hotel with me. Maeve can come and stay as well. As long as that's okay." He looks at Brenda.

She nods, looking over at me. "I don't have a problem with that."

Maeve's eyes widen and she smiles, meeting my gaze, a silent conversation passing through us within seconds.

"That sounds great." I grin over at Lucian, the nervousness that had started to gather dissipates. My body relaxes.

"Perfect." Lucian settles in a seat with his own plate.

"Let's eat." Maeve smiles.

THE HOTEL IS glass and steel, tucked downtown where the buildings are too tall to count the floors. A doorman opens the car door like we're royalty. Another doorman opens the front door. The hotel is grand with white and gold accents. We make our way across the lobby to the elevators. Lucian hits the button for the top floor. We walk down the carpeted hallway to the double doors.

The doors opened with a soft click, and we step into a suite that doesn't feel real. Cream-colored walls are framed by gilded crown molding. Plush rugs are layered over glossy marble floors. A chandelier dripping with crystals hangs above the sitting area, casting prismatic light across velvet armchairs and a glass coffee table that probably cost more than my old house.

FORGED IN BLOOD

Floor-to-ceiling windows let in the city skyline, the kind of view that makes everything feel high above the world. There's a faint scent of roses and fresh linen in the air — not overpowering, just enough to smell expensive. To the right, double doors open to a king-size bed covered in silk sheets and a headboard upholstered in soft gray suede.

"Wow..." Maeve and I say in unison.

It isn't just luxury. It's curated perfection. Like every detail has been chosen for someone who expects nothing less.

And for a second, I don't know where to stand. I don't know how to exist in a space like this.

Lucian leads us down a short hallway and motions to a smaller bedroom with two queen size beds.

"You both can rest here. I had them bring up a few things—clothes, toiletries. If you need anything else, just tell me. Maybe in a day or two, if you're feeling up for it, we can go shopping."

Maeve's eyes are comically wide. "Do we have a limit?"

I smack her arm with the back of my hand, shooting her a look.

Lucian chuckles. "It's okay, it's a fair question. No, no limit." He looks over at me. "Go crazy, get whatever you like. For both of you. I'll have some men with us to help carry the bags."

My mouth drops open as Maeve bounces up and down.

"No way." She squeals beside me. "Thank you, Lucian!"

Lucian smiles at her. "Thank you, Maeve. For taking care of my girl when I couldn't."

Maeve beams, and my chest warms at the sight.

"I'll let you ladies get to it. Feel free to order room service if you get hungry. I'll just be down the hall. Maybe we can have dinner together tonight, if you're not too tired?"

"Thank you. Dinner sounds great."

Lucian nods, and his footsteps retreat down the hallway.

The bedroom is modern with blackout curtains and clean sheets. Maeve runs and jumps into one of the beds. I crawl into the other, curl around a fluffy pillow. It smells like fabric softener. The mattress hugs my body.

"Oh, I could get used to this. It's so comfy!" Maeve groans as she stretches.

"This bed is like a cloud." I lay back and close my eyes, and before I know it, I'm falling fast asleep.

6 FIRST TASTE

The next morning, I wake up to the smell of pancakes and syrup. Maeve sits cross-legged on the bed beside me, grinning over a silver-domed tray like a gremlin who's just stolen treasure.

"Lucian said to get whatever we want. So, I ordered the works." She lifts the lid with a flourish. "You're welcome."

There are pancakes, waffles, scrambled eggs, hash browns, fruit slices arranged in a spiral, and two tiny glass bottles of fresh-squeezed juice. Also? Whipped butter in a rose shape.

My stomach growls loud enough to answer for me.

"You know this is like... ten breakfasts, right?"

"Exactly," she says, handing me a fork. "We deserve ten breakfasts."

After a lazy morning, I head into the bathroom. I turn on the water and let out a happy sigh just looking at the water pressure. The water quickly heats, and steam fills the room. I step inside and groan softly as the water hits my skin. Maybe hot water does heal all. As I use the fancy soaps, the scents swirl and fill my lungs. The grime of everything goes down the drain and my muscles relax. I can't even remember the last time I had a hot shower. Or ever where I wasn't rushing to get through it.

For the first time, I feel clean. After getting dressed and settling on the couch with Maeve, Lucian brings me different treats that he remembered from my childhood. My favorite is a delicate custard tart, topped with strawberries. Maeve's favorite is the chocolate cream puff.

He takes Maeve and I to the aquarium. We marvel at all the fish and stop at every exhibit. We get little jars with floating jellyfish in them from the gift shop.

The next day, Lucian takes me on a walk around the hotel. We talk and with every word my body relaxes. I learn more about my grandparents, my Grandma Gracie. She was strong, confident, and she didn't take shit from anyone. I'm honored to have her name and I'm determined to live up to it.

Maeve pulls me out of bed the next morning with one mission: retail therapy. She ignores any protests and drags me into one boutique after another. Lucian and his men trailing behind us. As a CEO it must be nice to have security guards. Silk blouses, pleated skirts, and sunglasses I could never justify buying. I try things on with mounting skepticism, but Maeve? She's lit up.

"You're hot," she says as I turn in the mirror. "Own it."

Lucian insists on buying me multiple pairs of shoes. If I even look at a pair for a second too long, he calls an attendant to get it in my size to try on.

I'm trying on a pair of boots with boxes surrounding me on all sides. I stand to walk around in the boots then look in the mirror.

"What do you think of these?" Lucian tilts his head. "They look great on you."

"They feel good. It's kind of weird. I don't know when the last time I got a pair of new shoes. Always just got what I could get for cheap at the thrift store."

Lucian's face frowns.

"Your mom didn't get you shoes?"

I stare down at my feet. "When I was around eleven or twelve she really just stopped paying much attention to me at all. She was always high or passed out."

Lucian's silent for a moment, then he steps over boxes to me, placing his hands on my shoulders.

"I'm sorry, Gracie. You deserved more than that."

"It's not you who should be apologizing." I raise my face to his. "I was taken from you."

His eyes scan mine then he pulls me into a hug. "I'll always be here for you now. Anything you need, I'll get it for you."

By the end of it, the guards carry so many bags Maeve and I can't stop laughing.

"That one looks like he might tip over." She cackles.

Lucian chuckles with us.

That afternoon, we hit the pool. Maeve sunbathing in oversized sunglasses and a cherry red bikini, her headphones in. I wear an oversized T-shirt over my suit, ankles dangling in the water, watching the clouds pass. The bruises are now a yellowish green, but mainly, I can't stand to look at my scars.

"Iz?"

I hum, turning to look at her.

"Don't stay here for me."

I pull my feet out and walk to her, sitting on the lounger beside her. "You're my sister. You would be the only reason I'd stay."

She slides her sunglasses up onto the top of her head, looking at me. "Because you're my sister from another mister, I want you to have a better life. You go, get to know your dad, and make a better future for yourself."

My eyes water. "I don't want to leave you."

"You're not." Maeve sits up. "No matter what happens, I will always be here for you. Only a phone call or text away. You've been through hell; you deserve a slice of nice."

I hold her gaze, seeing the truth in her eyes. "I do want to know him." I stare at my feet.

"I know you do. He's the only parent who seems to actually give a damn. So, fuck this hellhole and going to community college. Go get your fancy on."

I laugh. "I love you."

"Love you, too." She winks, lying back.

I mirror her.

"What if my step-sister is evil?"

"What's her name again?"

"Dakota."

Maeve sighs. "I mean, most stories, the stepsister is an evil bitch."

"True, but the way Lucian describes her, I have a tiny bit of hope that she won't be."

"For your sake, I hope she's not. You've dealt with enough."

The car smells like leather and something expensive I can't name. The seats are too soft, like they're trying to lull me into comfort, but all it does is make me feel more out of place.

Maeve's beside me in the backseat, chewing on a piece of gum and bouncing her leg like we're headed to a field trip.

Lucian sits up front with the driver, occasionally glancing back to check on us.

I grip my new duffel bag in my lap like I'm holding onto reality itself. Like if I let go, this will all slip away. When we pull through the gates and onto the private airstrip, I pinch myself.

"Holy shit," Maeve whispers, pressing her face to the window. "That's a jet."

Not just any jet. Sleek, white, and shining in the morning sun like something out of a spy movie. It looks like it's never known the words coach or economy.

My eyes widen. "We're flying in that?"

Lucian turns in his seat and nods. "Yes. It's more comfortable this way."

"I've never even been on a plane," my voice barely above a whisper.

He studies me for a beat. "Then I'm glad your first flight will be one where you're safe."

Maeve practically has her head out of the window. "There's a carpet. There's a literal carpet on the tarmac."

The car stops. The driver opens my door before I can find words.

Lucian steps out and offers me a hand.

Maeve follows, spinning once to take it all in. "God, this is some movie shit."

"I don't belong here," I murmur, my feet sticking to the ground.

Lucian turns to face me. "You do. Whether you believe it yet or not."

Behind him, a steward is already loading my bags. Another person waits at the foot of the stairs to the jet.

Maeve nudges my arm. "Go. Live it up. I'll hold it down back home. I'm going to call and text you every single day until you block me."

I turn to her, heart lodged in my throat. "I'd never block you. You sure you'll be okay?"

She shrugs, but her eyes are glassy. "You're the one getting on a spaceship, Isobel. I'll be fine."

I pull her into a hug that doesn't feel long enough.

"I'm going to miss you," I whisper into her hair, the tears welling.

"Not as much as I'm going to miss you." She sniffles.

"Ride or die, forever."

"Ride or die, forever."

When I turn back to Lucian, he's watching us with a softness in his gaze.

"You ready?" he asks.

I don't say yes. I just nod and step toward the stairs. The sun reflects off the panels of the jet. My first time flying... straight into the unknown.

The inside of the jet is quieter than I expected. The air itself knows it's supposed to be rich and still. The carpet beneath my shoes is cream-colored and soft enough to sink into. The chairs aren't chairs at all—they're armchairs, wider than the twin bed I grew up on, upholstered in butter-soft leather with little silver buttons that probably do things I don't understand.

Lucian gestures for me to sit wherever I like. I hover by one of the windows before lowering myself into a seat.

There's a blanket, a silk pillow, headphones, and... a menu?

"Is this real?" I whisper, flipping the small booklet open. I blink. "You can order steak. On a plane."

Lucian settles into the seat across from me. "They'll ask if you'd like anything once we're in the air. Don't worry. It's all included."

I look around again in disbelief.

A steward comes by with a quiet smile. "Miss Ashthorne, would you like sparkling or still water before takeoff?"

"Uh… just normal water, please," I manage.

The steward nods and disappears behind a curtain.

I glance at Lucian. He has one ankle perched on his knee, leaning back in the seat with his arms relaxing on the rests.

"I feel like I'm living someone else's life."

"You're not." He folds his hands in his lap. "This is yours."

"Wait, you always have access to this?"

"Yes."

I let out a shaky breath, then glance out of the window. The tarmac stretches out below, the sky pale and cloudless. Everything feels too still. The engines hum to life, a soft vibration under my feet. My heart races. My fingers grip the chair.

"Hey," Lucian leans forward. "Look at me."

I do.

"You're safe."

The jet begins to move, taxiing smoothly down the runway. I clutch the armrests like they're lifelines.

My breath catches as the ground falls away. My stomach drops. I watch as trees shrink and buildings turn into toy blocks. The sky opens wide around us like it's been waiting for us.

"I'm flying," I say, half in wonder, half in disbelief.

"You are." Lucian smiles.

I STEP out of the car. The sun warms my face. Seagulls cry over head. I fill my lungs with the salty air.

Lucian steps beside me. "Have you ever been to the beach before?"

"No." I shake my head. "At least not that I can remember."

Lucian smiles as we walk towards the sand.

"I used to take you to the beach every weekend in the summer. It's one of the most relaxing places to me. I wanted that for you too." He stops at the sands edge, stepping out of his shoes.

I copy him. The moment my feet hit the sand, I'm giddy. The water gleams ahead of us.

Lucian takes my shoes. "Go. Run." He nods toward the water.

I start running toward the water.

Running through sand is harder than I imagined, but I push through. When I reach wet sand. I roll up my jeans before stepping into the cool water. It laps around my ankles and the sound of the waves soothes me.

My eyes stare out into the water. The wind kisses my face.

Fear and awe tangle together. I feel small, but not in a way that makes me want to disappear. More of the vastness of the unknown. What life is about to bring. With each crash of the waves washing over my feet, a piece of the darkness loosens its grip.

Lucian walks up beside me.

"You know, I made myself a promise that as soon as I found you, I'd bring you here." Lucian smiles out at the water.

"Here we are." I smile up at him.

"My mom always brought me to the beach as a kid too. And eventually I'd come on my own and let the waves take my worries away. Let it quiet my mind."

"I can see why." I stare back out at the waves.

We stand there for a moment, the ocean filling the silence between us. I try to picture him younger, before the power he must have now as a CEO, the responsibility. Just a boy with sand between his toes and salt in his hair.

"It's strange," he says, his voice low, "being here with you now. I never thought I'd get the chance. I never gave up, but it was hard to hold onto the hope as time went on."

I look up at him. The hard lines of his face soften.

"I understand that. I learned that hope can be a dangerous thing to hold onto. It can hurt as much as it can heal."

He nods.

"I missed so much," he whispers.

"I did too." My voice breaks, but I don't look away.

"I'm just so happy you're here now." Lucian smiles squeezing my shoulder gently. "We'll make new memories."

As another wave rolls in, I let myself believe him.

7 ASHTHORNE HALL

The car slows as the wrought-iron gates open. Ashthorne Hall sits beyond them like something out of a movie. Grand and old, with ivy clinging to the stone columns. The gravel drive winds in a perfect curve around a fountain that's taller than the car.

I glance at Lucian, who's watching my face.

"Welcome home."

The car stops, and before I can move, someone's already opening my door. A man in a suit offers his hand.

The gravel crunches under my boots. The air smells like rain and roses and money.

Lucian steps out beside me. "You don't have to be nervous."

"I'm not nervous," I lie.

He gives me a look but doesn't call me on it. Just gestures toward the wide front doors, which swing open as we approach.

Inside, the foyer is all marble floors, vaulted ceilings, and golden light pouring in through stained glass. A chandelier sparkles above us like a constellation frozen in crystal. My reflection follows me in the polished floor—oversized hoodie, scuffed shoes, hair in a messy braid. I look like a stray.

"Isobel," Lucian says softly, stepping closer. "This is your home."

I swallow hard. "It feels like a museum."

He smiles faintly. "It's warmer than it looks."

A woman steps forward from the hall—tall, sleek, with perfect posture and cool eyes. She's in her forties, maybe. Impeccably dressed.

"This is Elara," Lucian says. "House manager. She runs the estate. Anything you need—clothes, toiletries, space—just tell her."

"Welcome, Miss Ashthorne," Elara says with a graceful nod, like I'm royalty instead of a stray dragged in off the street.

"Nice to meet you." I try to force a smile onto my face, but I'm not sure I succeed. "Please just call me Isobel."

"Would you like a tour?" Lucian gestures.

"I'm going to need a map."

"That can be arranged." He chuckles.

A large living room with a fireplace and cushioned seats. A formal dining room with a long, opulent dining table.

We pass a portrait of a woman in a high-necked gown with a hawk perched on her arm.

"She looks like she'd stab someone with a knitting needle."

Lucian glances over. "That's Margot Ashthorne. Your great great great great grandmother. She probably did."

We push through a set of double doors, and it's like stepping into a dream.

Books line every wall, floor to ceiling, with rolling ladders and iron balconies along the second level. There's a spiral staircase winding up into the soft light that filters through the stained-glass dome overhead. Velvet chairs in deep blues and emeralds are scattered around a sunken fireplace. It's warm here, even though no fire burns.

"This is my new favorite room." I look around in awe.

"I'm not surprised." Lucian chuckles. "Come back whenever you want."

"I definitely will." I smile as he leads us back out. Albeit, somewhat reluctantly on my side.

He shows me the kitchens—somehow bigger than the dining room—then the back terrace where the gardens stretch toward the tree line.

The gardens roll out in layered tiers with hedges trimmed to perfection, beds bursting with soft peonies, lavender, and strange flowers I don't even recognize. Stone paths snake through them, curving around marble statues half-sunk in ivy and time. There's a koi pond, of course. There's always a koi pond in rich people movies. But here it's real, orange and white shapes drifting beneath lily pads.

We head down one of the stone paths, and he shows me the greenhouse. It's all glass and iron bones, full of filtered sunlight and the smell of damp moss. Inside, it's warm and misty, alive with vines, herbs, and exotic plants that stretch for the ceiling. There's a little table and two wrought-iron chairs tucked in the corner.

"I used to come here when I needed to think," Lucian says, brushing his fingers across a lavender stalk. "Still do, sometimes."

After the greenhouse, he leads me toward what looks like an outbuilding—stone, similar to the rest of the estate, but newer.

He punches in a code, and the door slides open into a modern dream.

It's a gym. Full floor-to-ceiling mirrors, polished floors, free weights, machines I don't know the names of, even a boxing setup in the corner. There's a small fridge filled with water bottles, and sleek storage cabinets stocked with everything from towels to wraps and protein bars.

We exit through a side door, and the path curves again—this time to a hidden courtyard. And there, nestled in a serene oasis, is a pool.

Long and light blue, surrounded by chaise lounges and trailing vines. A glass wall to the side reveals a pool house, stocked with towels, speakers, and —yes—a minibar.

I blink. "This is insane."

Lucian gives a small laugh. "It's a lot. I know."

"It's not just a lot. It's another planet."

Lucian leads us back into the house, showing me which way to his office if I ever need him. My head is spinning as we make our way to the main foyer where Elara is just walking in from the other side of the house.

"Miss Isobel, your room has been prepared. Would you like to rest before dinner?"

"Oh, yes, thank you." I smile at Elara.

Elara leads us up the stairs, her heels whispering against the marble while my boots land like gunshots. I try to walk quieter, but everything about me feels too loud here — the weight of my steps, the beat of my heart, even the breath I hold in my lungs. The staircase curves upward like something carved into a palace, wide and elegant, flanked by gold-dipped sconces and intricate railings that gleam beneath the chandelier's light.

Every painting we pass feels older than the country — oil portraits of men in military coats and women in silk gowns, their gazes heavy and all-knowing, as if they can see straight through me. The hallways stretch on, lined with wainscoting and antique tables topped with flower arrangements and crystal bowls I'm afraid to even look at too hard.

We stop at the end of a hallway at a set of double doors.

"Welcome to your room," Lucian says as Elara opens the doors.

The room is... breathtaking. No, *unreal*. I stepped through a mirror and landed in some princess's daydream.

It's massive, at least twice the size of the living room back home, with ceilings so high I could stack five of me and still not touch the molding. The walls are a soft stormy gray with faint silver detailing that catches the light. One entire side of the room is windows, draped in gauzy white curtains and heavier blackout panels, all tied back with braided cords. The late afternoon light spills in and sets the room aglow.

The bed sits in the center like a throne, canopied, four-posted, carved from deep wood with velvet hangings. The comforter is thick and pale silver, layered with plush pillows in shades of ash, ivory, and charcoal.

There's a massive walk-in closet built into the far wall, doors wide open, revealing rows of hanging clothes. All new. All clearly chosen for me. I spot the clothes we bought with Maeve already unpacked and hanging with yet even more clothes. All my new shoes Lucian insisted on are lined up in neat rows.

A full wardrobe, multiple pairs of shoes. I'm speechless. Warmth spreads through my body and I want cry. I don't feel deserving of any of this. But Lucian, *my* dad, cares about me.

I pull out one hanger, running my hand down a soft knit sweater, the color of oatmeal. Before Lucian, I never owned anything that didn't belong to someone else first. Never chose what I wore based on comfort, just... what didn't itch. What I could get that fit. What didn't show the bruises. But now, I have endless options, all of it new.

A desk sits beneath the window with a sleek laptop already charging. A soft reading nook is tucked into the corner beneath built-in shelves, and the shelves... are full. Books I've only ever seen in libraries. Spines in leather and gold, others in soft pastels. Art books. Fiction. Poetry. A few graphic novels.

There's a full-length mirror near the closet. No cracks, no missing pieces. The girl in it doesn't look like she belongs. I look like I'm trespassing.

Lucian comes from behind me. "If there's anything you need, we can have it here by morning."

My eyes feel like they might pop out of my head. "This is all for me?"

"Yes," Lucian says with a little chuckle.

"I—" My voice sticks. I clear my throat. "This is... too much."

"No," he says, his tone firm. "It's not even close to enough."

"My old bedroom is smaller than the closet."

My hands shake a little as I run my fingers over the quilt. It's absurdly soft.

The room smells like fresh linen and something faintly floral. No mildew. No cigarette smoke. No mold creeping in from the walls.

The kind of room you don't have to lock.

For a long moment, I stand there. I don't cry. But something shifts inside me. Like this is the first breath after drowning.

Lucian touches my shoulder lightly. "We'll give you some time to settle in. Dinner is at seven if you feel up to it."

I nod, still absorbing everything. He leaves, and Elara follows, giving me one last nod before pulling the doors closed with a gentle *click*.

And then... Silence.

Not the kind I grew up with. Not the sharp, dangerous kind that came before yelling or slamming doors. This silence is *soft*. Safe. Wrapped in thick carpet and heavy curtains.

The first thing I do is walk back to the doors. Running my fingers over the cool antique brass handles... and find a keyhole. A tiny, polished key already sits in the lock.

Turning it slowly—*click*—I feel the lock slide into place. From the *inside*. I test the knob. It doesn't budge.

A laugh catches in my throat, soft and disbelieving. A door that *locks*. Not to keep me in, but to keep everyone else out.

Just me. This is mine.

I drift through the space slowly, touching everything just to make sure it's real. The rows of books. The windowsill cushion, still warm from the sun. The silver-rimmed lamp beside the bed.

I sit on the bed and it's like I'm sinking into a cloud.

The tears come out of nowhere. Not loud, not ugly—just quiet streaks down my cheeks as I bury my face in a pillow that smells like lavender and clean cotton.

This room is mine. No yelling outside the door. No footsteps I have to hold my breath through. No fear. No Daniel.

THE AIR IS warm and faintly perfumed, carrying the distant scent of rosemary and garlic, sharp and inviting, threading through the corridors. It lures me forward, toward the dining room, where I'm supposed to sit as if I belong here. My stomach twists, part nerves, part hunger, and I keep my gaze straight ahead, shoulders squared, pretending I don't feel the weight of every step or the grandeur pressing in from all sides.

I feel like I'm being watched, even though I haven't seen anyone. The sconces flicker with soft golden light.

The double doors at the end of the hall are already open.

Lucian stands as I enter. He's at the head of a long, elegant table, the kind you only ever see in movies. A chandelier spills soft light across a white linen runner, flanked by silver and crystal. Everything gleams.

And at the far end of the table, a girl sits.

She straightens immediately when she sees me. Blonde hair pulled into a neat low ponytail, sharp cheekbones, pink lipstick. Her dress matches her nails, and the moment I meet her eyes, she lights up with a smile that's so bright it throws me off balance.

"You're here," she says, standing up. "Hi! I'm Dakota."

She crosses the room with the eager steps of someone who's been waiting for this moment.

Lucian's voice cuts through the hum in my ears. "Isobel, come in. This is my wife, Adrienne. And this—"

"I'm her stepsister," Dakota finishes, beaming. "Technically. But who cares about technicalities?"

Adrienne rises too, elegant in that unbothered way only rich women seem to master. She offers me a small, cool smile. "Welcome, Isobel. I hope your room is comfortable."

"It is," I say, still trying to find my footing. "Thank you."

Dakota gestures to the seat beside her. "Come sit. I saved you a spot. I mean, technically the housekeeper did, but I told her to."

Lucian gives a quiet chuckle and pulls out my chair as I cross the room. I sit down, feeling like every movement is being documented, but Dakota's warm gaze never wavers.

"I can't believe you're real," she says as the first course is placed in front of us. "I've known about you for a while now, well, I knew there was someone. I just didn't think I'd actually get to meet you."

"Yeah. Me neither." I manage a small smile, still unsure what to do with this version of events.

"Lucian told me everything," Dakota says, reaching for her glass of water. "I mean, not everything-everything. But enough. And I just want you to know. I'm really glad you're here. Seriously."

Her voice is open, a little nervous even.

"Thank you," I say, my voice quiet.

For a beat, the room settles. Cutlery clinks against porcelain. Adrienne sips her wine. Lucian watches me with something close to relief.

Dakota twists her fork between her fingers, then leans in just slightly.

"Do you… like it here so far? I know it's a lot all at once, but I really hope it doesn't feel awful."

That catches me off guard. I blink. "It's… not awful."

Dakota lets out a soft laugh. "Okay, that's fair. We'll work our way up to kind of okay next."

Lucian chuckles under his breath. Adrienne even smiles behind her glass.

I reach for my water glass and take a slow sip, glancing sideways at the girl who — hours ago — I had prepared myself to hate. She's nothing like I expected. And even though I don't fully trust it yet… I want to.

Dakota picks up a slice of bread from the basket and offers it to me first.

"Trust me," she says. "The chef's sourdough is basically a religious experience."

I take the bread. It's warm and fluffy. A perfect crunch on the outside with a light inside.

"That's amazing." I take a bite of duck. It's sweet, rich, and probably the most expensive thing I've ever eaten.

Dakota glances down at her plate. "I know this is weird. I've never had a sister before."

"Me neither," I admit. Maeve has always been like a sister to me, but this was official.

Her smile softens. "Well… then maybe we can figure it out together?"

I meet her eyes. There's nothing fake there. Just honest, maybe slightly awkward, hope.

I nod slowly. "Yeah. Maybe we do."

Lucian exhales, his shoulders dropping, and for the first time all night, I realize my shoulders aren't as tense. Adrienne even has a faint smile as she reaches for a second pour of wine.

The conversation shifts after that, less stiff, less formal. Dakota asks what I think of the house so far, and I tell her about the painting in the hallway that I swear moved the first time I walked by. She laughs, snorting a little before she covers her mouth with a hand.

"Oh my god," she says. "That one creeped me out as a kid, too. I used to run past it every time I had to go to piano lessons."

"I knew it. It's haunted."

Lucian chuckles under his breath. "It's eighteenth-century. Not haunted, just expensive."

"I don't think those are mutually exclusive." Dakota nudges me and winks.

Adrienne stays mostly quiet, but there's no more frost in her gaze, just quiet observation. Occasionally, she makes a small comment—about the menu, about Dakota's weekend schedule—but she's not hostile. Just distant. Reserved. And right now, I can live with that.

"Do you like school? Are you good at it?" Dakota asks.

"I mean, it was hard with my situation." I take a much-needed drink of water.

"You already seem smart." Her voice is sincere. "And I bet you're crazy brave, too. Just walking in here tonight, knowing you'd be sitting across from strangers. I'd be freaking out."

"I kind of am," I admit.

After dessert—some fancy, sculpted thing with chocolate ganache and gold flakes that looked more like art than food—we linger around the table, sipping drinks and trading a few stories. Nothing too deep. But it's something. It's more than I expected.

Eventually, Lucian rises. "I have a call in five," he says, looking to Adrienne with a nod.

She rises gracefully, her napkin folded with precision. She leans over to kiss Dakota's cheek, then nods at me. "Good night, Isobel."

"Good night."

As she disappears through a side hallway, Lucian turns to me. "I'll see you in the morning."

"Yeah. Okay." I nod.

He pauses. "I'm glad you came."

Then he's gone.

The room falls into a comfortable silence. Dakota stands, stretching slightly, and picks up her water glass.

"Do you work out? I'm going to need to work off that chocolate."

"I don't. I've never worked out before."

"Well, do you want to come with me tomorrow? You don't have to do anything, I'd enjoy your company and getting to know you. And if you want to, I can help you with anything."

I hesitate, then think fuck it.

"Sure, tomorrow." I nod.

She nods. "Okay. Tomorrow."

Then, before I can leave, she adds quietly, "I meant it, you know. I'm really glad you're here."

THE MOMENT I shut the door behind me, I lock it. The click is quiet, but it fills the whole room like a shout. My chest rises and falls as I lean back against the door.

The quiet in the room is golden and still, lit by the warm glow of the chandelier above. Everything is untouched: the soft bedding, the neatly folded clothes, the elegant desk tucked beside the window. It all looks like a magazine spread, like it belongs to someone else.

Dinner went better than I expected. No jabs. No raised voices. Dakota smiled at me, even made space at the table when she didn't have to. Still, something in me buzzes with tension. Like I've been braced for impact so long, I don't know how to stop.

I pull the sweater over my head, toss it onto a chair, and grab my phone. My thumb moves on instinct, tapping Maeve's name.

It rings once. Twice.

"Hey," she says, warm and familiar.

My pounding heart seems to slow and I can take a deep breath.

"How's castle life?"

I huff a quiet laugh. "You have no idea."

"Ooh, that good already?"

"Dinner was... honestly not what I expected."

There's a beat of silence. "That sounds suspiciously not terrible."

I smile. "I met Dakota. My... stepsister. She's my age. Beautiful. Composed. She looks like a Barbie."

Maeve hums. "Sounds like she's one of those 'perfect on paper but secretly a viper' types."

"Actually... no. She was nice." That surprises even me as I say it.

"Wait. Nice, nice? Or, like, 'smiling shark' nice?"

"She made room for me. Gave me the good bread. Even asked if I was okay. She seemed like she genuinely wanted to get know me."

Maeve lets out a soft breath. "Wow. Okay. That's... weirdly wholesome. I was ready to sharpen my claws."

"I was, too." I pace a slow circle on the rug. "I think I went in expecting a fight. I was bracing for it. But it didn't come. Now I don't know what to do with the fact that she might actually want me here."

"Maybe," Maeve says gently, "that's allowed to feel good."

"I want it to. I really do."

"Then start there."

I sit down on the bed, folding my legs beneath me. "Adrienne was quiet, but... not mean. I don't think she knows what to do with me either."

"You're a walking plot twist," Maeve says. "They had to recalibrate their whole family dynamic. They had time to get used to the idea of you, but interacting when you're actually there is a different scenario entirely."

I laugh under my breath. "I keep thinking I'm going to wake up and none of this will be real."

"Isobel, this is real. The bed you're sitting on? Yours. The weirdly formal dining room? Also, yours. And if anyone makes you feel like you don't belong, just remember, you do."

I nod, even though she can't see me. "I'm trying."

Maeve's voice softens. "You don't have to win them over in a day. You don't have to prove you deserve to be there. Just exist. Be you. That's more than enough."

Tears burn and I try to blink them away. "You always say the right things."

"I'm your best friend. It's literally in the job description."

I lay back on the bed, the duvet soft and heavy across my legs. "I wish you were here."

"I do too. But I'm only a call away. You got this, Iz. You've survived worse. Now you get to figure out what it means to live."

I close my eyes. "One marble hallway at a time?"

"One fancy light switch at a time," she corrects. "And claim the good bathroom before Dakota gets any ideas."

"I'll keep that in mind," I laugh. "But I actually have my own bathroom."

"Lucky bitch." Maeve's smile fills her voice. "I only hate you a little for that."

"Sorry." I wince.

"No! Don't you dare apologize, Isobel Ashthorne. You enjoy all the perks. I'll enjoy them when I come and visit."

We fall quiet, the line buzzing softly between us. My heart aches, missing my best friend.

Then Maeve says, "I hope you sleep okay tonight."

I don't answer right away. Just let her voice settle into the quiet of the room.

"Me too," I whisper.

"If not, text me. I'll send you memes. Or a playlist. Or possibly threatening audio messages you can play on a speaker near Adrienne."

That makes me smile.

"Thanks, Maeve."

"Always."

I end the call, set the phone down, and crawl beneath the covers. The sheets are crisp and expensive. It's a completely new world.

I still feel like I don't quite fit. But... maybe I could.

8 FIGHT OR FLIGHT

The house is dark. Just creaking wood, rotting carpet, the static buzz of a broken lamp.

The air is heavy, too thick to breathe. I know I'm dreaming, but that doesn't stop it from hurting.

The floor groans outside the door. Then his voice. Low. Slurred. Too close.

"Think you're better than us now, huh?"

The door flies open.

Daniel's in the doorway, backlit by the flickering TV in the other room. The haunting laugh track echoes in my ears. Shirtless, eyes red-rimmed and wild. He moves fast, always faster than I think he should. The belt's already in his hand.

I back away, hit the wall. My voice is gone. Legs locked. The dream never lets me scream.

He raises the belt. Crack. White-hot pain across my arm. Crack. The skin on my back burns.

The floor shifts beneath me. My knees buckle. I taste blood. I hear my own breath ragged and helpless.

He leans down, hatred burning in his eyes.

"Ain't no one comin' for you, little bitch."

My heart is like a wild animal trapped in a cage. I'm drenched in sweat, lungs gasping for air. For a second, I don't know where I am. The room's too big, too quiet.

My senses start to return. Soft sheets. Heavy blankets. A silk pillow under my head.

A warm breeze from the window stirs the curtains.

And the door—

Still locked.

I'm not there.

I'm *not* there.

I'm not *there*.

My breath stutters, tears rising too fast to stop. I throw off the covers and press my feet to the cold wood floor just to feel grounded, to make sure I really am here.

The dream clings like smoke. His voice still echoes.

I wrap my arms around myself, curling forward. My hair sticks to my face, damp. I reach out—fingers trembling—and switch on the small lamp beside the bed.

Light floods the space.

No cracked drywall. No duct tape over windows. No bloodstains on the carpet.

This is my room. Ashthorne Hall. Safe.

My throat aches. I wipe my face with the edge of the blanket. My phone sits on the nightstand like a lifeline. I almost reach for it.

But instead, I whisper to the empty room.

"I'm safe. I'm safe. I'm safe."

I don't even try to go back to sleep.

BY THE TIME I wander downstairs, sunlight is pouring through the tall windows like something out of a movie. Everything in Ashthorne Hall looks less haunted in the daylight.

The dining room is quieter than last night. Just the soft rattle of porcelain and the smell of coffee and something buttery drifting from behind swinging doors.

Lucian smiles as I enter. "Morning."

He's in a dark gray sweater and slacks, somehow looking both expensive and approachable. His hair's still damp from a shower, pushed back from his face.

"Morning," my voice is hoarse.

He gestures toward the table. "Help yourself."

I sit. The chair doesn't creak. The table doesn't wobble. There's a place already set for me—white China, a glass of orange juice, a linen napkin folded like a flower.

Lucian sits across from me and sips his coffee. "I heard you were up late. The night staff mentioned the TV."

I stiffen. But he holds up a hand. "No one's monitoring you, Isobel. Just... making sure you're okay."

I nod, eyes flicking to the covered plates in front of us. "I didn't sleep much."

"Do you want to talk about it?"

I shake my head. "Not really."

He doesn't press. Just lifts the lid on one of the dishes and reveals a small stack of golden pancakes with berries and powdered sugar. The other plate has eggs, toast, and what looks like some kind of fancy bacon. Not a single thing touches another.

"I used to hate when food mixed."

"I remember." Lucian chuckles.

"You remember that?" My eyes widen.

"I remember everything I was allowed to know."

I study him. "Even the dumb little stuff?"

He looks at me then, truly looks. "Especially that."

"Well, I eventually got over the food touching thing. I didn't have much of a choice."

I reach for the toast just to have something to do with my hands.

He adds, voice gentler now, "No one expects you to adjust overnight. Take your time. Set your own pace. Anything you want or need, you got it."

"Can I get that in writing?" I smile, raising an eyebrow.

Lucian smiles into his coffee. "I'll have my lawyer draft it this afternoon."

We eat in comfortable silence for a while. Lucian refills my orange juice without asking, and when I finally clear my plate, he pushes a small plate of croissants toward me.

"You're trying to fatten me up," I murmur, half-teasing.

He raises a brow. "This isn't about fattening. It's about giving you back your strength."

I tear off a piece of croissant and chew slowly. It's buttery and soft. I don't say thank you out loud, but I think maybe he hears it anyway.

Dakota skips in, wearing a blue matching work out set and a small white jacket.

"Good morning!" She gives us a big smile.

"Morning." I take a long sip of coffee.

"Good morning, Dakota." Lucian smiles.

Dakota slides next to me, pouring herself a glass of orange juice. "We're going to the gym today. Isobel said she'd keep me company." Dakota bites into a crispy piece of bacon.

"Oh, really?" Lucian's eyebrows rise. "I didn't know you work out."

"I don't." I shrug.

"We're going to get to know each other and if there's anything Isobel wants to try, I said I'd help her," Dakota adds.

"Well, I'll try to stop by and see how it's going." Lucian's phone rings. Reaching into his pocket, he pulls it out and glances at the screen. "Sorry, girls, I've got to take this."

"No problem," Dakota and I say in unison.

I give her a small smile.

Lucian's eyes soften for a moment before he turns, answering the phone with a stern greeting before walking out.

Dakota sets me up on a treadmill, and I walk in a steady rhythm as I watch Dakota move from one machine to the next. She lets me know that she has a trainer coming shortly.

She asks me a lot of the basic things. What's my favorite color? *Black.* She tells me that's not a color. *So, blue.* What's my favorite TV show? *I don't have one, never had time to watch.* Favorite movie? *Same answer as before.* Favorite food? *Couldn't really be picky since I didn't have many options.*

She has a small crease between her brows by the time her trainer arrives. Dakota twists her hair back into a tight braid. I stop the treadmill and move next to the boxing ring, dabbing my forehead with a towel and drinking some water.

Dakota steps into the ring with a tall, broad-shouldered trainer. He circles her like a shadow, barking commands that she answers with fierce precision.

Jab. Cross. Elbow. Sweep.

She moves like she's done this a hundred times. I can hear the power behind each move.

My breath catches as I watch her land a brutal hook to the trainer's padded side, followed by a low kick that knocks him slightly off balance. He grunts in approval, nodding for her to go again.

Lucian stops beside me. I can't help the jump. His arms are crossed, as he watches his stepdaughter without a word. His expression was unreadable.

I can't look away for long.

This was the same girl who'd passed the bread at dinner with a polite smile. Who looks like a walking doll. But here—she is something else entirely. Sharp. Unyielding. Fierce. She moves with a type of grace that is equally deadly.

"I didn't know she could fight like that," I say, a bit of awe in my voice.

Lucian glances at me. "She's been training since she was ten. It started as a way to channel her energy. Now it's part of her discipline. Her edge."

I nod slowly, still watching Dakota drive her fist into the padded mitt with a satisfying crack.

A strange feeling tightens my chest. Not jealousy. Not envy. Something deeper.

Need.

"I want to learn."

Lucian turns fully toward me.

"I want to learn how to do that," I say, my voice quiet but firm. "To defend myself. To fight back. I don't ever want to feel weak again."

There's a beat of silence. Then he nods once.

"Good," he says. "We'll start tomorrow."

And just like that, something inside me shifts and clicks into place.

"That would be perfect." I beam up at him. "Thank you."

I'M TRYING to copy the stretches Dakota showed me when Lucian steps in with a woman with wine-colored hair. They laugh and it dawns on me that I've never seen Lucian talk and joke like this with anyone.

I push myself up off the ground and rub my hands down my leggings.

"Isobel, this is my good friend, Savannah Riley. Savvy, this is my daughter, Isobel."

Savvy extends her hand out with a wide smile. "It's an honor to meet you."

I take her hand. Something about her just emanates warmth and comfort. "It's nice to meet you."

"Savvy is one of the best fighters and trainers I know. She agreed to help out and teach you this summer." Lucian crosses his arms, his smile big and easy.

"Sounds good." I return their smiles.

"I'll leave you ladies to it." Lucian squeezes my shoulder. "Thanks again, Sav."

"Oh, no thanks needed!" she returns with a bright smile. "It's truly my pleasure."

Lucian heads out, and she turns back to me, taking a deep breath. "Ready?"

I exhale heavily. "As ready as I can be."

Savvy spends the next hour teaching me different workouts and building a circuit that I can do when she's not around. Then she teaches me the proper fighting stance. Feet shoulder-width apart, slight bend in my knees, weight balanced, hands up, elbows in. She teaches me the basics. Guarding, footwork, breathing, blocking, parrying, and how to throw a proper punch.

By the end of hour two, I'm drenched in sweat while Savvy looks like she just started to work out. We settle on the floor to take a break.

"How do you know Lucian?" I take the water she hands me gratefully.

"We grew up and went to school together actually. I've known your dad since we were little kids." She takes a swig of her water, then smiles at the memories that must be playing in her mind.

"Your dad was always so nice to everyone, but he had a few dorky years before growing into the man he is today." She laughs under her breath.

"Really?" I smile trying to think of Lucian as anything other than powerful. Dorky?

"Can you tell me more about him? What he was like to grow up with?"

"You want embarrassing stories." She pokes at me.

I nod eagerly. "I mean, if you're willing to share them."

Savvy laughs and it's a light but full sound. "Your dad has these friends, Max, Preston, and Derek. I'm sure you'll meet them soon. They've been thick as thieves since elementary school. They banded together over fruit snacks and juice boxes and have been that way ever since."

"Max, he's the troublemaker, always daring everyone to do things. While Preston is very proper and craves order, Derek is very 'go with the flow' but usually helps Max with all the shenanigans."

"Oh boy."

"Yes, anyways, we had a class trip to this ice-skating rink. There was this girl Lucian was trying to impress, and when she asked him if he knew how to, he said yes. When in fact, your dad did not skate. He had never skated."

"Oh no." I gasp but laugh.

"Right, but he couldn't back out now. It would require admitting incompetence, and at that time, Lucian would rather perish than admit defeat." Savvy laughs, shaking her head.

"So, the moment he steps out onto the ice, he's slipping and sliding like a newborn deer trying to stand and walk."

We both laugh. "Oh my gosh! What happened next?"

"He's gripping the wall like it owes him money, meanwhile, his legs are going every which way and he can't stand still for longer than a few seconds.

"The girl asks if he's okay and he insists he's 'warming up'. But ten minutes pass, and he does not leave that wall. A child skates past him—backwards."

I fall back, laughing at the mental image.

"Eventually, Max tries to teach him. 'Push and glide,' he said."

"Push and glide." I giggle.

"So, your dad pushes, and glides… directly into the barrier. The crash was so loud I swear the whole place went silent." Savvy is laughing so hard she's wiping at her eyes.

"Your dad just lies there for half a second, dignity in shambles, then sits up and announces that 'the ice is uneven'. We were crying laughing."

"Oh, that must have been so embarrassing."

"Yes, safe to say, he did not impress the girl." Savvy takes a deep breath while still laughing.

"For weeks afterward, people would ask him if the floors were uneven."

"That's freaking hilarious." My cheeks hurt from smiling.

"It really is." Savvy stands up and offers me a hand. "That's my one Lucian story for the day. Let's get back to it." She helps me up.

"If he ever asks, tell him Max told you all these, okay?" She winks.

9 TRUTH OF THE HEIR

The next day, as I'm walking through the house, I hear laughter floating through the halls.

I follow the sound and find Lucian and Savvy sitting with three other men.

"Gracie, come in! I want you to meet my friends!" Lucian waves me in.

"Hi, Isobel." Savvy smiles.

"Hi." I give them a small smile. Part of me wants to turn and run back out of the room with all the eyes on me.

"This is Max, Preston, and Derek."

Max is tall with chestnut hair and gentle brown eyes. He gives me an easy smile and a wave. "Nice to meet you, Isobel. It's crazy to see you all grown up."

Preston gives me a serious but polite nod. "Hello." His voice is deep, his locs are pulled away from his face in a low ponytail.

Derek gives me a big smile. "You look so much like Lucian." His dark hair is styled neatly.

"Come and sit with me." Savvy pats the seat beside her and I follow.

"Nice to meet you all," I say and turn to look at Lucian. He's relaxed in his seat with a big smile on his face.

"So," Max says, leaning forward before anyone else can speak, his grin widening. "You're the legendary Gracie. I feel a little cheated. Lucian made it sound like you'd be taller."

Lucian scoffs. "Ignore him."

Max only laughs. "I'm kidding. You've got his eyes, though. Lucky girl."

I blink, unsure how to respond, but Derek chuckles.

"He's been jealous of Lucian's eyes since we were kids." Derek adds smoothly. "Man has no filter. You can ignore him most of the time." He shoots a look at Max, whose mouth has dropped open.

"You take that back!" Max says.

"No." Derek replies.

Max tackles Derek and laugh as they wrestle. Preston moves aside, his eyes smiling but never fully laughing.

Savvy gives me a warm smile, I must be failing to hide the tension. "The boys were just reminiscing about their glory days at Blackmoore."

"Is that a high school?" I ask no one in particular.

"It's a private elite college." Lucian answers. "Specializing in focusing more on certain areas of study."

"They maintain higher standards than most colleges." Preston adds.

I nod. "I see."

"Lucian was the golden boy." Derek takes a drink.

"Except the floors were uneven." Max snickers.

The room fills with laughter and Lucian hurls a pillow at Max with surprising accuracy.

"Do you have plans for college?" Derek asks.

I open my mouth, then close it again. My pulse quickens.

I swallow. "I really hadn't thought too much about school. I never thought I'd be able to afford it."

"Well, good thing Lucian's loaded so you can do whatever you want now." Max smiles.

Lucian rolls his eyes.

"But I didn't apply anywhere."

"You're an Ashthorne, you don't have to apply." Preston shrugs.

"There's a spot for you at Blackmoore Academy, since you're part of the Ashthorne legacy," Savvy says.

"Is school something you want to do?" Lucian asks, leaning forward.

"If I don't, what would I be doing? Become a spoiled, rich brat that just lies around?"

"She's got it." Max claps, laughing.

I shake my head with a small smile. "I'd rather go to school. I want a better life, but I don't want things just handed to me."

Lucian beams. "That's my Gracie."

"You can let us know how the floors are." Max cackles.

"Have you ever been ice skating?" Derek's eyes sparkle.

"You're all insufferable." Lucian groans.

THE SUMMER PASSES in slow motion—each day softer than the last, like the universe is learning not to touch me so roughly.

Training with Savvy every morning is the highlight to my day. Max and Derek join us on occasion, and I get to learn different fighting styles.

I ask Savvy why they all learned to fight and she said it was just a part of their lives. Being in security and living among the elite, they needed to learn how to protect themselves.

The training with Savvy is brutal but necessary. At first, my body feels foreign. Awkward. Weak. I bruise easily, forget to breathe, mess up the footwork. But I don't quit.

Dakota joins me sometimes, offering quiet tips between rounds.

"Keep your elbow tucked," she says. "Pivot from your core. You'll hit harder."

She's not competitive about it. Just supportive. Sometimes we stay after Savvy leaves and spar a little. She pulls her punches but never underestimates me. I start to appreciate that more than I expected.

Strength training becomes part of my daily rhythm. I lift. I run. I fall. I try again. Slowly, I start to see the changes—my body stronger, my breath steadier, my mind quieter. I don't flinch as easily. I stand straighter. I look in the mirror and see someone who could fight back if she had to.

Piece by piece, bruise by bruise, I'm taking myself back.

I'm building myself. Something I wasn't allowed to do before. I'm learning who I am, who I want to be.

I don't want to be the quiet girl who flinches at every noise.

I want to live up to my Grandma Grace and the Ashthorne legacy.

I won't be a doormat anymore. With this determination, my training session with Savvy this morning has me feeling better than ever.

We're taking a break from my training when the question bubbles out of me. "Did you know my mom?"

Savvy looks at me with sad eyes; it's not pity I don't think. "I did."

"What was she like?" I'm suddenly starving for the pieces Savvy may have. "I don't have many memories of her... before."

Savvy sits, patting the mat in front of her. I join her and cross my legs.

"I think you should ask your dad to tell you more about her. I liked her, don't get me wrong. We were even friends, but I don't think I'll have the insight you're looking for on her."

I nod.

"She was always going on about how she couldn't believe someone like Lucian would love her. They met in college. Your mom had Lucian head over heels for her with her fiery personality."

"Your dad, naturally, always wanted to impress her. Max dared him to give her a big romantic speech. But of course, he went above and beyond that. He decided to write her a poem."

"A poem?" I grin.

"A long poem. Complete with Shakespearean cadence and dramatic pauses. It was a whole thing." Savvy giggles, and I join her.

"He decided to recite this poem to her in the middle of the lawn. It was cheesy and hilarious but she loved it. And that's really all that mattered." Savvy reached over squeezing my hand.

"Thank you." I smile back.

I'M CURLED up on the chaise in the library, trying to finish a book I've restarted four times, when a soft knock sounds.

Lucian leans in, his expression careful. "Gracie. Can I speak with you for a minute? In the study."

The way he says it makes my stomach drop.

I nod, set the book aside, and follow him down the hall. The study is warm and dimly lit, all polished wood and deep leather. There's a small fire burning low in the hearth, even though it's summer.

Lucian closes the door behind us.

I sit in the chair across from his desk, suddenly aware of how small I feel in this room.

He lowers himself into the seat opposite me. "I wanted to talk to you about Blackmoore Academy."

Anxiety creeps in my chest. "Did they reject me?"

"No, they didn't." He chuckles.

My brows scrunch in confusion. *Then what about it?*

"There's really no way to say this gently. I'm the current head of the Guild."

"What's the Guild?"

"It's... It's a thieves' guild."

I blink.

"I'm sorry, what?" I breathe. I couldn't have heard him right.

"It's not what it sounds like," he says. "At least not entirely. The Guild is older than Blackmoore. Older than most countries. We deal in secrets. In power. In leverage. And we keep the balance between the other guilds and the elite who rule behind the scenes."

My heart pounds in my ears. "And you're in charge of it."

"I am," he confirms. "And one day, you'll be expected to take my place."

I stare at him. "You're joking."

"I wish I was."

A strange chill passes through me. "Why me?"

"Because you're my daughter. And because you survived. You adapted. You've seen what it means to have nothing — and still hold your head up. That's what the Guild needs in a leader. And what I need in an heir."

"That's insane." A strangled laugh escapes me. "What about Dakota?"

"She's not my blood; she could never take my place. But she'll be an initiate, just like you."

I feel like my brain has checked out for the day. The workers in there decided they were done and just left. I can't fully process the words, they haven't fully sunken in yet.

I swallow hard. "So, what now? I train to be a thief?" I let out a shaky breath. "I mean I've stolen to get by but this sounds like diamond heists and stuff that people see in movies."

Lucian chuckles. "Yes, sometimes it is like that. But to be a leader, you'll need to not only be a thief, but a strategist, negotiator, and ghost."

I stand and start pacing the room. "Is this why my mom ran? She found out about this?"

Lucian shakes his head. "No, your mom always knew about the Guild. When I knew I wanted to spend my life with her, I let her know. Everything it would mean if she tied her life to mine. Gave her an out. But she told me she didn't care. That she wanted to stay."

I huff out a breath, running my fingers into my hair. "This is insane. How is this real?"

Lucian stands and moves to me, placing his hands on my shoulders. "I know this is a lot to take in, but I didn't want you going to school and being blindsided by this. You've been training with Savvy all summer, but you'll have additional classes at school that are for the Guild."

"You didn't think to tell me before?"

"You wanted to train, I wanted to give you time to settle in," Lucian says.

"So Savvy, Max, Preston, and Derek are part of it too? That's why they know how to fight."

Lucian nods. Letting everything sink in.

"Everyone who goes to Blackmoore, are they a part of it?"

"No, it's a secret society. The Guild has a lot of power over Blackmoore, which is how we're able to hide our movements, and teenagers like you are able to start your training early."

I nod as my brain processes his words.

"There's a competing family. The Ravencourts have always tried to take the power away from the Ashthorne family. You'll want to stay away from his son, Jace, and anyone he associates with."

"Ravencourt," I repeat. "Is he in the Guild?"

"His father, yes. Jace will be an initiate like you, but he's had far more training than you. As will most of the others."

He moves back to his desk. "I've long suspected their family had something to do with the death of my parents. The man who hit my parents, I uncovered that his family received a large sum of money after his death. I just couldn't trace it back to them."

My jaw drops, his body is stiff. He looks up at me with fire in his eyes. "That is why I'm telling you to stay away from them. I have to remain impartial as the leader and treat Jace the same as any other initiate. But I can't stand the idea of anything happening to you at their hands."

I nod. "Okay, I'll be careful."

I'm the heir to a thieves' guild.

And somehow, the man on the other end of the desk—the one who brought me safety, who gave me this second chance—is the most dangerous of them all.

"Do you want to attend? This is still your choice. If you don't want to go, to have any part of this, then you can choose a different path."

I take a deep breath.

"What happens if I choose to not go?"

"Then our family legacy ends here with me. But don't let that sway your decision. I love you, and I will always will, regardless of what you decide."

I sit with his words for a moment. This legacy, this Guild. Savvy and her stories of Blackmoore pass through my mind.

My dad, he's giving me an option to not carry on our family's legacy if I don't want it.

But something in me does.

"I want to go." I raise my chin and let him see the confidence in my eyes. "I want to carry on the Ashthorne legacy. I want to be more. I want to be like Grandma Grace."

Lucian smiles, pride beaming in his eyes. "You already are so much like her, Gracie. I'm proud of you."

He walks back around, wrapping me in a hug.

"You're stronger than you know."

10 BLACKMOORE ACADEMY

The city turns into winding roads through dense forest past iron gates, stone bridges, and long-forgotten statues tangled in ivy. The world feels quieter here.

The car slows, the trees part, and I see it.

Blackmoore Academy rises like something out of a forgotten fairytale. Gothic spires pierce the sky. Black stone walls stretch wide and tall, covered in climbing ivy. The building is sharp-edged, sprawling, ancient.

It looks like it was built to keep things out—or keep them in.

I gulp.

The car pulls up to the front circle drive. A massive stone fountain gurgles at its center, water spilling over a statue of some winged creature with blank eyes. The flagstones gleam under the overcast sky.

My heart pounds as the driver opens the door.

Lucian steps out first. He's dressed sharply, as always. His hand lingers on the doorframe. For a second I wonder if he's second guessing my decision to come here.

Then he turns, opens my door, and offers me his hand. I take it.

The wind hits me first—cool and tinged with the scent of pine and rain. The air tastes different here. Thinner.

Blackmoore looms in front of us, all shadowed arches and hard lines. Dakota moves around the car and joins us.

"Isn't it amazing?"

I nod, smiling despite the nerves tightening in my chest. "It doesn't feel real."

"It will." Her hand lingers lightly on my arm before she tucks a loose strand of hair behind her ear. "Come on, let's go get settled in."

Lucian raises a brow but doesn't argue. He just gives me a nod and a small, proud smile.

I look at him. "You're not staying?"

"I have some business to take care of today." His eyes are apologetic. "I tried to reschedule but it couldn't wait."

I nod, trying not to cling. "Okay."

He leans down, pressing a kiss to the top of my head. He opens his arms, and I step into them, wrapping my arms around him. He squeezes me tightly.

"I love you," he whispers into my hair.

Dakota and I watch as his car rolls back out of the driveway. I tighten my grip on my bag, draw in a shaky breath. The pressure of the Ashthorne legacy sitting on my shoulders. Knowing what hides beneath Blackmoore, in the shadows. It's overwhelming. I steel my reserves.

I can do this.

"Ready?" Dakota asks.

I nod, and we head inside together, side by side.

The entryway is massive—vaulted ceilings, marble floors, chandeliers like upside-down forests of crystal. Students pass us, but I don't flinch. Not with Dakota next to me.

She chatters as we climb the staircase. "Your schedule's been uploaded to your account. And I talked to the housing director, so you're on the same floor as me. Three doors down."

"That's... perfect," I say, stunned.

She nudges me with her elbow. "I thought so."

North Wing feels like a place carved out of time—arched ceilings, tall windows, and long stretches of echoing stone. Students stand in clusters, lean against window ledges, glance up as I pass. I pass a group of girls and hear their whispers.

"...that's her..."

"...Ashthorne's kid..."

"...kind of pretty, I guess..."

I keep walking. Shoulders straight. Chin up. Eyes ahead. Heartbeat pounding. *Don't let them see you sweat.*

By the time I reach the third floor, my legs ache and my hand hurts from clenching my bag so tight.

"This is you." She says.

The door is tall, dark-stained wood with black iron hinges. A silver key sits in the lock; it clicks open with a satisfying, solid sound.

I step inside—and freeze.

My room is nothing like I expected.

The ceiling is vaulted, beams exposed and painted deep charcoal. Two tall arched windows line the far wall, spilling soft afternoon light across the stone floor and rich woven rugs. A queen-sized canopy bed sits centered, its frame brushed black metal, layered with cloud-colored sheets and a thick, plush comforter. A writing desk. A wall of bookshelves. A wide armchair nestled under one of the windows. A couch set in front of the large dresser with a TV sitting on top. A small kitchenette area. En-suite bathroom and a walk-in closet.

"This room is beautiful." I walk in.

"Right?" Dakota follows me in, the heavy door shutting behind her. She slides the lock into place.

A slow breath rattles out of me. The lock on the inside settles my nerves a bit.

"We're actually lucky. Some girls have to share their rooms. But thanks to Lucian, we don't." Dakota takes a seat on my couch.

"Oh, yeah, that is nice."

I wander the space like I'm walking through a dream. Everything smells faintly of cedar and clean linen. I run my hand along the cool glass of the window.

There's a small panel by the door—a sleek intercom system. I press it and a clear, robotic voice chimes:

"Breakfast begins at 7:00 A.M. in the East Wing dining hall."

"Blackmoore wouldn't let anyone just be late." I chuckle.

"Definitely not." Dakota giggles. "The intercom is nice but it gets annoying quickly."

"I could see that."

"Well, I'll let you finish settling in." Dakota stands up and crosses over to me hugging me again. "I'm so glad you're here!" She squeals.

"Me too." I smile, hugging her back. "Thanks for walking me."

"Of course, what are sisters for?" Dakota squeezes my arms once more before unlocking the door and slipping out.

THE INTERCOM BUZZES TO LIFE, crisp and cold.

"Good morning, students. Breakfast begins in thirty minutes."

I jolt upright in bed, momentarily disoriented. It takes a minute to get my breathing under control when it finally clicks in my brain that it's the intercom. I can see why Dakota says that gets annoying.

The soft sheets tangle around my legs. For a second, I think I'm still dreaming. Then I remember. I'm at Blackmoore. No yelling. No doors being kicked open. No footsteps outside my door.

Just quiet. I let myself breathe that in before I swing my legs over the side of the bed.

The closet is already stocked with uniforms. Dark green tailored blazers with the gold Blackmoore crest, gray pleated skirts or slacks, crisp white shirts. I pick a skirt and shirt and slide them on with careful, mechanical movements.

Everything fits perfectly. Like it was made for me.

I move to the bathroom. My toothbrush is already in a glass. The soap smells like vanilla and honey from the night before.

I tie my ash-brown hair back in a loose half-up knot, and for once, it behaves. It falls in soft waves down my back.

Back in the bedroom, I slip on the blazer and pull the tablet from the desk to check the map and schedule again.

My bag's already packed with school supplies that Lucian had delivered last night. Notebooks, mechanical pencils, smooth pens, different colored highlighters, everything brand new and expensive feeling.

It makes me nervous to touch any of it.

At the last minute, I glance at the mirror. My reflection looks... strange. Not in a bad way. Just different.

I grab my keys and head for the door.

Click. The lock slides open.

I leave the broken girl from high school behind. I'm determined to fill this role, to be Isobel Grace Ashthorne.

Time to find out what kind of school Blackmoore really is.

THE AIR IS brisk in the stairwell as I make my way down from the third floor, the scent of fresh coffee and something sweet—maybe cinnamon—guiding me toward the dining hall.

My boots echo softly on the polished stone. A few other students move past me in pressed uniforms, talking quietly.

I keep my head high.

The dining hall is cavernous.

Vaulted ceilings stretch overhead like a cathedral, chandeliers hanging low on chains of dark brass. Long banquet-style tables line the room—polished wood, silver trays, and elegant place settings that'd look more fitting in a five-star restaurant than a school cafeteria. Food is set out buffet-style along one wall, gleaming under warm lights. Eggs, pastries, berries arranged like someone painted them.

Fresh bread, citrus, and roasted coffee beans fill my nose. My stomach growls.

Students stream in through arched doorways, laughing, gossiping, and dragging their blazers off to toss them over chairs like royalty. Everyone knows where they're going. Everyone has a place.

I grab a tray and fill up a plate. I'm hungry but the way my stomach keeps flipping, I'm unsure if I should eat at all.

Dakota's already seated at one of the long tables near the tall windows, sunlight casting soft gold through the glass and into her hair. She's laughing at something one of the girls next to her has said, one hand wrapped around a coffee mug. She looks so at ease. Effortlessly at home.

And then she sees me.

Her face lights up. She lifts her hand and waves me over, making space on the bench beside her.

I'm surprised by how much relief that tiny gesture brings. I cross the room, heart thudding a little too fast.

"Morning," she says as I slide into the seat next to her.

"Hey," I manage, setting down my tray. "Hope I'm not crashing anything."

"We're sisters now." She nudges my arm. "You're supposed to sit with me."

I let out a quiet breath of a laugh and look down at my plate.

Her voice lowers slightly, just for me. "Did you sleep okay?"

I nod. "Better than I expected."

"Good. Today's going to be a whirlwind, but I've got you. Don't stress too much about first impressions. Most people know each other from high school."

I glance at her, surprised again. "You're... really good at this."

She shrugs and pops a piece of toast in her mouth. "Being nice?"

"Being a person."

She snorts. "Don't tell anyone. I have a reputation."

I smile and she gives me a wink.

"Okay," she says, tapping her spoon on the edge of her plate for attention. "Everyone, this is Isobel—my sister."

The heads around the table turn. A mix of girls and a couple of boys, all perfectly put together in their tailored uniforms and sleek hairstyles. They look like they belong on the cover of a magazine titled Elite & Effortless.

Dakota gestures down the line. "That's Callie, Brynn, Evie, Tammy—don't let her borrow your eyeliner—and that's Rowen. The only boy here with an actual personality."

Rowen gives a lazy salute with his juice glass. "Welcome to the madhouse."

I nod, trying to keep track of the names. My brain latches onto Brynn = red lipstick, Callie = high bun, Rowen = personality. The rest blur into a wash of designer perfume and private school polish.

"I love your hair," Brynn says, tilting her head slightly. "Those waves are so soft. Is that natural?"

"Oh—uh, yeah." I tuck a strand behind my ear and try to smile. "Mostly."

"Seriously, you're stunning," Callie says with a little grin. "Like, your bone structure? Unfair."

I blink. "Oh. Thanks. Um... yours too."

Smooth, Isobel.

Dakota laughs beside me. "Get used to it. They compliment like it's a competitive sport."

"We just speak the truth," Tammy says, tossing her hair.

I reach for my coffee to hide the heat creeping up my neck. Compliments aren't something I know what to do with. I spent most of high school trying to be invisible.

Dakota notices. She leans in just a touch and says under her breath, "You're doing fine. Just eat your toast."

I glance at her, grateful, and take a bite. The toast is buttery and warm. The tension in my chest starts to loosen, just a little.

"You have a schedule yet?" Brynn asks, spearing a piece of melon.

"Yeah," I say between sips of coffee. "It was preloaded on my tablet."

"Ooh, let's see." Callie leans in, eyes bright. "What do you have first block?"

I pull the school tablet from my bag and wake the screen. I scroll to the timetable.

"Advanced Literature." I look around the table.

Callie leans in again, glancing at my tablet.

"Wait—first block is Mr. Carrick's Lit class?"

"Yeah. Room 204?"

"Oh my god," Tammy groans. "You got Carrick? I've heard he assigns a five-page essay after every unit and calls them 'casual reflections.'"

"It's not that bad," Brynn says, stifling a smile. "Unless you forget to annotate. Then it is that bad."

"Don't listen to them," Dakota says, brushing a strand of hair behind her ear. "Carrick's intense, but he's fair. And he actually loves what he teaches, which helps. You'll be fine."

"Anything I should watch out for?" I try to calm the hoard of butterflies in my stomach.

"Poetry Unit." Rowen snorts.

"It's emotional warfare," Callie adds.

Laughter ripples around the table, and I find myself smiling. The noise of the dining hall swells around us—cutlery clinking, low conversations, the occasional laugh echoing off the stone arches. I look around at the table, at Dakota next to me, at the faces watching me not with suspicion, but curiosity and... welcome.

It's new. It's weird. It's overwhelming.

I'm halfway through my juice, listening to Brynn and Callie argue over some celebrities and who is better looking when Callie stops mid-sentence, her mouth hanging open.

Silence seems to spread around us. I follow Brynn's gaze over my shoulder.

Four of them.

They move with the kind of presence that can't be faked—like the world tilts slightly wherever they go. Every head turns. Conversations cut off mid-sentence. Chairs scrape as people scramble to get out of their way.

The first one leads the pack. Tall, fit, with a face carved from stone and eyes like polished frost. His hair is nearly black with a cool, ashy undertone. Smooth, sculpted waves, brushed back, not a hair out of place. His uniform is immaculate. His expression is cold, his jaw sharp.

Next to him, a boy with lazy confidence in every step, his tie loosened like he couldn't care less about rules. His grin isn't aimed at anyone in particular, but it feels like a dare all the same. He runs a hand through dark, tousled hair, laughing under his breath like he knows something we don't. A glint of a lip ring on his lower left side. He's definitely not as intimidating as the first one.

Behind them, the largest of the group walks with a kind of quiet menace. Shoulders broad, jaw tight, hands shoved in his pockets like he's holding himself back from cracking knuckles or necks. People clear out of his way like he's a wildfire in a uniform. He doesn't walk so much as prowl. His hair is a light blond, shaved close on the sides, messy on top.

And trailing a step behind is a lean, almost lanky one. A tablet in his hand, earbud in one ear. He doesn't bother posturing. Doesn't need to. His gaze flicks over the room once—over round, silver rimmed glasses—before going back to his screen. Brown hair falling back over his eyes.

They pass by tables like no one else exists.

But everyone else sees them. Worships them.

Don't get me wrong, I have eyes. They are all incredibly good looking. But they scream danger. I've had enough of that.

The tables around them seem to bend in their direction, students perking up like sunflowers toward the light—if the light were cold, untouchable, and dressed in black and silver.

I take another bite of my fruit, slow and steady.

This must be Blackmoore royalty.

Quietly, I lean toward Dakota. "Okay, who are they?"

Dakota follows my gaze and smirks. "Oh. That's the Blackmoore Four."

"The what?"

"It's stupid," Callie cuts in.

"They're not a real group or anything," Brynn adds. "Just... a collective legend."

"They're all legacy students," Tammy says. "Super elite, they ran the high school. No one really knows what they're studying half the time."

"They're kind of like the school's personal myth," Dakota says, tapping her spoon to her bowl. "Scary-smart. Scary-skilled. Scary-hot."

I snort. "Great. So, they're a walking red flag."

"Basically," Callie says, sipping her smoothie. "But the kind that makes everyone want to run right into traffic."

"Do they have names? Or is it like no one dares to speak their name type thing?" I ask the girls, grinning.

"Oh, they definitely have names." Evie giggles. "I hear girls moaning them all the time."

Dakota rolls her eyes, leaning into me. "That one"—she nods subtly at the first boy— "is Jace Ravencourt. He's like the silent leader. He never speaks unless he has to."

The boys sit down only a table away. Jace looks like an aristocrat. High cheekbones, nice nose, strong jawline.

That's Ravencourt? Ugh, of course he's hot.

"He's... intense."

Dakota smirks. "That's one word for it."

"I've named him the cold prince in my head."

"I love her commentary." Evie giggles.

"The tan one leaning back like school's a joke? That's Luca Silvain. He's got teeth behind the charm. Don't fall for it. He flirts with literally everyone."

I glance at him. Tousled dark hair, lazy smirk, glint in his eye that says he enjoys pulling wings off flies just to see what happens. He catches me looking and winks.

I look away fast, heat creeping into my cheeks.

"Then there's Tex Ward," Tammy says. "You don't want to meet him in a hallway alone. Came from nowhere."

He's massive. Brooding. Scar on his eyebrow and sleeves rolled up to show the ink lining his arms. He's not slouched—he's coiled.

"And the last one?"

"That's Noah Vexley. The hottest tech genius. Doesn't talk much. Quiet, smart, scary when he wants to be," Rowen finishes off.

I nod.

He's pale, slight compared to the others. His dark brown hair falling over his glasses while he taps away on a tablet.

I'm unsure if I'm supposed to feel intrigued or warned.

"Want me to walk with you to your first block?" Dakota offers, already collecting her bag.

I blink, surprised. "Sure... yeah. Thanks."

She flashes a smile—genuine, easy. "Let's survive your first day, Ashthorne."

I smile back, nerves still fluttering in my stomach. But suddenly, they feel lighter. Like maybe—just maybe—I'm not doing this alone.

We stand, and the rest of the table calls out good lucks and "you'll do great" as I follow Dakota into the current of students.

Maybe I will survive this place.

Maybe I'll even belong.

11 BLACKMOORE FOUR

The classroom smells like old paper and eucalyptus cleaner. The walls are lined with dusty bookshelves, and sunlight cuts through tall windows in golden slats. I slip into a seat near the middle—not too close to the front, but not in the back where it's easy to disappear.

My fingers brush the sleek school tablet on my desk as I glance around. Students file in, most of them already talking to each other. Some toss their bags down like they've been here forever. I keep my spine straight and my mouth shut.

This is fine. I'll just get through class, take notes, and leave.

A chair scrapes nearby.

I don't look.

Then a voice—low and smooth—says, "You always sit alone, or is this just a first-day ritual?"

I blink and glance up.

Luca Silvain is leaning on the desk next to mine, his tie still loosened from earlier, dark brown curls falling into his light brown eyes. There's something too perfect about his smile—white teeth, sharp canines, full mouth, and just enough mischief to make it dangerous. The lip ring catches the light when he grins. He's smiling like we've been flirting for years. Like this is a thing we do.

I freeze. "Are you... talking to me?"

His grin widens. "Depends. Are you Isobel Ashthorne?"

"...Yeah."

"Then yeah," he says, dropping into the seat beside me without waiting for permission. "I'm talking to you."

My brain scrambles. I have no idea what to say. Popular boys don't talk to me. Especially not the boys everyone else stares at like they're carved out of legend and unbothered wealth. How does he even know my name? Then I remember Lucian. Of course, people would know his long-lost daughter. He was with Jace, is he in the Guild too?

Lucian's voice echoes in my head. My hackles rise.

He watches me like he's waiting for something, his elbow propped on the desk, fingers loosely twirling a pen.

"Luca," he offers, like we're friends now. "You'll want to remember that."

I blink at him.

"You've got a nice poker face," he says, nodding to me. "Jace owes me twenty."

"You've already bet on me?"

"Well, of course," he says with that flirty smile that must get him all the girls, head tilting. "Impressive."

"Thanks?"

He leans in enough that I catch the faint scent of some expensive cologne and peppermint. "So... Advanced Lit. Either you're smart, or someone seriously overestimated your reading comprehension."

I lift a brow. "You always this charming?"

"Only when I'm trying to impress someone," he says without missing a beat.

A breath of a laugh escapes me before I can stop it.

He grins like that was exactly the reaction he was aiming for.

I open my mouth to respond, but something makes me pause. I feel someone watching me. I glance across the room and—there he is.

Sitting three rows up, in the very center like he owns the damn place. Jace Ravencourt. Dark hair, sharp profile, back perfectly straight. I can feel his attention like a blade across the back of my neck.

Judging. Waiting.

Not smiling. Not speaking.

Luca observes me with the lazy attention of a cat playing with its toy. He leans forward on one elbow.

"You've got the look, y'know," he drawls, voice low enough that no one else can hear. "The whole tragic, dark past thing. Haunted eyes, mystery girl vibes. You're lucky—some people pay for that aesthetic."

I try and fail not so scowl, a little taken back by the change. "You talk to everyone like this?"

He shrugs one shoulder, grinning. "Only the interesting ones."

"I could show you around," he says, quiet and dangerous. "Blackmoore's a labyrinth if you don't know the right doors. And I happen to know all of them. All the best places to do dirty things in." He winks.

I fold my arms. "Thanks, but I don't trust guys who flirt like it's a sport."

Luca's eyes spark—amused again. He likes the pushback. "That's fair. But maybe I'm just being nice to the new girl."

"Maybe I don't need nice."

He tilts his head, like I've just confirmed something for him. "No. I bet you don't."

Then the smile fades. And just like that, the temperature drops.

I knew it. They were testing me. Using the charmer first to try to lower my guard. *Sneaky move, Ravencourt.*

He leans back in his seat, all trace of warmth gone from his voice. "Still," he says, tapping a finger on the desk, "you should be careful."

My stomach knots.

"New girls tend to break easily around here," he finishes. "Would be a shame if all that sharpness you're pretending to have turned out to be paper-thin."

My jaw tightens, and he smiles again.

Not kind. Not playful.

Predatory.

A voice from the front of the room calls for attention as the teacher begins organizing the day's lecture.

Luca glances forward, then back at me. "Catch you after class, Ashthorne?"

It's not really a question.

I nod—slow, careful. "Sure."

He gives a lazy salute with two fingers and turns back to the front like we didn't just have a bizarre, surreal moment.

I stare at my tablet for a beat too long before finally forcing myself to focus.

THE BELL SIGNALS the end of second block and the beginning of lunch. Students begin to file out of class, Evie launching into a story about how one of the history professors once caught a kid cheating and made him recite the Academy's founding doctrine backwards.

I'm only half-listening.

Because I can feel him behind me. Footsteps that don't rush but don't stop either. Predator pace.

Evie says her goodbye to me and turns down the hall.

As soon as we're alone, he speaks.

"You took your time finding your place."

I turn. Jace Ravencourt stands there—hands in the pockets of his pressed uniform slacks, posture relaxed, but his pale grey-blue eyes sharp.

"I didn't realize I had one," I say.

He steps closer. Not enough to crowd, but enough to unsettle. It's too quiet.

"You do now." He leans down slightly. "Or at least, you think you do."

I narrow my eyes. "Do you always talk in riddles or is this just a 'me' thing?"

He tilts his head, studying me like I'm a glitch in a perfect program. "You're not what I expected."

"Great. Disappointing rich boys since day one."

His lips twitch, not quite a smile. "Not disappointed. Intrigued."

"I'm not here to entertain you."

"No," he says, taking a measured step closer, "you shouldn't be here at all."

My fists clench at my sides. "If you've got something to say, just say it."

Jace's voice drops.

"You think because the vultures circled you and didn't strike, that you're safe?" His gaze flickers down, then back up. "You see, Ashthorne—this place doesn't work like the world you came from. Here, the knives are hidden behind perfect smiles. And the second you forget that..."

He taps a finger against the crest on my blazer. "You bleed."

I hold his stare. "Thanks for the reminder then."

His expression doesn't change, but there's something dangerous in the silence that follows. Like he's calculating how deep he could cut if he wanted to.

"Good," he says at last. "I'd hate to be bored."

He looks down his nose, like I'm nothing more than a speck of dirt. Then he turns and walks away like nothing just happened.

Like he didn't leave frostbite behind with every word.

I walk fast, needing to get out of that hallway. Out of the air he left behind.

It's colder now. Like he took the warmth with him.

I'm halfway down the east wing when footsteps pound on the tiles behind me.

"Isobel!"

I turn just as Dakota skids to a stop beside me, a little out of breath.

"I wanted to catch you and walk with you to lunch," she says, looking me over. "What happened?"

I force a shrug, even though my pulse is still racing. "Ravencourt happened."

Her eyes widen. "Wait. He talked to you?"

"Mm-hm." I keep walking, hoping she won't press. "It was… something."

Dakota keeps pace, her brows drawn. "What did he say?"

"Nothing worth repeating."

Dakota groans.

"He thinks I shouldn't be here."

She nudges me gently with her elbow. "Yeah? Well maybe he's just pissed someone new isn't falling in line."

"I'm not here to fall in line," I mutter.

Jace's voice still echoes in the back of my mind.

Here, the knives are hidden behind perfect smiles.

THE NEXT BLOCK I have after lunch is Biology. The desks are long tables arranged in trios. I scan the room, looking for an empty seat.

But I see them.

Two of the four boys are already seated.

Cause why wouldn't they be here.

Tex is sprawled across the back corner like the desk personally offended him. One leg stretched out, arms crossed, eyes half-lidded. As if he's daring someone to give him a reason to care.

Noah's adjusting something on his tablet. His fingers move fast, precise. Not once does he look up.

A knot twists in my stomach when I realize the only open seat is between them.

This had to be planned.

I keep my face neutral and make my way over.

As I pull the chair back, Tex doesn't move, but I can feel his eyes rake over me. Not in the way Luca looked. This is different.

Like he's watching for cracks.

I sit. Noah spares me a glance over the rim of his glasses, then returns to his screen. No greeting. Not that I expected one.

A woman in a sleek navy coat walks in, heels echoing sharply against the tile. "Welcome to Biology. Team assignment is with who you're sitting with. Work efficiently."

Splendid.

Noah sighs. "Great."

I glance over. "Don't strain yourself with enthusiasm."

He lifts a brow. "I'm just not a fan of dragging dead weight."

Tex snorts.

I don't even look at him. "Then keep up."

Noah actually pauses at that. The corner of his mouth twitches—something between amusement and disbelief.

"Alright, Ashthorne," Noah murmurs. "Let's see what you can do."

The tray lands on our table with a wet *thunk*. A preserved fetal pig. My stomach twists for a half second—then settles. I've seen worse.

Tex picks up the scalpel like it's a weapon. "You ever even done one of these before?"

I pull on my gloves. "You ever stop talking?"

Noah grins at that. "Oof. I like her."

I glance over the instructions on the projected slide, then point. "Start the midline incision at the sternum. Cut shallow or we'll tear through the lower organs."

Tex narrows his eyes, but he does it. Clean, steady. I hold the tissue back with forceps. Noah angles the light. We fall into rhythm.

"Digestive or respiratory?" Noah asks, peering over the pig.

"Digestive," I say at the same time as Tex.

His gaze flicks to mine. "You actually know this?"

I nod. "Liver's right there. Dark brown, lobed. Stomach's tucked under the left lobe. That tube you just nudged? That's the esophagus."

Noah whistles low. "Okay, overachiever."

"Guess I'm not dead weight after all," I murmur, lips twitching.

Tex doesn't answer. He just starts cutting again—slower this time, more careful. I catch him watching me from the corner of his eye as I point out each part with precision.

By the time we've labeled the major systems and entered our data, our tray is the cleanest one in the room. Noah logs the results while I remove my gloves with a satisfying snap.

Tex leans back, arms crossed again—but this time, it's not a wall. It's evaluation.

"You're not bad," he says finally.

I arch a brow. "That's your version of a compliment?"

Noah laughs. "That's practically a love letter coming from him."

I smile faintly, but inside, something steadies.

THE HALL IS quiet when I get back from class.

My feet drag. I'm tired — not just from school, but from always being on alert since the 'Blackmoore Four' entered my day. I'm already counting down to a hot shower and some quiet relaxation before diving into homework.

But then I see it.

My door. My key is sitting in the door lock.

I freeze. My heart stutters.

I know I locked it. I remember the way the key clicked when I turned it. I had the key. I pat my pocket and search my bag. It's not anywhere. I look back at the key sitting in the lock.

I push the door open slowly.

Everything looks the same... at first. And then it doesn't.

My pillows have been fluffed, but they're facing the wrong direction. The window's cracked open just slightly — and I always close that. There's a notebook on my desk that was tucked in the drawer, now laid out with the page open.

Not vandalized. Not messy. Just... touched.

Like someone went through everything I own and then put it all back just enough to drive me insane.

My breath catches. I walk in. Careful. Slow.

The hoodie I always read in? Gone from my bed.

A necklace I've never worn? Sitting neatly on my pillow.

And worst of all—the framed photo strip of me and Maeve... turned face down.

My skin prickles.

Not a single thing is technically damaged. If I report it, they'll say nothing was stolen. No harm done.

But I know what this is.

This was intentional. They wanted me to know they were here. That they could come back anytime they wanted.

And there would be nothing I could do about it.

I make sure my door is locked.

I sit stiffly on the edge of my bed, phone gripped in both hands. The silence in the room presses down on me, heavier now that I know someone's been here. Touched my things. Rearranged my world just enough to unsteady it.

I hate how my fingers shake when I open Lucian's contact.

He answers on the second ring.

"Isobel?"

"Yeah. It's me," I say. My voice is too thin. I swallow, trying to thicken it with steel. "I need a favor."

"Anything."

I stare down at the turned-over photo of Maeve. Right where someone left it.

"I need another lock. A better one. Something they can't pick or swipe the key or... whatever. I just—" I stop. Breathe. "I need this room to be mine."

Lucian's voice is quiet for a beat. "Did someone break in?"

"Yes," I say, even though technically... no one would call it that. "Not in a normal way. Nothing's missing. But someone was in here, and they wanted me to know it. They were deliberate."

His silence sharpens. I can almost hear him mentally snapping his fingers at someone. Making a list. Fixing it.

"Do you know who did this?"

"I have an idea but there's no proof."

"I'll handle it," he says. "I'll have a specialist come tonight. Not just a better lock, but a full security system. This won't happen again."

A knot in my chest loosens. Not all the way—but just enough that I can breathe again.

"Thanks," I whisper. "Really."

He lowers his voice. "I promised you'd be safe. I meant it."

When we hang up, I stand. I walk to the window and slam it shut. I pull the curtains. I straighten the photo of me and Maeve, flipping it upright again.

They think they can scare me? Fine.

But they're not taking this room from me.

I spend the next hour going through all my things, putting them back where they belong, while meticulously looking around for any shred of evidence to confirm my suspicions.

But they were careful. They left nothing behind.

Checking my phone, I make my way down to the dining hall. I grab a sandwich and some snacks to take back to my room to eat in peace.

Shortly after I finish my dinner, there's a knock.

"Max! Preston!" I smile.

"Hi, Iz!" Max steps inside, giving me a quick hug.

Preston follows and offers me a high five.

"Lucian said some people broke into your room?" Preston asks.

I roll my eyes, shutting the door behind them. "Nah, someone must've lifted my key. They just did it to mess with me."

Max's playful smile disappears. "Who's messing with you?"

I giggle. "Calm down, it's okay. Nothing I can't handle. If anything, I'm being hazed."

Preston lifts an eyebrow, studying me. "If you say so."

The first thing they do is remove the lock entirely. It's dismantled in less than two minutes.

In its place, they install a high-tech thumbprint lock with a secondary six-digit code. A small screen glows softly above the knob, and I'm shown how to set my print, my backup pin.

"No override," Preston says. "Well, except Lucian. But only yours works. Not even school administration can get in."

"But if you want to add anyone, you can calibrate it with the app we'll install on your phone."

Good.

Then come the cameras.

Three total — one just above the door, another in the far corner facing the windows, and a third angled to cover the entire room in a wide sweep. They're tiny. Sleek. Matte black. Easy to miss if you're not looking for them.

Motion detection. Night vision. Audio pickup. All encrypted. All synced directly to a secure server only I can access.

They set up an app on my phone. It pings when there's motion and I'm not in the room. Records anything suspicious. Saves clips instantly.

"There's a panic feature," Max holds out a small pendant. "Press and hold for three seconds, and it'll alert us and the campus emergency response. Someone will be here in under two minutes."

I take it.

It's light. Cold in my hand.

They test everything. Show me how to lock and unlock the system manually, how to review footage. The door clicks shut with a mechanical hum that feels solid. Permanent.

By the time they leave, it's well past dark.

I stand in the middle of my room and breathe in the silence.

Safe. This room is mine again.

I walk over to the nightstand and place the pendant next to the photo of Maeve and me — upright this time. Just the way I like it.

Then I curl up on my bed and open the app. I scroll through the live feed of my own room, watching the quiet. The stillness. I watch until my eyes drift close and I fall asleep.

.

12 ASSHOLES

*I*t's pitch black. My ears ring from the silence. Anxiety threatens to take over. I remind myself to breathe.

Light floods the space, my eyes burn.

"Get out." Daniel's voice is gruff.

I scramble to get out. He grabs a fistful of my hair and throws me against the wall.

"Hurry the fuck up. You're so slow."

I grit my teeth against the pain as I stand. I keep my eyes trained to the floor.

"Did you hear anything?"

"No."

He slaps me, my whole body crumpling against the wall.

"No, what?" he spits..

"No, sir." Silent tears run down my tears.

"You pathetic, weak, excuse of life. Such a waste of space. Crying over a little slap." He grunts, yanking my arm so hard it nearly pops out of the socket.

I'm suddenly in the living room, cheek rubbing against the carpet.

The deranged laugh track blares in my ears.

"You'll never be anything." His fingers dig into my hips.

I try to move but I'm tied down.
"Such a good girl for your daddy."
I scream.

The sun barely cuts through the drawn curtains when the alarm buzzes on my phone. I groan, rolling over, the sheets twisting around my legs. My body aches like I ran a marathon in my sleep.

Even here—behind locked doors and motion sensors—I couldn't stop it.

By the time I drag myself through the shower and into my uniform, I feel like a ghost wearing my own skin. I line my eyes in kohl to hide the tiredness. Tame my hair into a ponytail. When I finally step out into the hallway, everything feels too bright.

Too loud.

I keep my head down throughout the morning, the nightmares following me like a cloud.

Before third block starts, I take a seat up near the back, hoping to blend in. I should've known better.

Jace slides into the seat behind me. I feel him before I even hear him — that cold presence like a knife drawn quietly in a dark room.

"Rough night, Ashthorne?"

His voice is low and smooth, a private whisper against the back of my neck.

I stiffen, straightening without turning around. "Why? Looking to send a sympathy card?"

A soft chuckle. "Not exactly. Just thought you looked a little..." He pauses. "Haunted."

I clench my pen tighter. My hand stills over my notebook.

"Must be the lighting," I mutter, not trusting myself to say more.

He leans in, voice dipping even lower. "You're not sleeping well. That's a shame." A beat. "Blackmoore's supposed to be safe, isn't it?"

I turn just enough to meet his eyes. Blue. Cold. Studying me like a question he already knows the answer to.

"Get a hobby," I say quietly.

He smiles—if you can call that twist of his mouth a smile. "You are my hobby."

Then he sits back, completely at ease. The teacher starts the lesson. I don't hear a word of it. I feel the burn of his stare between my shoulder blades the entire time.

I KNOW something is wrong the second I step into the atrium on my way back to my dorm.

It's too quiet. Not the good kind, either. The kind that hums under your skin and makes your instincts curl up like a cornered animal.

Too late now. They're waiting.

Tex perches up on the arm of a leather couch like a predator scanning for prey. Luca, sprawls nearby with an apple in hand, a lazy smile as his eyes track me. Noah's already staring at me, the blue glow of a tablet reflected in his face. And Jace, of course. Standing. Silent. Watching.

I move to walk past, pretend I don't see them—but Noah lifts the tablet, and my name flashes across the screen.

ISOBEL GRACE ASHTHORNE

My blood runs cold.

"What the hell is that?" I ask, voice low.

Noah smirks. "Just some light reading. School files are surprisingly easy to access when you know where to look."

I lurch forward, hand outstretched. "Give it—"

"Did you know," Luca interrupts, grinning lazily, "you've moved... what, six times in the last five years?"

Tex whistles. "That's gotta be a record."

"Foster homes. Group homes. Temporary placements," Noah lists, flicking through the file like he's swiping a menu. "Oh, here's a fun one—'removed due to suspected domestic abuse.' But no charges were ever filed."

Jace doesn't say a word. Just watches me. Waiting.

My mouth dries. I can't breathe. It's like they've cracked me open without touching me.

"You read my file," I say, voice hoarse. "You violated—"

Luca laughs. "Violated? Sweetheart, that would require rules. There are none for people like us."

"It's funny," Tex says. "You act like you're so tough. But this? This is who you really are."

I take a step back, but the door feels miles away.

"Damaged," Noah murmurs. "Disposable."

"I'm not," I whisper. "I'm not—"

"You're a charity case," Jace says, finally breaking his silence. His voice is razor-sharp and soft all at once. "A broken little girl Daddy couldn't keep hidden anymore."

Something inside me cracks. I want to scream. I want to hit them. I want to disappear. But I won't give them that. Not a single tear. Not an inch of weakness. I belong here. I won't run from my legacy.

I meet Jace's gaze, and, somehow, I manage to stand taller. My voice shakes, but I make it work.

"You had to dig through my file to find something to hurt me with," I say. "Must be hard, being so powerful and still that pathetic. I've survived a lot worse than four spoiled assholes in blazers with nothing better to do with their time."

The smirk fades from Luca's mouth. Noah's fingers pause over the screen. Tex's expression darkens.

Jace narrows his eyes. "You'll regret that."

I already do. But I don't show it. I just walk.

Even though I feel like my legs might give out any second, I walk. I don't look back.

THE TREES LOOM OVERHEAD, the branches clawing like they want to pull the night down with them. Someone has strung fairy lights between trunks, their glow flickering gold through the dark like fireflies on a sugar rush. Music pulses in the distance, carried by the wind and the laughter of too many rich kids with too few consequences.

Dakota tugs at my sleeve. "You sure you're okay? We can bail. Say the word."

I adjust the leather jacket around my shoulders. "It's fine. I'm not going to let them get to me."

The woods are alive with commotion—bottles clinking, shadows dancing between fire pits, someone already shrieking with laughter near the edge of the clearing. The energy is feral, different from the marble halls and cold glances of Blackmoore Academy. Out here, no teachers. No uniforms. Just teenagers and trouble.

Dakota nudges me as we step fully into the clearing. "That's Cressida Lorne. Junior council. And over there's Felix, he's—well, kind of a jerk but his family bankrolls a lot of the academy's events. He's a sophomore."

"And the host?"

She tilts her head toward the center bonfire. "Tall guy in the black hoodie, sipping something from a flask. That's Kellan. Sophomore. Trust fund anarchist. Throws these 'forest ragers' every few weeks. Teachers pretend they don't know."

I take it all in, the way people melt into each other, conversations sparking, cigarettes glowing like embers between painted nails. Someone already has a speaker on full blast, blasting bass that makes the dirt hum underfoot.

Then I feel it.

That shift in atmosphere. Heads turning. A subtle ripple of tension passing through the clearing. Dakota stiffens beside me.

"They're here," she mutters.

I don't have to ask who.

From the shadows, they emerge one by one—black coats, lazy grins, danger glinting in their eyes. Jace walks with intent, clearly expecting people to move aside like he's royalty. Luca wears a smirk with a cigarette tucked behind his ear, dragging his fingers through his hair. Tex shoves someone out of his path with his shoulder without even looking at them. Noah brings up the rear, the lights reflecting in his glasses.

Jace's eyes meet mine. No smile. Just that quiet calculation. I don't look away.

Evie and Brynn appear at my side with two plastic cups in each of their hands, breathless and flushed.

"I bribed the guy with the good stash," Brynn grins, offering me one of the cups. "Tastes like lighter fluid, but it'll do the trick."

Evie hands Dakota the other cup.

I accept it, eyeing the liquid warily before taking a small sip. It does taste like lighter fluid, with maybe a hint of lime.

"God, that's awful," I cough.

"Exactly." Dakota grabs my free hand. "Now c'mon. We don't come here to stand around."

I hesitate. The clearing has turned into a writhing mess of limbs and sound—bass thumping through the speakers, people grinding, hands roaming. I'm not used to this kind of chaos. It makes my skin buzz, but not entirely in a bad way.

Dakota tugs me again. "Come on, sister."

I follow her and the girls into the fray. The crowd swallowing us whole.

Heat and sweat and laughter blur together. Dakota twirls, her curls bouncing as she dances. Evie and Brynn dance next to us wildly. I keep my movements smaller, guarded, but let the beat settle into my bones. For the first time in a while, I'm not watching the world move around me. I'm in it.

Evie leans close, yelling over the music, "See? Not so bad!"

I smile—an actual one, I think—and raise my cup toward her in mock salute. "Maybe a little bad."

We spin back into the rhythm, surrounded by strangers but cocooned in our own reckless energy. I almost forget the boys in the shadows, watching like wolves waiting for prey.

Almost.

I can feel eyes on me. I turn away from them. *Let them watch, let them all watch,* the little voice inside my head chants encouragingly.

I take another gulp of the lighter fluid, forcing it down. Letting the warmth spread through to my fingertips and down to my toes in my black combat boots. I let my hips swing more, my eyes closing, and my head falling back. The simple tight navy dress I'm wearing is soft against my body as I move.

Hands wrap around my waist and hot breath fans my ear.

"Let's dance, sexy." He squeezes my hips.

My eyes flash back to the dusty carpet. Ice replaces all the warmth in my body. Daniel's voice echoes in ears.

"What's wrong, baby?" He pulls me against him, grinding against my ass.

My chest tightens. *No.*

"Get off me," I mumble. It's hard to get the words out, but it seems the guy doesn't get the memo, and his hands travel up and down my sides, then further grabbing my ass.

Something inside me flicks on like a light, and I whirl around and knee him in the balls.

He groans, doubling over.

"I said. Get. Off. Me," I growl at the guy, feeling stronger now.

"You bitch," he hisses through his pained grunts.

I glare daggers at him then scoff, turning away and grabbing Dakota's hand, dragging her behind me to an area where a large white sheet is strung up between two trees.

"Are you okay?" Dakota looks over me. "What an ass."

"Yeah, just... flashbacks." I shiver. "Had to get some air."

"I understand." Dakota gives me a small smile.

I let the clean air fill my lungs and exhale all the negativity out of my body.

"What's that for?" I nod to the projector some guys are setting up.

"They always do like a slideshow of photos of people and videos people submit. AV club likes to put shit on." Dakota shrugs

"What an interesting thing to do at a party." I crinkle my brows.

"Dakota!" Brynn calls, waiving frantically.

"Are you going to be okay?" Dakota squeezes my hand.

"Yeah, I'll be fine. Go." I give her what I hope is a reassuring smile.

Dakota goes to Brynn, who pulls her into the throng of people dancing. I turn and watch as the projector clicks on, and pictures of different parties are shown. Some people laugh at the various poses and pranks that have been done so far this year.

My eyes sweep across the party. Red cups tilted, secrets spilled, and everyone looks so at ease.

This is their world, and I'm just discovering it. I catch flashes of familiar faces in the crowd—Dakota, Brynn, Evie, Callie, and farther off, the boys. The bonfire creates dancing shadows, laughter buzzing like static all around me.

The music slices off mid-beat, leaving behind a jagged silence that makes the crowd falter. A sharp screech of feedback crackles through the speakers—shrill and sudden, like the scream of metal on metal.

Heads turn toward the DJ, whose hands are up in confusion. Conversations die mid-laugh. Even the firelight feels colder, like the forest itself is stumped.

A low hum starts from the speakers.

"No—please don't—"

My heart stops. I slowly turn toward the screen.

The video is grainy but unmistakable. My dorm room. My bed. The nightlight in the corner. The shadows warping the space.

And me. Curling in the sheets, breath ragged. Thrashing.

"Stop—please—Daniel, stop—"

The crowd falls silent. My stomach plummets as if I've stepped off the edge of a cliff.

I know this nightmare. I know it like I know the shape of my scars, the hollow of my chest where trust used to live. I lived this night a hundred times before—but never like this. Never with the world watching.

"I won't tell—I promise—"

There is something so obscene about hearing the words with my voice cracking in terror, echoing across the clearing.

A few people laugh—uneasy, confused.

Someone mutters, "Is this… is this real?"

I can't move. I can't breathe. Then the laughter grows. Bolder now. Cruel.

"Holy shit, what's wrong with her?"

"Is this a movie? Did she record herself having a mental breakdown?"

"This girl's psycho."

I'm still watching, frozen, as my own body screams on-screen. I whimper, gasp, and claw at the sheets like they are ropes that could keep me from being dragged under.

I can feel every eye. Every whisper.

They took this from me. The safety of my room, where I fall apart. They dug it out and fed it to the sheep.

The video cuts off with a sharp click. Then the music resumes like nothing ever happened.

But the sound keeps echoing in my skull. The begging. The breathless panic.

Everything I work so hard to keep hidden—on display.

I barely register the voices around me now, shouting, mocking, laughing. The burn behind my eyes. My nails are digging into my palms. The way the earth tips sideways beneath my feet.

I turn slowly to look across one of the bonfires burning, seeing the four boys I know are responsible for this stunt. They stand just beyond the flames, their faces lit in flickering gold and shadow. Jace in front, arms folded, watching me with that unreadable, storm-slick stare. Luca leans in to say something to him, smirking, like this is all some private joke. Tex looks bored, and Noah is tapping on his phone, probably queuing up the next round of humiliation.

I don't move. I keep my spine straight and my chin high. My face burns —anger or shame, I can't tell—but I meet Jace's gaze and don't look away.

They want a reaction. They want me to crack, to give them a reaction.

I won't.

But inside, something fortifies.

As if I'm slammed back into my own body, I realize that I'm still frozen in place, still standing in front of the screen that projected my nightmares. My cup slips from my fingers and hits the dirt with a soft thud, liquid splashing out around it.

I blink, but the scene is still there. My worst moment on loop. My breathing. My begging. My terror. Broadcasted like a joke.

"Isobel..." Dakota runs up, and I push past her.

I can't. I'm too busy trying to hold myself together.

Laughter crashes around me. I'm drowning.

My stomach churns. My lungs can't take in air. My heart slams so hard against my ribs it feels like it's trying to break free and run without me.

I walk as calmly as possible back out of the forest. Past all the laughing people, teasing and taunting. Past the people making out and grinding on the dance floor. Past people moaning in the darkness. I hold it all in all the way till the edge of the forest, then I run.

13 SURVIVE

The next morning feels like a punishment, too bright, too normal for how hollow I feel inside. My eyes are puffy, my throat scratched raw from crying until there was nothing left in me. I haven't even changed out of the sweatshirt I threw on the night before. Everything still smells like bonfire and embarrassment.

I sit on the edge of my bed, staring at the wall where the camera once was. It's gone now. But the damage has already been done.

My hands shake as I pick up my phone.

It rings twice.

"Gracie?"

Lucian's voice is low, calm.

I open my mouth to speak, then close it again.

"What's wrong?" he presses.

Something tightens in my chest. I blink fast, pressing the heel of my palm into one eye. "They... they showed a video of me. From my room. Everyone saw it. They're watching me, Lucian. Laughing at me. Like I'm nothing. Like I'm a game."

His voice hardens. "A video? What kind of video?"

"Just me," I say quickly. "Just me... crying. I was having a nightmare. It wasn't supposed to be anyone's business."

A breath on the other end. "The cameras—your room is secure. That shouldn't be possible."

"It was before the cameras were installed. When they broke into my room the first time." My voice cracks, ugly and vulnerable. "I thought they just messed with my stuff, but they hid a camera."

Lucian goes silent again, but I can feel him thinking, calculating. "I'll look into the breach immediately. You know I will."

"But that's not..." I bite my lip hard enough to sting. "I don't think I can do this."

His voice is quieter. "I understand. But if you come home now, they win. And I didn't raise a daughter who lets cowards win."

I press my forehead into my hand. "You didn't raise me at all."

That makes him pause.

"No. But I'm here now. And I'm not letting you run."

I don't say anything. Don't have it in me.

My breath hitches. I hate crying, hate the way it makes me feel weak and messy and exposed, but the ache in my chest won't stop growing.

"Then tell me what I need to do."

Lucian's voice, calm and unwavering, carries only one word, "Survive."

"If anything, that's all I know how to do. I've already survived worse."

"That's my girl."

I SPEND the weekend in my room after Dakota told me a nifty perk of being an Ashthorne; I can order room service. Not having to go down to the food hall to eat is truly the cherry on top.

Monday rears its ugly head. The cafeteria buzzes with chatter and clinking trays, but it all goes silent the moment I step inside. The air changes. Everyone already knows.

Eyes flick in my direction. Mouths twist around barely hidden smirks. The weight of every stare crawls across my skin.

They want me to shrink, to fold into myself. They want my embarrassment. But I'm not giving them anything. I imagine the strength my grandma had, all from Lucian's stories, and I channel her.

I keep my chin high, walking straight to the breakfast line. Gripping the tray a little too tightly, I shuffle forward before grabbing some eggs and fruit I won't eat.

Laughter rises from a nearby table. Different theories and guesses at what the video is about float around me.

The tray shakes just slightly in my hands. I don't look. I don't break. I've heard worse. But it *feels* different.

The cafeteria shifts again, as heads turn to watch Jace, Luca, Tex, and Noah move through the room as if they own it.

Luca spots me first. His grin spreads slow and cruel. "Morning, starlet," he calls across the room. "Didn't know you had such a flair for dramatics."

A table erupts in laughter. My ears ring. I keep walking.

Then Jace's voice slices through. Cold. Loud enough to carry. "You should be grateful. Most people don't get *this* much attention on their first week."

I freeze mid-step. The tray in my hands feels stupidly heavy. He's looking straight at me. Daring me to crumble. Waiting for the fallout.

"She didn't ask for your opinion." Dakota's voice cuts clean through the noise.

The entire room seems to stop.

She's standing at her table with a full tray in hand, her friends behind her like a wall. Callie, Brynn, Evie, Tammy, and Rowen—all watching with expressions that range from mildly pissed to *full-blown ready to throw down*.

Dakota walks toward me, heels tapping like punctuation. She stops at my side, looks past me to the boys.

"Don't you have anything better to do? Or are you just that obsessed with her?"

Callie lets out a loud *oof*.

Brynn mock-clutches her chest. "Damn. That's embarrassing for you, Jace."

Tammy bites into a strawberry and mutters, "Creepy."

Luca opens his mouth, but Rowen beats him to it. "Shh. Let the grown-ups talk."

Jace's expression cools further somehow, but he doesn't respond. Just turns and walks off, the others following.

Dakota turns back to me, her voice dropping. "Come on. Sit with us."

I nod, stunned, and follow her back to their table. The moment I sit down, Callie scoots her tray closer.

"Your eyes are actually insane," Brynn says, studying me like I'm some painting that just arrived.

"Don't listen to any of those people; they just thrive off the drama." Evie rolls her eyes.

I'm caught completely off guard. Compliments? From popular girls? To *me*? Are they backing *me* up?

"Oh. Uh. Thanks," I mumble.

Dakota slides into the seat beside me, smiling like nothing just happened.

"Ignore them. They're loud, not interesting." She hands me a napkin. "You okay?"

I nod. "Yeah. I think I am."

And I mean it.

I BARELY WALK OUT of my last class before my alert pings again — a soft chime that sounds like a gunshot after the day I've had.

> **New classes. Required attendance. No exceptions. Please see below.**

Great. Because nothing says 'welcome to your villain origin story' like surprise after-school activities with the people who most want to destroy you.

I trudge across campus, every step a reminder of the whispers in the hallway, my own voice echoing in my head like a broken record.

Multiple guys reenact my video from the party. I try not to scowl, but I'm pretty sure I fail.

My limbs feel heavy, the kind of tired that settles in your bones and stays there. I don't even look at the class name. Don't care.

I just want this day to end. Pushing open the heavy wooden door, I expect some kind of lecture hall or maybe a weird elective.

Instead, I step into something that looks like it belongs in a Bond villain's basement — sleek black floors, reinforced walls, weapons racks gleaming along one side. A training room.

A man in a fitted black jacket glances up from a clipboard near the front and gives me a brief nod. "You're late."

I can't do anything but stare.

"Look who finally decided to join us," Luca purrs from the side of the room.

His voice fills me with dread.

And there they are. All four of them. At least Dakota is here too. Relief washes over me at the friendly face.

Luca, lazily perches on a bench like he's posing for a magazine cover, twirling a throwing knife between his fingers. Jace stands rigid, watching me with that same cold, unreadable expression. Tex leans against the wall in the back, looking like he has better places to be. And Noah, already typing something into a device strapped to his wrist, eyes me over the rims of his glasses.

"Awesome," I mutter under my breath, making my way to the far edge of the mat, as far from them as possible.

Dakota opens her mouth, but the instructor clears his throat. "Welcome to Combat Fundamentals. This is a guild-verified practical, not an academy course. You will be watched. You will be graded. And you will not enjoy it."

He pauses, eyes settling on me. "But you'll learn. Or you'll fail."

I'm not even sure I care which.

The instructor scans his clipboard again. "Ashthorne."

I lift my chin.

He points to a narrow hallway off to the left. "Changing room. Training uniforms are waiting in your size. You've got two minutes."

No one else moves. No one else needs to change, they are already changed. Of course. I nod stiffly and duck through the door.

Inside, the room is cold and bare—metal lockers, a bench, and a single matte-black uniform folded neatly on the counter. I peel out of my uniform with shaking fingers. Slip into the training outfit which clings like a second skin—slick and tactical, high-collar, long-sleeves, and black from neck to heel.

I look ready to break into a museum.

By the time I step back into the training room, I can already feel their eyes.

Luca lets out a low whistle.

Noah doesn't even try to hide the once-over he gives me.

Jace's expression doesn't change, but I feel the weight of his gaze.

Dakota gave me a reassuring smile,

"Better," the instructor mutters, like I'm a tool finally polished.

I take my place on the mat next to Dakota, crossing my arms tight over my chest.

"Partner assignments," the man barks. "These are not optional."

"Ashthorne. Ward."

Tex doesn't say a word. Just jerks his chin toward the mat. Dakota squeezes my hand in silent support.

I walk toward him, every step heavier than the last. Luca has a look of amusement on his face while Noah has something close to pity. I hate both.

We take our positions.

"Basic blocking drill. Switch every five strikes," the instructor calls out. "Begin."

I brace myself, raising my hands. I barely have time to react before Tex moves.

Strike. Strike. Strike.

His movements are precise, effortless, like he's been doing this since birth. I stumble back after the fourth hit, barely catching the fifth with a shaky forearm block.

"Switch," the instructor says.

My turn. My strikes are hesitant. Clumsy. I barely graze him. He doesn't flinch once, doesn't even blink. When I finish the fifth, he doesn't wait. He advances again, faster this time.

I block the first two, then he clips my side with a sharp jab that knocks the wind from my lungs. I cough, doubling over slightly, trying to breathe.

"You done?" he raises an eyebrow.

I look up at him. "No."

Another round. Another barrage of hits I barely deflect. My skin stings. My arms tremble. Sweat slicks down my back.

"You're weak," he mutters. "You flinch before I even hit you."

I straighten. "That won't last."

Tex's eyes flick over me. "You sure about that?"

I swallow the knot in my throat. "I won't break," I say through my teeth.

He looks at me for a beat longer than necessary. Something flickers in his gaze — not approval. Not sympathy. Just... interest.

Then he turns away without a word.

I'M NOT sure what I expected from Advanced Strategic Theory, but I feel like I'm not supposed to be there. I have to sit through pages of tactical jargon and theoretical scenarios that I barely understand. The instructor is a former guild tactician, and she speaks like everyone already has ten years of espionage experience. And who knows, maybe the boys do. I take frantic notes while Dakota takes neat bullet points next to me. Jace has his chin resting on his hand, Noah is engaged, and Luca keeps shooting me winks. Tex is so relaxed he might've been asleep if his eyes aren't open.

And if I thought Advanced Strategic Theory was overwhelming, Guild

Ethics & History is infuriating. It is a crash course in the Guild's past – coups, betrayals, and oaths scrawled in blood.

I mean, really, who knew a thieves' guild would need to have an ethics class?

By the time I drag my sore body down the hall to the last door on my schedule, I'm hanging by a thread. My arms ache from drills with Tex. My brain throbs from Strategy and Ethics. All I want is to curl into bed and sleep for a week.

FIELD TRAINING

Lovely.

The moment I step inside, I know I'm in trouble.

The room looks more like a war room than a classroom. Thick maps line the walls. Gear lockers stand open along the back, displaying grappling hooks, lock picks, and other tools I don't have names for. A weapons rack stretches along the far side, full of training blades and blunt staffs.

And they are all there. Again.

There are others, too. But they don't matter.

A tall woman with a buzzcut and a scar down her throat claps her hands. "On your feet. Field prep begins now. If you're tired, good. You'll be worse in the real world."

I stiffen.

She points at me. "New girl. You're last on the roster. You'll be the runner today."

"Runner?" I echo.

"You'll find out."

Everyone else is already moving, collecting packs, tools, gear I've never touched. I hesitate for a beat too long and someone shoves a bag into my arms.

"Try not to get lost, Ashthorne," Jace mutters as he passes, his voice just loud enough for others to hear.

I swallow my pride, clutching the straps tighter, and step into line.

Whatever this is... it isn't school anymore. It's boot camp.

The instructor's voice cracks like a whip through the tension in the room.

"Today's drill is a live simulation."

Whispers spread. Packs shuffle.

"You have five minutes to gear up. Runners will deliver the objective. Guards will keep them from doing so. Roles are randomized."

A screen flickers on behind her. Names began to shuffle.

I hold my breath as they click into place.

Runner: Isobel
Guards: Jace, Tex, Noah, Luca

When will I escape these guys?

I feel his eyes on me from across the room. I don't look at him. If I did, I might flinch. And I won't give him that.

The instructor turns, handing me a slim satchel. "Inside this bag is your target: a marked document. You must deliver it to the red building at the far edge of the grounds. Your path will be monitored. The guards are allowed to use any non-lethal force to stop you. If you don't make it in thirty minutes, you fail. Understood?"

I nod. My fingers are already sweating on the strap.

Jace passes behind me with the casual confidence of someone who never fails. "Try not to trip over your own ego," he says softly.

I don't answer. I'm too busy trying not to vomit.

The whistle splits the air, and I run.

The moment my feet hit the trail leading into the simulation zone, the terrain changes—dense trees, half-buried stone paths, knee-high grass concealing God-knows-what. The satchel bounces against my back with every step, the strap already digging into my shoulder.

I have thirty minutes. And the predators are already out there.

Leaves whisper above me. I duck low and veer off the path. I don't know if they've already been deployed or are just waiting in the shadows, but I'm not about to make it easy for them.

My breath comes fast. I count it. In, two, three. Out, two, three.

I scramble over a fallen log and drop into a shallow ravine, knees scraping against the dirt. The satchel stays close—I keep one hand on it like it's my lifeline.

Somewhere deeper in the woods, a twig snaps.

I freeze. Another snap. Closer.

I dart to the left—and nearly slam into Luca, who appears from behind a tree. He's twirling a knife in one hand.

"Boo," he says, grinning.

I don't wait for him to strike. I spin and run the other way, lungs burning, heart thudding against my ribs like a warning drum.

His footsteps are close behind mine.

"You're quick," he calls, still laughing.

I spot a narrow break between two trees and dive through it, branches snagging at my hair. I slide down a small slope, breath tearing out of me. Mud streaks my uniform, and the satchel nearly slips—but I catch it.

I don't look back.

I burst into a clearing and nearly run headfirst into Noah, crouching behind a low stone wall with some kind of scanner device in his hands. His eyes snap up as I skid to a halt.

"Oh. You're here already."

He doesn't move to block me. Just tilts his head and mutters, "Ten out of ten for reckless speed."

Then he reaches behind him and presses a button on a device strapped to his wrist.

The trees around us hum. A low, static buzz that disorients me for just a second. I stumble—long enough for him to lunge forward and try to grab the strap of my satchel.

I duck and roll, knocking into his legs. He curses as I push past, cutting through the far edge of the clearing and vanishing into the trees again.

Halfway there.

I'm bleeding from one palm, knees scraped raw, sweat soaking the inside of the suit. My vision blurs at the edges, but I don't stop.

Tex comes out of nowhere—pure power, a wall of muscle and fury. He doesn't say anything. Just raises one arm and blocks the narrow path ahead of me.

I change direction, vaulting over a mossy boulder and barreling into thicker brush. I hear his footsteps behind me—closer, heavier—but slower than Luca's was.

Still, it is enough. Enough to push my body past its edge.

I stumble up a gravel incline, shoes slipping. My breath turns to ragged gasps. Then—finally—I see it.

The red outbuilding.

It sits like a relic of a forgotten war, rust creeping up the corners, a single window covered in grime. It is only twenty feet ahead. Then I feel it.

The shadow at my back. The static charge in the air. I turn just in time for Jace to slam into me.

He doesn't knock me to the ground. Just pins me—fast, efficient, clinical. One arm braces across my chest, the other grabbing the strap of the satchel and yanking it hard enough to choke.

My body locks.

"You don't belong here," he murmurs, breath cold against my ear. "You're just a name with blood behind it."

I elbow back, catching him in the ribs. He grunts, and I drop low, twisting out from under his arm and shoving him off.

"I survived worse than this," I snap, chest heaving. "I'm not some pampered, pretty little princess. I earned every damn scar."

His eyes flash—not with mockery this time, but something darker.

Then he smirks. "We'll see."

I don't wait. I sprint those last twenty feet, adrenaline fueling my every step, and shove the satchel into the objective locker. It clicks shut.

A loud buzzer blares through the zone.

Objective complete.

I drop to my knees in the dirt, gasping, limbs trembling. My whole body burns. I hear the others approaching, their footsteps slower now, less urgent.

I look up to see Jace standing at the edge of the clearing, watching me with a look that isn't quite anger… but isn't admiration either.

Something inside me hates how unimpressed he looks. His jaw is tight, his clothes immaculate, not a speck of dirt on him. I hate that he still looks composed. I hate that I'm shaking.

"You're bleeding," Noah calls as he approaches. "Just a heads up."

"Yeah," I rasp. "I noticed."

The instructor, Briar, stands by the objective box with a clipboard and a steel gaze. "Let's break it down."

"Ashthorne," she says, voice loud enough to cut through the tension. "You completed the mission. Bag intact. Not bad for a first timer."

'Not bad'. I'll take it.

"But," she continues, stepping closer, "you were almost intercepted three times. Your evasion is fast but sloppy. You relied on instinct, not technique."

I nod, too winded to argue. I'm not sure my legs will even work right now.

"You're bleeding," she adds, pointing to my scraped palm and the torn edge of my sleeve. "In the field, that's a weakness. Next time, wrap it. Don't let your enemy smell blood."

I nod again, slower this time.

Her gaze flicks to the boys.

"Ravencourt," she says sharply.

Jace raises a brow.

"You made contact too late. She reached the objective. Explain."

He shrugs one shoulder. "She was faster than expected."

Luca coughs out a quiet laugh, but Briar doesn't so much as blink. "Excuses are for the dead."

Jace's mouth curves slightly, but he doesn't argue.

She turns to the others. "Silvain. You played. Next time, commit. Vexley—good placement, but your trap was too slow to trigger. Ward—strong form, poor timing."

Tex gives a grunt of acknowledgment, jaw flexing.

Then Briar looks at all of us. "You think this is a game? That your bloodlines make you untouchable?"

Her gaze lands on me. "This girl outran you. Outmaneuvered you. And some of you underestimated her because she doesn't look the part."

Jace's jaw ticks.

"Don't make that mistake again," she finishes. "Class dismissed."

14 WELCOME

The days start to blur, the bruises don't.

The new classes are harder than I thought possible. Strategy lectures that make my head spin. Guild ethics where every answer feels wrong. Combat drills that leave me gasping for breath, my muscles screaming before we even hit the halfway point.

And always... *them*.

They take turns picking me apart.

Jace never touches me during sparring, but his words cut like blades. *"You're not fast enough." "Maybe you'd be better at playing victim again." "You're wasting space."* He never raises his voice. He doesn't have to.

Luca teases with a grin and a voice like silk, but there's venom behind it. *"Nice stumble, sunshine. Want me to tattoo a target on your back so they know where to hit next time?"*

Tex is worse in silence. He hits hard and holds back just enough to remind me he's *choosing* not to break me. His eyes are haunted. And when I catch him staring too long at the scars on my arm, he looks away in disgust.

Noah barely speaks. When he does, it's surgical, like he's dissecting me. *"Emotion makes you predictable." "If they know where your weaknesses are, they'll never stop exploiting them."*

They don't let up. I don't back down.

Every time I get knocked flat on the mat, I stand up. Every stare, every shove, every cutting remark—I swallow it like bitter medicine and keep going.

I train until my knuckles bleed. Run laps and simulations until I throw up. I learn. Adapt.

I'm not leaving until I earn my place here and every last one of them knows they picked the wrong girl to underestimate.

The school looks older at night. Colder. Shadows move differently. The hallways are dead silent when I creep out, dressed head to toe in black. My hair tied back in a sleek ponytail.

I follow the directions that were sent. Down a back stairwell. Behind a locked panel that opens with a thumbprint I don't remember giving. The air changes. Damp stone. Hidden heat. The weight of something ancient presses against my ribs.

Two massive oak doors, carved with the Guild's crest—a fox head and a blade—open easily as I push.

The chamber beyond is lit by fire. Torches flicker in sconces. Candles burn on iron stands. A wide circular space stretches out like a coliseum, shadows rising into an unseen ceiling. At the center, a black stone table. Around it, maybe twenty figures, all in black, masks obscuring most of their faces.

Except one.

Lucian.

He stands at the head of the table, tall and composed in a charcoal suit, no mask on, only power.

And to the side are rows of initiates that I've seen in my Guild classes, including the four boys.

They don't wear their uniforms. Just black, plain and clean.

I walk and take my place next to Dakota.

Lucian raises his hands.

"Tonight," his voice commanding, "we welcome a daughter of legacy. A name thought lost. A bloodline reclaimed."

My chest tightens. I don't want more spotlight on me.

"This is Isobel Grace Ashthorne," he continues. "My daughter. The rightful heir to the Ashthorne seat."

Some heads turn toward me. Others stay stone-still.

"She will begin her initiation this month," Lucian says. "As all of you once did."

He turns to me. "Step forward."

I do. I press my hands to my thighs.

"Do you accept our code?"

I nod.

"Say it," he prompts.

"Steal from anyone, never from the Guild. No killing—not unless the choice is death or the fall. And above all—honor above chaos. We do not burn the world to rule it. We slip through its cracks to own it quietly."

"And our creed?"

"Honor amongst thieves, bound by blood."

"Welcome to the shadows, Isobel." Lucian smiles.

A small box is placed in front of me. Dark green velvet. Inside, a gold, intricate ring with a purple-red stone.

"The stone is an Alexandrite, to represent your birth stone. It changes colors in different light sources. The Guild mark is underneath the stone, embedded in the gold."

"It's beautiful," I whisper.

"Every ring is designed for each initiate to wear for the rest of their Guild career. Wear it with pride. Or not at all," he says.

I slide it on. The ring feels heavy on my finger. Not from the weight — it is featherlight, the gold shines. But from what it means. Legacy. Power. Expectation.

Lucian gives me a subtle nod, then gestures with two fingers. I step back in line. Dakota grabs my hand and squeezes it.

There is a space between the boys and me, but the space between us is electric with tension. The air around the boys always feels charged — like lightning could strike at any moment, and they'd *enjoy* the chaos.

One by one, initiates are called up and given their rings.

Then across the circle, a masked woman rises.

"Quarterly reports. Eastern Sector. Inventory discrepancies noted."

A man steps forward, bowing his head slightly. "A rogue cell in Prague. Handled quietly."

The words are vague but cold. *Handled.*

Another figure reports on political funding, another on surveillance updates. I catch phrases like 'extraction team', 'coded ledger breach', and 'vault breach contained'.

My stomach flips. This isn't just a secret society. It's an empire. With rules, reach, and ruthlessness.

I listen and watch. Because if I'm going to survive this world — if I'm going to rule it — I have to know how it works.

The final reports end. One by one, members began to slip back into the shadows.

But Lucian doesn't dismiss us. Instead, he steps to the center of the chamber, eyes sweeping across the circle, then landing on the six of us still standing near the table.

"The Guild thrives because we remember what it takes to earn your place," he says. "Legacy may open the door, but blood, skill, and sacrifice are what keep you inside."

He turns to us — to *me* — last.

"Now comes your first task."

Lucian gestures, and a second Guild member — a tall man in a sweeping black coat, face covered by a sleek, hawk-like mask — steps forward, holding a small metal box.

One by one, we are called by last name.

"Ravencourt."

Jace steps forward and takes his envelope without a word.

"Silvain."

Luca's mouth twitches. He bows and saunters back with his task in hand.

Lucian shakes his head.

"Ward."

Tex steps forward stiffly.

"Vexley."

Noah scans the envelope like he can see inside.

"Brennan."

Dakota steps up and takes the envelope.

And then. "Ashthorne."

My name echoes against the stone. It feels heavier than ever, because there's meaning now. I step forward. The man holds the envelope out but doesn't release it right away.

"Good luck," he says, voice muffled behind his mask.

Lucian meets my eyes. I take it.

After we're dismissed, after the torches are snuffed — I open the envelope alone in my room.

It holds only a dark green card with gold ink:

Infiltrate Sablehall Auction. Acquire the Sunrise Ruby, 25.59 carats, value-estimate: $30.42M. Deliver within 7 days. All tasks must be completed alone.

I exhale slowly and flip the card over.

There, in smaller writing, it reads:

We'll know if you cheat. We'll know if you fail. Welcome to the Guild.

15 RECON

The training mats smell like sweat and rubber. I'm already winded — two drills in, heart racing, ribs sore. Tex doesn't go easy. He never does. But he also doesn't smirk like the others. No taunts, no sneers.

Just relentless, silent pressure.

"Again," he says, arms crossed.

I scowl, drop back into stance, and lunge.

He catches my wrist mid-air and uses my momentum to send me tumbling. I land with a hard thud on the mat, knocking air clean out of my lungs.

"Your balance is better," he mutters, offering a hand.

I don't take it. Instead, I roll to my feet, chest heaving. "Yeah, well, nearly dying builds character."

His mouth twitches. Not quite a smile. We reset.

Between drills, he circles me, sweat darkening the collar of his shirt.

"You read your task?"

His question makes my hackles rise. "Yeah."

He keeps circling. "What is it?"

I hesitate.

I know better than to trust any of them. And yet...

Tex isn't like the others. He isn't kind — not even close — but he doesn't *toy* with me like Luca or shred me like Jace and Noah. He mostly watches as if waiting to see what I do. Still, I shake my head.

"I'm not telling you."

He raises a brow, stepping back. "Why not?"

I meet his eyes, tired and flat. "Because you've all been making my life a living hell since the second I got here. I don't want you making *this* harder, too."

He blinks once. Doesn't speak.

For a moment, he stands there, jaw tense, like he wants to argue — or maybe admit something — but doesn't know how.

Finally, he turns away and tosses me a towel. "Fine."

I catch it. But before I can say anything else, he mutters, almost too low to hear.

"I hope you survive it."

And just like that, he walks off the mat.

I sigh and follow him over to the heavy punching bags. I watch silently as he tapes up his hands, trying to commit it to memory so I can tape up my own.

He takes his stance. His bag rattles with brutal precision. Every strike is clean, efficient. Controlled fury.

I silently tape up my own hands, watching him out of the corner of my eye. I try to copy his strikes with the bag next to his.

No taunts. No barking commands. Just... working.

I focus on the bag and keep in mind everything I've been taught this far. Sweat drips into my eyes, and I pause to wipe my forehead. That's when I feel his gaze.

"You're not bad at this."

I raise an eyebrow. "Careful, Ward. That almost sounded like a compliment."

He huffs a short laugh and drops his gloves, pulling the wraps off his hands.

"You ever fight before all this?"

"Not like this." I shrug. "Mostly stayed small and fast. Easier not to be noticed that way."

He nods slowly. "Yeah. I know what that's like."

I'm taken aback by the personal confession. I wait for the usual silence to return, but instead, he leans back against the wall.

"I didn't grow up like the others." He glances over. "I had a mattress on the floor. Moved foster homes nine times. One of them had bedbugs. Another had a guy who locked us in the closet when we 'talked back.'" His jaw tightens as the memories pass in front of his eyes. "You learn real quick either to disappear or fight."

My hands freeze on the tape I'd been unwrapping.

"I'm not saying this for pity," he adds. "Just figured... you'd understand. More than anyone else here."

I don't say anything at first. Just meet his eyes, something flickering between us. Then I nod. "I do."

We stand there for a second. Not training partners. Not enemies. Not Guild initiates. Just two people who have been through hell and learned how to fight their way through it.

He pushes off the wall, grabbing his towel, and tosses me a protein bar on his way out.

"Eat. You're gonna need it."

I SPEND the next couple of days mostly in silence, focusing on my task. I have five days left. I've gathered as much intel as I can based on the Guild files we are given access to, but I know I'll need to do some recon. I'll have to go tonight and maybe even tomorrow.

The academy is unnervingly quiet at night. I move through the stone halls like a ghost, each step muffled by the boots I've taken from the Guild armory. Black hoodie, black gloves, hair tied back, nothing to catch the light. My bag is packed with recon gear.

I turn the corner near the east wing stairwell, only to slam straight into a solid wall of muscle.

"Shit." I stumble back, heart spiking.

Tex.

His hoodie is half-zipped, his hands in his pockets, and he looks at me like he's only half-surprised.

"You don't look like you're sneaking out at all." There's a bit of laughter in his voice. Like he's caught a child playing dress up.

I square my shoulders. "Should've known you'd lurk around in the dark."

He gives a half-smirk. "Better than getting caught."

There's a beat of silence between us.

"You going after your task?"

"Why does it matter?"

He shrugs, gaze unreadable. "It doesn't. Just curious if you are stupid enough to try it alone."

"I *have* to do it alone," I snap. "I don't really have a choice."

He steps a little closer, shadows catching across his jaw. "You have to do the task alone, but you don't have to do recon alone."

I open my mouth, then shut it again. He studies me a moment longer.

"You're right not to trust us," he says. "But don't confuse that with isolating yourself from other initiates. There's a difference."

"I can't afford to have any of you make this harder," I repeat.

Tex tilts his head. "You think I'd sabotage you?"

"I think you've all made it your personal hobby to watch me fail."

"I grew up in a piss-soaked apartment with police sirens for lullabies. And I failed the only person who ever mattered to me." His voice is low and honest.

My breath catches.

"I'm not the enemy, Ashthorne." He looks at me, something raw behind his eyes. "Not tonight."

Everything in my brain screams to walk away, to not talk to this broody brute and just get on with it. But something in my gut tells me to consider it.

"I'm not dragging you into this."

"You're not dragging me anywhere," he chuckles. "You wouldn't be able to. I'm choosing. That's how Guild loyalty works. Or... supposed to."

I scan his face one final time, and my gut wins.

"Fine. Keep up." I walk past him, and he follows.

Tex takes us to a hidden garage where the Guild keeps vehicles for students. He hops into a nondescript car and motions for me to get in.

I give him directions as he drives, following the GPS on my phone.

Sablehall's exterior doesn't look like much. A three-story building with frosted glass, iron trim, and just enough disrepair to seem forgettable. But underneath... a renowned auction house. And I'm supposed to rob it.

We crouch behind a dumpster across the street. I pull out my tablet, flipping through the blueprints again. Tex peeks over my shoulder.

I scan the perimeter. Multiple guards. Security drones. An access keypad on every door. Everything about this place was designed to make people quit before they tried.

Tex taps my shoulder. "Motion trigger above the second window."

"You've done stuff like this?"

He doesn't answer right away. "Once."

I don't press. Don't need to. We sit there in silence for a beat, eyes on the building, breath clouding the night air.

I keep my gaze on the flickering drone light above the security gate, but something gnaws at me. Earlier, he said he'd failed someone. I fight the urge to ask, but curiosity wins out. I turn slightly toward him, voice quiet.

"You said... that you failed someone."

The silence stretches.

"I won't use it against you," I add. "I just... want to understand."

His jaw flexes. "She was nine," he says after a moment. "My little sister. Ellie."

My eyes widen.

I don't know what to say.

My chest aches. I want to ask more, but I don't want to shatter whatever fragile thread we've managed to build between us.

Still, a question slips out. "How did you end up here? In the Guild?"

Tex lets out a breath — something between a scoff and a sigh.

"After Ellie... I didn't have anyone." He leans back against the stone wall, eyes focused on the horizon. "So, I left the house we were in. Started fighting underground. Bare-knuckle. Stealing what I needed to get by. Ran with a bad group of guys. Eventually got arrested, was looking to spend time in Juvie."

My brows lift.

"Then a fancy lawyer showed up with Gideon Ravencourt and they said they could offer me a different life. I was the last remaining heir to the Ward family. I was the illegitimate son from an affair. But my father's 'real' son died in a car accident. So, he wanted me to represent him in the Guild."

"Wow," I whisper.

He nods. "So, I said fuck it. And went to live with the Ravencourts."

I study him in the dark. The sharp lines of his face. The way he keeps his fists loose, but always half-curled.

"Do you talk to your dad?"

He shakes his head, making a face. "Nah, he wants nothing to do with me. I'm just the guy who does the dirty work while he gets to keep his status and Guild connections."

I know without a doubt, I'm blessed to have a dad like Lucian.

"You're not what I expected."

He looks over, a faint smirk. "And you're not what we expected either."

I don't respond to that.

"So yeah. I know what it's like to be helpless. To be too late. That's why I fight. Not for the Guild. For *her*. Honestly, if I wasn't recruited to join the Guild, I'd probably be dead."

The silence between us hums like static.

I reach down and tighten the strap on my glove, unsure what to do with the ache in my chest.

"I'm sorry." The words feel dumb.

He just nods. "We should move. Guards rotate in six."

16 SABLEHALL

The night has come. The forest around the vault is unnaturally still. Even the wind feels like it's holding its breath as I crouch behind the tree line.

Patrolling guards in sleek black uniforms and night-vision lenses. No flashy logos. No names.

I check the time. 2:17 a.m.

Everything I wear is matte: gloves, suit, even the pins in my hair. A thin sheen of sweat lines the back of my neck despite the cold.

From the undergrowth, I pull a case the size of a small lunchbox. Inside is the gear I selected from the Guild armory.

EMP click puck. Limited range. One-time use.

Tension cable. Ultra-thin. 150 lb. capacity.

Liquid glass cutter.

I clip the case to my belt, heart pounding like a drumbeat inside my ribs.

Time to move.

There's a weak spot in the fencing on the southeast corner. Not a flaw — a flaw meant error. This was intentional, a discreet utility access buried beneath a false patch of soil. Tex clocked it during recon.

I dig my gloved fingers beneath the mossy layer and find the edge of the steel grate. It groans faintly as I lift it — then swing it up on silent hinges.

Beneath, a service tunnel the size of a crawlspace. Barely lit. Air damp and sour.

I slide inside, feet first.

The tunnel is narrow enough that my shoulders scrape the walls. Somewhere above, I can hear the faint whir of a security drone moving across the courtyard. I keep low, counting the paces in my head.

Fifty-six... fifty-seven... there.

A small hatch door with a biometric panel.

I pull the fingerprint foil from my pouch — a print lifted earlier from a borrowed coffee cup in the Sablehall delivery truck. Another one of Tex's little gifts.

The light blinks green. The hatch hisses open.

Behind it — a narrow stone stairwell, ascending into darkness.

The old stone stairwell narrows the higher it goes. I brush my gloved hand along the wall for balance. No creaks, no buzz of electricity. Just air and pressure and darkness.

When I reach the top, I crouch low and peek around the bend.

A hallway stretches ahead, gleaming with polished black tile. Thin, silvery lines crossing like a web.

Laser tripwires.

I inhale through my nose.

Okay. We trained for this.

I pull the guild tablet from my pack and activate the overlay. The interface flickers, casting faint light across the hallway. With a flick of my finger, I load the infrared grid map.

The tablet lights up — every laser thread glowing bright orange on screen.

They aren't static. They *move*. Rotating in slow, hypnotic patterns.

Of course they do.

I strap the tablet to my forearm, sync my motion sensors, and wait for the Guild's program to find the rhythm. There. A ten-second window. I drop low and twist through the first set, breathing slowly as I pass inches from a beam that could set off a silent alarm and call down guards like hellhounds.

Twist. Roll. Slide. Hold breath. Keep moving. Breathe.

The hallway seems to stretch, each section harder than the last. At one point, I have to flip fully horizontal to slip beneath a pair of crisscrossing beams while hovering inches above a pressure-triggered tile.

My shoulder grazes a hair too close — and the light on my tablet flashes red.

I freeze. The sensors pause.

But nothing happens.

My heart doesn't start again until I reach the far end and collapse, silent, behind a statue of some forgotten saint holding a sword.

The room ahead is a quiet kind of majestic — high ceilings, dark marble floors, recessed lighting casting gold shadows across polished surfaces. It was built to impress and intimidate. A single spotlight shines down on the pedestal in the center of the vault, and in the middle of that, under a delicate bell of glass, sits the Sunrise Ruby.

Even from here, it glows.

I creep to the railing, crouching low as I unclip the compact rope coil from my harness. My fingers move fast and sure. I fix the grappling hook into a carved stone notch along the balcony ledge and give it a hard tug.

Secure.

I loop the harness strap around my waist and thighs, check the line, and then climb onto the ledge. My boots balance on slick marble. Thirty feet below, the vault's pressure sensor floor surrounds the pedestal. No landing. Just hang and hope the tension in the rope holds.

I lean back gradually, letting my weight shift until I'm suspended fully over the drop. My heart pounds, but my breath stays steady.

In. Out. No fear.

I walk down the wall backwards, lowering myself hand over hand. The silence is broken only by the squeak of my gloves against the rope and the low whir of climate control above.

Fifteen feet.

Ten.

Five.

My boots hover inches above the floor. Close enough that I can see the tiny pressure sensors tucked into the tile seams. I twist slightly in the air, adjusting my angle until I'm directly above the case.

The ruby gleams up at me, blood red, impossibly smooth.

I pull the glass cutter from my hip pouch and flick it open with a click that sounds too loud in the stillness. Steady. I score a circle, then brace my gloved hand beneath it as I ease the pane free.

No alarms.

No weight shift.

Good.

I reach inside.

The ruby is heavier than it looks. Perfect in my palm.

For a second, I just stare at it. Thirty million dollars in my hand. Enough to change lives. End them. Start wars. But to me, it's just a task. One more step toward proving I belong here.

I slip it into the padded case on my belt and place the replica. I begin to ascend, fast and smooth, hauling myself up by the rope. No celebration. No wasting time. The longer I stay, the higher the chance of someone noticing.

I back away from the ledge and unhook my gear, every movement precise. My pulse is still elevated, but adrenaline has sharpened me, not rattled me.

I've done it.

But it isn't over yet.

I use the liquid glass cutter on one of the top windows. I slip out of the opening, feeling like Catwoman. I reattach the glass, rotating it to match, wiping away any smudges. From a glance, no one would ever know I'd been here.

I cross to the east side where the building backs up against a luxury office complex. I measured the distance already, but it still doesn't help my nerves. I only have a minute in between the guards changing for this jump. It's eight feet across, a solid two-story drop. I look around checking for guards, stepping back.

Deep breath.

Sprint.

Jump.

My boots slam against the gravel of the opposite rooftop and I quickly roll. A motion sensor light blinks on. I duck low and sprint to the service stairwell door. I pull pins from my hair and shove it into the keyhole, moving until I feel the familiar click.

I wrench the door open and take the stairs as quickly as possible. I stop at the second-floor office level, right above the street. Not wanting to risk getting caught on the lobby's camera, I move my way to one of the windows, pushing it wide enough for me to slide through.

One leg, then the other.

I hang for a second, then drop into the alley below, knees bending, palms kissing the concrete to break the fall.

I'm out.

No alarms.

No alerts.

Just my footsteps fading into the night.

THE GUILD CREST on the old chamber door shimmers faintly as I press my palm to it. It hisses open. The Guild chamber. Cold air. Dim lantern light. The scent of old parchment and steel. Smoke.

I move quietly down the stone steps, still in my stealth gear, hood shadowing my face. When I reach the floor, I pause.

They are all there. The four boys stand off to one side — Jace with a scowl permanently etched into his icy face, Luca smirking because I don't think his face knows any other position to be in. Tex still and unreadable, and Noah tapping at something on his watch with a glint of calculation in his eyes.

And then there are the others.

Ten masked Guild members in dark cloaks line the circular dais like silent judges. Their masks gleam — gold, fox-shaped, inhuman. All eyes on me.

Lucian stands at the center, unmasked, tall and perfectly composed in his dark coat.

"Isobel Ashthorne," he says, voice cutting through the hush. "You stand before the Guild to confirm completion of your initiation task. Do you have the ruby?"

I don't answer. I step forward and open the case from my belt. I open it slowly, revealing the Sunrise Ruby.

Gasps whisper through the room.

Lucian nods once. He steps down and takes the case from my hands with precision, setting it on the table. He extracts the ruby in between his fingers, the light catching on the faceted edges.

Even the masked ones lean in.

Lucian sets it on a scale on the table. One of the masked members holds some sort of device to it.

"Verified," one of them says, the voice hollow through the mask.

"Confirmed," says another.

Lucian looks back at me. His eyes are bright. I bask in it.

"You've done well."

I don't know what to say. My throat is dry. My body wants to collapse. But I stand straight.

Then, to my left, Jace scoffs. "She got lucky."

"She earned it." Lucian whips his head to look at him.

Another masked Guild member steps forward. "You've taken your first step, Isobel Ashthorne. But this is only the beginning. There will be more. Harder. Deeper. Blood and shadows. Prove yourself again... and you may yet survive us."

I nod once.

A pause. Slow, echoing *knocks* — three — from the masked members' staffs against the floor.

Acceptance.

Lucian steps back toward me, lowering his voice. "Go get cleaned up. And rest. You'll need it."

I turn, and as I climb the steps to leave, I catch Jace's eyes — dark and stormy. Challenge. Intrigue. Maybe even... concern?

Good.

I DON'T MAKE it to breakfast. I barely make it out of bed.

Muscles I didn't know exist ache. I slept like the dead last night and still feel half buried. But I drag myself into my uniform, pull my hair into a low bun, and shove my sore feet into boots.

Outside my room, the hallway is quiet. I don't make it five steps before someone is suddenly *there*.

"It shouldn't have been possible. Not for someone like you."

There it is. The same tone they all use — like I'm still beneath them. A stray dog that has wandered too close to a table hosting a feast.

I tilt my head. "And yet... here I am."

Is he really going to do this before I can get caffeine?

"Did he help you?" Jace's eyes narrow to slits.

"Who?" I know exactly who he means, but its fun to poke the bear.

Jace leans in like he can intimidate the truth out of me.

"Lucian. Your dad." He rolls his eyes. "Did he give you shortcuts? Codes? A back door?"

I stare at him. "Everything I got, I worked for."

His expression cracks for a heartbeat, just enough for me to see it. The uncertainty.

"You expect me to believe you pulled that off without help?"

I take a slow step toward him, barely an inch between us now.

"I don't give a damn what you believe, Ravencourt. I did what I needed to do. You can keep circling like a vulture, but it won't change the fact that I'm alive."

"For now," he grits out.

He holds my gaze, something simmering behind his eyes — not anger, exactly. Obsession? Frustration? Intrigue?

I start to walk away.

"You know what I think?" Jace raises his voice. "I think you're starting to believe the lie that you're more than what you came from."

I slowly turn back around.

"You say that like it's a bad thing."

He takes a single step closer. Calm, a predatory gleam in his eyes. "It is. When you start thinking you belong here. Like you're one of us. Like this place won't chew you up and spit you out the second you slip."

"Newsflash, Ravencourt. I've already been chewed up. This place doesn't scare me. *You* don't scare me."

He studies me, head tilted, like I'm a puzzle with pieces that don't fit where they should.

"What are you doing?" He's quieter now. "Really. Because it's not just about Guild training. Not just about legacy. You've got something to prove."

"Don't we all?"

"No." He says it like a truth carved in stone. "The rest of us are born into this. We don't have to prove anything. You do."

I cross my arms. "And that terrifies you, doesn't it?"

That smile — razor-thin, not quite reaching his eyes — falters. "It annoys me," he says. "There's a difference."

"Well, you're going to be real annoyed when I keep rising." I step past him, brushing him intentionally, and add over my shoulder, "Better get used to it, Ravencourt. I'm not going anywhere."

I don't have to look back to know he's still standing there.

THE LECTURE DRONES ON. My hand is cramping from notes, and my eyelids feel like they weigh five pounds each.

I can feel them before I even look. Tex drops into the seat beside me with all the subtlety of a wrecking ball, and Noah slides into the one on my other side.

Business as usual now, apparently. No one speaks right away.

I keep writing.

Noah leans in just slightly, his voice pitched low so it won't carry. "So... you're still here."

"Disappointed?" I mutter without looking up.

He lets out a quiet laugh. "Honestly? A little impressed."

I arch a brow at him. Noah Vexley is casually leaning back, stylus twirling between his fingers, the corner of his mouth quirking like he knows exactly how annoying he can be.

"How was it? Committing your first crime?" Noah asks.

"Who said it was my first?"

Tex sits there, broad arms crossed, staring straight ahead like the words on the screen have pissed in his Cheerios. "Jace is furious."

"Pretty sure his face is stuck like that." I continue writing.

That makes Noah chuckle. "I think he's trying to decide if he wants to kill you or kiss you."

I shoot him a look. "Let him try either. I'm good at ruining things."

Tex exhales through his nose. Not a laugh — more like reluctant approval.

"Why is glycolysis conserved across nearly all life forms?" the instructor asks.

My hand twitches like I should raise it, but I don't.

The instructor calls on someone else.

Noah nudges my elbow.

"Next time," he murmurs. "You've already got their attention."

I don't answer.

"Tex loves being right," Noah says with a grin, tilting his head toward the quiet brute beside me.

I eye Tex. His eyes stay locked on the screen, jaw tight.

"That's because I usually am," Tex mutters. "Saves time correcting everyone else."

"That's his version of a compliment," Noah stage whispers.

"You two talk a lot." I glance back and forth between them.

"Sometimes," Noah's tone shifts subtly. "You're breaking rules no one thought to write down."

I face him fully. "Sorry to disappoint."

"You didn't," he says — no grin this time, all curiosity. "I just don't get it. Why keep going? Why not tap out after what we did? After everything?"

Tex shifts then, looking at me. There is no amusement in his eyes, no mocking. Just quiet calculation and beneath that... something like guilt.

I meet both their gazes without flinching.

"Because when you've been through hell," I say, "You'll do anything to stay out of it."

That silences them for a long moment.

Even Tex blinks, gaze darkening — not with challenge, but recognition. He understands that one. Too well.

Noah leans back, tapping something half-heartedly on his screen again.

"Alright," he says, almost like a vow. "Let's see how far you make it, Ashthorne."

I DUCK into the back courtyard behind the east wing, where the stone benches are warm from the sun, and no one ever seems to go unless they want to sneak a vape or skip class.

I need silence.

I've barely sat down when I hear footsteps behind me—light, casual, and very much *on purpose*.

"Is there a reason you're here, or are you just following me for the ambiance?" I ask.

Luca rounds the bench and drops into the seat beside me, sprawling out like he usually does. His shirt is unbuttoned at the collar, tie hanging loose like everything else about him—too relaxed to care, too smug to be challenged.

"Thought you were hiding," he says.

"I'm not hiding," I mutter.

"Right. Of course not." He cracks an easy grin. "You're just meditating in the shadows like a broody little gargoyle."

I turn my head to glare at him, and he actually smiles wider.

"See? There she is."

"Do you annoy everyone this thoroughly, or am I special?"

"You're absolutely special," he says, deadpan, then adds with a wink, "But yeah. I'm an equal opportunity menace."

I don't want to laugh, but the corner of my mouth twitches before I can stop it. He notices.

"Careful," he says, mock-serious. "Keep smiling like that and people will start thinking you like it here."

"People already think too many things."

Luca smiles a lazy smile and leans back, resting his hands behind his head. "I'm just a fan of awkward silences and bitter girls in stolen hoodies."

"You must be *thriving* then."

He chuckles low in his throat, head tilting toward me. "I thought maybe the claws had dulled."

I shoot him a look. "You're always so annoying. Do I bring out your special flavor of unbearable?"

"You bring out a lot of things, Ashthorne."

That earns him a slow blink from me, unimpressed. He grins wider like he's *expecting* the eyeroll and likes it.

"Relax. I'm not here to bite. Not unless you want me to."

I ignore the statement. "Why are you here, then?"

He looks out over the hedges for a second. "You're interesting. New toy in the sandbox. No one knows what to do with you yet."

"I'm not here to entertain you."

"No," he says, smile fading just a little. "But you're making it awfully tempting."

Luca tilts his head, his charm fading just slightly. "This place eats people alive. But you... You keep looking like you're about to bite back."

I don't respond. Don't need to.

He stands up, brushing invisible dust from his pants, then looks back down at me.

"You're full of sharp edges, Isobel Grace Ashthorne. But I can't tell yet if you're a blade or a trap."

"Maybe I'm both."

Luca's grin returns, slower this time. "Even better."

He walks away without another word.

17 PRESSURE

Jace

My phone vibrates against my leg. I reach into my pocket and glance down. My fingers grip the phone before I slide my thumb across the screen.

"Jace." His voice sharp.

"Father."

"How is it going with the Ashthorne girl?"

I stare ahead at the common room doors. Looking around me. The hallway is empty. "Fine."

A short, amused breath crackles through the speaker. "From what I've heard, it does not seem fine," my father says. "She needs to be broken down, Jace. Completely. We cannot allow her to gain favor or strength. Weakness is what keeps her from becoming a threat. Do you understand?"

"Yes, father."

"She knows nothing of our world," he continues, voice tight. "Nothing of what it means to lead. You wouldn't want to follow someone like her, would you?"

A trap. He always phrases his expectations as questions.

"No, I wouldn't."

"Good." His approval is almost worse than disappointment. "You, Jace, were born to lead. I carved you into a weapon for that purpose. Honed you to perfection. Do not make me question my craftsmanship."

My fingers tighten around the phone until I'm worried it'll crack. "She completed her first initiation task," he reminds me, tone curdling. "That is a failure on your part."

Shame. Anger. And under it, something I refuse to name.

"She refused to share with Tex what her task was. She has no reason to trust us."

"Sounds like an excuse." His voice has that familiar edge.

"I will find something," I say. "Something effective."

"See that you do."

A pause, long enough to make me wonder if he's hung up.

"I raised you to be ruthless. Not merciful."

"I won't let you down."

"You better not."

The line clicks. I reach up, loosening my tie, just the slightest bit. Then push through the doors to the common room.

Noah's at the desk, typing, the glow of his laptop screen reflecting off his glasses. Luca is sprawled across the couch behind him, legs dangling over the armrest, his tie loose and blazer missing. Tex sits rigidly in a chair, scrolling on his phone.

"There he is," Luca drawls, sitting up with a lazy stretch. "Thought you died."

"Got held up." I slide into the seat next to Noah. "Find anything?"

Noah nods, swiveling the laptop over so I can see his screen. "Yeah, found a police report. Open investigation."

"What did she do?"

"She didn't do anything. She's the victim."

Victim?

That catches me off guard.

I saw the school pictures Noah was able to pull from her last school. She looked like a street rat.

Dull, brown hair yanked back, strands falling everywhere, oversized hoodie, hollow cheeks, eyes too big for her face. No smile. Plain.

"What happened?" I ask.

Noah clicks a folder. The screen fills with tiny thumbnails.

"She claims her stepdad raped her." Another click. "Here. Hospital records."

The page is cold, clinical text.

"She was brought in by some random man that almost hit her with his car. She stumbled out into the street and passed out. She was rushed into surgery for internal bleeding from a tear in her liver. Evidence of rape so they waited until she woke up for the kit."

My jaw tightens. I don't flinch, but I feel the others go still.

Tex walks over to stand behind us. "When was this?"

"A couple of months ago. On her eighteenth birthday." Noah pushes his glasses up on his nose.

I flip through the images, enlarging one after another. The bruises. Torn skin. Fear in her eyes.

Perfect ammunition.

"Blow them up," I say. "Print them. We'll have people put them up all over the school so she can't escape it."

"No," Tex barks out.

I turn, his posture is stiff, fists clenching and unclenching.

"That's fucked up," he says. "Think of something else."

"Why do you care?" I ask.

"I don't," he shoots back too quickly, making my eyes narrow. "But no one deserves to have the worst day of their life thrown in their face."

"She needs to leave." I lean back in my chair. "Go back to the shithole she crawled out of."

"Why?" Luca tilts his head, baffled. "I mean, sure, I get it, if she takes over, you don't get to, but who cares?"

The pressure starts behind my eyes. My father's voice echoes in my head.

"I care." My tone is ice, no room for argument.

"She doesn't belong here. She wasn't raised like us. Didn't earn anything. Why should someone like her run the Guild when we've been training for it for years?"

The room is silent.

Noah resumes typing. "This just feels a little...extreme."

Tex's jaw works, fists tightening again like he's fighting the urge to swing. "I don't like it," he states.

"I don't care." I stand, smoothing my hand over my uniform. "She needs to go. This is the best way to achieve that."

"This is pretty brutal," Luca mutters, a frown on his face. He leans back on the couch again.

I turn to meet Tex's eyes. "So, what will it be? Are you with us? Or against us?"

"You're going to push me out because I said I don't like your idea?" Tex narrows his eyes.

"Yes." My voice doesn't waver. "You're here because of the Guild. I'm protecting the Guild. So, decide—are you in or out?"

Tex holds my gaze for a minute. Tension thick between us.

Without a word, he walks out of the room, slamming the door behind him.

"Make it happen." I turn and leave the room without a second glance.

18 RAGE

Tex

My blood is boiling. My skin itches but I just roll my neck. Darkness creeps in the corners of my vision. I suppress the rage that threatens to explode out of me. My fists are balled, and the need to punch something, someone, is so strong, I think about turning back around.

The door behind me opens.

"Stop," Jace commands.

"Shove it up your ass," I call back, continuing to walk.

His footsteps are behind me.

"What did you just say to me?" Jace grabs my shoulder.

I whip around, lifting my arm to throw him off. "Don't. Touch. Me," I say through gritted teeth, eyes narrowed.

I'm shaking with the amount of rage that flows through me. I'm so close to breaking free of all the restraints I put on myself.

"What's your fucking problem?" Jace steps up to me, fire burning in his eyes.

"My fucking problem is you," I spit back, squaring my shoulders.

Jace's eyes narrow at me. "You best remember your place." His voice lowers, a tone I recognize as danger to anyone else. But not to me.

"I'm not your dog to order around. I know all your posturing. Don't forget that."

"I'm not posturing. You're acting out, and I want to know why." His eyes scan over my face, looking for a crack he can wiggle into.

"Are we just throwing our morals out the window? Just going to trust daddy dearest all of a sudden?"

Jace's jaw flexes, his shoulders stiffen. "You're here under my father's dime. Or have you forgotten that?"

"Oh no, I could never forget your dad paying for your own personal guard dog." I turn, my fists balled so hard I'm convinced they're stuck.

"I don't need you to protect me." Jace steps in front of me.

"Right." I roll my eyes, trying to step around him again.

He steps into my path.

"You're really asking me to punch you." I growl.

"I'll have you thrown out if you keep going after her," he calls to my back.

I turn to look at him, keeping each movement controlled. "You're going to throw away years of friendship over this girl?"

"Aren't you doing the same thing?" Jace fires back.

"Fuck. You," I grit out and turn back around.

I need to get away from him, this conversation.

"You're compromised. I'll send someone else to get information since you can't even get her first task."

I don't respond. I don't stop. Just keep walking.

I can't allow him to send anyone else. They won't protect her like I will.

I only hope she'll forgive me for my sins.

19 GHOST

The morning starts like all the others. A too-cold shower. My hair pulled back into a ponytail. My uniform clinging to skin still tender from training. I check to ensure my door is locked like always, turning off the alarms on my phone. My boots echo down the dorm hall as I head toward the main building.

At first, I don't notice anything different. The whispers? Normal. The stares? Expected. This school thrives on spectacle, and I've been the main event since I arrived.

But then— I see the first one. Taped to the hallway bulletin board, between club flyers and weekend notices.

A black-and-white photo.

My face. Swollen eye. Split lip. Bruising. My face sunken in like a Tim Burton character.

I turn and see more black-and-white photos slapped on the walls.

One showing faint fingerprint bruises blooming across my collarbone.

Another picture's bruising around my wrists Another of my back with every bleeding belt gash I endured that night. More pictures plastered of all the scars on my body.

X-rays showing bones that never healed properly.

My stomach drops.

The world narrows. My breath catches.

The pictures multiply the more I look around. Another on the girls' bathroom door. Multiple pasted to lockers. One fluttering from a stairwell railing like a flag.

They're everywhere.

Each one is a crime scene. Each one is me.

I don't know how I move. I don't know when I tear one from a wall, hands shaking. My fingers smudge the cheap ink like blood. My own wide eyes stare back at me from the paper — dazed, haunted.

Someone walks past me, laughing. Another turns their face away. I hear the shutter of a phone camera click.

"She's in the hallway. She saw it!"

"Someone go get a picture—no, video it!"

A voice I don't recognize mimics a moan. Another says loud enough for me to hear, "I heard she wanted it."

A hand brushes my shoulder as someone walks past, whispering too close in my ear, "Did it feel good? Or just familiar?"

I whip around — no one's there. They're already blending into the crowd, grinning. Phones are out everywhere. Recording. Laughing.

Screens light up with my face, my body, my trauma. Spliced apart into ink and paper, like I'm not even human.

I stagger toward the nearest wall and tear another one down. My fingers tremble so hard I can't rip it clean. The paper folds and bends and creases and still, there's so many more.

The hallway closes in around me. Too many eyes. Too many voices.

The ground tilts. My stomach lurches. It's hard to breathe.

And that's when I see them. The four boys. Lined up like a painting of apathy and judgment.

Jace in his usual stance, watching a test unfold. Luca's lips twitch with something that might be amusement or regret. I can't tell. Noah doesn't even blink. And Tex... his fists are balled, eyes dark, like he's ready to swing at the world. But he doesn't move.

Not one of them does anything. Because they did this. They wanted me to break. To leave.

I push past the whispers. Past the photos. Past the laughter and the horror and the stares. I won't cry. Not now. Not here.

But every step burns. Every photo is a wound flayed open again. And every photo message screams the same thing:

You are not safe. You are not wanted. You are broken.

I don't even know how I get back to my room.

Every inch of my body is buzzing.

I kick off my shoes and crawl into bed fully dressed. I drag my blanket up over my head and let the darkness swallow me whole.

FOR THE NEXT WEEK, I order all my meals to my room. I email teachers saying I'm sick. Dakota comes to check on me every day, but I just can't let her in.

I show up to training because I'm determined to keep improving. But I say nothing. I run drills. I take hits. I hit back harder. Then I leave.

The first day, Noah makes a comment, something half-clever about my silence. I don't even look at him. Some boys ask if I like it rough.

The next day, Luca makes a joke, I don't care. I don't answer. More boys try to proposition me, telling me they'll give it to me how I like it.

Jace watches me. I feel his eyes following me around. I don't acknowledge him either.

And Tex—he actually tries.

"Isobel." Quiet, pleading. Almost remorseful.

But I don't stop walking. I don't lift my eyes. I become a ghost moving through a battlefield. Not broken. But not whole either.

The only thing I hear is the sound of the laughter. That too-real memory of hands brushing past, words thrown like knives, and all of them standing there. Watching.

Someone tries to grab me. I turn around and break his nose.

The day after, the four of them linger in the hallway like ghouls. I'm determined to continue ignoring them, keeping my head held high.

Jace sticks his leg out, my hands and knees catching my fall.

"That's a nice position." Luca laughs.

"Down at my feet where you belong, Grace."

Apparently, Jace has had enough of my silence. I spin around and punch him in the balls. He doubles over with a groan, his face level with mine. I grab his pristine shirt and bring him closer to me.

"Don't *ever* call me Grace again," I grit through my teeth.

I push him back. He coughs and heaves deep breaths.

"You're going to pay for that." He pants.

"You can keep throwing venom my way, Ravencourt. But it won't make a difference." I turn and catch the small smile on Tex's face.

THE TORCHES FLICKER against stone walls, casting long shadows that dance like specters around the chamber. I stand at the edge of the circle, just like before, but this time, the space between us feels heavier. Different.

Lucian sits at the center dais, his fingers steepled. The others whisper in low tones, the hum of judgment in the air like static before a storm.

The boys are here too — the same boys who turned my life inside out, again.

Jace, silent and stiff, like he's waiting for a fight. Luca, too still to be bored, too sharp to be calm. Noah, face unreadable behind his mask, but I catch him glancing at me and then looking away. And Tex... not looking at me at all.

I don't acknowledge them either. I don't need to. The room settles when Lucian rises.

The normal updates are given. Different sectors, different jobs, different missions. I'm barely listening. Right before the meeting is usually wrapped up Lucian gives me a look that I can't decipher.

"There has been... discord among some of our initiates."

His voice is cold. Controlled.

"Acts unbecoming. Lines crossed. And though we do not regulate personal disputes, there are codes we do not violate — even among thieves."

A beat of silence.

"What happened this past week—the distribution of unauthorized material involving a Guild initiate—is not just a cruelty. It is a breach of discretion. Of honor."

The word hits the room like a dropped dagger. Honor.

I stare ahead, jaw locked.

Lucian continues. "Trust is currency in our world. Without it, we are nothing but rabid dogs with knives."

He surveys us all. "So. You want to play the game? Fine. Play together."

A shuffle, murmurs between the elders.

"Ravencourt, Ward, Silvain, Vexley."

"Sir," they answer in unison.

"Recite our creed."

"Honor amongst thieves, bound by blood."

Lucian nods.

"Your second initiation will be completed as a team. You rise as one… or you fall as one."

I glance sideways — Jace's jaw ticks. Tex dares to look at me.

I don't give him anything.

Lucian's voice cuts again. "You've all passed your first tasks, but the Guild does not function on solo acts. Trust—whether earned or forced—is nonnegotiable."

His gaze sweeps across each of us. Jace. Luca. Tex. Noah. And finally, me.

"Your second initiation will be completed as a unit."

Jace shifts beside me, jaw tight.

"You will infiltrate a secured convoy transporting black market weapon prototype—originally stolen from the Guild. These people are highly dangerous. Lethal. And the buyer is a known Guild traitor. You are to infiltrate, retrieve, and return the cargo."

My throat tightens.

"If one of you fails," Lucian says evenly, "you all fail. And failure...means removal from the Guild track. Permanently."

The silence that follows is suffocating.

"The route is protected. Armed. And mobile. You'll have to strike fast, in coordination, and adapt in real time. You leave tomorrow at nightfall. You will be supervised, and if you so need it, they will step in and help you. But you are all driving this mission. Act as if they aren't there."

No further questions are allowed. Barely time to breathe. The boys begin to filter out.

Jace is the last to go, tossing one last sharp glance over his shoulder as if expecting me to follow. I don't.

Lucian doesn't look at me right away. He waits until the heavy iron doors seal with a deep groan, until the hush of the chamber settles like dust in the air.

Then he speaks. "Gracie."

His voice is softer now, no longer the Guild master addressing his initiates, but a father speaking to his daughter. I turn to face him but I don't approach. My shoulders are tight, my arms crossed to hold myself together.

He steps down from the dais slowly, revealing the weary lines around his eyes. He looks furious. And regretful.

"I should have stopped this before it got this far."

I don't respond. I'm too tired. Too raw.

Lucian sighs, rubbing a hand down his jaw. "I've let you walk into fire expecting you to endure it... and you have. But what they did... those photos..."

His jaw flexes, barely contained anger beneath his calm.

"It crossed every line this Guild holds sacred."

I swallow hard.

"Why didn't you say something before? Why didn't you stop them?"

Lucian's eyes meet mine. "Because I needed to know who they were when no one was watching. And I needed them to see who you are without my shield."

I blink, stunned. A twisted kind of test.

"So, I'm your pawn."

"No," he says instantly. "You're my daughter."

He steps closer. "And I've seen enough to know this place doesn't deserve you yet. But that will change."

I let out a shaky breath. Some part of me wants to ask him to pull me out of here, to tell me I don't need to fight so hard anymore.

But the other part—the part that's still burning—wants to win.

"They won't stop," I say quietly.

Lucian nods. "Then don't give them the satisfaction of seeing you break."

He reaches into his coat and pulls out a small metal token—sleek and dark, stamped with the Guild crest. He presses it into my palm.

"Whatever you need for this task, you'll have it. From me. No questions asked."

I stare down at it. Cool. Heavy. For the first time since the photos went up… I feel steady again.

"Thank you," I whisper.

Lucian watches me closely as I slip the token into my pocket. But his expression shifts—like there's still one more truth he's weighing, something heavier.

"There's something else," he says. "I should've told you earlier."

"What?" I stiffen.

He exhales through his nose, the kind of breath a man lets out before ripping open old wounds.

"Shortly after marrying Adrienne, I made a deal."

I don't move. "With who?"

"Gideon Ravencourt." His gaze darkens.

"Why? You told me to stay away from them but you made a deal?"

"I know." Lucian sighs, dragging a hand down his face.

"What kind of deal?" My stomach drops.

"I was desperate," Lucian admits. "Your mother vanished with you, and every trail went cold. I searched for years. And finally, I made a deal—if I hadn't found you by the time his son started initiation, the Guild leadership would be transferred to him."

The words echo in the chamber like a hammer hitting stone.

I blink at him, stunned. "You were going to give everything to them?"

"I was getting pressured. They wanted to ensure I had an heir to train to take over. And without you, I didn't. And Ravencourt... he's been waiting."

The pieces slam into place.

Jace's hatred. His constant need to challenge me. The way all four of them look at me like I'm stealing something that was promised to them.

"So that's why he hates me."

Lucian's jaw clenches. "Among other things. But yes."

I stare past him at the old stone walls. At the flickering torches. At the truth.

"He was supposed to have it all."

Lucian nods once. "Until I found you. Until you walked into this Guild."

"The Blackmoore Four isn't new." Lucian continues, "It's always evolved depending on which family with the highest ranking has their child in school. For me, you know Max, Preston, and Derek. You were supposed to choose your Blackmoore Four. But since you were missing for high school years, the next family were the Ravencourts. Thus, Jace chose his four."

Silence stretches.

"But you have power now. You've survived and they can't even begin to fathom that. You are to inherit the Guild, the Ashthorne legacy," Lucian says.

"But if I fail," I whisper, "he gets what he wants."

"If you give up, yes," Lucian confirms. "But I know you, Gracie. You don't bend easily—and you sure as hell don't break."

My throat tightens. I look down at my ring. The stone glinting in the light. The intricate vines on the band.

Jace Ravencourt thinks this was his birthright. Let him keep thinking that. Let him watch me take it from him.

"Then I guess it's time I make him regret ever thinking it was his."

Lucian nods his approval. "I want to tell you the reason I couldn't ever let him take control."

I'm sure this is going to be good.

"Gideon doesn't just want power. It's not about legacy or pride. He wants to reshape the Guild."

He pauses, and for the first time since I met him, there's something like fear in his voice.

"He believes the Guild is outdated. That we should evolve. Start taking on high-value contracts the old codes forbid. Including assassinations. Murder. Covert killings for the highest bidder."

My blood runs cold.

"He wants to turn us into killers for hire. Remove the rule about no bloodshed. And if I hadn't found you, if I hadn't named you as heir, he would've had full authority to do just that."

The air feels too thick. Like the walls themselves are pressing in.

"We only take lives when it's necessary. That's how we've been able to fly under the radar for as long as we have. Taking lives carelessly is how you get attention drawn to you. And when you're trying to move through the shadows, the spotlight is not what you want."

I think of everything I've endured to get here. Every bruise. Every fight. Every cruel word. I thought they hated me because I was the outsider. Because I'm his daughter.

But it's bigger than that.

"He doesn't just hate me because I exist," I whisper. "He hates me because I'm standing in the way of a Guild soaked in blood."

Lucian steps closer, voice firm. "Exactly. You're not just a threat to Jace's inheritance. You're a threat to their entire vision. They'll keep testing you. Pushing you. Trying to break you so you'll walk away and they can go back to the plan. But if you stay…"

He places a hand on my shoulder. "You don't just protect your place. You protect the Guild's soul."

"And if I fail—"

"He takes control. And the Guild becomes a weapon in the hands of a man who thinks honor is weakness."

I let out a shaky breath, the weight of it crashing down. No wonder they want me broken.

"And Jace?" I whisper. "Does he believe that too?"

Lucian hesitates. "He was raised to. Trained to. But what he truly believes... only he knows."

I don't reply. I can't. My mind is racing. Fire licking at the edges of my resolve. They tried to humiliate me. Now I know why. And it only makes me more certain.

"Then I'll make damn sure they never get what they want," I say, voice steady, low. "Not from me. Not from this Guild."

Lucian just nods. Silent. Proud.

"Good," he says. "Because they have no idea who they're dealing with."

20 ALL FOR ONE

The wind bites colder at the edge of one of the Guild's warehouses, where an unmarked van and unmarked bikes wait, humming like living things. Black gear. Black masks. A wall of silence as we load up.

No stars above tonight. Just a moon like a blade's edge.

I strap on my utility belt, fingers trembling only slightly as I adjust the fastenings on my gloves. Tex silently double-checks his weapons near the bikes. Jace stands near the exit, still as stone, arms crossed, eyes narrowed like he's calculating how many of us are going to screw this up.

Noah passes me a discreet comm device, brushing my fingers briefly. "It's encoded. I'll be in your ear if anything goes to hell."

"Nothing is going to hell," Derek calls over us.

"I mean, you can give them hell." Max laughs.

Preston rolls his eyes, tapping away on his own tablet.

Luca pulls his mask up over his face and says, "Try not to die, yeah? I'm still trying to decide if I like you."

"Same," I say, deadpan.

He chuckles and disappears into the van.

Max drapes an arm over my shoulder. "Definitely no dying. Your dad would throw me off a cliff if I let anything happen to you."

I giggle and nod. "I'll do my best."

Max disappears behind the van.

Tex stops beside me just as I reach for the zip-up on my vest.

"You ready?" His voice is quiet. Less armor than usual.

"As I'll ever be," I say.

"Stick close to me."

"I can handle myself."

"I know," he says, not moving. "But if something goes wrong out there, I'd rather it be me."

The words hang there between us, suspended like breath in cold air.

I give him a tight nod, heart thudding louder than it should.

From up front, Jace snaps, "Let's go. The clock's already ticking."

We climb on.

No backing out now.

I wrap my arms around Max's waist.

"Hang on." His voice comes through my comms.

The night air rushes against my skin, whipping strands of hair loose from the tie at the base of my neck. We crouch behind a ridge of outcropped rocks overlooking the black stretch of desert road that cuts through the hills like a scar.

Below us, the convoy begins to appear — three matte-black transport trucks surrounded by two unmarked SUVs. The vehicles move fast but not recklessly. The Guild's intel was right. This route is lightly patrolled and distant from major cities. No one is supposed to know what's moving through here.

But we do.

"On my mark," Jace murmurs beside me, voice crisp in my ear through the comms. "Riders first."

"Copy," I whisper back, fingers curling in the sleek black gloves Lucian gave me from the armory. The high-tech friction coating should help with grip when I make the jump.

We're mounted on three slim bikes, engines muffled to near-silence, painted to vanish into the shadows. We wear black Guild suits woven with nanofiber — skintight, flexible, designed to repel minor damage and boost stealth. Noah sits in the unmarked van, ready to go.

"Initiating in three... two... one."

The wind rips across my helmet as we speed along the canyon road. Silent shadows trailing the convoy of matte-black transport trucks. They move like beasts with metal skin—three long-bodied haulers, armored and unmarked, with a rear-guard van tailing just far enough back to shoot without question.

"Get ready to jump." Max instructs.

I lick my lips, heart pounding as I steal a glance ahead. The others peel off, one by one. Jace vaults first, like he's born for it—precise, effortless. Tex vaults next off Derek's bike. Luca salutes before jumping off Preston's bike, and in that moment, the sick thrill hits my gut.

It's now or never.

Max pulls up close. I rise up, bend my knees, and jump.

Free fall. For half a heartbeat, the world is air and speed and adrenaline.

Then my boots slam into cold steel, my fingers grab the ladder bar just in time to avoid being thrown. I haul myself up and onto the roof of the truck —just in time to see Luca locked in a brutal fight.

One of the guards has climbed up through a hatch. Dressed in matte-black armor, he slashes at Luca with a hooked blade. Sparks fly as steel clashes. Luca ducks and spins with liquid grace, his dagger flashing.

But a second man is climbing out behind him. I see the blade and where it's aimed.

"Luca!" I shout.

He turns a second too late. I don't think. Just run.

My boots pound across the truck roof as I launch myself toward the second guard, tackling him at full speed. We go down hard, rolling toward the edge. His elbow cracks into my ribs, but I shove back, desperate. My hand finds his throat and I drive my elbow into it again. He sputters, clawing at me.

We hit the edge—my boot slipping on the smooth metal. He twists, trying to take me with him. I wind and shove, hard. He falls.

His screams are devoured by the wind.

I scramble away from the ledge, my chest heaving, blood in my mouth. The truck still roars beneath me, moving like a monster on rails. When I look up, Luca is staring at me—one hand clutched over his shoulder where blood seeps through his fingers.

I stumble over. "Are you okay?"

His face is unreadable for a moment—eyes wide, lips parted like he doesn't know what to say. Then he gives a crooked, blood-soaked smile.

"You—you tackled a guy off a moving truck," he says.

"Yeah. You're welcome."

"Didn't think you liked me that much."

"I don't."

Derek steps up and applies a quick pressure bandage on Luca's shoulder, then we drop down the open hatch into the truck's interior.

"Good stuff." Preston places a hand on my shoulder.

The world narrows to cold walls and the sound of Luca's labored breathing.

He teeters, and I catch his arm before he can fall.

"Don't you dare pass out on me."

"I'll try to stay conscious for your sake, sweetheart," he rasps.

Smartass. Even while bleeding.

Luca's still alive. Still here. And I made sure of that.

No way am I letting this vampire be the reason I fail.

The inside of the transport truck is a stripped-down vault—steel walls lined with welded racks, crates strapped down tight with military-grade netting. The stolen prototype weapons are here. I can feel it.

But we don't have time to celebrate. My comm crackles.

"Rear guard van is on the move," Noah's voice comes through, sharp and clipped. "ETA ninety seconds."

"Copy," I whisper, already moving.

Luca sways, grabbing one of the crates for balance. Blood still drips down his arm but he motions toward the vault door leading to the cab. "You go. I'll cover the gear."

I don't argue.

I sprint down the aisle, scanning crates as I go. Looking for matching model numbers as they're shown in my HUD.

"Thirty seconds," Noah calls. "I've locked the driver's route, but they'll override it soon."

"Buy us more time," Jace snaps.

The truck jolts. I crash into a crate as something explodes nearby.

They're trying to stop us.

The back doors shudder, then there's a horrible screeching sound as they are ripped open—not by force, but by tech. Someone has hacked the electronic seal.

Two men in black-clad armor climb in, guns raised.

My body moves before my brain can catch up. I grab a crowbar off the rack and hurl it, nailing one in the chest. He staggers back. The other fires.

The blast sears past me, slamming into the wall. I duck, roll, and kick a crate toward him—it knocks his legs out, just enough for me to lunge. My knife finds the space between his armor plates. He screams, and I yank it out.

"On your right!" Max yells.

Another attacker, this one from the upper vent. *Seriously?* I whirl just in time to block a strike from his shock baton. It jolts up my arms and I bite my tongue. Holding in a scream.

He comes again. This time, I duck, catch his wrist, and twist hard. The baton drops. I headbutt him—helmet to visor—and he collapses with a grunt.

I stand over him, panting.

The truck skids again. The back doors are still wide open, the road a blur beneath them.

Behind us, Noah's van hugs our tail, just far enough for Jace, Tex, and Preston to cling to the edge, faces grim, arms braced on the reinforced frame.

"Throw it!" Jace barks, his voice ripping through the wind.

Luca yanks open the nearest crate, sweat dripping into his eyes. "Got it."

I grab the first wrapped prototype, fingers slipping slightly from the blood still dripping down my wrist, and heave it across the open gap. The wind catches it—

Tex lunges and nabs it with both hands, nearly losing his balance.

"Again!" Jace orders.

Luca pulls another out, grunting, his wound clearly slowing him. "This one's heavier—"

"I got it," I say, shoving him aside gently. I brace my foot, wind up like a pitcher, and launch the case toward Jace. He catches it one-handed, his strength absurd, and shoves it behind him into the van's holding bay.

The truck jostles again.

We almost lose footing.

"Speed bump in ten—hang tight or you're roadkill," Noah calls out.

Luca wobbles as the truck jolts, and I grab his hoodie just in time.

"You okay?"

He nods, teeth gritted. "Last crate."

We drag it together, set it just inside the open threshold. The wind howls, the canyon flashing by in a blur of jagged rock and pine.

Jace meets my eyes.

"Together?" I call.

He nods once.

Luca and I heave, and Tex catches it, both feet planted wide as he slides it into the van. "That's all of them!"

"Jump!" Jace yells.

My heart pounds in my throat. The van looks so much farther than it did a second ago.

Luca turns to me, breathing hard. "You ready?"

"No," I say honestly, then take off running anyway.

We jump—leaping from steel to steel, weightless in freefall. My knees slam down hard on the van, and I skid, fingertips clawing for purchase.

Jace's hand snags my arm. "Got you."

He hauls me up just as Tex grabs Luca. The adrenaline doesn't drain out of me—it rips away, like someone's snapped a cord and left me raw and frayed.

Luca collapses against the van's wall, breath hitching as he pulls off his helmet.

"Luca?" I pull off my helmet and shift toward him, reaching for his shoulder.

My hand comes away slick—his entire left side is soaked red, the bandage barely holding.

"Shit," I breathe.

"Move back, Isobel." Derek's hands are gentle as he pushes beside me.

Derek's fingers prod at the opening.

Luca blinks slowly, head rolling back. "Just... restin' my eyes."

"Hey, hey." I lean in, slapping his cheek lightly. "Stay with me, Silvain."

"He's losing too much. That blade must've clipped an artery or something." Derek grumbles

Noah slams on the gas. "ETA five minutes. I've already called ahead. Guild med team's prepped."

"Floor it, Vexley." Max calls.

Derek grabs the rest of the bandage roll and presses it tighter, anchoring it with both palms.

"You saved my life back there." Luca's lashes flutter.

Jace sits opposite, silent, eyes locked on Luca.

"Didn't want you to get skewered." I give him a small smile.

"It would've... ruined my pretty face." Luca's breathing is shallow. He looks pale.

"Don't be a damn idiot," I say, my throat closing.

"Can't help it," he whispers, mouth twitching into the ghost of a grin. "It's the charm."

And then his eyes roll back and his body sags.

"Luca!" I yell.

Tex presses two fingers to his throat. "He's still got a pulse—barely."

The moment the van skids to a halt at the hidden Guild chamber, the back doors fly open. Two masked medical operatives rush in with a stretcher.

"Vitals are fading," one says. "We've got him."

I don't want to let go. I don't realize I'm still holding onto his arm until they pry my fingers away.

Jace silently steps aside, allowing them to lift Luca out.

As they carry him away, I watch the blood trail on the floor, my hands still stained crimson.

I hated him. But now all I can do is hope he doesn't die.

I'm numb, nauseous, and exhausted. But there isn't any time for that. Max, Derek, and Preston lead us down to the Guild chamber. The Guild chamber doors swing open with a low mechanical hiss, revealing the half-moon of masked figures already assembled. The obsidian walls reflect the pale torchlight, casting long, flickering shadows. I can feel the eyes on me.

My boots echo too loudly against the stone as I step inside.

Lucian stands at the far end.

"You completed the objective," one of the masked elders says from his left.

"Yes." My voice is low but steady. "The weapons have been secured."

"Casualties?"

"Luca Silvain got injured; he's in medical now," Derek says from behind me.

Another Guild elder leans forward. "And the mission compromise? Did anyone see your faces?"

"No." I shake my head. "We stayed dark the whole way through."

Lucian finally steps forward. "They succeeded," he says, not as my father, but as Guild Master. "Despite a more complex route and heavier resistance than expected."

"Impressive," says a figure with a silver embroidered hood. "Perhaps the girl is more than just a legacy name."

I can feel the backhand in that compliment. But I don't rise to it. I just stand there, arms loose at my sides, blood on my sleeves, trying to breathe through the ache in my chest.

A new voice speaks. "You led?"

"I acted," I reply. "We all did. It was teamwork."

Lucian gives a slight nod. "Initiation task two: complete."

The room murmurs in approval—low, like distant thunder.

Then the main doors open again. Jace, Tex, and Noah stride in, clothes torn, skin dusted with dirt and blood. Tex has a torn sleeve and a cut on his temple. His jaw works and he rolls his shoulders. Jace... his eyes meet mine once, sharp and searching, but he says nothing.

Lucian's voice rings out again. "They fought beside her. As a unit. They passed not just the test but proved cooperation under fire."

"They passed?" one of the masked councilmen says slowly.

"They did," Lucian answers. "All of them."

A slow ripple of nods followed. The Guild has seen us. And—for now—accepted us.

Lucian raises his hand and the room falls silent again, the weight of his presence immediate and absolute.

"This isn't the end," he says, his voice echoing through the stone chamber. "From this point forward, you all will rotate actively for Guild missions, you will remain under supervision by senior guild members."

My pulse jumps. *Active missions? That feels... fast.*

"Hey! We are not seniors. We're just experienced." Max whines.

Lucian chuckles and continues, "You've passed your second initiation task, but the third is still ahead. Between now and then, you will be sent out regularly. Real assignments. Real consequences."

Noah shifts beside me, eyes flicking up toward the council. Jace remains perfectly still, unreadable. Tex's jaw twitches. None of them speak.

"The missions will not be ceremonial," Lucian says, his gaze sweeping across the five of us. "You'll be briefed only when assigned. You'll work as a team, or you'll fail. And failure is not tolerated."

A pause.

"You want to wear the crest of the Guild?" His voice drops low. "Earn it."

There is a final nod from the council. The torches hiss with a fresh burn. The chamber, heavy with tension moments ago, suddenly feels charged.

Lucian gives me one last glance—just for a second—and then turns away, his cloak swirling as he leaves the chamber.

THE STERILE LIGHTS of the Guild infirmary waiting room buzz faintly overhead, a soft hum that only makes the silence between us heavier. I sit curled in one of the chairs, arms wrapped around my middle, eyes fixed on the scuffed floor tiles like they can offer answers.

Across from me, Tex leans forward, elbows on his knees, hands clasped tight like he's trying to keep himself from punching through the wall. He hasn't spoken since we arrived. Jace stands by the far window, posture tense, his neck still stained with a splash of Luca's blood. His fingers twitches at his sides, like he isn't sure what to do with the rage coiling just beneath his skin.

Noah sits beside me, hood pulled up, earbuds in. Every now and then, he taps his foot or cracks his knuckles. Restlessness masked as calm.

No one says it, but we are all thinking the same thing. *He lost so much blood. Too much blood.*

The moment Luca collapsed in the back of the van, it felt like time fractured. His blood had soaked through the bandages. My hands still carried the ghost of it, sticky and warm and terrifying. He'd joked on that van like he wasn't about to bleed out. Like it was all some game.

I had to stop the bleeding, to keep pressure. I had to hold him together. Now all I can do is wait.

A clock ticks somewhere. It's too loud. Every time the door at the end of the hall creaks, my pulse skips a beat.

Still no word. Still no Luca.

I'm not sure how much time passes. Noah sits up, lowering his hood and pulling out his earbuds. For a moment, he just stares at me.

"What?" I can't take him just staring.

He doesn't say anything. He turns to stare at Tex. I follow his gaze to Tex, his eyes moving over to me.

"Well?" I look back and forth between them. "I'm too tired for this shit, can you guys just get the torture or whatever you're about to do over with already?" I sink back in my chair.

"There's something I found I think you ought to know," Noah says slowly.

"No," Jace barks before Noah can say anything else.

When I look over at him, his eyes are shooting lasers at Noah. His facial expression a clear warning.

I watch as an entire conversation passes between them in complete silence. I obviously wasn't invited. The only thing I know is that whatever Noah wants to say, Jace does not want me to know about it. Noah turns to me again.

"I looked into your file, to research who you are and what we could use against you," Noah says.

"Obviously."

"We found files on your stepdad, Daniel."

I feel like a bucket of ice water is thrown over me. *They're going to bring this up here? Now? While we're waiting for Luca? Are they serious?*

"It's not about what he did to you." Tex walks over and crouches in front of me.

"Then what about him?" My voice is small.

"When I got into your file, there were redacted documents embedded underneath. Buried deep, like someone doesn't want anyone to ever find them. But they were Guild-marked," Noah says.

"What does that mean?" My voice cracks.

Tex leans forward. "It means your stepdad wasn't just some random scumbag. He was a Guild member."

I can't speak. The floor shifts under me — not literally, but in that vertigo way where everything I thought I knew tilts sideways.

"No way," I breathe.

"Rogue Guild," Jace says. "Years ago. He broke one of the codes. Not just stealing — he killed someone. A Guild operative. It's how he got exiled."

My mind reels. "He… he killed someone? And the Guild…"

"Erased him," Noah finishes. "Scrubbed him from the records. That's why it wasn't in anything the police knew. But the Guild keeps receipts. Quiet ones."

"He disappeared underground," Tex adds. "Made enemies. Made deals. When he took you and your mom… it wasn't random. He knew what he was doing."

I shake my head, the air feeling too thick to breathe. "No. No, that's not... My mom took me away. She said she ran because my dad was dangerous."

Jace's jaw flexes.

Noah looks down again. "That's what she believed. Or needed you to believe."

"What does that mean?"

"It wasn't a kidnapping," Tex says. "Not technically. We believe it was a revenge plot. Daniel was dating your mom right before she met Lucian."

"No." The words feel fragile. Weak. "She wouldn't..."

"He manipulated her," Noah's eyes soften behind his glasses. "She was young, scared, and had a history of drug use. I can only imagine that he used her addiction against her."

My throat closes. A thousand images flash through my mind — my mom, distracted and strung out, clinging to promises no one else could hear. Her frantic whispers when she thought no one was listening. The way she used to flinch at shadows in motel windows.

"She really believed she was doing the right thing," I whisper.

No one says anything. But their silence is answer enough.

The weight of it all presses into my chest.

"So what?" I say, too loud, too hollow. "You're saying... I was some kind of revenge plot?"

No one answers.

Noah's voice is softer now. "We thought we were tormenting a rich girl with a throne waiting for her. We didn't know the full story."

Jace looks away. "None of us did."

For once, none of them are smirking. None of them look amused. Just grim. Tight. Like they are standing in front of a storm they don't know how to stop.

"I'd have told her when she was ready," came a low voice from behind us.

I turn. Lucian stands in the doorway, his coat still dusted with rain, his expression unreadable but unmistakably tense. The room is silent.

"You weren't supposed to tell her." His eyes flick to each of them in turn

—Jace, Noah, Tex—his voice calm, but deadly. "That wasn't your truth to reveal."

"She deserved to know," Noah says, not backing down.

"And she would have," Lucian replies. "From *me*. In a way that wouldn't tear open any decent memory she managed to salvage of her mother."

His gaze lands on me, softer now, regret simmering just under the surface. "You've been through enough, Isobel. I wasn't trying to protect her—I just... didn't want to destroy what little peace you had."

I pick at my nails. I don't know what to say. My thoughts are too loud. A war between old loyalties and new truths rage in my head.

"I get it," I finally say, voice quiet. "But it's too late now."

Lucian nods slowly, eyes dark. "I know."

He draws a slow breath, the tension in his shoulders loosening slightly. "Luca made it through surgery," he says, the exhaustion clear in his voice. "The doctors were able to stop the bleeding and stabilize him. He's resting now, and you'll be able to see him later—after you've all had some time to recover."

A collective exhale fills the space.

"He's okay?" I ask, almost afraid to hope.

Lucian gives me a tired but steady nod. "He's strong. Stubborn, too." A faint flicker of something—maybe pride, maybe just relief—passes through his eyes. "He'll pull through."

I slump back against the chair, the adrenaline draining from my system all at once. My limbs feel heavy. My head throbs. But underneath all that... a thread of calm.

Lucian looks at us all. "Get some rest. Eat. Shower. You've earned it."

Then, to me alone, with a faint gentleness in his voice, "We'll talk more later."

And just like that, he's gone, the door closing softly behind him—leaving us all in the thick silence of aftermath and everything that still lingers unspoken.

21 ONE FOR ALL

The antiseptic tang of the recovery wing clings to the back of my throat as I step inside. Everything is too white. Too sterile. Too quiet. Except for the steady beep of machines.

Luca looks smaller in the hospital bed.

Pale. Hooked up to wires and monitors, a thick bandage wrapped around his side, stained faintly where they went in. His curls are a tousled mess on the pillow, darker than usual against his sickly skin.

But he's breathing. Alive.

Tex is sitting near the bed, arms crossed but eyes soft. Noah perched at the windowsill with his ever-present tablet, typing something out—but even he looks up as I walk in. Both nod at me in silent greeting.

Jace stands at the far wall. His eyes meet mine for a single second before flicking away like I'm nothing more than dirt under his shoe.

The frost is back. The cold prince taking up his mantle once again. The kindness he showed after the convoy mission has iced over.

No one says a word. I move toward the side of the bed and look down at Luca. "Hey," I whisper, voice rough. "You didn't die. Good."

His lips twitch. Barely. But it was there.

"You sound disappointed," he murmurs, voice hoarse and weak, but laced with that same lazy charm. "Was hoping to collect on my dramatic death speech?"

Tex snorts, and even Noah cracks a smile.

I sit on the edge of the chair beside him, trying not to let my emotions show. "You scared the shit out of me."

"Didn't mean to." He coughs, wincing. "But... thanks. For not letting me bleed out on top of a moving truck."

Jace shifts by the window, the scrape of his boot on the tile loud in the quiet room. He doesn't look at me but I can feel the chill coming off him.

Whatever fragile understanding we built has shattered. Again. He sees me as a pest. A problem he needs to solve. And currently I'm invading his space with his friends.

Tex stands, giving Luca's ankle a light pat. "We'll give you two a minute," he says, nodding to me then Noah before nudging Jace toward the door.

Jace doesn't move. Not until Noah gives him a look.

"Let's go. He doesn't need your scowling to interrupt his flirting." Noah pulls at him again.

Jace doesn't move. Noah tugs hard and he follows. The door clicking softly behind them, and just like that, we are alone.

For a moment, we just sit in the silence. The monitors beep, steady and slow, a reminder that time hasn't stopped even if it feels like it should have. I fold my arms across my stomach, not knowing what to do with my hands. Luca watches me with tired eyes, half-lidded but still sharp underneath.

"You've been quiet."

I shrug. "Just... processing."

"They told me they told you, about Daniel."

I don't respond. I'm not sure I can.

Luca shifts slightly, sucking in a sharp breath when the movement no doubt tugs at his stitches. "You don't have to sit here, you know. I'm not going to die now. Boring part's over."

"I want to," I say.

"You saved my life." He smiles.

"Don't get used to it." I sit back in the chair.

"Thank you." No grin, no smugness, no charm. Just sincerity in his face, bare and unguarded.

My brain short circuits. I think I'm in shock.

"I mean it, you don't owe me anything." He shrugs then winces. "Hell, I wouldn't have even blamed you if you didn't do anything. I mean, it's not like we were the welcoming committee when you arrived."

"You really think I'd just let you get stabbed?"

He shrugs. His eyes drop to his hands, fingers picking at the edge of his blanket. "You know my dad left when I was a kid?"

I blink. "Really?"

He nods. "He couldn't take the pressure, didn't want to be a Silvain anymore. So, my mom raised me."

"Oh."

"She taught me how to smile the right way, how to pick out the right suit. How to work the charm my father gave me."

I didn't expect that.

Luca tilts his head toward me. "And then she died. Heart failure, they said. I thought it was all the lies she weaved. You learn fast how quickly people close doors when you stop being useful."

I swallow, throat tight. "I'm sorry."

He shrugs with a weak smile. "Don't be. It taught me how to smile through hunger. How to turn charm into a weapon. And eventually, the Guild notices, and with my last name. I belonged."

A beat passes. Then another. His voice drops low, almost hesitant. "I didn't come to Blackmoore to play dress-up with the elite. I came to make sure I never ended up powerless again."

That hits something in me.

Because isn't that why I'm here too?

To reclaim the power I was denied. To never feel helpless again.

I lean forward a little, meeting his gaze. "You're not as shallow as you pretend to be."

His smile is soft now. Sad. "Don't ruin my reputation."

I hesitate. Then reach out and curl my fingers lightly around his wrist, right below the IV line. His skin is warm.

"You scared me," I whisper.

"You... stayed."

"I did."

Luca blinks at me, something unspoken passing between us. Something real.

"I knew you were in love with me." He winks.

I roll my eyes and stand, stepping closer to the bed. "Rest, Luca."

"You'll be around?"

"If you need me."

"I think I do." And he doesn't say it to charm me.

"I'm so glad you're okay." Dakota hugs me as soon as I open my door.

I hug her back and breathe in her familiar scent.

"I'm okay. Luca's the one who got stabbed. My bruises will heal." I close the door behind her and lock it.

She flips on the coffee machine and starts making coffee for us.

"How is he doing?"

"He's good, still just as flirty as always."

"Well at least there's that." She scoffs.

We wait silently as the machine beeps, signaling that coffee is ready.

I sit on the couch with my mug, and Dakota sits next to me.

"We really haven't talked since the pictures..." Her voice is small.

I hesitate a moment and take a long sip of my coffee. "I'm sorry, I just... needed time," I say, choosing my words carefully. "After the photos, after all of it, I didn't want to see anyone. Didn't want anyone seeing me."

Her expression softens immediately, the tension in her shoulders bleeding away. "I figured that might be it. I would've holed up too."

I nod. "It wasn't just embarrassing. It—" I cut myself off, forcing the rest down. "It cracked something in me. I've been trying to piece it back together."

Dakota shifts closer, offering me a candy bag she's pulled out of her pocket. I take one so she doesn't worry.

"I get it," she says after a beat. "I wish I could've done more. I should've ripped those bastards apart."

"You've done enough," I say quietly. "Really. I just needed space to... recover."

"And now?" she asks, watching me. "You back?"

"Trying to be." I give a small, tired smile.

She flops back onto the couch with a sigh, her voice muffled by a throw pillow. "Good. Because if I have to keep pretending to be interested in Brynn's conspiracy theories alone, I might actually snap."

I laugh—really laugh this time. It feels like a bruise being pressed, but at least it's real.

"Deal," I say. "You bring the sarcasm, I'll bring the snacks."

"I'll owe you."

"You already do."

I lean my head back against the couch, closing my eyes for a second. Just taking in this moment with my sister. Maeve has always been a sister, but now I have another.

Dakota sits up again after a moment, hugging a pillow to her chest, observing me. The laughter is gone from her eyes now, replaced with something softer. Hesitant.

"Iz," she says, her voice quieter. "Can I ask you something?"

I nod slowly. "Yeah. What's up?"

She picks at the seam of the pillow for a second before speaking. "Those photos. From... you know. I heard rumors. Everyone's been saying awful things—half of them don't even know what they're talking about. But I didn't want to listen to any of it. I wanted to hear it from you."

My throat tightens. The room suddenly feels smaller.

Dakota doesn't push. She just looks at me like she's trying to leave the door open, not force me through it.

I stare at the floor. "It was real," I say, barely above a whisper. "That was me. And it wasn't a fall, or a fight I picked, or whatever version of events they're telling themselves to make it easier to swallow."

She nods, slowly. "Okay."

"I don't want to talk about what happened," I add, my voice sharper than I mean it to be. "Not yet. Maybe not ever. But... just know that it's real. And they had no right to invade my privacy like that."

Dakota's eyes glisten a little, and she nods again, more firmly this time.

"They're disgusting," she says. "All of them. What they did... it's not just bullying. It's evil."

I blink hard, jaw tight. "Yeah."

She reaches over and puts a hand on mine, just a light touch. "You don't have to tell me anything, Iz. Just... don't shut me out again. Please."

"I'll try," I whisper. "I'm just figuring out how to be again."

"I'll help you," Dakota says, her voice quiet.

And for a few minutes, we just sit there—no jokes, no jabs, no pretending. Just quiet understanding in the space between us.

Suddenly, she lights up like a sparkler and shoots upright. "Wait! Has anyone told you about the Halloween dance?"

I blink. "The what?"

"Oh my god, Isobel. You seriously don't know?"

I shake my head, and she gasps. "Okay. Blackmoore throws a huge Halloween masquerade every year—like, over-the-top decorations, dramatic lighting, illusions, maybe a DJ, maybe a string quartet depending on the mood. It's the one time the school pretends we're normal kids."

I arch a brow. "Sounds... dramatic."

"Exactly!" Dakota grins. "And this year's theme is Masquerade of Monsters. Think gothic, think eerie glam, think big. Everyone dresses up."

I sip my coffee. "That sounds cool."

"You're definitely coming with me. I don't care if I have to drag you in bedsheets and call you a ghost."

A quiet laugh escapes despite myself. "I don't even have a costume."

She waves that off. "That's what shopping is for."

I tilt my head, watching her. "Why do you care if I go?"

Dakota pauses, then offers a soft shrug. "Because you deserve to have one night that doesn't suck. Because I'm your sister and I want to show you a good time."

That makes my lips twitch. "You're not subtle."

"Wasn't trying to be." She winks. "So? Say yes?"

I hesitate. The idea of going to a school-wide event with everyone staring at me makes my stomach flip. But for once... I don't want to be the ghost in the corner.

"Fine," I mutter.

Dakota whoops and throws the pillow at me.

I HADN'T REALIZED how much I needed to get off campus until Dakota and I are driving through the wrought-iron gates of Blackmoore and into the crisp weekend air. Lucian insisted on the sleek black town car. The cobbled road curves away from the academy like a secret path, lined with old stone walls and the occasional enchanted lantern that flickers despite the daylight.

I take a deep breath and close my eyes for a moment. This week has been a blur. Between normal classes, and the homework and studying that goes with that, I also had training and the Guild classes that I needed to stay on top of. I also visited Luca, who is doing better. Noah and Tex have been friendlier when I've seen them in classes or in passing, but Jace is definitely back to shooting glares and ice looks my way.

Dakota practically bounces beside me, her cropped jacket flaring with every step. "You're going to love the boutique I found," she chirps. "It's goth-chic with just the right amount of spooky. Total masquerade dream."

I tug the sleeves of my hoodie over my fingers. "You've put way more thought into this than I have."

"Obviously," she says, linking our arms. "This is our makeover montage. I'm not letting you show up in sad girl black and call it a costume."

I let her pull me along, not fighting it. Spyglass Hill is picturesque in a carefully curated way—ivy crawling up bookstore facades, cafés with spindly chairs and steaming mugs by the window, and magical charm shops that pulse softly with wards and glamour spells. It doesn't feel real, but maybe that's why I can breathe a little easier here.

The boutique Dakota leads us to looks like it's been plucked out of a Victorian dream. The sign reads Hemlock & Veil, its windows fogged from inside with hints of velvet and lace. A tiny bell rings when we step in.

Immediately, Dakota scatters like a magpie, fingers skimming rows of velvet gowns and jeweled masks.

"Okay, something in blood red would be hot," she calls. "Or black with feathers. Or—oh my god—this one has silver beading that looks like constellations."

I wander, letting my fingers drift across textures. Most of it looks too glamorous for me—too bold, too much like I'd be pretending to be someone else. But then, isn't that what the masquerade is about?

My hand stills on a dress tucked to the side. Midnight black with long sheer sleeves, subtle embroidery curling like ivy along the hem. Understated. Elegant.

"You find one?"

I nod once. "Maybe."

"You would look dangerous," she says, pleased.

I glance at her. "And you?"

Dakota grins. "I'm going full vampire queen. If we're going to crash Blackmoore's perfect aesthetic, we might as well do it with fangs and vengeance."

That makes me laugh.

We spend the rest of the afternoon trying things on, getting pastries from the corner café, and arguing about masks. For a while, I forget the weight of secrets and scars. For a while, I just feel… like a normal teenage girl trying to choose who she wants to be.

We're halfway down the street when I catch my reflection in a salon window.

I pause.

The glass is half-fogged from the heat inside, but my face is clear enough — tired eyes, bruises finally faded, the same ash-brown hair pulled back in a low knot like usual. Tamed. Dull. Familiar in a way that suddenly makes my stomach twist.

I stare at her — that girl behind the glass — and I realize I don't want to see her anymore. Not like this.

"Hold up," I say, already turning toward the door.

Dakota stops mid-step. "What?"

"I want to go in." My voice doesn't waver, even though my pulse is racing. "I need a change."

She looks between me and the salon, her brows lifting. "A haircut?"

"More than that." My hand is already pushing the door open. The scent of product and warm air rushes over me. "Come on."

She hesitates for a beat, then her grin spreads. "Hell yes."

We step inside together.

They usher us into side-by-side chairs. A stylist with bubblegum pink nails runs her hands through my hair, clicking her tongue with excitement. "You've got great texture," she says. "Wavy like this? You should be showing it off, not hiding it."

I nod mutely, and she goes to work.

The scissors are fast and confident. The streaks of soft silver are even faster — feathered in under warm lights while Dakota flips through hair inspo on her phone and makes sure I don't chicken out.

When it's done, the stylist doesn't let me leave right away. "Sit. You've got all this, might as well learn how to work it."

She walks me through styling — how to coax the waves without frizz, what products won't weigh it down, even how to flick eyeliner in a way that makes my eyes look sharper, stormier. Stronger. When I finally spin around in the mirror… I don't recognize the girl staring back.

She's not prettier, not exactly. But she looks taller. Older. Like she's been through hell and clawed her way back out. Like she's not afraid to be herself anymore.

Dakota's eyes are shining. "Holy shit, Isobel."

I smile. "Yeah," I say quietly. "She's not so bad."

22 NEW HAIR, WHO THIS?

By Monday morning, the buzz is already alive in the air before I even set foot inside Blackmoore's grand hall.

It starts the second I walk out the dorms. A low hum of whispers, stares that stick longer than usual, heads turning in small clusters like a wave rolling across the courtyard.

For once, I'm not hiding behind oversized hoodies or a tangled bun. I scan over myself in the mirror. My hair down, bold, wavy, and freshly black with streaks of silver that shimmer in the light when I move. A new cut frames my face just enough to bring out the sharpness in my cheekbones and the steel behind my storm-blue eyes. The color contrast also making them pop. There's a touch of makeup — subtle, smoky — not to impress anyone, just enough to stand out.

I walk the halls head held high, shoulders square.

The dining hall is already full when I walk in. Same murmurs. Same stares. But this time, they feel different. Not pity. Not mockery.

Curiosity. Power.

I head toward the same table where Dakota and her friends are waiting. They shower me with compliments. I smile.

And then they walk in.

Blackmoore's golden four, dragging everyone's attention with them like gravity. But for once, they're not the center of it.

I am.

I don't even have to look up to know they see me. It's in the sudden stop of movement, the hitch in footsteps.

Then Luca's voice, smooth and amused, cuts through the space.

"Well, well. Who let the storm in?"

I glance up just enough to catch him staring. There's a pause. His eyes flick over me and he whistles low under his breath. "Didn't know Blackmoore had models now."

"I didn't do it for you," I say, buttering a piece of toast.

"Good," he replies, mouth tugging into a grin. "But damn if it doesn't look good on you anyway."

Tex gives me one of those unreadable looks from across the table, clearly still recalibrating. Something's shifted and he's not sure if he likes it or if he respects it too much to admit it.

Noah tips his head. "Bold move," he says. "But it suits you."

Then there's Jace.

Standing behind them, arms crossed, expression unreadable. Those ice-blue eyes locked on mine, trying to dissect me. For a beat too long, he just stares.

"New look. Same dirty mouth." he says.

He turns away, sliding into his seat without another word. I smile to myself, just slightly. Because they can all feel it. Something's changing.

And they don't know what to do about it.

"Hey," a voice says, warm, a little nervous. "Isobel, right?"

I turn. He's cute — in that boy-next-door way, all golden skin and floppy blond hair, a dimple starting to show when he smiles. He's not wearing the uniform blazer, just the button-down, sleeves rolled to his elbows.

"Yeah," I say, cautiously.

"I'm River," he offers, brushing a hand through his hair. "We're in Advanced Lit. together. I sit two rows back."

Right. The guy who actually takes notes. I give a half nod. "Okay."

He glances around, shuffling his feet. "I was wondering—um, there's this little café in town, they've got open mic nights and live music and all that. I thought maybe... would you wanna go sometime? With me?"

For a moment, the world tips sideways.

Not because he asked, but because of the four annoying assholes eavesdropping. Four distinct reactions hit me at once.

Jace. Still as a statue, like he's already decided this guy's beneath him. Tex. Crossed arms, unreadable. But he looks ready to take someone out. Maybe River. Noah. Raised eyebrows and that twitchy analytical look, like he wants to pull out a whiteboard and diagram what's happening. And Luca... smiling like he already knows how this ends, even if I don't.

I could say no. That would be the easy way out. Keep the waters calm. Don't poke the wolves.

But where's the fun in that?

I shift my stance and let my lips curve into a small smile. "Sure," I say. "I'd like that."

River grins. "Awesome. I'll message you?"

"Looking forward to it."

He waves awkwardly before heading off, probably rehearsing a victory dance the second he's out of sight.

Jace looks like he could snap someone in half.

Tex isn't moving, but his eyes burn.

I turn and keep walking, smiling smugly to myself.

I'м in the common lounge off the east hall, pretending to scroll through my tablet while I wait for Dakota. The space is mostly quiet — sun spilling across the marble in lazy gold stripes, a few voices murmuring from a table tucked in the corner. My hair's down again today, waves loose around my face, and I've finally gotten used to the new weight of people *looking*.

Which is why I don't jump when I feel someone slide into the seat across from me. Luca has a presence that's hard to miss. That faint smell of cedar and spice, the hint of smug confidence that walks into the room three seconds before he does.

"Isobel," he drawls, like we're old friends with shared secrets. Maybe we are, now.

"Luca." I don't look up right away, but I let him hear the edge in my voice. "Slumming it in the commoners' lounge?"

His laugh is a soft, rich sound. "Can't a guy seek out the woman who dragged him back from death's doorstep?"

I glance up at him. "You weren't dying."

"I was bleeding out on a speeding truck with prototype weapons strapped to my back," he says, placing a hand over his heart. "Pretty sure that qualifies."

I snort, but the image flashes too clearly — him on the roof of that transport, the way his body buckled, my hands slick with his blood while I put pressure on his shoulder in the van, how his body slumped when he passed out.

He smiles when I don't answer, something quieter in his eyes now. "You know, you didn't have to save me."

"I know," I say, voice barely above a whisper.

"But you did."

I shrug, throat tight. "Don't read into it. I'm never in the mood to watch anyone die."

His gaze sharpens. "You were shaking."

I look away, jaw clenching. "So were you."

He chuckles again, this time a little softer. "Touché."

Then he leans forward, bracing his arms on his knees, his voice dipping low and intimate. "So… you said yes to River."

I roll my eyes. "Did you come here to check my calendar?"

"No," he says, smiling with all teeth. "I came to figure out why you'd waste a night on him… when you could be spending it with me."

I blink. "You're serious?"

"Deadly."

"You—" I stop, shaking my head with a breathy laugh. "You were unconscious a few days ago."

"And now I'm sitting here, alive and intrigued."

I narrow my eyes. "You *tormented* me. Played a part in things that—" I swallow. "Things you can't take back."

"I never pretended to be good," he says. "But I'm not here to pretend. I'm here because you're the most interesting part of this place — and because you looked *insane* on that roof. Brave. Furious." His eyes flicker with something sharp. "Beautiful."

A lump rises in my throat before I can stop it. I look away again. "River doesn't play games."

"River doesn't even *know* the rules." Luca leans back, draping one arm over the back of the couch. "But I do. I know every angle, every move. You think he's going to understand you? See you? He'll run the second it gets complicated."

"And you won't?" I ask.

Luca's smile fades just slightly. "I've already seen complicated. And I'm still here."

That silence stretches between us, humming like a live wire.

I break it with a dry laugh. "Thanks for the unsolicited commentary."

He grins again — but there's something softer at the edges. "Anytime, baby. Just remember — when he inevitably bores you with his acoustic covers and awkward hand placement, you know where to find me."

And then he's gone, vanishing down the hall like he didn't just mess with the entire chemical makeup of my bloodstream.

I'M HALFWAY to my next class when a hand wraps around my arm and yanks me into an alcove. The hall is crowded, but no one seems to notice. I frown, my hackles are up and I'm ready to fight.

Not this asshole again.

His jaw is tight and his icy eyes burn into mine. I'm honestly surprised his back teeth haven't cracked with all that pressure he puts on them.

"What the hell is your endgame?" he spits.

I yank my arm free from his grasp. "Good morning to you, too."

He takes a step closer, all expensive cologne and fury. "You've been here what? Three months? And somehow, you've managed to screw everything up. You're poison." His eyes narrow.

My spine stiffens. "Excuse me?"

"Do you need me to say it again for you because you're slow? Did your stepdaddy hit you too many times in the head? Or was it the lack of oxygen when you were on your knees for him?"

I raise my hand and slap him across the face so fast I don't even realize until after I've done it.

"Fuck you." I move to step aside and walk away from him, but he grabs my arm and slams me back up against the wall.

"You fucking hit me," he spits in my face.

"You deserve it." I glare back at him.

We seem to enter some unspoken glaring match that I'm determined to win.

"I don't understand what they see in you," Jace says.

"What are you even talking about?"

"Tex is rebelling. Luca won't shut up about you. And Noah—" His jaw clenches tighter. "They're supposed to have my back, but all of them are tripping over themselves for *you*. You are ruining everything."

I blink once, tilting my head. "Sounds like a *you* problem."

His nostrils flare.

"I didn't ask for any of them to like me, or even talk to me. In fact, I've done everything I can to stay the hell out of their way. Maybe they're just tired of being your minions."

He scoffs, but I don't miss the flicker of something behind his eyes.

"You think you're special? You think that you are different than all the other pussy walking around these halls? Let me break it down for you. You're not. Just another girl with the same shit between her legs."

My blood boils and ringing begins in my ears.

"I've already been through hell, Jace. You think you scare me? Or that your opinion matters?"

He doesn't answer, just stares at me like he can't decide whether to hate me more.

I step around him, brushing his shoulder as I pass.

"I'm not here to break your little friend group," I say over my shoulder. "But if it's breaking, maybe it was never that strong to begin with."

THE CAFÉ IS warm and dimly lit. Cinnamon, coffee, and the smell of something sweet floats around me. I feel like any moment I'm going to become a cartoon following the scent trail.

River is already here. He looks cute out of uniform, wearing relaxed jeans, a faded gray long-sleeved shirt, and his tousled blond hair. Waiting by the window with two mugs in front of him. He spots me and stands with a genuine smile. "Hey, you made it."

"Yeah." I nod. "Wasn't sure this place actually existed or if it was just a rumor." I undo my black jacket and place it on the back of my seat. My cream color sweater matches the cozy vibes of the café.

"It's real. I promise the drinks don't suck."

I take a seat across from him. The window is slightly fogged from the warmth inside. The table is small enough that our knees touch. River slides one of the mugs towards me.

"I love the hot chocolate here. Thought I'd get one for you. It's a classic, but, if you hate it, we can get something else."

I raise the warm mug and let the chocolate smell fill my nose. The whipped cream on top mixes in with the rich flavor and its perfect.

"This is delicious." I lick my lips.

"I knew you'd like it." He beams, taking a sip from his own mug.

We talk while music plays. Nothing deep. Just simple things like music, weird Blackmoore rumors, his theory that the head of the history department might secretly be a vampire.

It's easy being around him. It's all light and warm. He doesn't push or pry. He listens, he laughs at the right moments. Makes eye contact without it feeling like he's trying to pry my brain open and study it under a microscope.

I feel like I could like that.

I watch the way his fingers trace the rim of his mug absently while he talks, the way he occasionally taps his foot against the leg of the table, keeping time with music playing.

At one point, he tilts his head slightly and says, "You're different than I thought you'd be."

"Different how?"

"I don't know. People talk you know? And trust me I know better than to believe everything I hear but there's something about you. Like a quiet strength. It's kind of magnetic."

I swallow roughly. I don't know what to say.

"That's really sweet." I clear my throat. "Sorry, no one's ever said anything like that to me before so I'm not sure how to respond." My cheeks heat.

"No worries." He shrugs. "You're not fake or pretending to be someone you're not like most people around here."

I glance down at the foam in my cup. There's a pang in my chest — not quite pain, not quite hope. Just something bittersweet that sits right beneath my ribs. *Is this what normal is supposed to feel like?*

"I don't always feel strong," I admit, voice low.

River doesn't tease. Doesn't push. He just says, "That's okay. You don't have to be."

I look up at him, caught off guard by the sincerity. For a moment, it's almost too much.

Before it can get heavier, he adds with a grin, "Also, I think I owe you a proper distraction. If I'm gonna have a coffee date with Blackmoore's most intimidating new girl, I better earn it."

"You think I'm intimidating?" I ask, smirking a little.

He lifts a brow. "You do kind of have resting murder face."

I laugh. "Wow. That's one for the yearbook."

River reaches across the table and his hand finds mine. "I've really enjoyed tonight with you Isobel." His eyes are full of warmth.

"Me too, River." I return his smile.

"Can I walk you back?"

"Yeah." I nod.

He stands up and helps me back into my jacket. I flip my hair out and he leads me through the café and into the chilly October air.

His hand is warm and steady in mine as we walk back towards the dorms. I'm not used to this kind of touch. I have to keep reminding myself that I'm allowed to have good things.

We talk as we walk. He tells me about his dog back home, a grumpy bulldog named Clive who apparently hates everyone but him. I tell him about how I've never had a pet, and he promises I'll meet Clive someday.

"He'll like you," he says with this quiet certainty that makes something strange flutter behind my ribs.

The campus glows under the lamps, patches of gold light breaking up the night. It smells like dew and pine and fresh-cut grass, my shoes making soft scuffs on the concrete with every step.

I glance at him once, just to study his profile. The slope of his nose. The way he smiles a little whenever I talk, even when I don't say anything funny. He looks like he means it.

When we reach my dorm building, I stop just outside the doors. My hand is still in his.

"Thanks," I say quietly. "For the drink. And the walk. And... not being an asshole."

River laughs, eyes crinkling at the corners. "I try my best."

"So... wanna do this again sometime? You know. No pressure. Just... talking. Tea. Maybe a bookstore next time?"

I don't answer right away. A small part of me — the bruised, hidden part — wants to keep everyone out. But another part, the one that sat across from him and *breathed* for the first time in weeks, whispers *why not?*

"Yeah," I say ducking my head. "I think I'd like that."

We're standing close now. Not close enough to suffocate. Just enough that I feel the heat from his body, the quiet question in the space between us.

He lifts his hand to brush a bit of hair away from my cheek. "Can I—?"

I nod before I can talk myself out of it.

He leans in slowly, giving me time to change my mind. I don't. His lips press gently to mine — warm, tentative, sweet. Not greedy. Not demanding. Just... kind.

It lasts only a few seconds, but it's enough to leave my heart thudding against my ribs like it's trying to learn how to beat for something good.

When he pulls back, his eyes search mine. "Goodnight, Isobel."

"Goodnight," I murmur, a little breathless.

River smiles and kisses my cheek then gestures towards his own dorm, he turns to look at me one last time with his hands in his coat pockets and a cute smile.

23 A KISS TO REMEMBER

I barely get two steps past the door when something hard slams into me. The breath whooshes out of my lungs as my back hits the wall, a sharp thud echoing off the marble floor.

Tex.

His arm is braced against the wall beside my head, eyes burning into mine. His jaw is clenched so tight I can see the muscle twitch in his cheek. He smells like smoke and leather and something darker. Wilder.

"What the hell—"

"Did you enjoy that?" His voice is low. "Did you like his lips on yours?"

My heart kicks up, but not from fear. It's the kind that comes when a storm rolls in and you know something is going to happen.

I swallow hard, trying to push past the heat of his body, the intensity of him so close I can feel it in my bones. "Move."

He doesn't.

Instead, he steps even closer, and it's too much. Too close. His chest brushes mine. His breath hits my lips.

"Did he make you feel anything?" he asks, quieter now — but somehow even more dangerous like that.

My spine stiffens. "Why do you care?"

"I don't," he says.

But it's a lie. He knows it. I know it.

He leans in, his eyes flicking to my mouth and back up again. "He doesn't even *know* you."

"And you do?"

Tex exhales through his nose like he's trying to hold something back. His fist curls beside my head.

"I know you don't like people getting close."

I clench my jaw. "Maybe I wanted to try."

His dark eyes stare into mine. I feel like he can see every part of me.

"You think a pretty face and soft hands is gonna fix it?" he spits. "You think he can make you forget?"

"No," I snap. "But at least he doesn't try to tear me down every time I take a damn breath."

That shuts him up.

For a second, we just stand there — two live wires sparking in the dark.

The next second, he kisses me.

It's brutal and hot and starved — as if he's been holding himself back for far too long and finally snapped. His mouth crashes into mine, and I gasp, the sound lost as he presses in closer, deeper, harder. His hands bury into my hair, pulling me against him like he can't stand even an inch between us. It's greedy and raw and full of everything he won't say out loud.

My back's pinned to the wall but my hands find his shirt, twisting into the fabric like it's the only thing tethering me to earth. I gasp into him, and that's all it takes for the kiss to deepen — his lips parting mine, his tongue brushing with a hunger that lights a wildfire under my skin. My knees go weak. My mind blanks. I forget my name. I forget where I am. Heat tingling and pooling in my core.

He growls low in his throat — the sound making my pulse stutter — and then he's lifting me, like I weigh nothing. My legs instinctively wrap around his waist as he presses me harder into the wall. His mouth never leaves mine, not for a second.

Like he wants to own every breath I take.

He tastes like trouble. And I want more.

When he finally pulls back, just enough to breathe, his forehead rests against mine. His breath fans across my lips that are still parted, stunned.

"I know for a fact," he breathes, "he doesn't make you feel like *that*."

Then he kisses me again. Slower this time. A deep, consuming drag of lips and tongue and heat that makes my bones melt. I feel every plane of his hard body as he presses against me, the rough fabric of my jeans rubbing against my clit and making me moan.

He trails kisses down my neck as my fingers curl into his hair and his rough hands make their way under my sweater and move across my waist.

"Tex." I breathe, "Stop."

He freezes, and slowly I slide down against the wall and him, legs shaky, body burning. I can feel his erection against me as he gently lowers me back down.

Before I can say anything, he turns and walks out. Like nothing happened. Like he didn't just soak my panties with a single kiss.

I close the door behind me with a soft click, but it might as well be thunder in the quiet that follows.

My legs are still trembling.

I lean against it, head tipped back, eyes fluttering shut as I try to catch my breath — but it's useless.

He's still there.

Tex.

On my skin, in my lungs, like smoke I can't cough out.

I press my fingers to my lips, swollen and tingling, and it's like I can still feel him — the rough drag of his mouth, the heat of his breath, the way he kissed me like I'm his and he was done pretending otherwise.

My heart won't slow down.

It pounds against my ribs like it wants to escape, like it doesn't know what to do with the storm he left behind.

He kissed me. He *wanted* me. No games, no venom, no walls. Just fire and heat and *want*.

I swallow hard and peel myself from the door, locking it behind me. I turn off the main light and slip into the bathroom. The mirror catches me in passing—lips a little swollen, eyes bright, cheeks flushed.

I turn, half-stumbling toward the bed. The silence in the room feels louder than anything, like it's pressing in from all sides. But still — I feel him.

In the way my hands shake.

In the phantom weight of him pinning me to the wall. In the heat between my thighs and the throbbing I've never felt before.

My fingers tremble slightly as I strip off my clothes, layer by layer. The softness of the fabric against my skin feels amplified, like I've been turned inside out. I slide into bed wearing just a camisole and underwear, trying to calm the fire he's left in me. But I can't. Not really. I curl beneath the blankets, covers pulled high, but it's no use.

Tex Ward is still with me — in every breath, in every pulse. I can feel his rough hands on my waist, in my hair.

I'm not even sure why I stopped him.

River.

His name drifts in like smoke under a door.

He was... sweet. Gentle. Said all the right things. Held my hand. Kissed me like I was fragile.

And for a moment, I wanted that. The ease. The quiet safety of someone who smiles with their whole face and doesn't come with jagged edges.

But that kiss didn't burn. It didn't *brand*. I didn't feel it throughout my body.

It didn't feel like I was standing on the edge of something dangerous and delicious.

Tex kissed me like he wanted to consume me. Like he'd been starving. Like he couldn't help himself.

And I kissed him back. I *let* him.

Worse — I wanted more.

I pull the covers tighter, burying myself in the cocoon of fabric like it'll muffle the truth.

River is the good thing. The *safe* thing. I should want him. I *do* want him.

Just... not the way I want Tex.

And that might be the most dangerous part of all.

I breathe in through my nose and out slowly. Try to center myself. But my skin is flushed, thighs pressed together on instinct. I can't stop replaying it—his mouth claiming mine, the way he said *I know for a fact he doesn't make you feel like that* as if he already knew what I was thinking. Like he *feels* it too. The effect I had on him. His erection.

I let my hand trail down, past my stomach. Tentative at first. I've never... really done this before. It was never safe in *that* house, and after... I've just been surviving. No one has made me feel like this. I'm left just... wondering what it would feel like if I permitted myself to want something.

My fingers dip lower. I shudder. Half from nerves, half from the way the ache inside me grows. I close my eyes and think about his voice in my ear, the scrape of his stubble, how his breath turned ragged against my cheek. How his body felt like it was vibrating with restraint.

I slide my hand into my underwear and gasp as my fingers brush over how wet I already am. It's startling—and a little embarrassing—but something about it thrills me too.

My clit is throbbing. I brush my fingers against it gently and gasp. I find a rhythm slowly, fingers circling just right, hips lifting. A breath escapes me, shaky and soft, and then another. I imagine Tex's mouth again. His heat. That possessive growl in his throat when he kissed me like I *belonged* to him.

A soft moan slips out before I can stop it.

My other hand grips the sheet as my thighs begin to tremble. It builds so quickly, unexpected and overwhelming. I can *feel* his hand on my body, his lips against mine. The way he kissed my neck, his hard body pressed against me. I try to stay quiet as my orgasm crashes, one hand fisting the sheets, my body arching, back curling off the mattress in a wave of heat and release.

My chest rises and falls, breathless and shaky, and I blink up at the ceiling in the dark. I feel flushed and raw and a little like crying—but not in a bad way. Just... overwhelmed. Because for the first time in a long time, my body feels like *mine*.

∼

I WAKE up with feelings I didn't expect. Electricity hums under my skin. My limbs heavy and warm under the blankets, body still humming with memory. Last night was mine. No one else's.

By the time I make it to the dining hall, the noise of conversation and clinking plates feels oddly distant. I scan the room automatically—habit, not paranoia, though sometimes they feel like the same thing.

Dakota spots me and waves me over. I make my way, still adjusting the sleeves of my sweater, hair loose and soft around my shoulders. As I slide onto the bench beside her, River appears out of nowhere and drops onto the seat across from us.

"Morning," he says with that easy grin, kissing my cheek. "You look... well-rested."

I don't mean to blush, but I do. "Morning."

Dakota raises a brow at me over her coffee like *girl, spill*, but I ignore her, nudging my tray forward and trying to focus on peeling the shell off a boiled egg instead of the way River's knee brushes mine under the table.

But then I feel that pull.

I glance up—and meet Tex's stare from across the hall. He's at a table with the others, angled just so, a spoon held loosely between his fingers. Noah looks from me to River with a flash of curiosity—and Luca, for once, looks serious, jaw set, drumming one knuckle idly against the table.

They aren't even pretending not to look.

I shift in my seat, aware of every inch of myself. River leans in closer with a big smile, voice low as he says, "You okay?"

I nod too fast. "Yeah, I'm good."

A snort escapes Dakota. "Clearly. You were glowing before you even sat down."

River gives me a look. "That a compliment?"

"It's an observation," she says, popping a grape in her mouth, but she winks at me behind his back.

I force a small smile and try not to look across the room again—but I can *feel* them. Like gravity. Like a loaded wire running straight through the space between us. My lips still tingle from Tex's kiss. I ache from the way I—

"Isobel," River says softly.

I blink. "Yeah?"

He smiles, gentle this time. "You zoned out there."

"Just thinking," I say. *About too many things. About too many people.*

Dakota kicks me under the table—friendly, playful—and I manage a real laugh.

But when I look up again, Tex is still watching.

RIVER SLINGS his bag higher on his shoulder as we walk the curved hall toward the east wing. The morning sunlight filters through the tall glass windows, casting strips of light across the polished floor, but all I can feel is the heat of his hand brushing mine.

"So," he says, giving me a sidelong glance, "dinner later? Or are you still trying to pretend I'm not charming?"

I laugh, low and a little surprised. "You're... mildly charming. Jury's still out."

He grins, pleased anyway, and slows in front of the classroom door. "I'll take mildly. For now."

I hesitate, unsure if he's going to lean in again like last night. But before I can overthink it, he bends and kisses me—its soft, with a warmth that stays just long enough to make my chest flutter. He smells like mint gum and clean laundry, and for a second, I let myself lean into the safety of it. The simplicity.

When he pulls away, I open my eyes—and freeze.

Tex and Noah stand just down the hall, both with unreadable expressions, both clearly having seen everything.

Noah is the first to move, raising his brows and muttering something under his breath to Tex. But it's Tex's eyes that lock onto mine. Not furious. Not even angry.

Just *burning*.

His jaw flexes once, then twice, like he's holding back words he knows will cut. His arms are folded tight across his chest, muscles tense under his shirt like he's barely keeping himself in check.

"Morning," River says, oblivious to the tension, giving them a nod before turning back to me. "See you after?"

I nod, but my gaze is stuck—trapped in the weight of Tex's silence.

River squeezes my hand and walks off, whistling, and I swallow hard as the silence stretches between me and the two boys still standing there.

Noah's voice breaks it. "Well, that was... something."

I turn toward the door without a word, but Tex's voice stops me cold.

"Still with him?" he asks. Low. Controlled. Dangerous.

I turn slowly, staring back at him. "Excuse me?"

His eyes drag over me—mouth parted, breath sharp. "Just wondering how many sweet words it takes to make you forget."

"Forget what?"

His laugh is humorless. "Everything."

I bite the inside of my cheek and say nothing. If I speak, I might scream. Or worse—admit how much his words sting.

Noah shifts beside him. "C'mon, man."

But Tex doesn't move. He just looks at me one more time—like I'm someone he doesn't recognize anymore—and then walks into the classroom.

Leaving me standing there with my pulse hammering and my stomach twisted into knots.

By the time I step into the classroom, my pulse has only just started to settle. My lips still tingle faintly, not from River's kiss—but from the fire Tex has lit in its wake.

I don't understand him. I don't understand *any* of them.

"Miss Ashthorne," the instructor's voice snaps me out of my head. "You're with Vexley today."

I turn toward the back corner of the room where Noah is already at one of the workstations, looking like he'd rather be anywhere else. His bright green eyes lift when I approach, unreadable as ever, but I catch the faintest twitch of amusement tugging at the corner of his mouth.

"Rough morning?" Noah says, sliding a laptop my way.

"You saw."

"*Everyone* saw."

I pull out the chair beside him and slump into it with a sigh. "Great."

He taps something on the screen. "Don't worry. This place has a two-day attention span, max. By tomorrow, someone will have set the science building on fire or streaked through the lunchroom or whatever rich kids do to stay entertained."

I don't smile, but I'm close.

He's watching me a little too closely, looking at me over the rims of his glasses. "You okay?"

"I'm fine," I mutter, even though my chest is tight and my stomach flutters from Tex's words.

Noah doesn't press. Instead, he turns the laptop toward me, launching whatever simulation or assignment we are supposed to work on.

I study the map, noting a pattern I didn't see.

"You're good at this," I say.

He shrugs. "I like systems. Patterns. Code makes more sense than people do."

I nod.

"So... what's the deal with River?"

I blink. "What?"

"I mean, he seems decent. For a normie. You into that whole golden retriever boyfriend thing?"

"Are you seriously asking me that in the middle of class?"

He smirks. "Just making conversation. Trying to keep my partner from spontaneously combusting under Tex's death glare."

I give him a flat look. "You're not funny."

"I'm hilarious. You're just in denial."

Despite myself, I crack a tiny smile.

And maybe Noah sees it—because his gaze softens, just a little.

"I know we give you hell," he says after a beat. "But... not all of us are trying to break you."

I look at him. "No?"

"No." He tilts the screen back toward himself. "Some of us just want to see what you'll do back."

CLASS ENDS FASTER than I expect, mostly because working with Noah is surprisingly easy. He didn't talk too much, didn't make things weird. He was just... steady. And he noticed things—small details I wouldn't have caught on my own.

When we submit the assignment, he leans back in his chair and stretches, his shirt pulling slightly to reveal a sliver of lean stomach. I look away quickly.

"So," he says, standing and casually slinging his bag over his shoulder. "You grabbing lunch?"

"Eventually."

The corners of his mouth curl into a lazy half-smile. "Need company?"

My brows furrow. "You want to eat with me?"

"Why not?" he says. "We worked well together. And if I'm seen with you, maybe someone'll finally try to hack me out of spite. It's been boring lately."

I snort, but I wasn't used to this—*attention*. Especially not the kind that made my skin warm in confusing ways.

As we walk out of the classroom side by side, I catch movement at the end of the hall. My eyes flick up—and there he is.

Tex.

Leaning against the wall, arms crossed, jaw tight. His eyes are locked on me.

Well—*us*.

He pushes off the wall slowly, not saying anything as we pass, but the heat in his stare scorches me from the inside out.

Noah notices. Of course he does.

As we step outside, he leans in just a little closer, his voice a low murmur by my ear. "You know, if I didn't know better, I'd say Ward's about two seconds from punching me in the face."

I roll my eyes. "Don't flatter yourself."

"Oh, I'm not. But I think you should know," he says, his voice dropping just slightly, "I don't really care who's watching."

I turn to look at him, unsure whether to be amused or unsettled. He wasn't flirting like Luca—smooth and disarming. Or like Tex—hot and electric. Noah's interest is quiet. He makes me feel like he's already thought about every outcome and is still choosing to move toward me anyway.

"Why are you doing this?" I ask.

He shrugs. "Because I like puzzles. And you, Isobel Ashthorne... you're a beautiful one."

I stare at him, throat dry, unsure how to respond. And behind us, is the weight of a stare still burning into my back.

24 BOYS, BOYS, BOYS

The dining hall is filled with its usual chaos, trays clattering, voices rising in swells of gossip and laughter. Noah guides us toward a quieter corner, away from the spotlight. I'm not sure if it's intentional, or just another one of his oddly considerate tendencies.

He slides into the seat across from me like we do this all the time. I'm halfway through biting into a sandwich when I hear someone behind me.

"There you are," River says, voice light, like we are in the middle of some casual rom com. "I've been looking for you."

Noah doesn't even glance up from his tray. "Found her," he says flatly.

River's smile freezes, the edges dropping a bit. "Mind if I sit?"

Noah finally looks at him — not irritated, not angry. Just calm. Calm like a warning before a storm. "I do, actually."

River blinks. "Seriously?"

"Dead serious."

"I'm not trying to start something," River says, his voice dipping lower, confused and annoyed. "I just figured—"

Noah cuts him off with a tilt of his head. "You figured you went on one date and that makes you special?"

River flinches slightly but covers it with a snort. "Isobel and I are talking. I didn't realize she had to check in with you now."

"She doesn't," Noah replies, still maddeningly calm. "But she also doesn't need you following her around like a puppy."

"Noah," I say, voice firm.

He doesn't look at me. Just says, "This isn't about your feelings, River. It's about respect. And if you actually gave a shit about her, you'd give her space."

River's jaw tightens. "Right. Because *you're* the picture of respectful."

Noah's voice drops to a near-whisper. "If we wanted background noise, we'd sit closer to the vending machines."

River clenches his teeth. "I just wanted to spend time with her."

"And I'm sure she'll call you," Noah says, already turning back to his tray, effectively dismissing him. "Later."

River looks at me, hurt flickering behind his eyes. I can't think of what to say.

After a long pause, he walks away.

I exhale, the silence between us suddenly thick.

"You didn't have to do that," I say quietly.

Noah doesn't look up. "Didn't have to. Still did."

"Why?"

He taps a finger on the table between us. "Because that guy doesn't see you. Not really. He sees some idea of you he can put on a shelf."

"And you think *you* do?"

"No," he says. "But I'd like to."

"But why so brutal? Like you didn't have to destroy the guy." I glance over my shoulder, not seeing River anywhere.

"Yes, I did."

"Why?" I turn back to Noah

He leans forward, voice low, almost too soft. "Because watching him kiss you felt like swallowing broken glass."

I stare down at my sandwich, appetite gone. The weight of eyes on me still lingers — not just from the surrounding tables, but from the seat across from me. Noah doesn't say anything else. Just eats, calmly, like he didn't just dismantle a boy with just a few choice words.

"Why are you telling me this?"

"I want to." He shrugs.

I gape at him. "I don't know what I'm supposed to do," I admit, voice low. "It feels like... too much. All of it. Everyone watching. The looks..."

"Because you're not used to being wanted," he says with a shrug. "That doesn't mean it's wrong."

"But it *feels* wrong," I whisper. "I'm doing something I don't know how to do."

Noah leans back, his arms crossed, studying me like I'm a particularly complex puzzle he's determined to solve. "You don't know how to be wanted without a price attached."

That strikes a little too close to home.

"Don't analyze me," I grumble, eyes back on my tray.

He smiles, but it's not mocking. It's warm. "I'm not. I'm just telling you the truth."

A pause. Then, casually, "This is dating, Isobel."

"Huh?"

"This. Awkward meals. Mixed signals. Unspoken tension. Questioning if you're allowed to like more than one person. Trying to figure out if your ribs hurt because someone punched you during training or because someone kissed you too well the night before." He smirks. "Dating."

I let out a shaky breath, unsure if I want to laugh or hide under the table.

"I don't think I'm cut out for it."

"You are," he says, softer now. "You just haven't figured out *how* yet. But you will."

He picks up his juice carton, pops the straw, and takes a slow sip like he didn't just drop a truth bomb and leave it smoldering on the table between us.

From across the dining hall, Tex's stare is like a brand on the side of my face. And I don't even need to look to know Jace is watching too.

Too much attention. Too many possibilities. Too many ways to burn.

I regret turning down the deserted hallway when I see Jace, leaning against the wall.

Fuck. Can't turn back around now.

I roll my shoulders.

"Surprised to find you alone," Jace says.

I sigh. I know I shouldn't respond, but I take the bait anyways. "What's that supposed to mean?"

"Thought you'd be soaking up the attention from your little fan club."

"I don't have a fan club." I roll my eyes. "If anything, it's a smear campaign. You've had most people at the school teasing me for weeks."

"Okay then." He pushes off the wall, his hands in his pockets. "Your reverse harem."

He circles me, his finger brushing one of my curls off my shoulder. I suppress a shiver.

"I've been told it's called dating." I'm proud that my voice comes out even.

"You could call it that." He shrugs, his heat surrounding me.

Why does this asshole seem to have some sort of effect on me?

"I think you just like spreading your legs for anyone who gives you attention."

That snaps me right out of it.

I glare at him. "I haven't spread my legs for anyone. Not that it's any of your business."

He stops right in front of me.

"In fact…" I step up closer to him, pressing a finger into his chest. "If anything, you sound concerned someone else might get what you want."

I can't help the small smirk that spreads across my face as his jaw flexes, his eyes narrowing.

"I'm not concerned at all," he bites out.

"But you admit you want me."

"No."

"Oh, you're jealous." It's my turn to circle him.

"That's absurd." He huffs, it sounds forced.

"You feel threatened?" I smirk.

"Absolutely not," he snaps.

I hum.

Before I can think, I'm shoved up against a wall.

"What the—"

"Listen here, Ashthorne," Jace hisses into my face, "I don't know what game you're playing at here. But I'm Jace Ravencourt. I lead, and people follow. If anyone is threatened in this situation, it certainly is not me. I'm a man, while you play around with little boys. You can't even imagine being with someone like me."

I smile. "Sounds like you're afraid the little boys are winning."

He scoffs. "They aren't competition. You'll get bored of their amateur games, and you'll crave for a real man to make your legs tremble. And I won't be interested."

I press closer to him, smirking as his breath hitches, and position my lips right next to his ear.

"Trust me, I won't be looking for a man like you."

I duck under his arm and saunter away. Feeling his stare drill into my back.

I'M HALFWAY down the dorm corridor, just finished my training sessions, lost in thought, when I hear my name.

"Isobel."

I turn, startled. River stands at the end of the hallway, shoulders tense, jaw tight. He's ditched his blazer, rolled his sleeves up, and his easygoing smile is nowhere to be seen.

"I've been looking for you," he says, voice low but sharp around the edges.

"What's wrong?"

His brow furrows, and he closes the distance between us in a few long strides. "What the hell was that at lunch?"

"Lunch—?"

"With Noah." His hands flex at his sides. "He doesn't just *ask* me to leave, Isobel. He humiliated me. In front of everyone."

I wince. "I didn't ask him to do that."

"You didn't *stop* him, either."

That stings, because it's true. I didn't. I sat there frozen, trying to play neutral while the floor fell out from under me. Again.

"I didn't know what to say," I admit.

River exhales through his nose, looking away for a moment before returning to me with something harder in his eyes. "Is he your boyfriend now? Is that what this is?"

"No," I say quickly. "I... I don't know what anything is."

"Because from where I'm standing," he says, narrowing his eyes. "It looks like I've just been someone to kill time with until the others started noticing you."

"River, it's not like that."

"Then tell me what it *is*, Isobel." His voice softens, the anger thinning into something more vulnerable. "Because I like you. I really like you. But I'm not going to fight for someone who doesn't want to be fought for."

I look down at my shoes. My hands are shaking, just a little.

"I do want you," I whisper. "Or... I want to want you."

River's face twists in confusion. "What does that even mean?"

"It means I'm messed up," I say, voice cracking. "I don't know what I'm doing. It means I don't know how to do this. I don't know how to be normal. I've never dated anyone, and I'm still learning how to be safe in my own skin, let alone figure out who I want to give pieces of my heart to."

His expression softens slightly, the edge of anger and hurt dulling. "I'm not asking for all of you. I just want honesty."

That's when the weight in my chest turns prickly.

I look up at him. "Then I have to tell you something."

His brows knit.

"There was... a moment. With Tex." I feel my stomach lurch as I say it. "He kissed me. It wasn't planned. It just... happened."

River steps back like I've hit him. "When?"

"After our date," I say quietly, ashamed. "Right after you dropped me off."

His mouth opens, then closes. "So, that's why you were acting weird."

I nod, unable to meet his eyes.

He scrubs a hand over his face. "And now Noah's sniffing around too?"

"I'm not leading anyone on," I say quickly. "I'm confused and trying to make sense of everything and I didn't expect—any of it. I just... I'm trying to be honest. Like you asked."

He stares at me for a long moment, his expression unreadable. "You're honest," he says. "But that doesn't mean this doesn't hurt."

"I know."

He nods, then backs away another step. "Figure out what you want, Isobel. But maybe don't keep collecting hearts while you're doing it."

And then he turns and walks away.

I'M SHUTTING my room's door when a hand slams against it, stopping it cold.

I jump, heart leaping into my throat.

"Jesus—Tex?" My voice is shrill.

He leans into the doorway, filling the frame with all his muscles and contained rage. His jaw is hard, and his eyes are dark, unreadable.

"Of course." I roll my eyes. "What do you want?"

"To talk."

"Why?"

"Because River looked like he wanted to throw something when he left, and you look like you want to disappear."

I scowl. "That's none of your business."

"It became my business the second I kissed you."

"You mean the kiss you ambushed me with?"

He exhales a sharp breath, straightens up. "You kissed me back."

My jaw tightens. "Doesn't mean it meant anything."

"Liar," he growls.

The word slices through the space between us. I flinch — because it lands too close to the truth.

I push the door again, but he doesn't budge. "Move."

"No."

"Tex—"

"I'm not letting you walk away as if nothing happened."

"Why not?" I bite out. "So, you can say I belong to you now? That's how this works, right? You take, and you claim, and you break things just to see if they'll still want you after?"

He goes still at that. His gaze drops, lashes brushing his cheekbones. When he looks back up at me, there's something raw in him — a ripple beneath all the bravado.

"I don't want to break you," he says, voice low. "I don't want you ruined, Isobel. I just..."

I stare at him, breath caught.

"You make me feel something."

"It's too late," I whisper.

He flinches like I hit him. "Is it?"

I don't answer. I just stand there — staring at the boy who barged into my life like a wrecking ball and is suddenly looking at me like I'm the one who could destroy him.

"I came because I needed to know."

"Know what?"

"If I imagined it. The way you kissed me back."

My breath stutters.

He steps forward just enough to close the space between us, but not enough to touch. Not yet.

"Did you feel anything, Isobel?"

My throat constricts. I want to lie. I want to slam the door in his face and pretend it never happened. But I can still feel the ghost of his lips on mine. Still feel the fire he lit.

"I'm trying..." I whisper. "Trying to want something normal. Something easy."

"Does he make you feel alive?" Tex asks, and suddenly his voice is a raw thing — all gravel and thunder. "Because I know for a fact you make me feel alive."

My heart is hammering.

"Let me in," he says, softly.

He waits. And I hate how badly I want to say yes. To everything. To him.

I don't know why I do but I take a step back, letting him in. Tex doesn't smile. Doesn't smirk. He just walks in like he knows he's crossing over a line.

25 FIRST STEPS

The air shifts the second the door clicks shut. It's just us now. No uniforms, no assignments, no war games or politics.

Just me and him.

Tex doesn't speak at first. He takes one slow step closer, like I might bolt if he moves too fast.

"You shouldn't be here," I whisper. The words sound brittle. Useless.

"You let me in."

God, I did. I did.

I should be smarter than this. I should hold the line I keep drawing. But my chest aches and I'm so tired of pretending I don't feel it when he looks at me like this. As if I matter. Like I'm fire and he wants to burn.

"You kissed me like you meant it," he says, stepping into my space. "Don't lie and say you didn't."

I don't. I can't. My silence is answer enough.

His fingers come up, slow, tracing a line from my jaw to the edge of my mouth. "Still think you want normal? Something easy?" His voice is low now, intimate. Like a secret meant for just us.

And then he kisses me again.

His kiss feels like something feral, barely held back. His hands anchor at my waist, pulling me in until there's no space between us. I gasp, and he swallows the sound like he needs it.

I fist the front of his shirt without thinking, gripping tight, grounding myself in the weight of him. He doesn't flinch. Just deepens the kiss, tongue sliding against mine like he's starving for this.

I've never been kissed like this, not before him — like I'm wanted, claimed, devoured.

My back hits the wall, and I don't even register how we got there. One of his hands slides up my ribcage, not greedy, not fast — just enough to make my knees shake. He pulls back just enough to look at me, breathing hard.

"I've tried to stay away," he admits, forehead resting against mine. "Tried to convince myself this wasn't real."

"And?"

"And it's killing me."

I close my eyes. My pulse is thunder in my ears.

Because it's killing me too.

When I open them, I whisper, "Then stop pretending."

He kisses me again — softer this time, but no less intense. And this time, I kiss him back like I don't care who I'm supposed to be.

Just a girl.

Just a boy.

And all the fire between us.

His body is pressed to mine, mouth hot against my throat, and my hands fist the back of his shirt like I'll drown without the anchor of him. I can feel him—hard, insistent—and I'm losing track of what I'm meant to say, what I'm even trying to protect.

His hand trails down, slow and possessive, gripping my hip before sliding around to the front of my leggings. He doesn't slip underneath. Just presses.

Right there.

I jerk, inhaling sharp and fast, thighs clenching. His lips brush the shell of my ear. "You're soaked," he mutters, voice dark and reverent. "Tell me, Isobel —did I do that to you?"

I don't trust my voice, but I nod, already trembling.

His fingers flex, the pressure making my head tilt back against the wall. "Were you this wet last night too?" he asks, tone wrecked. "When you were alone in your bed?"

Heat floods my cheeks. My breath catches.

He leans in closer, nose brushing mine. "Did you touch yourself?"

A beat. Then, quietly, "Yes."

He groans. It rips out of him, low and guttural. His forehead presses to mine like he's trying to breathe through it. "Did you think about me?" he rasps.

My answer is barely a whisper. "Only you."

His hand moves away like it burns him, like if he keeps touching me, he won't stop. "Fuck." He paces a short step back, then forward again. "You have no idea what you do to me."

I exhale shakily, dizzy from the intensity.

"I want you." He kisses me again. "I want to be the one you choose," he says, jaw clenched. "I know what you went through. I don't want to push you."

My chest tightens. "Tex..."

His gaze flicks down again, hungry and tortured. "But god," he mutters. "You touching yourself to me? I can't stop seeing it."

My lips part.

He steps in again, eyes locked on mine. "Show me," he says roughly. "Show me what you did."

My breath stutters. And he moves his head like he's trying to shake the thought out.

The second Tex starts to pull away, I reach for him. "Wait," I whisper.

His eyes flick back to mine, stormy and confused.

I take a breath. "You asked me to show you."

He stares, silent. I can hear the rush of his breath, the thud of my heart.

"I want to," I say, voice steadier now. "I want to show you. I want you to see me... Just *me*."

His throat works. "Are you sure?"

I nod, stepping back from the wall, leading him with my eyes until I reach the bed, peeling my leggings off and sitting down. I ease back against the pillows, my knees drawn up. My chest hammering, but I don't look away.

Tex watches like he's afraid to breathe too loud and break whatever spell this is.

I slip my hand beneath my panties and press gently between my thighs, gasping at the sensation. I'm already so wet it's obscene. For a second, I close my eyes, grounding myself in the feeling—not shame, not fear—*desire.*

When I open them again, his jaw is tight, his fists clenched at his sides. An obvious bulge in his pants, I lick my lips.

"You don't have to just watch." It comes out in a pant, voice trembling but real. I want to see him. I *need* to.

His eyes darken. He drags the chair from the side of the room closer, sitting just to the side of the bed. Then, slowly, deliberately, he unzips his pants and frees himself.

He's already hard, my eyes widen.

Watching him wrap a hand around his cock while his gaze stays locked to where my fingers move over my clit—it lights something in me I didn't know I needed. Not just the want, but the *control*. I'm letting him see me, but I'm the one choosing it.

Tex groans, low and guttural. "Jesus, Isobel." He squeezes his cock, liquid shining at the tip.

My name in his mouth makes me shiver. Goosebumps pepper my skin from the heat of his stare.

Tex groans under his breath, his hand tightening around himself. I clench, wanting to feel him between my thighs. I moan louder than I mean to.

His reaction is instant: a stuttered breath, a ragged curse. "Wait."

I freeze.

"Take your hand out."

I obey.

He moves closer, his chair next to the bed, his hard cock jutting out towards me. My pussy aches. My legs are still spread to him. He moves slowly, his hand touching my panties, feeling the wetness. I inhale sharply as my clit throbs. I want him to touch me.

He moves my underwear to the side and his eyes darken as he looks at me.

"That for me?" he asks, voice thick. "All that... Is that because of *me?*"

"Yes," I whisper.

He groans, fisting his dick and I whimper.

"Good girl." He sits back, and I slide my hand back between my thighs.

His hand moves back to his cock as his eyes lock with my fingers. I watch him as his hand strokes up and down his shaft, how he circles the head. My fingers move faster; I feel like I'm dripping.

"Was this how you looked last night?" he asks, voice rough as his pace quickens matching me. "Were you this desperate for me?"

I nod, circling harder, my breath hitching.

"Answer me," he growls out.

"Yes, Tex." i moan.

He lets out a low, strangled noise, and his movements speed up as I work myself faster. My body is humming, on fire, every nerve lit up like I've never felt before. It's not just the pleasure—it's the power from seeing what I do to him.

"You're so fucking beautiful like this," he growls. "Strong. Brave. *Mine.*"

Tex watches like he's memorizing me. Like I'm something sacred and precious all at once.

The sound I make is halfway between a moan and a gasp. I'm so close, and when he leans in just a little more, eyes burning into mine.

"Let me see you, Isobel," he grunts.

I tip over the edge with a cry, my body trembling as I fall apart. My back arches, my toes curl and I stare into his eyes.

He follows moments later with a deep groan, chest heaving, jaw clenched as he spills into his hand.

We sit there, nothing but the sound of ragged breathing. The silence thick but not awkward. The air is heavy with the scent of desire and something deeper—something that feels like understanding.

He's looking at me with something I can't decipher.

"You wreck me, Isobel," he says, tucking himself back into his pants.
I smile—tired, trembling, and *proud.*
Because I did that. *Me.*

I WAKE up tangled in my sheets, my body still pliant and relaxed. The sunlight bleeds softly through the slats of the blinds, painting pale lines across my comforter, across my skin. My legs shift restlessly beneath the blankets, sensitive. A pulse still hums low in my stomach, like my body hasn't caught up to the fact that Tex is no longer here.

I touch my lips. They feel swollen. Branded.

Last night wasn't supposed to happen. But it did. And I let it. Wanted it. Craved it so badly it scared me.

The shame tries to creep in, slow and ugly, but I shove it back. I wasn't going to be ashamed for wanting something—for feeling alive. Not anymore. Still, my head throbs with the question. *What now?*

I kissed River. Said yes to him. Let him hold my hand. Let him believe there was room for him inside whatever version of a life I'm building. And maybe there was—until last night. Until Tex.

He sees me. Not the mask I wore around the school. Not the bruised girl in the file they hacked. *Me.*

And he wants me anyway.

I sit up slowly, pressing my palm over the space between my thighs. The ache is still there. Real. Heavy. He barely touched me, not really—but it's like my whole body has been marked by him.

Heat flushes across my cheeks.

God. I let him watch me. I wanted him to. I wanted him to see all of me, and the way he looked at me...

No one has ever looked at me like that.

I bury my face in my hands, heart pounding. This wasn't supposed to be complicated. I wanted a clean slate. A normal life. Someone safe.

Someone like River.

But River's touch didn't set me on fire. River didn't make me come undone with just a look and a low, hungry voice whispering my name.

My phone buzzes on the nightstand. I glance at it, already knowing who it is.

> River: Morning. Breakfast?

I don't answer right away. I can't. My fingers hover over the screen like responding might set off a chain reaction I'm not ready to face.

Because no matter what I tell myself... Tex has made me feel something I didn't know I could feel. And now, nothing else feels the same.

I SIT with River at a quiet table tucked near the windows, sunlight spilling across the tablecloth in soft gold. He looks freshly showered, his hair still damp and pushed back, his smile easy. He passes me a muffin from his tray. A peace offering.

"Sleep okay?" he asks.

I give a noncommittal shrug, tearing off a piece of muffin I don't really want. "More or less."

He nods, watching me like he wants to say more.

I feel it first. The slight change in pressure. The prickle of awareness at the back of my neck.

"Am I interrupting something?" Luca is all smooth lines and amused eyes as he slides into the seat next to me — not across, not nearby, but so close it makes River's jaw tighten. Luca doesn't even look at him. His full attention is on me, looking at me like I'm the most fascinating person he's ever set eyes on.

"You weren't invited." I raise an eyebrow.

"That's never stopped *me* before," he replies, unbothered. "Besides, I missed you."

River bristles, his hand going still around his coffee mug. "We were having a conversation."

Luca finally spares him a glance. "You'll live."

"Luca," I warn under my breath.

He leans closer, elbow on the table, his voice dropping low. "What? I'm just saying hi. It's not my fault if things get... uncomfortable."

River's smile is strained. "You always make things awkward?"

"Only when it's fun," Luca says, his gaze sliding back to me. "So... did you miss me?"

I roll my eyes, heat prickling beneath my skin. "You should be resting."

"I am," he says, not missing a beat. "Resting my eyes. On you."

River looks between us, clearly trying to piece together whatever the hell this is.

"You know," Luca says to no one in particular, picking up an untouched strawberry from my plate without asking, "I can't help but wonder what someone like *you* is doing with someone like *him*."

River's shoulders tense. "Excuse me?"

I open my mouth to shut it down, to snap at him, I don't even know, but Luca gets there first.

"Chill out, dude. I'm just saying. You don't really seem all that interesting," he dares River, biting into the strawberry with a grin. "Bit of a safe bet."

"And? You're the better choice?" River's eyes narrow.

Luca beams. "Exactly." He turns to me. "Even he says I'm the better choice."

"Okay," I cut in, holding a hand up to Luca. "Enough."

Luca holds up his hands in mock surrender, but the gleam in his eyes says *I'm not done.*

River looks at me, his voice softer. "You don't have to deal with that, y'know."

"I'm fine. I can handle Luca," I say, though my heartbeat begs to differ.

Luca leans back, folding his arms behind his head. "You *are* fine. That's the problem. I hope you do *handle* me." He winks.

I glare at him. There's no real heat behind it—the flush on my cheeks betrays me.

River stands, gathering his tray. "I've got to get to class."

"I'll see you later?" I already regret this circus.

He dips his chin, giving Luca one last glance before walking off.

The moment he's gone, Luca leans in again. "So... when are you going to put that poor lad out of his misery?"

I scowl. "I don't know what you're talking about."

"Then tell me this," his voice as smooth as velvet. "When he kissed you, did you feel butterflies?" His smile curves knowingly.

"How do you even know about that?" I already know the answer. I stand too fast, tray rattling. "Never mind, you are *so* infuriating."

I walk away to the sound of his laughter.

26 HALLOWEEN

The rest of the week passes in a blur of tension and distractions. Whispers still follow me down every corridor, and a few girls look at me with outright malice. Maybe because the boys who rule Blackmoore's social hierarchy have started orbiting me instead of shoving me out into the cold.

But none of it matters right now.

Not the photos. Not the whispers. Not the guilt.

Because Saturday night is right around the corner. The annual Blackmoore Halloween Dance.

It's all anyone can talk about. Dresses. Masks. Dates. Drama. Even the instructors have backed off a little, as if giving us space to breathe before another inevitable storm.

And through it all, Dakota is relentless.

"I'm not letting you bail," she says, yanking open the door to my room Saturday afternoon, garment bags slung over one arm.

I slip behind the folding screen she's set up and ease the dress on. When I step out, Dakota whistles.

I turn to look in the full-length mirror. The girl staring back is bolder, more confident. Storm-blue eyes framed by smoky liner. Lips soft and glossed. My now silver-streaked black hair has been curled into soft, elegant waves that fall over my shoulders.

I look... lethal.

"Damn," Dakota whispers, stepping beside me. "If they weren't already obsessed, they're about to lose their minds."

A flush creeps up my neck. "You think so?"

Dakota meets my eyes in the mirror. "I know so."

I stand in front of the mirror admiring her work. I'm blown away.

My black lace mask frames my eyes perfectly. The corseted dress hugs like it's molded to me. The slit reveals just enough leg to be dangerous.

For a moment, I let myself believe that this night can just be fun. I can laugh and dance like a normal girl and not some girl that's trying to get into the thieves' guild.

Maybe, just for a few hours, I can be more than what those boys try to reduce me to.

THE MOMENT I step into the hall, it's a whole different world.

Everything shimmers.

The chandeliers cast flickering gold over marble floors and draped velvet. Students spin in elegant masks, gliding between columns of smoke and shadow. A DJ plays something dark and lilting from the dais, the haunting music echoing under the arched ceilings like something out of a twisted fairytale.

Dakota squeezes my hand as we descend the stairs. "Heads up," she murmurs, smirking. "Because everyone is looking at you."

She isn't wrong. Conversations dull. Movements slow. A ripple of stares spread like fire through dry brush.

I hold my chin high and let the silence wrap around me like a second gown.

Let them look.

They watched me break.

Now they can watch me rise.

Dakota breaks off to find her date, her laughter trailing behind her. I stay at the edge of the dance floor, pretending not to notice the way people part around me like water. It isn't fear. It's curiosity.

Then they arrive.

Tex dons all black, mask a shiny gold. Luca is in dark green velvet with a devil-may-care grin that doesn't quite reach his eyes. Noah is in sleek navy, his hair a little messier than usual — deliberately so. And Jace, regal in tailored gray and wine red, a predator in polished armor.

For the first time... their eyes don't scan the crowd.

They are looking at me.

Tex reaches me first, his gaze sweeping over me from head to toe, jaw dropping ever so slightly.

"You look..."

"Different?" I offer with a tilt of my head.

He smirks. "Delicious."

Heat rises in my cheeks. Before I can answer, Luca steps in. "Forget dangerous. You're stunning, sweetheart. Don't let anyone close unless they deserve it."

I give Luca a smile. I've never felt beautiful, never been told anything. But to have them looking at me like this? Like I'm some big discovery in the museum? It makes me feel good.

Confident.

Like maybe I'm not just a girl trying to fill her family's legacy.

I'm just Isobel.

Noah's voice comes from behind me, lower, more intimate. "We might need to revise the dress code. This? This is criminal."

And Jace? He doesn't speak. He just looks at me like I'm a bomb he hasn't finished defusing yet.

My pulse thrums in my throat. I'm used to being the center of their attention — but not like this. Not when it isn't cruel.

A slow song drifts in, and I turn to step away, feeling overwhelmed. But Tex is already offering a hand. "Dance with me."

I place my hand in his, feeling his rough palm against my fingers. He pulls me onto the dance floor as if it was inevitable — as if I belong there, with him, in his arms. The music is sultry, threaded with shadows and a beautiful kind of haunting. Around us, costumed silhouettes move in time. But in that moment, it's just us.

His hand finds my waist, the other holding my hand tenderly. My skin buzzes from the contact, memory and sensation colliding like sparks on a fuse.

My cheeks warm.

We start to move, swaying back in forth. I don't miss how his thumb brushes along my side, over the bare skin his hands have touched before. There's no mask between us tonight — not really.

"You look more like yourself," his voice low.

I scan his face. "You barely know me."

He smirks, but it softens just enough to make my chest ache. "Yeah. But I like what I do know."

We dance in silence for a beat, the air heavy with everything we won't say. His palm tightens against me, like he's holding himself back — from what, I'm not sure. Or maybe I am.

I look up at him, our faces just inches apart. "You keep looking at me like that."

"Like what?"

"Like you want to kiss me."

"And if I do? Claim you as mine in front of everyone?" Tex's eyes are dark with desire.

"I'm not an object to be claimed." I lift my chin.

Tex's eyes drop to my lips.

"I remember everything about that night," I say, the words breathy. "I haven't stopped."

He exhales like I've caused him pain. "You're dangerous when you're honest," he growls.

"But you like danger." I smile.

His gaze stays on me, searing and unflinching, as though nothing else in the room exists. "You look incredible tonight."

I give a small, self-conscious smile, my fingers tightening where they rest on his shoulders. "Thanks. It's... kind of weird. Everyone looking at me."

He leans in, his mouth near my ear. "Let them look."

I shiver and laugh softly, the sound surprising even me.

We move in slow circles, lights flickering around us. I'm aware of every touch, every breath. His eyes keep dropping down to my lips like he's going to kiss me.

But he doesn't.

Instead, after a beat, "Go out with me."

"What?"

"Not now," he says, smile tugging at one corner of his mouth. "Not like this. Just—soon. You and me. Just us."

The song ends before I can respond, and someone brushes past us, jarring me.

Tex glares at the guy. I put a hand on his chest. Meeting my eyes, he nods and steps back, his hand sliding from my waist but lingering for one last second. "Think about it, Isobel."

Then he's gone, swallowed by the crowd.

The next song kicks up, faster, brighter — something with a heavy bass that vibrates through the soles of my heels. Before I can fully process what's just happened with Tex, Dakota grabs my hand and hauls me toward the center of the dance floor.

"Okay, brooding boy break over." Her eyes sparkle. "Time to dance like no one's watching."

"I think *everyone's* watching," I glance around at the sea of masked and glittering students.

Dakota rolls her eyes. "Then let's give them a show."

I laugh and let her pull me into the music. We dance like we're just two girls at a sleepover, like none of this, the Guild, the cruelty, the boys matter. Just sweat, adrenaline, and pounding rhythm.

Dakota twirls dramatically, nearly bumping into someone, and we both crack up. I toss my hair back, the new weight of it swinging behind me, and letting the tempo carry me.

It feels good. *Free.*

For a few minutes, I'm not the girl everyone whispers about. I'm not Lucian Ashthorne's heir. I'm just Isobel, spinning under spooky lights, laughing with my sister. I let myself have fun and I don't care who's around.

After a few songs, I tell Dakota I need some air. She asks if I want company, but I assure her I'll be fine and for her to keep dancing.

The cold hits me as I open the door — crisp and biting after the heavy warmth of the dance floor. I step outside the hall, letting the door fall shut behind me. The silence wraps around me like a familiar blanket. My lungs ache for the clean air, my skin flushed and buzzing from too much, too many stares, too many emotions I don't know how to name.

I walk to the edge of the terrace, placing my hands on the stone railing, letting the night sky wash over me. I tilt my face upward, letting the moonlight find me. The cool breeze lightly caresses against my heated skin. For a moment, I breathe and admire the beauty of the night.

Then I hear the soft shift of footsteps, the creak of expensive leather shoes. "Didn't think you'd run from your own spotlight."

My spine stiffens.

"Of course *you're* out here," I sigh, not turning around. "What? Tired of glowering from the shadows?"

"No."

The simplicity of his answer makes me blink as I turn slowly to face him.

Jace stands near one of the stone columns, hands in his pockets, looking like something carved out of shadows and steel. His usual cold prince expression set in place.

We stare each other down, neither apparently willing to break first. The air between us whirrs with tension. Jace moves, his steps syncing with the faint bass from inside. My heart skips.

He stops so close I can smell him. It's a delicious smoky scent, with a trace of something darker. I mentally kick myself for wanting to lean in closer.

"You're incredibly stubborn." His voice travels through my body as he breaks the silence.

I scoff, masking the flutter. "Talk about the pot calling the kettle black. You're the broody gargoyle here. Lurking in the shadows, watching me."

Jace's eyes narrow, his jaw flexing. "I was out here first. So how do I know *you* didn't just follow *me* out here?"

"Trust me, if I knew you were out here, I wouldn't have come out."

His blue eyes narrow. A hint of danger glints in them. "You really think new hair and a little makeup makes you irresistible? Please. They're only humoring you. Desperation still shows."

Fire flashes through me, white-hot and violent. My blood feels like it's boiling, searing through every vein. Heating me from the inside out.

"Fuck you, Jace." I don't have to stand here and listen to this. I shove past him

"No, *fuck you*." Jace eats my strides in two steps, his chest almost brushing against me. "You are the one who came and fucked everything up. You are the one stringing my friends along like little puppies. You are the toy they keep fighting over."

I stare at Jace in disbelief. "You're mad that they actually have a brain of their own? That they aren't blindly following your orders? Maybe the problem isn't *me*. It's *you.*"

Rage flares across his face, which seems to be the only emotion he can't mask. He stalks forward, his presence alone pushing me back until I hit a column. His hand braces against the column next to my head. I can feel his warmth. My body reacts to him, and I hate it.

"You think you've got me all figured out?" he murmurs, so close his lips are inches away from mine.

"I don't want to figure you out. I want you out of my face and leaving me alone."

"Liar."

My heart slams so hard against my ribs I'm worried it's bruised. I should shove him away. I should say something, anything. But I don't move.

His eyes flick over me as his jaw flexes, something conflicted on his face.

My tongue brushes along my lips, something coming to life within me I don't understand. I can't help the pull I feel toward him, even if he's a massive asshole.

Jace exhales, rough and angry, stepping back, taking his warmth with him.

"Go back inside, Ashthorne. Before you start something you can't finish." He shoves his hands into his pockets, and I can't help but admire the stance.

27 CRY ME A RIVER

The bass thuds through the marble halls as I slip back inside, my fingers still cool from the autumn air. I haven't been gone long, just long enough for my head to stop spinning from my encounter with Jace.

My eyes scan the room for Dakota, but I can't see her in the sea of masks and glitter. I keep to the edges of the room and make my way to the punch table. I grab a cup and fill it, just to give myself something to hold.

"Wow."

I turn and River is smiling whilst leaning on the table behind me. He looks handsome in all black.

"You clean up good." His eyes drag up and down my body. There's something that feels off with him.

"Thanks." I smile tentatively and step closer to him.

"Dance with me." He leans in, speaking low in my ear.

I smell it, the smell of alcohol. He's different because he's drinking. Before I can answer, he takes the punch cup from my hand and puts it down on the table, taking my hand to the dancefloor.

The music is loud and upbeat. A girl to my left tosses her head back, grinding against some guy in a devil mask. He grips her waist as they move.

River turns me and pulls me flush against him, his hands tight on my hips and he starts to move and grind against me. His movements match the beat, shameless, and uninvited. His breath ghosts over my neck.

Panic flares in my chest, my body locking up. It's too much, too close, too familiar. I try to step away but his grip tightens further, almost bruising.

My eyes flash back to a different pair of hands, equally as rough, gripping my hips and grinding into my ass.

"You smell good." River presses his erection into me.

"Don't," I gasp, barely audible. I try to jerk away from him.

He doesn't hear me—or doesn't want to.

"Hey," I snap louder, twisting away hard enough to make him stumble. "*Get the hell off me.*"

"Relax, baby," River slurs, his hands moving up and down my body, squeezing me in different places. "We're dancing." He grabs my ass hard.

"I said no," I bite out, louder this time. My voice shakes, but it doesn't break. "*Back. Off.*" I push his hands off me.

One second River's in my space, the next, he's not. Luca wedges himself between us with a grin that doesn't reach his eyes.

"Yo, River," he says, light and easy, but his body is steel. "Didn't your mom ever teach you what *no* means?"

River blinks, frowning. "We were just dancing, dude. Fuck off."

"Were you?" Luca tilts his head. "Because it looked like you were about half a second from catching a fist to the jaw."

There's something coiled behind Luca's smile. Something dangerous.

"Fuck. Off." River steps up to Luca.

"No." Luca puffs his chest, staring down at River. "What are you going to do about it?"

"Why don't you mind your own business?" River sneers.

"See, the thing is… this pretty girl *is* my business."

That's all it takes. River shoves Luca back, and Luca shifts, pushing me out of the way. When he turns back around, River swings. Sloppy but fast.

Luca ducks, quick and sharp and counters with a clean shot to River's ribs. They crash into a table. Cups clatter to the floor, someone screams.

The music stutters, students shout and scramble out of the way. River launches again, this time grabbing Luca's collar, and they slam into the wall near the punch table. Luca grunts but doesn't back down. He twists free, drives his elbow into River's side, and shoves him hard enough to stagger back into the crowd.

"*Stop!*" I yell, the sound tearing out of me before I even think about it.

But they don't. They're locked in it now—adrenaline, pride, maybe something uglier underneath. My stomach churns. The lights are too bright. The bass too loud. It feels like the whole room is spinning.

"*Luca!*" I say again, louder this time, panic rising in my throat. "Stop. Please."

That gets through. His head snaps toward me. Just for a second.

It's all River needs.

He catches Luca across the jaw with a lucky shot. Luca stumbles, blood blooming at the corner of his mouth.

I gasp, hands covering my mouth.

But Luca straightens—wipes the blood with the back of his hand—and looks at River with a dark, bloodthirsty, smile.

Then faculty storms in. Two teachers push between them, one shouting orders. The crowd parts with a collective breath.

River shouts something I don't catch as they drag him back. Luca doesn't answer. He just watches me.

My hands are still trembling.

The dean's voice echoes over the sound system, demanding order.

I stand in the middle of the chaos, everyone staring, whispers swirling again like ash after an explosion.

This is my fault.

MY MIND IS a messy jumble as I walk back to my room on autopilot. I slam the door shut behind me and press my back against it, heart still racing. The hallway feels like it's following me, voices echoing in my head even though I know I'm alone now.

Stupid. That's what it was. Stupid and loud and messy.

I should've stayed outside. I should've never come back in. I should've walked away when I smelled the alcohol on River. I should've stopped him, I shouldn't have frozen. And Luca... he came to help me.

My breath hitches.

The room is too quiet. Too neat.

I don't know whether to cry or scream. So, I do neither. I just sit on the edge of the bed and press the heels of my palms into my eyes.

There's a hard knock at the door.

I don't answer.

A beat. Then another knock. Firmer this time. "Isobel. Open up."

I clench my jaw and yank the door open. Tex's eyes scan me instantly, his expression thunderous.

"You okay?" his voice is rough.

I step back.

He stalks past and closes the door behind him. I press my back to it, exhaling like I can push the tension out. He doesn't speak, just waits. Giving me the time to find the words.

"River was drunk." I close my eyes. "I smelled the alcohol on his breath. Then his hands are all over me and he says something that reminded me..."

I can't finish the sentence.

"You want me to beat the guy up again?" he asks casually, like he's asking if I want coffee.

Despite myself, I let out a soft laugh.

"Pretty sure Luca already took care of that."

"Yeah, well. I've got a stronger punch."

I open my eyes and look at him. "Why are you here?"

He shrugs. "Figured you could use someone who wasn't trying to fix anything. Just... be here. I wanted to make sure you were okay. You ran out of there pretty fast, which is impressive in those heels."

I huff out another laugh and look at him. Really look.

And something in my chest eases.

"I hate that it got to me," I admit. "I hate that he made me feel small."

Tex nods. "Yeah. Been there."

He doesn't ask questions. Doesn't offer platitudes. Just exists next to me like he's holding space for whatever I need.

"I feel stupid," I whisper.

"You're not."

"It was all my fault."

"No." Tex walks up and grips my chin in his big hand, lifting my face up to his, his blue eyes burning with fire. "This was not your fault."

"But—"

"River was drunk, you said it yourself, he didn't understand what the word 'no' means." Tex's voice is firm. "He should've never put his hands on you like that."

I let his words sink in and sigh. He opens his arms, and I step into them. His arms are warm and secure. My head quiets.

"I'm so tired of this. Of fighting. Of trying to breathe when it feels like everyone's trying to shove my head under water."

He pulls back just enough to look at me, brushing a tear from my cheek with his thumb.

"The good things don't come easy. You're going to make it to the other side and you're going to be stronger for it."

The words undo me. I close my eyes, lean into his touch as he tucks my hair behind my ear and rests his forehead gently against mine. For that moment, it's just us. The feel of his arms around me like armor.

His breath is warm against my cheek, and I don't move. Not right away.

I don't want to leave the safety of his arms, don't want to pull away from the only place that feels steady in a world that keeps trying to knock me off balance.

Then I look up at him, eyes searching, and I kiss him.

Soft at first.

A question.

His hand clenches at my waist, but he doesn't move. Doesn't respond. My heart is thundering now, the ache in my chest too big, too loud.

"I need this," I whisper against his lips. "Please, Tex. I need you."

His eyes close like he is at war with himself. "You're upset."

"I know."

"You should rest."

"I don't want to," I say, more desperate now. "Make it stop. Please."

He looks at me like I'm breaking something in him just by asking. Then I kiss him again. Deeper, firmer, and this time he kisses me back.

And when he kisses me… it's not careful.

It's like he's been holding back for days, weeks—months, even. His hand cups the side of my face, calloused fingers grounding me, thumb brushing under my jaw as his mouth claims mine.

I gasp into him, and he swallows the sound.

He walks me backward until the back of my knees hit the edge of the bed, and he pulls away just enough to look at me—his chest heaving, eyes dark.

"Tell me this is what you want," his voice is hoarse.

"I wouldn't be asking if it wasn't. I want your hands on me, not his."

Something in him disintegrates. His mouth crashes against mine again, hungry and rough. His hands move up into my hair, exposing my neck to him.

He kisses down the side of my throat and across my collarbone. His hand travels up my thigh, the slit giving him easy access. He grabs my ass tightly and pulls me against him.

"Tex," I pant, "untie me." I turn around, pressing my ass against him, feeling his hard cock press back into me.

His fingers brush over the fabric of the corset. I arch slightly as his fingers toy with the ribbons, tugging gently, undoing them one by one until the laces loosen and the bodice gapes open at the back.

His fingertips trace the spaces between each ribbon, slowly sliding down the length of my spine, featherlight.

I flinch.

It's small. A flicker of panic in my breath, a tremble in my shoulders—but he notices. Tex stops.

His hand stays right where it is, barely resting on my lower back.

He speaks into my ear. "Hey." His forehead rests against the side of mine. "I'm not going to hurt you."

"I know," I whisper, but my voice cracks. "It's not that. It's just... they're still there."

His hand moves again, carefully this time, not down—just across. Comforting. A steady weight.

"I've seen them," he says, brushing a strand of hair away from my face. "That night. When the pictures were everywhere."

I tense. His hand reaches around, tilting my chin to look back at him.

"And all I could think was how fucking strong you must be to have lived through it."

Tears burn behind my eyes.

"You're beautiful," he murmurs, kissing my cheek, then the corner of my mouth. "Every scar, every line. Not because they define you—because you survived them. You're still standing."

I blink fast, swallowing a lump that comes from nowhere.

"I don't want you to hide from me," admiration thick in his voice. "Not your scars. Not your fire. I want all of you, Isobel."

My breath hitches and I nod.

And when he kisses me again, it isn't to devour—it's to worship.

Tex's hands skim over the open back of my corset, now loosened and slipping down my body. I let it fall. The cool air kisses my skin, but it's nothing compared to the heat of him—his body, his gaze.

I whirl around to face him, pushing his jacket off and unbuttoning his shirt.

His body is all muscle and defined lines, scars mapping their way across tanned skin. My eyes drag over every inch—his broad shoulders, the sculpted ridges of his chest, the way his stomach tightens under my gaze, the veins that climb up his arms.

I press my hand to his abdomen, fingers splayed and feel the heat of him. He stills beneath my touch, watching me with something fierce in his eyes.

"You're beautiful," I say before I can stop myself. Not in the fragile, pretty way—but in the carved-from-survival, devastating way. A body built to endure.

He clears his throat. "I've never been called that before."

"You are." I lean in to press a kiss to the scar on his side. "All of you."

Tex pushes the rest of my dress down, letting it pool around my ankles. He pushes me back onto the bed and stands over me. His eyes trace over my breasts, my nipples pebbled. The black lace thong is the only thing left. He undoes his pants, and they drop to the floor, leaving him standing there in just plain black briefs. His cock is outlined by the fabric.

I lie back, chest rising and falling, and he follows me down, pressing a line of kisses from my collarbone to the center of my chest. Each one unravels a knot inside me.

His hands frame my ribs, reverent, as though I'm something divine. I arch into him, silently asking for more.

He groans low in his throat. "You're going to drive me insane."

"Good," I all but purr, my voice hoarse with need.

His mouth captures mine again, this time deeper, more demanding, while his hand slides down over my bare stomach, past the waistband of my thong. He hesitates—just long enough to glance up and meet my eyes.

I bite my lip, pleading with my eyes.

He slips his fingers beneath the fabric. I'm dripping for him.

"Fuck," he growls.

"You do this to me," I admit, heat rising.

His lips smash mine again as his fingers stroke through me, slow and teasing. My thighs tremble around his hand. I run my hand up into his hair, burying my face in his neck as my hips move of their own accord.

"That's it," he says, breath hot against my skin. "Use me. Let me take care of you."

My body obeys before my brain can catch up, heat building, cresting like a wave about to break. His fingers move in perfect rhythm, the pad of his thumb circling just right. I moan as pleasure hits me all at once.

I shatter with his name on my lips.

He kisses me through it, gentle now, hand stilling as I throb beneath him. My whole body pulses with aftershocks, my breath ragged.

When I open my eyes, his are already on me.

Tex strokes his knuckles along my cheek. "I've never wanted someone the way I want you."

"Me either," I breathe.

Tex gives me a devilish smirk as he drags his tongue down to my breast, circling around my nipple then sucking it into his mouth. I moan and he kisses down my stomach. I lift my hips as he pulls off my panties.

"I've thought about this." He kisses along my hip. "About you." His eyes molten. "About tasting you."

Then his mouth is on me.

Warm, slow pressure makes my entire body jolt.

"Tex... sensitive."

"Don't worry, baby, I got you." He smiles. His tongue moves with purpose, teasing and relentless, and my hips buck before I can stop them. He grips my thighs tighter, holding me still as he devours me like he has all the time in the world—like this was what he'd been starving for.

My fingers thread into his hair as pleasure coils low and tight, overwhelming in its intensity. He groans when I pull him closer, the vibration sending another wave crashing through me.

"You're so fucking sweet," he mutters against me. "So good..."

One hand moves away from my thigh and his fingers plunge into me as he continues feasting on me. I moan loudly, my hips grinding against his face and fingers, chasing the release that is just there.

He growls against me, sucking my clit hard into his mouth, pressing his tongue against it, flicking it furiously.

I come undone, everything melting away. I press against him as he continues to pump his fingers in and out of me, prolonging my release. My body tingles, my toes curl. His name on my lips over and over like a chant.

He moves up my body and grinds his hard cock against me, straining against his pants, moaning into my mouth as we kiss.

"I want to make you feel good."

He looks into my eyes. "You're in control, babygirl."

I kiss him, pushing myself up, and he backs onto his knees without breaking our kiss. I shift and slowly push him to lay on his back.

"My turn indeed." I climb on top of him.

I watch his breath catch as I kiss down his chest, taking my time. I grind myself against his cock, just a thin layer of spandex separating us. My pussy clenches with the thought of him sliding inside me, but I'm not sure I'm ready to go there yet.

"Isobel, you don't —"

"I want to." I place my hand on his chest and move myself further down.

I need this, not for validation or approval. But because I want to take back every part of myself that has ever been claimed without consent. I want to feel powerful in my own skin again. I want to be the one to unravel him.

My hands slip beneath the waistband of his boxer briefs. I watch his abs flex as I tug them down and exposed him fully. My cheeks flush with heat, but I don't look away.

His body is truly a work of art. All hard lines and tensed muscle, veins, strength wrapped in control, but not with me. With me, he gives me the reins.

I wrap my fingers around his thick cock, slowly stroking once, remembering how he did it to himself when he watched me that night, and the groan he lets out goes straight through me.

"Jesus," he breathes, head falling back. "You're going to fucking ruin me."

I don't answer. I just lean in and brush my lips over the tip — soft, testing. He jumps in my hand, a low curse tumbling from his lips. His skin is soft and smooth, like velvet. I run my tongue over it, and he moans. I'm so turned on by his moans. I need them on repeat.

Then I slide him into my mouth, inch by inch.

His hand finds my hair, not to force or hold, just grounding himself. The control in his body begins to splinter apart, and I can feel it in the way his hips buck slightly, the way his breathing comes in jagged pulls.

"Fuck, Isobel—" My name comes out like a prayer and a warning all in one.

I hollow out my cheeks, trying to remember everything I've ever heard, read, or imagined. But more than that — I just listen. To his body. To the way he mutters my name, the way his thighs tense beneath my palms, the way he gasps when I swirl my tongue just right.

I have power. I have him unraveling.

I keep moving my head up and down, pressing my tongue against him. Letting him hit the back of my throat, and he curses, and my eyes look up to him. His gaze locks with mine, heavy with desire. He continues guiding me, his hand in my hair.

I pick up speed, my hand playing gently with his balls. He groans, his fingers tightening against my scalp.

He's shaking by the time he swears again, and then he's spilling into my mouth, hot and salty and overwhelming. I take all of it, because I want to.

I pull back slowly, wiping my mouth with the back of my hand. My lips tingle, and my throat burns a little, but I feel... proud.

And when I look up, Tex is staring at me like he's never seen me before.

His chest rise and falls like he'd just fought a war, and the awe in his expression makes my cheeks heat again for a whole different reason.

"You're incredible." His voice is rough but filled with admiration.

He reaches for me, hand sliding behind my neck to pull me close again, and I go willingly — breathless, trembling.

He kisses me and his hand slides between my legs once more.

"You're dripping." He bites my lower lip gently. "You love sucking my cock don't you?"

I nod, and as I lie next to him, he leans over me.

"Can't leave you dripping like this." He smiles, sucking my nipple into his hot mouth.

His fingers work expert circles on my clit again and I'm so close already.

"Rub yourself," he commands into my ear.

My hand snakes down my body, and he pushes two fingers into me. It's perfect, my body squeezes around him as he picks up speed and I rub my clit in tandem. With my other hand, I pull him to me and kiss him hungrily, and before I know it, I'm coming again. I moan loudly into his mouth as he works me through my release. Wave after wave, my body shakes. When he finally stills, we're both panting and his eyes find mine.

My limbs feel like jelly as he places a soft kiss to my lips.

"Let's get you cleaned up." He moves and offers me his hand, and I take it.

28 AFTERMATH

The room is quiet, lit only by the soft glow of the bedside lamp, shadows pooling in the corners. The silence between us is warm and full. Like something sacred has settled there and neither of us wants to disturb it.

Tex is behind me, his chest pressing against my back, one arm wrapped securely around my waist like he has no intention of letting go. His other hand traces slow, lazy patterns along my hip — shapes that don't mean anything but somehow say everything.

I watch his fingers glide gently along my skin, dipping under the edge of the sheet and back out again, dragging warmth in their wake. Each stroke makes me shiver, not from cold but from how present he is. From how gentle he can be, when the world has only ever known him as dangerous.

His thumb brushes a spot just above my hipbone and lingers there. "Still with me?" he asks, his voice low and raw and sleepy.

I nod, the corner of my mouth tilting up. "Still here."

"You didn't flinch that time."

"I know."

He presses a kiss to the curve of my shoulder. "You're incredible."

I don't know what to say to that. So, I just reach for his hand and lace our fingers together, grounding myself in the moment. His hand is bigger, rougher — but it fits with mine like we are two pieces that have been battered by life in just the right way to match.

"You're not what I expected," I murmur.

"Good or bad?"

"I haven't decided yet."

He laughs, a soft, hoarse sound that rumbles against my spine. "Fair."

We lie there, tangled in each other, and I feel safer and more seen than I have in a long time. There is no pressure in his touch, no expectations. Just quiet. Steady. Real.

And I find myself wishing time would freeze right here.

Just for a little while.

I shift onto my back so I can see him better, and he glances down at me. His expression is open in a way I rarely see — stripped of his usual hard edges. It makes my chest ache.

"When I was a kid," I say slowly, "I used to lie awake and pretend I was someone else. Someone stronger. Someone who didn't flinch every time the door opened."

His hand tightens around mine.

"I don't think I ever stopped pretending," I admit. "But lately... I don't know. It feels like I'm finally starting to become that girl."

Tex stares at me for a long moment, and something flickers in his eyes. Pride? Pain? I can't tell.

"You are," he says softly. "You already are."

Silence stretches between us, heavy with things we aren't quite ready to say. Then he rolls onto his side, propping himself up on his elbow, his gaze pinned to mine.

"You make me feel like I could actually have something good," he says, almost like he doesn't mean to say it out loud.

I swallow hard. "You deserve something good."

I trace my fingers lightly over the back of his hand where it rests on my stomach. "What happened to Ellie?" I whisper.

He stills. For a moment, I'm not sure he'll answer.

"We were stuck in this foster house. Adults who didn't give a shit about the kids they were fostering, just the check that came with them. I used to tell her bedtime stories about breaking out, about stealing enough to buy a new life. She believed me."

His voice cracks, just slightly. "One night, there was a fight. Local gang came to collect what they were owed. Guns. Screaming. I told her to hide in the crawlspace." He swallows. "But a stray bullet hit her, and by the time I went to get her, she was gone."

Everything in me clenches.

"I'm sorry," I whisper, my chest aching for this man.

"Don't be."

"What was she like?"

His voice comes low and rough against the shell of my ear. "She had this gap in her front teeth, which she was really self-conscious about. I used to tell her it made her look fierce."

There is a smile in his voice, but it's cracked.

"She wanted to be a dancer," he continues. "Used to tie pillowcases or sheets around her waist like tutus. Said she'd be on a stage one day, spinning so fast the world would disappear."

I can feel the ache in his chest like it's my own.

"My mom died after Ellie was born. That's when my dad, well, Ellie's dad, started drinking. Eventually, he lost his job, then us. But no matter what happened, I made sure Ellie and I stayed together."

He looks past my shoulder, like he's letting the memories play before he speaks.

"She used to collect rocks," he says, his voice low. "Not pretty ones, not crystals or polished stones. Just the ones she found on sidewalks or playgrounds. She said they were 'rescued.'" A short breath of a laugh leaves him. "I once found one in my shoe before a fight. She snuck it in there. Said it was her 'lucky pebble.' In fact..." He leans over and fishes something out of his pants. He wraps his arms around me, holding up a palm-sized grey rock with white speckles. "I still carry it around with me. It truly is a lucky pebble. It's kept me alive all these years."

The fondness in his eyes makes my eyes sting.

"She sounds like she was clever," I murmur, smiling into my pillow.

"She was. Way too clever. She had this habit of making up words when she didn't know the real ones. Like when she couldn't remember the word for violin, she called it a 'shoulder guitar.' And everyone just… went with it."

I can hear the fondness in his voice now, more than the pain. Like the fog of loss has briefly lifted, letting the sun through.

"She was obsessed with pancakes," he continues. "Wouldn't eat anything else if she could help it. Once told me she wanted to marry a stack of them." He paused. "And she had this laugh. God, it was like… It just filled up a room. This big, snorting, bubbling thing that made everyone around her start laughing too, even if they didn't know why."

My throat tightens. "She sounds amazing."

"She was," he says, his voice far away. "She used to draw with sidewalk chalk all over the concrete outside our building. Said she was decorating the world. And when it rained, she'd cry like she was losing her friends. But the next day, she'd start over. Never stopped drawing."

I can see her in my mind now — barefoot on sun-warmed pavement, hair wild, coloring her little world bright.

"Thank you for telling me about her," I whisper, reaching back to run my fingers along his arm.

His lips brush my shoulder. "She would've liked you," he says again, quiet and certain. "You would've made her feel safe."

My chest aches, but it is a good ache. A full one.

"Stay," I say, breathless. "Just for tonight."

He nods and pulls me against him, skin against skin, wrapping around me like armor. And for once, I sleep without dreaming.

THE NEXT MORNING, I wake up to a message on my tablet that I need to be at Dean Everett's office at ten. My stomach clenches. No explanation. Just that.

Tex stirs behind me, his arm tightening briefly before he blinks awake. "What's wrong?"

I sit up, already reaching for my clothes. "The school messaged. Said I need to be at Dean Everett's office at ten. Didn't say why."

Tex sits up too, frowning, his hair a sleep-rumpled mess. "I'll get changed. I'll meet you down there."

I pause at the edge of the bed, turning to look at him. He reaches for me, cupping the back of my neck and pulling me in for a kiss. It's soft, but there is something fierce beneath it—something protective.

"Whatever it is," he says, brushing his thumb along my jaw, "we'll handle it."

I nod, letting his steadiness anchor me. He kisses my forehead before my dorm door shuts behind him. Then I pull on leggings, a loose black tee, and boots, tug my hair into a quick ponytail, and slip into the hall. The air is brisk and quiet.

By the time I reach the corridor outside Dean Everett's office, I slow to a stop. All four of them are already there.

Tex leans against the wall, arms folded across his chest, wearing a dark long-sleeved shirt he must've thrown on. Noah stands beside him, scrolling absently through his tablet like he isn't wound tight beneath the surface. Jace paces in a slow, deliberate line, hands in his pockets and jaw tight. And Luca—Luca looks like he just rolled out of bed and dared anyone to say something about it, his usual lazy grin nowhere in sight. A bruise blooms across his jaw.

Guilt floods my chest. They all look up when they hear my boots on the floor.

Jace is the first to speak. "Took you long enough."

Tex pushes off the wall. "It's not even ten yet. Chill."

Jace continues to glare at me. I give it to him right back.

"What are you even doing here?" I cross my arms over my chest.

Jace scoffs. "I go where I want."

"Okay," I mock, rolling my eyes.

The office door opens then, as if summoned by the weight of our silence. The assistant nods. "You can come in now."

They aren't walking ahead of me like they usually do. They walk with me. Whatever is about to happen... they are choosing to stand beside me.

Fluorescent lights hum overhead, bouncing off the polished wood of Dean Everett's desk and the rows of bookshelves lining the walls. It smells faintly of coffee and old paper. I barely register any of it—because all I see is him.

River sits in one of the chairs across from the desk, a scowl etched deep into his face. One eye is swollen nearly shut, the skin around it darkening to an angry bruise. His lip is split, the dried blood flaking. His hair is messy like he couldn't be bothered. He looks like hell.

And when he sees me, his jaw clenches tighter.

"Sit," Dean Everett says without looking up from the tablet in his hands.

We do. I end up in the middle, flanked by Tex and Noah, while Luca drops into the chair beside the window like he couldn't care less. He doesn't even glance at River. But his fists are still curled.

Everett finally looks up.

His gaze scans the room, heavy with authority. "I want to be very clear. Fighting is grounds for suspension—potential expulsion if deemed serious enough. You are not above the rules just because your parents are generous donors or you hold academic privilege. This school maintains its standards for everyone."

No one speaks.

Everett sets his tablet down. "I've reviewed the footage. It shows Mr. Silvain and Mr. Hale engaging in a physical altercation at the Halloween dance. But I also know it started long before the first punch was thrown."

His eyes land on me. I sit a little straighter.

"I understand this incident had something to do with you, Miss Ashthorne. That makes you a witness." He pauses. "So now, I'd like to hear your version. What happened last night?"

My palms are damp. I lace my fingers together and try to steady my voice.

"I'd just come back inside from the terrace," I say slowly. "River came up and asked me to dance." I swallow.

Out of the corner of my eye, I feel Tex tense.

"The music was... loud. People were dancing close." I continue. "He pulled me against him. It was more than I was comfortable with, and I tried to step back. But he didn't let go."

River scoffs.

"Mr. Hale," Dean Everett warns, not even looking at him.

My voice is quieter now. "He was holding my hips. Grinding against me. I told him to stop, but he didn't. That's when Luca stepped in."

Dean Everett turns to Luca. "Is that true?"

Luca leans back, arms folded. "Yeah. I saw she wasn't okay, so I got in the middle. Told him to back off."

"And then you hit him?"

Luca's mouth twists. "No. He shoved me first."

Dean Everett looks at River again. "Is that accurate? Don't forget I have footage."

River glares at me. Then at Luca. Then down at the floor. His jaw moves like he wants to spit out something vile—but instead, he mutters, "Yeah."

Dean Everett leans back in his chair, fingers steepled. "Miss Ashthorne, thank you for your honesty. I understand this wasn't easy to talk about. Given the context, it's clear this was a defensive escalation rather than an unprovoked fight."

His gaze shifts back to River. "Mr. Hale, you are suspended for one week, effective immediately. Any further incidents, and you'll be removed from Blackmoore entirely."

River's fists clench on his knees. But he doesn't argue.

Everett nods to the rest of us. "You're all dismissed."

We stand slowly. River doesn't move. Just before we step out of the room, Everett calls, "Miss Ashthorne?"

I turn back.

"I appreciate how you handled this. You showed maturity. That matters here."

I nod, too numb to answer. Then I walk out, the boys falling into step around me.

29 FREE

The second the classroom door opens and Dean Everett's assistant calls my name, my stomach drops.

Every eye follows me as I rise from my seat, shoving my things into my bag with more force than necessary. I catch Dakota's concerned glance, but I don't stop. I just need to get out of that room.

The walk to the dean's office feels longer than usual. The hallways are quieter. The air colder.

When I open the door, my pulse stutters at the sight of Lucian standing by the tall window, arms crossed, framed by morning light. His posture is stiff, jaw tight. Dean Everett stands as I enter but doesn't say much—just nods and steps out, leaving us alone.

Lucian turns. The look on his face tells me its nothing good.

"What happened?" I ask, my voice flat, throat dry.

"Daniel has made bail."

My mind empties. A buzzing starts in my ears.

"Bail?" I repeat, as if I haven't heard him right.

Lucian nods once, every line of his face tense.

"W-what? How?" My body feels like it's been disconnected. "The detective told me he was denied bail."

"He appealed and the judge granted bail. He has shown good behavior while in jail."

"But he has no money."

"It looks like he was wired money from offshore accounts. I'm still trying to trace it back." Lucian runs his hand down his face. "The important thing is that you're safe here," Lucian says. "Blackmoore has layers of protection. He can't touch you."

I laugh, hollow. "He abused me for years, Dad. Nothing stops people like him."

His expression cracks for a moment—softness, guilt, rage, helplessness flickering through. He crouches in front of me, leveling his gaze with mine.

"I will not let him hurt you again," he says, low and fierce. "I promise you that. You're also a different woman. Even if he did manage to get close to you, you've had training since then. You know how to fight back."

I nod, barely. But the chill has already settled in my bones.

When I stand, Lucian pulls me into a tight hug, kissing the top of my head.

"You're going to get through this, Gracie. We will handle Daniel. You're strong. I love you."

One second I'm sitting there, his words still echoing in my skull—Daniel's been released—and the next I'm standing outside my room, hand trembling as I press my thumb to the lock. The soft click of the door unlocking sounds too loud in the silence, echoing in my bones.

I step inside and shut the door behind me, the seal of it clicking into place like a coffin lid. My breath is tight, shallow. My body moves on autopilot—straight to the control panel by the wall. I open it with a swipe, checking each camera one by one. Hallway feed: clear. Dorm lobby: empty. Exterior motion sensors: quiet. I cycle through again. And again.

I check the backup system on my phone, making sure the data stream is active, that the alerts are functional, and that the feeds are encrypted. I reset my passwords even though I know no one could get in.

He is out.

Free.

The man who carved me open without lifting a knife. Who made my own home a battlefield littered with landmines.

I walk into the bathroom. Close the door. Turn on the hot water until steam fills the room. I don't step into the shower. Just stand there, staring at my reflection in the mirror as it slowly fogs over, softening my edges until I'm just a blur. I turn off the water.

My hands shake. I go back into the bedroom and recheck the cameras.

Still nothing.

Still safe.

Still, a trapdoor in my chest threatens to open and swallow me whole.

I sit on the edge of the bed and stare down at my hands in my lap. I flex my fingers. Open. Close. Breathe.

The silence is so loud it roars.

I don't cry. Don't scream. Don't punch the wall even though I want to.

Instead, I do the only thing I can—I follow the motions. I clean my already clean weapons. I organize the bag by my door. I recheck the perimeter alerts.

Because if I let myself stop, even for a second, I know the spiral will come. And I can't afford to drown. Not now. Not when I've fought so hard to climb out the last time.

Not when he is out there.

Free.

And I'm not.

The shrill chime of the motion sensor alarm nearly stops my heart.

I freeze where I stand—halfway between the closet and my desk—adrenaline slamming into my veins so hard it makes my vision tunnel. My eyes flick to the monitor on the wall. The camera feed shows the hallway outside my dorm door.

Four familiar shapes.

My heart doesn't slow, but it shifts—away from panic and into something tighter, heavier. I move to the door and unlock it, not even waiting for the knock before pulling it open.

Jace is in front, flanked by Tex and Noah. Luca trails behind, his hands shoved into the pockets of a worn bomber jacket. They are all still dressed in their uniforms like they dropped everything the second they heard.

Maybe they did. Lucian must've told them. Of course he did.

Noah is the first to move. He crosses to me with that calm steadiness he always carries, like his presence is meant to slow the world down.

"I'm so sorry," he says, his voice low.

Tex's eyes sweep the room like he's ready to move if anything is out of place. "You check everything already?"

I nod. "Three times."

He still walks over to the window and tugs on the latch to double-check. Meanwhile, Luca hovers near my bed, looking at me the way someone might study a wounded animal, like he wants to offer comfort but isn't sure I'll take it.

He shrugs, hands in his pockets. "Wasn't gonna sit through another ethics lecture when I knew you were spiraling."

"I'm fine," I lie.

Jace stands by the bookshelf, his arms folded, his jaw tight. "Clearly," he says flatly.

I shoot daggers his way. "What are you even doing here?"

"Guild obligation," Jace says.

"Cut it out, she's part of the team now." Luca slaps a hand against Jace's chest.

Jace scowls.

Tex drags a hand down his face. "They never should've let him out. Ever."

"I know," I whisper. "I know. But they did. And now…"

"Now you don't have to worry about it," Jace cuts in. "Because we're already handling it."

I blink. "Handling what?"

He looks at me, eyes cold in a way that makes me feel like I'm not the one he's angry at for once.

"From this point on, you're not alone," he says. "One of us will be with you at all times. Classes, training, meals, walking across the damn courtyard. You're not stepping anywhere without backup."

My mouth drops open.

Luca flops into the chair near my desk. "Say goodbye to your alone time, pretty girl. We even argued over who gets first shift. It got dramatic."

Noah snorts. "You wrote your name on the notebook in glitter pen."

"It was strategic," Luca replies. "She needs someone with charisma."

Tex shakes his head. "She needs someone who can put a guy in the ground if he shows his face."

"I don't need any of you to—"

"You do," Luca says, cutting me off. "Not because you're weak. Not because you can't handle yourself. But because you shouldn't have to."

The room goes quiet.

He continues. "You shouldn't have to watch the door. Or flinch when someone moves or makes a sound. You shouldn't have to sleep fully dressed and ready to fight. That's not living. That's surviving, and you've survived enough."

My chest aches.

Luca's tone softens, just barely. "We're not going to let you do that alone anymore. We're a team."

"And at night?" I ask, because the silence is always at its worst then. "What about when—"

"One of us will stay," Jace says. No hesitation. "Every night. We'll rotate. We already cleared it with Lucian."

I shake my head, not out of defiance, just because I don't know what to do with that kind of safety.

"You don't have to do that. You don't even like me."

"We want to," Noah says.

"We're going to," Tex adds, crossing his arms.

"You don't get to scare us off, sweetheart," Luca says. "You're stuck with us now."

For a moment, I just stand there, wrapped in a hoodie that's too soft, surrounded by four boys who don't hesitate.

They're not just protecting me. They're choosing me.

The tears hit before I can stop them. Not sobs, just a few hot drops, rolling silently down my cheeks.

Noah steps closer. "Is it okay if I?"

I nod.

He pulls me into a hug, warm and solid, anchoring me to the ground.

Luca grabs the front of Jace's shirt, dragging him over and throwing his arms around us.

Luca holds Jace's arms in place. "Get in here Texy, time for a group hug."

Tex rolls his eyes with a sigh but gives in.

Not crushing, not overwhelming, just surrounding. Shoulders brushing. Arms overlapping. A cocoon of warmth and steel and we've got you.

I close my eyes.

And for the first time since Lucian gave me the news... I feel like I might actually be safe.

30 THE CAGE

The boys have stayed all day in shifts, unofficially, cycling in and out under the radar. They act like it's casual. Like it isn't strange that four elite Blackmoore boys are spending the afternoon camped out on the floor of a girl's room, swapping stories, arguing over which energy drink is actually poison, and flinging cards across the floor with deadly accuracy.

They stay. They make it feel normal.

But night comes. And with it, the restless itch under my skin.

I sit on the edge of my bed, fingers twisting in the hem of my hoodie, while the others talk in low tones near the window. It isn't claustrophobia, it's something deeper. Like if I stay still too long, he wins. Like every second I spend hiding means I'm still his.

I stand without thinking. Four sets of eyes snap toward me.

"I can't sit here," I say. "I need to move. Go somewhere. I don't care where."

Tex's jaw ticks. He glances once at Jace, then back at the others.

Noah's the first to nod. "Yeah. Okay."

Luca straightens, a grin already forming. "I know just the place."

"We all do," Tex adds, voice low. "You'll like it."

I blink. "Wait—what?"

Noah is already pulling his phone out, tapping quickly. "Give us ten. We'll meet back here."

Luca's halfway to the door. "Get dressed, pretty girl. We're going out."

"Out where?"

"You'll see." He winks, then disappears through the door.

Noah tosses me a soft smile and follows.

Tex pauses in the doorway. "We'll make sure it's clear. Just be ready."

And then it's just me and Jace.

He's leaning against the bookshelf, arms folded, like he never once relaxed all day.

I look at him. "Aren't you going to go change, too?"

He shakes his head once. "I can wait."

"You don't have to."

"I know."

He doesn't move. Doesn't offer more.

I shift, suddenly unsure. "Why you?"

Jace's eyes meet mine. The space between us stretches tight. He sighs.

"Couldn't risk leaving you alone with any of your admirers. What? Scared to be alone with me?"

I throw up my arms and huff. "Why are you even here?"

He pushes off the bookshelf, dropping his arms. He's stiff.

"Well?" I ask as he continues to stare.

"I know who's bankrolling Daniel." His voice is low, like he's trying to keep from spooking an animal.

My eyes widen. "How? My dad doesn't even have an answer."

His jaw flexes. "Well, Lucian doesn't have access to my father's servers like I do."

My jaw drops. "We need to tell my dad! He needs—"

"No," Jace barks, storming to me.

"What?" I breathe.

"We can't be rash." His eyes bore into mine. "My father has backup plans for his backup plans. We can't let him know we're on to him. We need solid proof. It's just taking Noah time to track it down."

I stare at him. "Your father released the monster who terrorized the last thirteen years of my life. You can't expect me to just let this go."

"I'm not saying that." Jace runs his hands through his hair, then grabs my arms. "Just give me time. I know you have no reason to trust me but I know my father better than anyone. I'll figure out a plan."

I stare. This is probably the most unguarded I've seen him.

"Fine." I lift my arms to push his hands off.

Jace takes a step back and I can see the wall being resurrected.

"You should get changed."

I glance down. Hoodie. Pajama shorts. Bare feet. *Right.*

Jace moves toward the couch as I head to the closet.

I stare at my clothes like they might give me answers.

They didn't say where we're going. Didn't say what to wear. What to expect.

Just to get dressed.

My first instinct is practicality, black leggings, my most broken-in black boots. Comfortable, flexible, nothing that can snag if things go sideways.

But something in me itches to be bold.

Not like a target. Not like prey.

But like Isobel Ashthorne.

I grab the sheer black top I've never worn, a little clingy, subtly glittered at the sleeves. Underneath, a lace bralette that offers enough support and coverage in a pinch, but peeks just enough to make a statement. I throw on my cropped leather jacket, the one with reinforced lining, hidden snap compartments stitched into the hem.

The jacket's heavier than it looks. So am I.

I tuck two daggers into my boots, hilts barely visible above the laces. A third blade slips into the lining of my sleeve, secured by a magnetic catch. A fourth rests flat along the inside panel of my jacket, angled for easy reach.

Just in case. Not because I'm scared. Because I'm prepared.

I lean over the vanity counter and swipe on eyeliner, dark and sharp. Add a little shimmer at the inner corners. Nothing too heavy, just enough to feel like armor.

When I step back and catch my reflection, something shifts. Not pretty. Not delicate. Lethal.

I inhale. Straighten my spine. Then I step out into the living room.

All four of them are already there — changed and waiting.

Noah's in dark jeans and a navy crewneck, hands shoved into his pockets. Tex has a black tee stretched across his arms, worn jeans and boots scuffed from use. Luca's in some impossibly expensive leather jacket with dark jeans. Jace wears all black — fitted shirt, a coat slung over his shoulder.

The moment they see me, everything stills.

Luca's brows shoot up. A low whistle slips out before he grins. "Well, damn."

Tex doesn't say anything, but he doesn't blink. His hands open and close at his sides.

Noah blinks then looks away, a slow flush climbing up his neck.

And Jace... Jace just stares.

There's no chill in his gaze. His mouth opens slightly, then he shuts it again, jaw clenched.

"Too much?" I ask, suddenly self-conscious. I glance down, tug at the edge of my jacket.

Luca's already shaking his head. "Nope. Absolutely not. Ten out of ten. Would risk arrest."

"You're not wearing that dagger sheath I gave you," Noah says, eyeing my jacket with subtle approval. "But you did compensate. Clever."

Tex grunts. "You ready?"

I nod once. "Where we going?"

Jace's voice is the one that answers. Low. Certain.

"You'll see."

The car ride is quiet, but it hums with tension.

I keep trying to guess where we're going, but the path doesn't make sense. We take two different service roads, then turn down a gated drive I didn't even know existed behind the east courtyard. Jace drives. The others joke around in the back, half-whispers and snorts of laughter.

But I can feel the shift.

The way Tex bounces his knee. The way Noah keeps checking the rearview mirror like he's watching for a tail.

Even Luca's grin is tighter than usual.

"Are we going to get arrested?" I ask, only half-joking.

Jace doesn't look over. "Not unless you bring a weapon into the ring."

"Wait, what?"

We stop.

A sleek steel door waits at the bottom of a narrow ramp, cut straight into the stone foundation. Jace punches in a code. The door slides open with a hiss.

Heat rushes up from the darkness.

Bass-heavy music thumps beneath the ground. Dim lighting flickers across rusted pipes and exposed brick. And voices, dozens of them, rise in a low roar that smells like sweat and blood and adrenaline.

Luca turns and grins. "Welcome to the Cage."

Noah leans in close enough for only me to hear. "Guild tradition. Off-the-books. Every few weeks, they open the floor and let people settle scores or just show off."

I blink. "And people bet on it?"

"Obscene amounts of money," Luca says with a big smile.

Tex tugs off his jacket and tosses it over his shoulder. "Rules are simple," he says. "No weapons. No killing. Everything else? Fair game."

"And you're fighting?" I ask, turning to look at him.

Tex shrugs like it's nothing. But there's a flicker in his eyes.

"Was already signed up before today. Figured I'd still go a round or two. Burn some things off. You okay with that?"

The truth is, I should feel tense. Nervous. Something. But instead, heat blooms under my skin.

I nod. "Yeah. I want to see."

He studies me for half a second, then nods once. "Good."

He plants a quick kiss on my lips before turning to head in a different direction.

I stand, blinking as he casually strolls away.

"Did he just..." Luca points at Tex, eyes wide.

"Indeed, he did." Noah exhales heavily.

My brain is just coming back online. *He kissed me in front of everyone.*

"Come on, let's go," Jace growls.

The stairwell opens into a massive underground pit, a wide circle surrounded by steel rails and tiered stone benches. Lights hang from chains above, throwing stark shadows across the floor. A crowd is already gathered, some in uniform, some in sweatshirts and boots, all leaning in like they're watching something sacred and violent unfold.

And in the center, the cage. No mats. Just concrete and bloodstains and the hum of something like an animal waiting to break free.

Noah finds us a spot along the lower railing. Luca disappears briefly to flirt with the person running the bets. Jace stands just behind me, eyes sweeping the room.

Tex reaches over his head and pulls off his shirt then steps through the gate.

Roaring cheers, whistles, and shouts of his name fill the space. Apparently, he's known here.

His opponent is taller, broader, and cocky as hell. He smiles and taunts Tex.

Tex takes the first hit, a brutal jab to the jaw that turns his face but doesn't move his body.

Then he smiles.

And unleashes hell. It isn't elegant. It isn't clean. But it's devastating. Every punch lands with the kind of finality that says don't get back up. His opponent does anyway. Twice. The third time, he stays down.

The match ends with a roar. I can't stop staring. My heart is hammering, not from fear, but something wilder. Something hotter.

Tex in a fight is something else entirely.

It isn't reckless. It's controlled violence; every move is instinct.

Beside me, Luca whistles low. "Think he was showing off for you."

I glance up at Jace, who's still watching the ring.

"He always fight like that?"

"No," Jace says.

The crowd is still buzzing from Tex's win.

He steps out of the ring like he just went for a run — jaw tense, knuckles bloodied, sweat dripping down his spine. But his eyes find mine the second he crosses the gate. He says nothing, just gives the smallest nod like *you saw that*, and I nod back like *hell yes, I did*.

He disappears from view as he makes his way up to us. He grabs a towel from a crate near the wall and leans against the railing beside Luca, who hands him a bottle of water without looking.

"Who's next?" Noah asks, glancing toward the ring.

There's a pause.

"I'll go," Jace says.

Three heads turn.

Even Luca blinks. "You sure?"

"Have some things to work off." He's already pulling off his coat, folding it neatly over the railing beside me. His black shirt fits too well. His sleeves roll up in one smooth motion. The holster on his hip is unclipped and passed to Noah, who takes it wordlessly.

Jace steps toward the ring with that slow, unhurried stride like he isn't walking into a fight, but into a meeting he fully intends to dominate. My breath catches before I even realize why. Because this isn't like watching Tex.

This isn't heat. It's chill. Calculated. Quiet. Lethal.

"Who's he up against?" I ask.

Tex gives a tight shrug. "Doesn't matter."

"Why?"

"Because no one beats Jace in the Cage."

Noah nods. "He doesn't go in often. But when he does…"

"It's always good," Luca finishes, watching the pit with a hungry gaze. Like he's ready to devour the violence Jace is about to bring.

Jace steps into the ring and the noise changes.

It doesn't spike, it drops. Like the crowd knows better than to scream at a loaded gun.

His opponent is already in the ring, broad, heavily inked, cocky in that *I think I'm the main character* kind of way. He grins when he sees Jace and rolls his neck like this is going to be fun.

It isn't. The second the match starts, Jace doesn't hesitate. He doesn't waste energy. Doesn't circle or bait.

He strikes.

Fast. Precise. No flair. No drama.

Every movement is exact. Controlled. Like he's mapped the entire fight in his head before he stepped into the ring.

His opponent goes for a haymaker. Jace slips it like smoke and buries an elbow into his ribs so hard the man stumbles a few steps before recovering. But Jace doesn't let him. He's already there, a knee to the gut, a palm to the throat, a sweep that drops him like a puppet whose strings have just snapped.

The guy tries to get up. Big mistake.

Jace steps in again, heel slamming down an inch from the guy's head. Not a hit, a threat. A warning.

Stay down.

The crowd is dead silent. Luca's eyes shine with mirth. The match is called. And Jace just... steps back.

Like he wasn't one second away from shattering someone's spine.

He wipes the sweat from his brow with the back of his arm, breath steady, jaw clenched. No gloating. No emotion. Just that calm, unreadable mask.

Heat rushes through my body. Maybe I'm more messed up than I thought. Because his violence is exciting.

He leaves the ring and his eyes lock with mine.

I don't move. Because suddenly, I understand something I didn't before.

Tex fights because he's burning. Jace fights because he can.

Because power isn't the tool, it's the baseline. And he only shows it when he chooses to.

He stops in front of me. Still breathing a little hard. Still glistening with sweat.

"You should be careful staring like that..."

"Like what?" My voice is breathier than I would like.

"Like you like what you see." His muscles flex, every vein popping in his arms. "I might take it as a challenge."

31 FIGHTER

I tear my eyes from Jace, shaking out the heated fog clouding my thoughts, when the words leave my mouth.

"I want to fight."

Noah turns to me so fast it's almost comical. "You what?"

"I want in," I say, louder this time. "I want to fight."

Luca blinks. "You mean like... metaphorically?"

Tex's brow furrows. "Isobel—"

"No." I straighten my shoulders. "I don't want to sit on the sidelines. Not tonight. Not after today. I want to bleed it out, same as you."

A beat of silence.

Jace is the only one who doesn't look shocked. He's watching me like he already expected this.

Noah steps in front of me, expression soft but protective. "I'm not saying you can't... I'm just saying maybe we think this through. The Cage doesn't go easy."

"I don't want easy," I snap.

Luca lifts both hands, palms out. "I mean, personally I think it's kinda hot, but—"

Jace cuts him off. "She's in."

Everyone turns.

"What?" Noah says.

Jace doesn't blink. "She wants in. She's in."

"You're serious?" Tex asks.

"Completely."

I narrow my eyes. "You're not just saying yes to prove a point?"

He meets my gaze evenly. "I'm saying yes because I know what this night means. And because you won't forgive yourself if you don't take the shot."

Something twists in my chest.

Jace glances toward the edge of the ring where the matchmaker, a heavily tattooed man in his thirties with an iPad and a headset, is scrolling through the night's lineup.

"I'll get you in." He disappears into the crowd, moving with that same quiet command he carries everywhere. The other boys hover around me like an informal security detail, all three tense.

"You don't have to prove anything," Noah says.

"I'm not."

"You've already made your point," Tex mutters.

"Exactly. And now I'm going to make it with my fists."

Luca whistles. "Remind me never to piss you off."

Jace returns a minute later. "You're up next."

I take a slow breath.

Then pull my jacket off and toss it to Noah.

He catches it without comment.

I tug my sheer top over my head, leaving just the lace bralette underneath. The air hits my skin and makes everything feel sharper.

I tie my hair into a high ponytail and flex my fingers.

Jace leans against the railing, arms crossed.

"You better not have given me someone easy," I say, cracking my neck.

He scoffs. "Please. You think I'd let anyone go easy on you."

Jace and I move downstairs. We move to the entrance under the guys; they won't be able to see us from this side. The concrete feels colder near the edge of the ring.

The lights overhead flicker against steel beams, casting long shadows across the walls. The current match is still going, two older Guild guys circling each other like wolves, both bleeding, both refusing to give an inch. The crowd's eating it up.

I stand just outside the gate, heart steady, breath even. My fingers twitch, not from nerves. From anticipation. Jace stands beside me. He hasn't said much since we left the others. His presence is solid. Heavy without pressing. He watches the ring, calm. He's probably already calculated the outcome.

The roar of the crowd swells as one fighter slams the other into the floor. Dust kicks up. Someone yells for blood.

"Is this your way of getting rid of me for good? Letting someone beat me to death in a fight?"

Jace's eyebrow arches, then he scoffs, shaking his head.

"Why'd you say yes?"

He looks at me again, waiting for me to elaborate.

"To the fight," I add. "You didn't even hesitate. The others did. But not you."

He studies me for a moment, eyes unreadable.

"You need this. Not to prove anything to us. Not to be strong. But you need to feel that you're not a victim. Not tonight."

The crowd screams again. A whistle blows. The match ends. Blood and sweat stain the floor. My name is called over the speaker. Jace turns fully to face me.

"You go in there," he says, "and you fight for yourself. Not for anyone else. Not for what he did. For you."

A beat.

"Just don't break anything you can't bandage. Lucian might actually kill me if you do."

I smile.

"I make no promises."

The gate swings open. The world narrows. I step into the ring.

The noise fades behind me, a distant echo of voices, boots on concrete, the metallic slam of the gate locking behind me. The lights overhead burn white-hot, casting long, stretched shadows across the floor. It smells like copper and dust and old sweat.

Across from me, my opponent steps in. She's tall, wiry, with muscle and coiled tension. Her eyes flick over me once and she smirks like she's already decided how this is going to go.

Good. Let her.

She's older. Her knuckles are taped and bloodied; this isn't her first fight. But that doesn't scare me.

It focuses me.

The ref steps into the center. No introductions. No rules. Just a hand lifted, then dropped.

Begin.

She comes at me fast, a straight punch aimed at my jaw, sharp and sudden.

I duck under it, the motion instinctive, clean.

She follows it with a knee — fast — but I twist, catching it on my hip instead of my ribs. It still hurts, but pain's never been a thing that's stopped me.

I snap back with an elbow to her side, then pivot and drive my boot into her shin. She stumbles, just a bit, and I close the distance, slamming my shoulder into her chest.

We hit the ground hard.

The breath punches out of me, but I recover first, twisting on top of her.

She snarls, grabbing my ponytail, yanking back hard, but I let her. Use the momentum to swing my body around, wrench her arm across her chest and jam my knee into her sternum.

A satisfying crack.

She grits her teeth and bucks up, knocking me off. We roll across the concrete. My shoulder scrapes raw against the floor, friction-burn and blood.

We both come up fast. This time, she hesitates. I spit blood. Smile. And that's when it shifts. She comes in reckless, annoyed now. Sloppy.

Big mistake.

I block the first hit, then jab once, quick into her gut. Not enough to drop her. Enough to wind her. Then I spin low, hook her ankle, and drop her flat on her back.

Her skull thuds against the floor.

The crowd howls. But I barely hear them.

She's dazed, still moving, but slower now. Her limbs are heavy. I close the distance, plant my boot beside her ribs, and crouch.

"Don't underestimate me," I say, breathing hard.

She snarls something. I can't hear it over the roaring in my ears. Doesn't matter.

She reaches up for one last grab, but I catch her wrist midair, twist it behind her back, and press my forearm to her throat.

"Yield," I grit out.

She fights it. For two long, ugly seconds, she fights it.

Then taps twice on the floor.

The ref shouts. The whistle blows.

It's done.

My heart's pounding in my ears, breath coming in hard, shallow pulls, but I don't feel weak. I feel alive. My skin hums. My fists still clench and unclench at my sides like they haven't caught up to the win yet.

I step back. Stagger. The pain's sinking in now, my ribs ache, and I'm bleeding from somewhere near my elbow. Doesn't matter.

I won. I fucking won.

Every nerve in my body is buzzing. Electricity is alive under my skin.

The gate swings open again, and the first thing I see is Jace. He doesn't smile. Doesn't cheer. He just offers his hand.

I take it.

He pulls me out of the ring, steady and sure.

"Better?" he asks under his breath, he looks down at our hands then drops it.

I blink. "That was..."

His gaze drags over my body and I feel it. The noise of the Cage fades until it's just us, the air between us pulled taut. Humming with adrenaline. I should step back. Back away from this man who's been nothing but an asshole to me. But tonight, he understood what I needed. I'm caught in his orbit, aware of every inch of space between us.

His jaw tightens, something dark flickering in his eyes, but it's not anger. It looks like restraint.

I grab his shirt and pull him to me, our lips crashing together. For a moment, he's stiff, but then his arms wrap around me, one hand cupping the back of my head to hold me to him.

He pulls away, panting, eyes searching mine.

"I'm not fragile," I pant, gaze steady. "Neither are you."

Something snaps.

Jace lifts me, and my legs wrap around him. He walks up to the far wall, hidden in the shadows. As soon as my back hits cold concrete, his lips are back on mine.

"You have no idea what you've started," he growls into the kiss, nipping at my bottom lip.

His lips move across my jaw, trailing down to my throat. I gasp and his hands are hot against my skin, every touch another zap of electricity. My hands tangle in his hair as a soft moan escapes me.

"Jace..." I breathe.

"Mine." He bites the base of my neck.

My eyes fly open and my hands push against his chest. "Excuse me?"

Jace's eyes are wild, a storm raging behind them.

"You're mine." He breathes. "I gave them all a chance. They swung, they missed. But you? You're looking at me, not them. You feel this. And you know exactly who you belong to."

I blink, the electricity fading fast. I unwrap my legs and slide down his body. I fight back the groan that the friction creates.

"Say it. You're mine."

"You don't get to demand that I'm yours, Ravencourt. That was just heat of the moment, nothing more."

I step aside but Jace mirrors me. "Try to run, Isobel. I'll catch you. Every time. And you'll thank me when I do."

I push him aside and head toward the stairs, making my way back to the others.

Noah waits with a towel already in hand, Tex nodding, and Luca grinning like he won the lottery.

Luca whistles. "Remind me never to bet against you."

Noah hands me the towel. "You good?"

I grin, patting the towel over my face and nod. "Yeah," I say. "I'm really fucking good."

The crowd is still murmuring as we make our way up the next stairwell, but it's different now. I hear it.

"That was Ashthorne's kid."

"Did you see that finish?"

Their voices aren't pitying. They're not whispering tragedy behind their hands anymore.

I walked into the ring and rewrote my name.

Jace walks ahead, one hand shoved in his pocket, the other still close to me, not touching, but near enough that I could grab it if I stumbled.

I don't. Not after his claim.

I kinda want to fight again, though, just because of that. I'm not an object to be claimed.

Noah lingers just behind me, his jacket now draped over my shoulders. I didn't ask. He didn't offer. He just did it, and I let him.

Tex walks on my other side, jaw tight, quiet. But there's a tension rolling off him that isn't anger, it's pride. Fierce, silent pride.

And Luca?

He's already halfway up the steps, yelling to the guy who runs the board. "Run me my money, baby! I told you she'd wreck her!"

I blink. "You actually bet on me?"

Luca grins over his shoulder. "Please. I saw that fire in your eyes the second you tied up your hair. Best odds I've had in weeks."

"You're the worst," I mutter.

"I'm the richest," he corrects, tossing a wink back at me.

"Feel like we should be concerned about your gambling tendencies," I mumble. Noah laughs.

Outside, the night air is sharp and clean — too cold for the sheer bralette I'm still wearing, but I barely feel it. Everything's tingling. My blood's still running hot. We drive back to campus and electricity thrums through me.

The gravel crunches under our boots as we walk across the path back toward the dorms. The lights from Blackmoore's towers glow through the trees, pale gold and stately.

It should feel like returning to a cage. But it doesn't. Not with them walking beside me.

Not with my knuckles split and my pulse still singing.

Not after tonight.

Luca nudges me with his elbow. "So. When are we forming an underground tag team?"

"You'd slow me down," I say.

He gasps. "Unbelievable."

"I'd pay to watch that," Noah says.

"I'd pay to refuse to watch it," Tex mutters.

Jace hasn't said anything since. He's walking just ahead, calm as ever. But when I glance up at him, I catch it — the flicker of a smile at the corner of his mouth.

It's small. But it's real. My heart stops for a moment.

We reach the dorms. They stop with me at the door like it's instinct.

"Shift schedule still stands," Jace says. "One of us is in your room every night."

Tex looks at me. "You want it to be me tonight?"

Jace shifts, a smirk on his lips.

Oh no, we can't have that.

I smile at Tex, "Yeah."

Jace raises a brow, but he doesn't argue. He just steps aside. Tex walks inside, sweeping the room, checking corners, making sure I don't have to.

THE HOT WATER stings where my skin is raw — shoulders scraped, elbow bruised, a cut across my ribs from hitting the ground wrong.

But I don't care.

I stand under the spray until the ache turns clean. Until the dirt and sweat and blood swirl down the drain and the water runs clear.

When I step out, I pull on one of my oversized tees — soft and worn — and a pair of shorts. My hair's still damp, pulled into a loose braid down my back.

Tex is waiting on the couch.

He's set out a small first-aid kit on the table, not the bulky institutional one from the dorm, but a sleek, matte-black, Guild-issued pack. *Of course.*

He doesn't look up right away. Just gestures for me to sit.

I do. He kneels in front of me. The moment stretches, quiet except for the rustle of gauze and antiseptic swabs.

"You don't have to do this," I murmur.

"I know. But I want to take care of you."

He takes my arm, his touch light— fingertips grazing along the scrape at my elbow. It's not deep.

"You should've iced this already," he says.

"I was busy." I shrug then wince.

The corner of his mouth twitches — the barest hint of amusement. "You almost dislocated your shoulder."

I lift my chin. "But I didn't."

He doesn't argue.

Just dabs the cut with something that stings. I hiss, and he pauses immediately, not pulling back but softening his pressure.

"Sorry."

I shake my head. "Don't stop."

He wraps the gauze with practiced precision — crisp, clean, controlled. Of course he's done this before. For himself, probably. For the others. But he's quiet with me. Focused.

He finishes wrapping the scrape on my arm and reaches for another antiseptic wipe.

"This one might suck."

I shift slightly, lifting the hem of my shirt to show the bruise forming under my ribs.

He stills.

Then he nods once and kneels a little closer. The cloth is cool against my skin. The contact burns anyway.

"You fought well," he says.

"Thanks."

"No, I mean it." He looks up again, gaze locking with mine. "You didn't panic. You read her. Adapted."

"I learned from the best."

Tex smiles, and I realize it's the first one since we've been alone.

"What's wrong?"

His hand pauses for a beat but then continues. "I just don't like seeing you hurt. The only marks I want to see on your body are the ones I leave."

"But I'm not hurt, per se. I won, Tex. I just… needed to fight." My breath catches a little.

I'm not broken glass anymore. I'm a sword still cooling from the forge.

"I know," Tex says, standing smoothly.

He tucks the last piece of gauze back into the kit and clicks it shut. Then, without another word, he heads over to one of the duffel bags tucked near the door.

I blink. I didn't even see them.

Of course, the boys brought supplies. Probably took shifts packing while I was changing earlier.

Before I can ask, he disappears into the bathroom.

The door clicks shut behind him, and for the first time all night, I'm alone.

The silence settles in around me.

My limbs ache. My ribs throb dully. But beneath the physical exhaustion is something else — something sharper. A kind of clarity.

I fought. And I won. Not just the match, the *moment*. The fear. The helplessness I didn't even know I was still carrying.

And the most unexpected part of the night? That kiss.

Jace claiming me.

My blood boils again. How dare he?

He thinks after all the shit he's put me through that a kiss will just erase it all?

No, it was just the adrenaline, and he was there. That's it.

But he didn't hover. Didn't doubt. He just watched. Supported. *Believed*. Considering he was telling me to fuck off at the Halloween dance a couple weeks ago…

It hits me all at once how rare that is, to be trusted with your own strength.

The bathroom door opens. Steam rolls out first, thick and curling into the room. Then Tex steps through.

Hair damp. No shirt. Just a pair of soft, gray sweatpants hanging low on his hips, the waistband slung in that effortless way that feels almost calculated. His chest is lean and cut with quiet definition, a few faint scars trailing across his ribs and collarbone.

I blink once. Hard. He tosses the towel into the hamper like he didn't just silence every thought in my brain.

He smirks.

"You're drooling." His deep chuckle makes me shiver.

"I am not!" I grin as he climbs into bed beside me.

I prop myself up on my elbow, and Tex does the same, his fingers tracing lazy lines up and down my side.

"I'm proud of you." He takes my hand, kissing my knuckles. "You were amazing out there."

"Me?" I laugh. "Talk about you! You were brutal. Vicious. Seeing you unleash like that. It was hot."

He lifts an eyebrow, pushing up to loom over me. "Oh really?"

I giggle as he lowers his lips to my neck. I sigh and I run my fingers through his hair.

"I wonder if you can show me how hot you found it." Tex's deep voice fills my ear as his hand slides down my body.

My pulse jumps. His fingers find my clit and pinch slightly. My fingers dig into his shoulders, and he kisses me again as his fingers rub me with perfect pressure.

"I find you very hot," I gasp as another jolt of pleasure moves through me. "I think you can feel that for yourself."

Tex smiles as his fingers move faster and faster. Everything from tonight pushes me over and my orgasm slams into me.

32 WAR

Noah stays the night after Tex. He brings tea he doesn't know how to brew and a book he doesn't think I'd want to read, but we end up talking until two in the morning. About stars. Algorithms. Stupid hypothetical Guild tech no one has ever actually built. Somewhere between him correcting himself mid-ramble and me laughing for real, his hand is holding mine. By the time I fall asleep, his arm is around my waist, and my head is on his chest. I wake up like that too. We don't talk about it.

The night after, Luca shows up like he's hosting a sleepover in a five-star hotel. He's wearing silk pajama pants with little dragons on them, black and gold, and carries a bag of snacks under one arm like it's a mission kit. Under the other a rolled-up poster.

"Movie night," he declares the second he walks in. "You need popcorn, sugar, and at least one unnecessarily hot guy in your bed. Lucky for you, I multitask."

I roll my eyes. "You're the worst."

"I'm the best worst."

"What's the poster for?"

He kicks off his slippers — yes, actual slippers — and unrolls the poster.

"Feast your eyes!" His voice is dramatic. "The Riven Altar is the hottest band. Been around for a while, I'm sure you've heard them before."

I shrug. "You'll have to show me."

"Do you live under a rock or something?" Luca gives me a look. "Anyways, you need some decoration on your walls. Plus, since I'm going to be staying here, I thought I might as well have something to make it feel a little more homey."

I roll my eyes as he tapes it up on the wall. Four veiled members stare back. Luca flops onto my bed like he owns it. I almost laugh. It's a familiar kind of chaos, Luca in motion. Loud and bright and impossible to hold still.

And maybe that's the point.

We watch some ridiculous spy rom-com he insists is "underrated genius," and for a while, I let it happen. He makes dumb commentary during all the dramatic music cues. Steals my candy. Drapes an arm behind me but never pulls me closer.

It's easy. Halfway through the movie, I pause it.

He looks over. "Bathroom break? Emotional breakthrough? You finally realized you're in love with me?"

I sit back, folding my legs under me. "Do you flirt like that with everyone?"

He raises an eyebrow, grin still in place but softer now. "Only with you."

I study him for a second. "Why?"

Luca's face freezes. Then, to my surprise, he shrugs. "Because it's fun. Because I like you. Because you're hot and terrifying and you never laugh at my jokes, but you almost do, and that keeps me chasing the high."

"Luca—"

"But," he says, sitting up straighter, "I'm not stupid."

I blink at him. He runs a hand through his hair, and suddenly the performance drops. Not gone, just quieter. More serious.

"We're not in a reverse-harem romance book," he says, smiling faintly. "And you're going to have to choose. Eventually."

My breath catches.

He meets my gaze. "None of the guys are rushing you. You know that. We're all just... orbiting. Waiting to see which way you turn."

I try to speak, but he cuts in gently.

"You don't owe us anything. But don't pretend we don't feel it."

I look away. But he's not done.

"I've known for a while it's not going to be me."

That makes my head snap back toward him. He's smiling again, soft and sad.

"It's okay. Don't give me that look. I've seen the way you look at them. At him. I'm not going to say who, I won't influence your choice. But it's not me."

My heart squeezes. "I'm sorry."

"Don't be. I like who I am around you. Even if it's just your favorite disaster friend who occasionally sleeps in your bed and flirts too much."

"You do flirt too much."

He smirks. "But you're used to it now."

I nod. He shifts, lying back beside me, hands folded behind his head. "I meant what I said, though. I like being near you. Even if it's not in the way I want. So, if you ever need someone to distract you, or annoy you, or sneak in midnight cupcakes..."

"You'll be there?"

He smiles without looking at me. "Yeah, pretty girl. I'll be there."

THE KNOCK COMES EARLY. I barely have time to sit up before the door opens, and Jace steps in, already dressed in full uniform. His eyes sweep the room, instinctively checking corners before they flick toward my bed and stop.

Luca is sprawled beside me, shirtless, arm draped casually over his chest, one leg tangled in the blankets. His eyes are still closed, but there's a smug curl to his lips like he knows exactly what this looks like.

Jace freezes. A flicker.

It vanishes almost as fast as it appears, buried under the familiar mask he always wears. Cold. Composed. Untouchable.

But I see it.

The flicker of something hot and sharp and possessive in his eyes. Jealousy. Then it's gone.

He steps further into the room, followed by Noah and Tex, both already suited up in pressed uniforms, collars straight and boots polished. Noah glances over at Luca, then at me, and raises one eyebrow. Tex doesn't say anything — just drops his duffle by the wall and starts checking over my gear.

"Emergency Guild meeting," Jace says, not looking at the bed again.

"Lucian's called in everyone," Noah adds, already at my desk, pulling out my blazer and holding it up for inspection. "Senior operatives. Regional leads. You name it."

"It's full War Room protocol," Tex mutters. "Something's going down."

Luca finally stretches, cracking one eye open. "Is it weird that I'm flattered they let me sleep?"

"Very," Jace deadpans.

Luca grins.

"Get dressed," I murmur, throwing a pillow at him.

The boys fall into motion like clockwork, throwing uniforms on, buttoning cuffs, tying ties. Even with the tension in the air, it's seamless. Like they've done this a thousand times. And maybe they have.

What stuns me more than the urgency is how natural this feels now. How I'm not just tolerated in this rhythm, I'm part of it.

By the time we head out, I'm in full uniform too, boots laced, jacket crisp, hair pulled back into a tight ponytail. Jace checks the hallway. Then we move.

When we reach the Guild building, I'm hit with it all at once.

The presence. The weight.

Guild members from every corner of the globe fill the grand chamber, older operatives in dark suits and long coats, younger recruits in sharp uniforms, commanders with scars and pins and reputations I've only heard whispered about. They speak in clipped phrases, different languages, and quiet urgency. There's no laughter. No small talk.

This isn't a meeting. It's a storm gathering. And I'm standing in the eye of it. My stomach twists.

Luca leans down beside me so his mouth is right against my ear, voice low. "Welcome to the big leagues, Ashthorne."

Noah gives my wrist a subtle squeeze. Tex stays close, scanning every face that passes.

And Jace... Jace is still watching the room.

The room quiets like someone flips a switch. Voices drop. Movement stills. Dozens of eyes turn toward the massive oak doors at the far end of the hall as they swing open with a heavy thud.

Lucian Ashthorne enters without ceremony, with Max, Preston, and Derek trailing behind him.

He's dressed in full Guild black, high-collared coat, gold insignia at his chest, shoulders squared with a kind of ruthless command that doesn't ask for respect. He demands it.

Jace stiffens beside me. Luca straightens from where he was lounging against the wall. Even Tex shifts his stance. Only Noah doesn't move, but his expression sharpens, gaze locked on Lucian's face like he's already calculating three steps ahead.

Lucian reaches the center of the room.

His eyes scan the crowd, not rushing, not lingering. Just marking.

Then he speaks. "In the Guild, we live by a code."

Silence. No one dares interrupt.

"We do what others cannot. We go where others won't. We act when others hesitate. But with that power comes discipline. Control. Purpose."

He pauses. "And the knowledge that taking a life is not a line to cross lightly."

His gaze sweeps the room again. "There are exceptions. There always have been. In combat. In self-defense. To prevent greater loss. These rules stand, and they will continue to stand."

He steps forward, voice hardening. "But he did not kill in defense. He killed because it suited him. Because it gave him power. Because it served his greed."

"Daniel Mercer," Lucian says, cold as steel, "was once one of us. He wore our crest. He took our oaths. And then he betrayed everything we stand for."

My chest goes tight. Like a rubber band being stretched to the absolute maximum. The boys are silent around me. Watching. Listening.

Lucian continues, "He took a life. And then another. And then," his voice falters, just briefly, "he took my family."

A flicker of emotion. Gone in a blink.

"He disappeared with my daughter. With her mother. Hid them from me. Lied. Manipulated. And now, after all these years, he resurfaces, not in peace, not in remorse, but with blood on his hands and a growing list of black-market contacts that point to something far more dangerous than one man going rogue."

He turns, voice rising. "He is recruiting. Building something. A shadow network of mercenaries, forgers, and weapon smugglers. We've intercepted messages. Watched transactions. He's planning something large. Strategic. And fast-moving."

Lucian's expression hardens to stone. "He's gearing up for war."

Murmurs spreads through the room, low, urgent.

Lucian lets it ride for a beat, then slams it still with his next words. "We don't sit back and hope men like him fail. We act. Swiftly. Quietly. With precision."

He draws a slow breath. "Over the next several weeks, you will receive new mission orders. Not one, not two... many. This isn't a single strike. It's a dismantling. A methodical takedown of his network. One piece at a time."

He pauses, and I swear I feel his eyes rest on me.

"This will not be easy. And it will not be clean. But I promise you this, Daniel Mercer will not win this war."

Silence follows. Thick. Absolute.

Then Lucian gives a final nod. "Briefings will begin within the hour. Dismissed."

Operatives begin murmuring. Moving. Pairing off. Orders are whispered. Names are passed around.

And just like that, the war begins. We don't make it far. We're barely out of the main hall when a Guild aide intercepts us, tall, stiff, earpiece in place, voice clipped.

"Director Ashthorne wants you in the South Briefing Room. Immediately."

No need to ask who 'you' means. Jace nods once and falls into step without hesitation. The rest of us follow.

The South Briefing Room is smaller. Quieter. Designed for strategy, not spectacle. Frosted windows line one wall. A sleek black table stretches down the center with built-in displays glowing softly beneath the surface.

Lucian is already there.

He's removed his coat. Rolled up his sleeves. His hair is still immaculate, but there's something fierce and restless in his posture, a tension like a drawn bow.

He doesn't waste time. "You'll be working as a unit," he says, as soon as the door closes behind us. "Effective immediately."

My heart kicks.

Noah sits at the head of the table and pulls up the holo-display. Jace remains standing behind me. Luca finds the chair nearest mine and spins it around backward before sitting. Tex leans against the wall, arms crossed, watching Lucian like he's waiting for a reason not to trust him.

Lucian's gaze falls on me.

"You're not a trainee anymore, Isobel. You're not on the outside of this. You're part of the team."

I nod, trying not to let it shake. He taps the table. A digital map flares to life, a cluster of red points webbing across cities, ports, and hidden airfields.

"This is what we know so far. Mercer has people in six locations tied to illegal weapons movement. Two of them are former Guild. One of them used to run extraction out of Cairo. Another specializes in digital surveillance, and we believe she may have breached one of our southern data vaults."

He points to a glowing dot near the center. "And here. There's been chatter about a prototype."

"Weapon?" Jace asks.

"Biochemical," Lucian replies. "Something Mercer's interested in. Something that doesn't just kill. It disables. Breaks control."

I stiffen.

Lucian doesn't elaborate. "You'll rotate across intel, recon, and field support over the next two weeks. Some missions will be hands-on. Others will require discretion and subtlety." His eyes flick to Luca. "Minimal collateral."

Luca offers a two-fingered salute. "I can be subtle."

Lucian doesn't look convinced. Then he turns back to me. "You'll train with the team daily."

"Understood," I say.

Lucian watches me for a beat longer. Then, quietly, "I don't expect you to be okay with this. I don't even ask it. But I do expect you to be ready."

"I'm good."

His jaw tightens, the only visible emotion he lets slip. "Good."

He straightens and looks at the boys. "Full loadout prep by morning. We start briefing the field teams in four hours. You have until then to decompress, rest, or get whatever it is you think you'll need."

He doesn't dismiss us. He just leaves.

By the time we get back to my room, I'm barely holding it together.

The door clicks shut behind Tex, and for a few long seconds, none of us speak. The quiet isn't awkward, it's heavy. Saturated. Like everyone's still carrying the echo of Lucian's words in their bones.

He's gearing up for war.

I pull off my blazer and drop it over the back of my desk chair. My boots follow, then my tie, my hair. I tug everything loose, like peeling away armor.

The boys move around me in practiced silence.

Luca grabs a bottle of water and flops onto the couch, tossing one to Noah without looking. Tex opens the window a few inches and leans against the sill, staring out at nothing. Jace stands near the bookshelf, arms crossed, brow furrowed. He's not looking at anyone, but I can feel the tension humming under his skin like a live wire.

Noah's the one who finally speaks. "So. Full-time training."

"They're squaring it with the school," Jace says. "We'll stay enrolled. Get credits. But Guild training takes priority now."

I sit on the edge of my bed. "What does that even look like?"

"Six to eight hours a day minimum," Noah replies. "Field simulations. Combat. Tech interface. Tactical theory. Debrief and prep rotations. Only one rest day. Until further notice."

Luca groans. "Goodbye, social life. I barely knew you."

"You didn't have one," Tex mutters.

"Still rude."

I let out a breath and lean forward, elbows on my knees. "So, this is it, then. We're… in it."

Jace looks over, his eyes finally meeting mine. "We've been in it. You're just caught up now."

No one contradicts him. And that's what really gets me.

Because for all their teasing and chaos and unpredictability, these four boys — my team — are already miles deep into this world. They've trained for it. Bled for it. Sacrificed things I can't even name yet.

And now I'm part of that equation. No more halfway. No more pretending I'm just along for the ride.

"I don't want to let any of you down," I say quietly.

Noah sits beside me and nudges my knee with his. "You won't."

Luca leans his head back against the arm of the couch. "Honestly, you're the only reason I haven't gone feral yet. If anything, we should be worried about disappointing you."

Tex grunts in agreement.

Jace doesn't speak. But he watches me like he's memorizing the lines of my face, like maybe if he looks hard enough, he can protect me with just that.

I nod slowly. "Okay," I say. "Then let's train. Let's fight. Let's burn his whole damn network to the ground."

I know they're thinking the same thing.

Because war is coming.

And I'm walking straight into the fire.

The others trickle out as the evening fades, Noah first, mumbling something about needing sleep before his brain melts. Luca follows, tossing me a wink and a half-hearted, "Don't miss me too much."

Tex lingers, checking the window locks and giving Jace a look before disappearing without a word.

It's just us now.

The room feels still in a way it hasn't all week. Like something is waiting.

I sit on the edge of the bed and glance over at Jace, who's by the desk, unbuttoning his uniform jacket. His shoulders are tight. Controlled. His movements precise.

"Jace."

He pauses but doesn't look at me.

I stand, wiping my hands down my legs.

Didn't think the control freak's ego would be so fragile.

I cross over to him. "Jace—"

I blink, and before I realize it, he's lifted me onto the desk, standing between my legs.

My eyes widen. His hand squeezes my sides gently as he leans in.

"Try," he murmurs, "to tell me you don't feel this too."

His fingers press into my hips, his eyes flicking down to my lips like he's seconds away from devouring them.

"Go on," he challenges, leaning closer, breath hot against my lips. "Lie to me."

I push him away, sliding off the desk.

He pins me back to the desk, one hand on my lower back, another around my neck.

He squeezes gently.

"You can push me away all you want, but I'm not a man that listens when it comes to you."

"You're insane." I lift my chin.

"Never claimed to be sane." He smiles.

I slide my phone out of my pocket, unlocking it.

He eyes my phone, his hand loosening. "Who are you calling?"

I tap a button, letting it ring out on speaker.

"Iz? Everything ok?" Tex asks.

"Everything's fine," Jace bites out, grinding his jaw.

"Ignore him. Can you come back? I want you to stay instead."

"No—" Jace says.

"Be right there," Tex says, then the line clicks.

Jace scowls at me as I grin up at him.

"It's my night," he growls.

"I don't care. It's my room and whatever I say goes." I step aside.

I look over my shoulder. He's staring at the floor, his brows furrowed, his hands frozen in place like he can't comprehend what's happened.

Before he can say anything else, Tex knocks on the door.

I skip over, opening it.

Tex sweeps in. "Jace being an insufferable asshole?"

"Isn't he always?" I lean against the doorframe with a giggle.

That seems to snap him out of whatever trance he's in. He straightens and turns robotically.

I wiggle my fingers with a smug grin. "Buh-bye."

Tex raises an eyebrow as Jace rolls his shoulder back and strolls out.

"This isn't over," he says, his voice low.

"It is for now," I say, shutting the door behind him.

33 THE CRUCIBLE

The training compound doesn't look like much from the outside. Gray walls. Reinforced steel doors. A biometric lock Noah breezes past with a casual flick of his wrist.

But the second we step inside, I understand why they call it the Crucible.

The air is cold. Sterile. Sharp with the scent of sweat, metal, and antiseptic. The lighting is artificial, bright but clinical. Hallways stretch out like arteries, each one labeled in stark black text: *Combat. Simulation. Tech. Recon. Conditioning.*

We head to Combat first.

Jace is already in uniform. Tex's sleeves are rolled. Luca's stretching like he's warming up for a football game, and Noah is muttering to himself while syncing his wristband to the system's database.

Me? I'm barely holding it together.

A week ago, I was worried about passing midterms.

Now I'm standing in a reinforced underground arena preparing to spar with elite-level operatives who have literally trained since childhood.

No pressure.

The training director, a sharp-eyed woman named Wren, walks in like a blade in boots. She doesn't smile. Doesn't introduce herself.

She just says, "Two-minute warmups. Then partners. Don't embarrass yourselves."

Luca whistles low. "She's cheerful."

"She'll knock your teeth out," Tex mutters.

"I mean, yeah, but with style."

They scatter without question, starting their drills. I'm searching my pockets when Jace appears at my side with a pair of reinforced gloves in my size.

"You always forget them." He shrugs.

"Thanks," I mumble, pulling them on.

"They're not going to go easy on you," he says under his breath. "So don't ask them to."

"I wasn't planning to."

His eyes linger for half a second longer, unreadable, before he nods and steps away.

I stare at him for a moment before taking a deep breath, mentally preparing for the day,

The warmup is brutal. Burpees, core drills, balance holds, quick-feet ladder sprints. I lose count after the first round. My lungs burn. My calves scream. But I keep going. Because none of them stop. And if I'm really part of this team now… I can't be the weakest link. I refuse.

"Ashthorne!" Wren barks.

I glance up, startled.

"Center mat. Now."

I jog over, glancing toward the others. Noah looks up from his set. Luca's already bouncing on the balls of his feet like he's hoping I'll get my ass kicked. Jace watches me closely. Tex doesn't even blink.

Wren holds up a pair of sparring batons. "Let's see what you've got."

I take them. The mat is colder than I expected.

Wren tosses me a set, lighter than they look, but solid in my grip. My palms are already slick with sweat, and I haven't even thrown a strike yet. She doesn't give me time to adjust.

"Ready stance," she says sharply.

I square my shoulders, knees bent, weight balanced like Luca showed me once in the lounge when he was showing off.

Wren nods. Then she moves.

Fast.

I barely block the first strike — a downward arc aimed at my shoulder — but it sends a jolt through my arms anyway. I stumble back two steps, breath knocked out of me before we've even started.

She doesn't stop.

A swipe at my ribs. A twist at my ankle. I pivot awkwardly, managing to stay on my feet, but my defense is clumsy. Unrefined. Every block is a second too slow. Every strike I attempt is batted away with precise, minimal effort.

It's like sparring a ghost with knives.

"Feet," she snaps. "Too slow."

I grit my teeth and readjust. She goes low next, a sweeping kick that knocks my balance sideways. I hit the mat hard.

Luca lets out a soft, sympathetic whistle from the edge. "She's still conscious. That's a win."

"Get up," Wren says.

I do. Again, and again. She doesn't go easy on me. Not even close.

But somewhere in the chaos, the clatter of batons, the sting of bruises blooming under my sleeves, something clicks. A strike lands. Light, but clean. A flick of my wrist catches her off guard just long enough for me to pivot out of her range.

She doesn't praise it. But she doesn't stop me either. We circle again.

I block her next hit high, drive my baton low toward her side, and miss by inches. She knocks me back hard enough I almost trip, but I don't. I steady. Plant. Push forward again.

By the end of the round, I'm heaving. Drenched. Shaking.

Wren lowers her batons.

"You're sloppy," she says. "But stubborn."

I blink at her.

"That'll keep you alive longer than skill in the field. Barely."

Then she turns to the boys. "One of you get her on strength conditioning before she dislocates something."

THE DAYS BLUR. Not in a lazy, summer haze kind of way. In a battlefield tempo, survival-is-a-luxury kind of way.

Every morning starts at five am. No exceptions. No excuses. No 'five more minutes.' The alarms they blast through the intercom system don't snooze, they scream. Having to cross the room to shut it off before coffee makes me incredibly cranky.

Tuesday, we bleed in combat.

Sparring. Conditioning. Weighted drills. More baton work. Jace runs drills with me until my arms feel like they're going to fall off, correcting my form every time I falter. Wren throws me across a mat twice and tells me, "You're improving." I'm not sure if she's lying or if I just don't break something.

Wednesday, we get tactical.

Lucian leads the strategy meeting. We sit at a round table in the South Wing, staring at rotating 3D holograms of known black market networks. Red lines connect faces to ports to labs and secret transfer points.

"Patterns," he says. "The war will be won by the ones who see the patterns first."

I speak up once, connecting a name I remember from Daniel's phone to a drop point in Budapest. Lucian doesn't smile. But he nods.

Noah scribbles everything into a secure Guild tablet and mutters, "Nice, Ashthorne," when no one else is listening.

Thursday, they shoot us.

Literally. Simulation day. Rubber rounds. Real vests. Real bruises. The scenario is a raid. Loud, hot, confusing. Smoke floods the room. Alarms blare. There's yelling. Flashbangs. Noah's screaming commands into an earpiece. Luca's behind me cracking jokes even as we're both getting pelted.

Jace goes silent and surgical, clearing a hallway like he's done it a hundred times.

Tex takes a hit shielding me. Later, I find a dark blue welt just under my collarbone. I press it gently and smile, because I didn't freeze.

Saturday is recon and stealth.

One full day of sneaking past cameras, pressure pads, noise traps. I fail miserably for the first two hours, get caught whispering, breathing too loud, stepping too hard.

But then Luca challenges me to beat his score. And I do. By four seconds. He doesn't let it go all day.

Sunday, we're immersed in a full scenario sim. We're split into pairs. Disoriented. Thrown into a pitch-black maze of abandoned rooms and coded doors. We have to get out using only what we know, tactical memory, combat instincts, and blind trust.

I get paired with Jace.

Neither of us speaks much. We move silently. Efficiently. When he lifts me over a ledge, his hands linger just a second too long. When I reach for him in the dark, I don't hesitate.

We make it out first. Lucian watches from the control deck above. He doesn't say a word. But I know he sees.

That night, when we all collapse in my room — sore, bruised, adrenaline still buzzing — there's something electric in the air. Something earned.

THE DORMS ARE UNUSUALLY QUIET. No drills. No alarms. And my room is... full.

Luca's on the couch, sprawled across it dramatically, a half-eaten protein bar resting on his chest like a fallen soldier. Noah is cross-legged on the floor with his tablet in his lap and at least three mugs around him, all in various stages of being forgotten. Jace leans against the wall near the window, reading something on his tablet with a focused crease between his brows. And Tex is in my desk chair, reclined slightly, one boot propped up, watching the room with quiet amusement.

I'm in bed still. For once, I don't have to move. My body hurts. Like I've been hit by a truck made of rubber bullets and regret.

"Is it normal," I croak, "to feel like I got thrown down a flight of stairs after only a week?"

"Normal?" Noah says without looking up. "It's practically a rite of passage."

"Speak for yourself," Luca mutters. "I'm ninety-eight percent sure my spleen detached yesterday."

Jace doesn't glance up from his screen. "You don't need a spleen to run recon."

"Then you can do recon next time."

"No."

Tex grunts, either in agreement or because he's stretching a sore shoulder. Could go either way.

I shift slightly under the blanket, eyes drifting across the room. It's absurd how natural this has become, waking up with them here. Living in each other's spaces. Learning to breathe the same rhythm.

There's something unspoken hanging in the air today, though. A stillness beneath the teasing. They're all thinking it.

The mission is coming.

Lucian hasn't said when yet, but we know it's close. The fact that today's been cleared of all training means we're being prepped. A short breath before the plunge.

I sit up slowly and stretch, wincing. "How are you guys not dead?"

Tex shrugs. "Been through worse."

Jace murmurs, "You get used to it."

Luca groans. "I refuse to believe that."

Noah finally looks up at me, his expression a little softer now. "But you haven't tapped out. That's the part that matters."

Their words hit me like a delayed shockwave. They're not just being kind. They're acknowledging me. As part of this. One of them. I press my back against the headboard and let the quiet settle. It's peace. Or at least, the closest thing we're allowed.

"I need air," I mutter, pushing off the bed.

No one stops me.

But Noah looks up from his tablet and sets it down, already reaching for his hoodie. "I'll come."

I nod once. That's all it takes.

We don't say anything as we head out of the dorm and down the quiet eastern path that snakes along the back edge of campus. The late-morning sun filters through the thinning trees, casting long patches of light and shadow over the gravel.

The silence is comfortable. Familiar.

It's not until we've walked a full five minutes without either of us speaking that I finally break it.

"Do you ever get used to this?" I ask.

Noah glances sideways at me, his hands in his hoodie pockets. "Used to what? The bruises? The danger? The pressure to be perfect at eighteen?"

I huff a laugh. "All of it."

He thinks about it. "No," he says. "But you get better at hiding the parts that hurt."

I stop walking. "That's not exactly comforting."

He shrugs. "You didn't ask for comforting. You asked for truth."

Fair. He always gives me the truth, even if I don't want to hear it.

We keep walking, slower now.

"I think I keep waiting for someone to pull me aside and say, 'Actually, you're not supposed to be here. We made a mistake.'"

Noah's voice softens. "Impostor syndrome. Fun."

"I'm serious."

"I know." He pauses, then looks at me. "But it's not going to happen."

I glance at him. He gives me that half-smile, the one that doesn't reach his eyes but still feels warm.

"You're here because you earned it. Not because of Lucian. Not because you're some pawn in a larger game. You're here because you keep getting up. Even when you have every reason not to."

I swallow. "I still feel like I'm behind."

"You are."

I blink.

"But so was I when I started. So was Tex. Jace too, even if he pretends otherwise." He nudges my shoulder gently. "It's not about where you start. It's about whether you survive long enough to catch up."

I don't respond right away.

The trees thin a little ahead, and we step into a patch of sun. I close my eyes for a moment and let the warmth settle across my face.

"I'm scared," I admit.

He nods like he expected that. "Good. The second you stop being scared is when you get reckless. And we can't afford that. Not with what's coming."

I glance sideways at him. "You think it's going to be bad?"

"I think it's already worse than we know."

I hum.

"What do your parents do?" I ask.

"They're corporate lawyers." Noah's voice hardens.

"I'm guessing they aren't stoked with you not following their footsteps."

He nods. "They were stoked when Jace chose me to be part of the 'Blackmoore Four' but they were not so stoked when I told them I'd be specializing in tech rather than law."

"Lucians successful in tech, how is that not good enough?" my brows furrow.

His jaw flexes. "My dad knows Lucian is successful in tech and security. But he just wanted me to continue the family business."

I bite my cheek.

"Well, you're clearly excellent at what you do." I look at him and give him a small smile.

"Thanks."

We fall silent again. But it's not heavy. Not really. It's clarity.

And I think that's what Noah gives best, not reassurance, not comfort. Perspective.

"Thanks for coming with me," I say softly.

He bumps my shoulder. "Thanks for letting me."

We take the long way back.

Neither of us says it aloud, but it's obvious. The path behind the east dorms winds around the small garden grove, its benches tucked between bare trees and half-frozen flowers.

Noah slows when we reach the quietest part of it — a sun-dappled alcove shielded from view — and turns to face me fully.

His eyes search mine, cautious but open.

"I know what's coming," he says. "And I don't want to go into it wondering."

I don't have to ask what he means. His hand brushes mine, fingers barely touching. His familiar warmth reaches for mine. And then he leans in. It's not sudden. Not demanding. Just a gentle press of lips. Warm. Steady. Honest.

My hand rests lightly on his chest, and, for a second, I let myself feel it, his heartbeat under my palm, the quiet exhale of breath between us.

But something in me doesn't reach back. I pull away slowly and carefully.

And Noah — being Noah — doesn't ask why.

He just nods. "You don't have to say it," he says softly.

There's no pain in his voice. No bitterness. Just a softness that almost breaks me.

"I wanted to be sure," I whisper.

He gives me a crooked smile. "So did I."

A beat of silence.

Then he adds, "You don't need to apologize for not feeling anything for me."

Tears prick my eyes, but I blink them back. "I do love you. Just... not like that."

"I know that too."

He squeezes my hand once, then lets go.
We start walking again.
And though something closes quietly between us, something else settles. Respect. Clarity.

34 FINALLY

The sun is lower when we make it back to the dorms, brushing the tops of the windows with fading gold. Noah and I walk in step, quiet but at ease now, the kind of silence that doesn't need to be filled.

As we round the corner toward the front entrance, I spot a familiar figure leaning against the rail just outside the lobby doors, hoodie up, sleeves pushed up, a lollipop tucked in the corner of his mouth like it's a cigar.

Luca.

Of course.

He glances up when he sees us and smirks like he's been waiting all day just to say something dumb.

"Look who finally emerged from their walk of feelings," he drawls.

Noah snorts, unfazed. "Don't be weird."

"I'm always weird. It's part of my charm."

Noah gives me a sidelong glance. "I'm heading up. You good?"

I nod. "Yeah."

He squeezes my hand once — not lingering — then disappears through the doors.

Luca watches him go. Then looks back at me.

"You told him, didn't you?"

I blink. "What?"

His lollipop shifts from one side of his mouth to the other. "Noah. You told him it wasn't him."

My eyes narrow. "How the hell did you know that?"

"I told you," he says, grinning now. "It's how you look at people."

I fold my arms. "You're guessing."

"I'm not." He kicks off the railing and steps closer. "You don't even realize you do it. You look at the people you want differently than the people you're trying to figure out."

I stare at him.

He continues, voice lighter but not unkind. "You were always kind to Noah. Careful with him. Curious, even. But you never looked at him like you were drowning."

"And I do that with the others?"

He tilts his head, considering me.

"Only a couple of us," he says eventually, and for once his grin dims. "But yeah. Sometimes it's like you're not even aware it's happening. You just... ache toward them."

The words land harder than they should.

Luca shifts his weight and offers the faintest shrug. "I'm not trying to make you feel bad. Or confused. I just... notice things. It's what I do."

He leans back against the railing again, gaze flicking up to the sky. "You know," he says, "there was a version of this story where I thought maybe if I kept things light and easy and fun, you'd fall for that instead of the messier stuff."

I glance at him, heart tight.

"But I see you now," he says, meeting my eyes again. "And I get it. I really do."

There's no bitterness in his voice. Just certain, Luca-style truth.

Luca doesn't say anything when we start walking.

He falls into step beside me like he always does, like we've done this a hundred times before. The quiet between us feels different now. No tension. No open-ended questions. Just something settled, gentle.

When we reach my room, the door's already slightly open.

Inside, Jace is leaning against the far wall, arms crossed. Still in his fitted long-sleeve, his watch glinting in the low light. His expression is unreadable, but the second his eyes meet mine, I feel it in my chest.

That weight again. That pull.

Luca sees him too, and he doesn't say a word. Just glances at me, then at Jace, and gives me the smallest, almost-smile. No teasing this time.

"Night, Ashthorne," he murmurs, stepping back into the hall.

The door closes behind me.

Jace doesn't move. Neither do I.

"Am I going to have to call Tex back here?"

"No." His jaw flexes.

Silence folds between us again, thick with everything we left unsaid. My heart beats too loudly.

He sighs, pushing off the wall and crossing over to the couch. He takes a seat, dropping his head in his hands.

"I just... I can't get you out of my head." His voice is raw. "I don't understand it." He looks over at me, his eyes pleading.

I walk over, each step tentative. I sit down beside him, leaving some space between us.

"Why don't you hate me? I'm a Ravencourt, you're an Ashthorne."

I sit back, staring up at the ceiling. "That's a good question... My dad did warn me away from you. But you were just always around, like a gnat."

Jace shoots me a look, and I can't help but smile.

"You know..." He clears his throat. "I've never felt this way before."

He sits back, looking up at the ceiling. "I've never really let anyone in, only the guys. But you, you got under my skin. I thought you were just an annoyance, an obstacle I needed to conquer."

I roll my eyes. He continues.

"But the more time I spent around you, I started seeing the cracks in my father's words. You weren't some stuck-up bitch, who thought she was owed the world, you weren't some broken girl we could easily manipulate. Everything we threw at you, you took it and kept getting back up. "His hands flex, the veins popping out. "You're infuriating. But I do respect it. You didn't deserve that. I'm sorry."

My eyes widen. "Wait, can you repeat that so I can record it?"

He shoots me a look. I ignore it.

"As much as you annoy me, I like you, Jace. I can see how much you care for your friends. You're a great leader, and you have a brilliant mind. As cruel as parts of it may be." I mumble the end.

He turns to look at me, his eyebrows raised.

"What?" I ask.

"I didn't expect it to be reciprocal."

"I mean, I don't like you all of the time. Most of the time you're annoying."

The sides of his mouth tilt.

"I definitely don't like you when you're being possessive." I cross my arms.

He chuckles; it's a different sound when it's not full of malice. "You can lie to yourself all you want, but I see the truth in your eyes."

I stand up, turning to glare down at him. "You can tell yourself whatever you want, Jace." I lift my leg to step over him. His hands reach up and pull my waist down.

I catch myself on his chest, my legs straddling him. My hair falls like a curtain around us. He lifts a finger, tracing my jaw, featherlight.

"I feel a pull to you. Tell me, Isobel, you feel it too, don't you?"

That breaks something open in my chest. I lean forward. I can feel the heat of him and the tension in his shoulders, like he's trying so hard to stay still.

I close the distance.

And he kisses me back, not rushed, not greedy. Just sure. Like he's known all along this was coming but didn't want to reach for it until I did. I let all the things I want to say pour into the kiss. It's not heat or hunger or the rush of adrenaline. It's gravity, it's grounding. Like I've finally found the place all my chaos stops spinning.

When we pull apart, my hands are still curled in his shirt. His forehead resting against mine.

"Okay," I whisper.

Jace's voice is a breath against my lips. "Yeah. Okay."

His breath is still warm against my lips. I'm not done. Neither is he.

The second time our mouths meet, it's different, no longer tentative or testing. This one comes with heat, with pressure, with weeks of tension finally snapping. His hands find my waist, firm and certain, like he's done holding back.

I sink into him without thinking.

His mouth is softer than I expected. Slower, too, not devouring. Tracing every angle. Like he wants to memorize me this way. I tilt my head, deepen the kiss, and he answers immediately, one hand sliding up my back, the other curling into the edge of my shirt.

My fingers tangle in his hair, pulling slightly, and that's when he exhales against my mouth, the sound wrecked and low it makes me weak.

His movements stay precise, controlled, but his restraint is fraying. I feel it in the way his grip tightens. In the soft curse he breathes when I nip at his bottom lip. In the way his body leans into mine.

His hands grip my hips like he's trying to stay grounded.

"Isobel," he murmurs, voice hoarse, "you're going to ruin me."

I smile against his mouth. "That's the plan."

He kisses me harder.

My shirt rides up. His fingers brush bare skin.

And for a second, we both still, breath caught, foreheads pressed together.

His chest is rising hard beneath my palms. I can feel the steady beat of his heart. His lips are red. His hands haven't moved. This version of him...it does something to me.

I feel bold, powerful.

Sexy.

"You're... addictive," he says roughly.

I smirk. "Well, you may need to detox then."

Jace narrows his gaze. "We both know you'll only be answering to me."

"Do we?" I sit back.

"Yes, because if it's already this good now... imagine if I loved you." His hands grip my hips.

"You're sure of yourself," I mumble.

"Oh, I'm quite confident in my abilities." He smirks and grinds his hips up into me.

I gasp as I feel his hardness against me. His hands slip under the hem of my shirt, pressing into my skin.

He sits up until his mouth is against my ear. "Let me show you." He nips my earlobe then kisses my neck.

I tilt my head, allowing him more access as his hands continue up my sides. He bites the base of my neck, and one hand tangles in my hair.

"Jace..." A breathy moan escapes me.

He growls into my neck. Gripping my thighs tightly, he stands and walks to the bed, dropping me down. I bounce slightly, looking up at him. He hovers over me, eyes dark with desire. Any restraint has snapped.

He lifts one arm over his head, pulling his shirt off in the way only skilled men do. I have to try not to drool at every sculpted muscle that flexes. The veins that run up his forearms, how his chest rises and falls with every breath.

He gives me a smug smile, and I want to wipe it right off his face.

"I've seen better." I smirk as his smile drops.

He crawls on top of me, hovering over my body. His breath light against my neck

"You're playing a dangerous game here, Ashthorne." His voice is rough.

"You're not showing me anything vastly different, Ravencourt." I continue to poke at the bear.

Jace sits back, pulling my leggings down and off in one swift motion. He drags his nose lightly up the inside of my leg, biting my thigh. I squirm.

He grips both thighs in his hands as he flattens his tongue against my pussy through my panties, the heat of his breath seeping through the fabric. He continues to lightly run his tongue back and forth, until my panties are soaked through.

"Jace," I warn.

He chuckles as he finally pulls my underwear off and dives back between my legs. My hands plunge into his hair, as my stomach tightens.

My body writhes as his tongue moves against my body. I moan and curse. When I look down to see his blue eyes watching me, another wave of pleasure flows through me. His gaze, it's hunger and admiration, all wrapped together.

With every flick and stroke of his tongue, the tension winds tighter and tighter.

"Fuck, Jace, yes." I moan as I pull him closer to me, my heels digging into his back, my thighs gripping his head, refusing to let him move even an inch.

The promise of pleasure comes closer and closer, as he brings me higher and higher. My legs tremble in his hands, and the look of him is enough to push me that last bit.

Before I can break apart, he pulls away with a smile.

"Jace!" I gasp, my hips trying to follow him.

He tsks.

"What the fuck?" I pant. My core aches, my clit throbs painfully.

"So needy for me." His face glistens. He licks his lips. "Absolutely delicious."

He lowers his mouth to me, starting again. He builds me up then pulls away, over, and over.

"Jace," I plead. My skin is covered with sweat, every nerve ending screaming for release. My legs tremble and I can't make them stop. "Please." I can barely find the words, my brain is scrambled. All I can focus on is the release he keeps denying me.

He enters a single finger, hissing. "So tight, so wet."

"Jace," I beg again as he moves a finger slowly in and out.

"You're stunning." His voice is rough. "Laid out and needy for me."

I whimper as he slightly speeds up. My breaths come in ragged pants.

"Open that pretty mouth and tell me who you belong to." His eyes lock with mine.

I throw my head back as he hits deep inside me. He freezes.

"No…" I whimper.

"Look at me," he says.

I obey.

He starts moving again, the pleasure building. "Say you're mine."

"No." I shake my head.

"Say it," he growls, as his fingers pump harder into me.

"No," I gasp and moan.

I need more. I'm so close. I need release.

"You're mine." He sucks my clit into his mouth.

I shatter, pleasure exploding through me as my hands grip in his hair, the bed sheets, my back arching off the bed. His fingers keep me riding the high.

Everything is sensitive. Every touch has my muscles jolting.

"I hate you." I pant.

"You love it, admit it. It was one of the best you've had."

I hate that he's right.

"You let me come, even though I didn't say I was yours." I nudge him with my thigh.

"But you did." He smiles, standing up.

I watch as his fingers unbuckle his belt, pushing his pants down his legs. He palms himself through his boxers, and I lick my lips.

"Come here," he demands.

I move down to him. I must be dickmatized.

"Lay on your back. Head towards me."

I obey.

"Open wide." He pulls his cock out, stroking it.

He's big and I want to lick every vein. The smooth pink tip has my mouth watering. I open my mouth, sticking my tongue out.

He slowly inserts himself into my mouth, pushing to the back of my throat, I swallow him.

"Good girl." He moans. "I can see my dick in your throat." He clenches his jaw.

He moves another hand to pull up my shirt, the air hitting my nipples. He slowly begins to thrust in and out of my mouth.

"Play with yourself."

I move a hand down to my clit, the other up to my chest, squeezing and pinching my nipple.

Jace groans and I clench; the sound is music to my ears. He starts thrusting harder and faster. I match his speed and moan.

"Fuck, yes, Isobel." His eyes don't leave my body. One hand grabs my other breast and squeezes.

The pain is delicious.

He continues thrusting in and out of my mouth, and I moan around him as I work myself.

"Isobel... I'm going to come." He moans.

I suck in my cheeks, wanting to taste him.

He speeds up, growling as he finds his release, which pushes me into mine. I greedily swallow him down while riding out my own.

"Good fucking girl." He pants. "Beautiful."

35 THE ONE WHO LISTENS

When I open the door, it takes my mind a moment to register what I'm seeing.

Savvy stands in my doorway, her wine-colored hair pulled back in a sleek ponytail, dressed in all black. But this time a guild crest is embroidered into her chest.

"Savvy!" I squeal, moving forward to hug her.

"Hey, Iz!" She catches me.

"I've missed you!" I squeeze before pulling back. "Come in!" I open the door wide for her and she follows me inside.

"I heard from your dad you had watchdogs, but I don't see any in sight." She smirks.

"I asked for some alone time. Since we've been training so much, I think they've eased up a bit."

"Well at least they listen." Savvy sinks onto the couch, and I join her.

"I just got back from an extended mission, or else I would've been back sooner to help supervise with the other three. How is everything going?" Savvy gives me a big smile.

"It's good." I return the smile. "I've learned a lot. But I'd probably be in worse shape if it wasn't for your crash course over the summer. Very sneaky by the way." I laugh.

Savvy rolls her eyes. "Your dad wanted to tell you in his own time so I just had to come up with excuses. The stories kept you distracted though."

I nod in agreement, smiling. "Now, I want Guild stories."

"Deal." Savvy leans on her elbow, propping up her head. "I've heard the Ravencourt boy has done quite the number on you."

The blush that spreads is instant, thinking about the night before. Savvy's eyes widen.

"Oh, Isobel... don't tell me..."

"He's annoying." I hide my face in my hands.

Savvy giggles. "Oh, lord help us, your dad might have an aneurysm. He updated me and said he was sniffing around but I didn't think you'd sniff back."

I groan.

I recount the night of the cage and everything since then, realizing how quickly Jace has been able to wiggle through my defenses that were previously so impervious to his bullshit.

Damn.

By the end, Savvy is tapping her chin, humming.

"It seems like Tex knew what he wanted and went for it, while it took Jace some time to figure it out."

I nod in agreement. "I don't know what I'm doing." I throw my hands up. "The things I feel for both of them are so different."

I stare up at the ceiling.

Savvy sighs heavily. "They are two very different people, but they don't seem to be rushing you. I mean Jace is claiming you with his macho man act, so I take that back." Savvy pauses. "Only you can know what's right for you."

I chew on my bottom lip. Tex is heat and desire. Jace is ice and control.

"I've never had a boyfriend." My voice is quiet. "Didn't even allow myself to have crushes because I knew it was useless. How am I going to know what's right for me?"

My mind races with pros and cons for each. I close my eyes and take a deep breath, trying to slow the stream.

Savvy sits up, putting a hand on my leg. "Only one of them feels like love. My advice is to pick the one that listens, who knows what you need without you ever needing to ask." She gives me a small smile. "But only you know who fits in that."

TEX STANDS THERE. Duffle slung over his shoulder. Hoodie pulled low. His expression is unreadable. He steps inside, dropping his bag in its usual place. I follow.

When he turns around, he just opens his arms when I step closer, and I walk straight into them like I always do. And it's the most natural thing in the world.

He holds me for a long time.

No words. No rush. Just his arms wrapped around me, his chin resting on my head, and the steady thud of his heart against my chest like a metronome only I can hear.

I pull back slightly, just enough to look up at him.

There's a softness in his eyes I don't see often, something quiet and unrushed beneath the storm. Only showing this side of him when we're alone. His hand brushes a strand of hair from my face, fingers lingering at my jaw like he's memorizing the shape of me.

"Rough week," he says, voice low.

"Understatement of the year."

He smiles — that crooked half-smile that always feels like a secret — and leans in to press his forehead to mine.

"You okay?" he murmurs.

"No," I whisper. "But I am with you."

His breath hitches, just a little.

His hands move up my body until they land on my shoulders, giving them a gentle squeeze.

"You're tense."

"How can I not be?" I throw my hands up. "We're about to go head-to-head with Daniel and I'm trying to remember that I'm some badass Guild member, not a weak little girl who was beaten up so he could feel strong."

Tex watches me, then pulls out his phone.

"What you doing?" I place my hands on my hips. "I'm talking to you."

"I know." He nods as he taps on his phone, connecting it to my TV, and upbeat music starts to play. "But I don't think you need another conversation, you need movement."

He walks over, taking my hands in his, moving me back and forth.

I scowl at him, and he laughs.

"You need to dance it out, Iz. Can't have you going into this mission with your shoulders at your ears."

He spins me around and tickles my sides. I giggle and squirm.

"There you go! Loosen up!" He claps to the beat, moving his shoulders.

I smile as I watch him. He moves his head side to side, making silly faces at me while he pumps his arms.

"I thought you were good at dancing." I giggle.

"I can be, but letting loose isn't about being good; it's about releasing the tension. Go with the flow." He shimmies around me, then does an awkward twerk against me.

We laugh together, and I jump and just let my limbs fall where they do.

He continues wiggling and making faces. His knees go in and out as he moves his arms in front of him, while bobbing his head like a chicken.

We jump together and sing. He raps "Baby Got Back" and doesn't miss a single word. Tex beams when I laugh, while every time I make him laugh, the tension drains out of me faster and faster. Each muscle in my body relaxing.

He wraps his arms around me, kissing my forehead, then my nose.

"There she is." He smiles down at me.

I roll my eyes at him, and he chuckles.

"You can't tell me you don't feel better." He kisses me.

"I do." I wrap my arms around his neck.

"You gotta have fun every once in a while."

"What is this 'fun' you speak of?" I smirk.

He grins and tickles my sides again, my legs threatening to crumple before he scoops me up in his arms.

"I will never get tired of hearing your laugh." He spins us around, and I laugh again.

"You're good at pulling it out of me." I kiss his cheek. "Thank you, Tex."

"Anything for you, Iz."

36 THE COLD PRINCE

Jace

I don't knock. I don't know why I've even come. Habit, maybe. Or hope. Or something in between.

The hallway's dim, washed in that pale kind of light that makes everything feel softer than it is. My hand rests on the doorknob, fingers flexing once.

She's probably asleep. Still, I open it. Quietly. Carefully.

And then I see him. Tex. In her bed.

His arm wrapped around her bare waist, my territory, like he has any right to touch her in her sleep. As if he's earned it, or she'd choose him if she were awake.

Her face is tucked into the space between his neck and shoulder. Her hand curled over his chest like it belongs there.

It doesn't.

There's a sheet, but it doesn't hide much. Not the flushed skin. Not the mess of her hair, spilling across the pillow. Not the way they're tangled together like they've done this before. Like they've always done this.

The beast inside me rages, seeing her in the arms of another man. She's mine. She belongs to me.

My breath catches in my throat, but I don't move. Don't make a sound. I just stand there, fingers still on the knob, watching them in silence like some kind of fucking ghost.

I watch the rise and fall of her breathing, that little crease between her eyebrows she gets when she's dreaming. Even now, even unconscious, she's fighting something.

And he thinks he can soothe her? He thinks he can be her comfort?

Ridiculous.

She has no idea how many enemies she's made just by existing. How many knives wait for her back to turn. And Tex—that idiot—sleeps like a rock with his guard down, while she curls into him like he's safe.

No one can keep her safe like I do.

My pulse spikes, slow and lethal.

And I hate it. I hate that it hurts. I shouldn't stare. Shouldn't imagine sliding my hand where he is. Replacing it. Taking what he pretends he owns.

She's not his.

She's mine, whether either of us likes it or not.

If he were awake, he'd see the danger in my eyes. The warning. The promise of his blood.

The things I'm willing to do to protect what's mine.

I grip the edge of the doorframe, fingers curling into the wood. I should look away.

But I don't. I let it hurt.

I was molded to serve a purpose, to be a weapon.

One day soon, she'll look at me and finally understand.

I'm not going anywhere.

And I will burn down the world before I let anyone touch her like this again.

37 READY OR NOT

The room still smells like Tex. Leather. Smoke. Something warm I can't name. He's in the bathroom now, brushing his teeth with his hoodie half-zipped and humming like the world isn't about to turn inside out.

I'm already dressed.

Black tactical pants. Ribbed base layer. My jacket is tailored to hide blades in four different compartments. My boots are heavy and worn in, comfort in the form of violence.

I don't feel nervous. Not yet.

Just... steady.

Focused.

I braid my damp hair back and twist it into a knot, then swipe on a little liner in the mirror before stepping into the main room.

Jace is there.

Sitting on the couch, elbows on his knees, a folder balanced across one thigh and a cup of coffee cradled in his hand.

He's already in mission clothes, black and sharp and perfectly put together. His sleeves are rolled. His jaw is tight. He doesn't look up right away when I walk in.

When he does, it's for half a second.

"Hey," I say.

"Morning," he answers. His voice is neutral.

Something in my chest goes still. Before I can say anything else, he lifts the file and flicks through a page without looking at me.

"Lucian wants us at the command wing in twenty. Briefing room four."

I nod. "Okay. Thanks."

I wait for something more, a flicker of sarcasm, a question, even just eye contact.

Nothing.

He doesn't even look angry. Just... quiet. Guarded.

I feel Tex step into the room behind me, brushing close enough that his fingers graze my spine in passing. He grabs something from the counter and mumbles about coffee.

I glance back at Jace.

He's already on his feet, file under one arm, finishing the last sip from his cup.

He doesn't look at either of us as he heads for the door. And something about that silence stays with me. Even when the others arrive. Even when we fall into step, a unit again, all black boots and loaded gear and steel in our eyes. Even when we reach the command wing and I see the others, Guild members from across the world, gathered in suits and weapons, voices low, tension high.

I feel it.

The way Jace walks beside me without saying a word. The way his shoulder never touches mine. The way his eyes flick toward me... and away.

Something's shifted. I don't know what.

But I feel it like a bruise I didn't know I had. And I don't have time to ask.

Because Lucian is at the front of the room. Savvy, Max, Derek, and Preston, standing in silent support.

Just his presence, commanding, composed, and cold enough to cut steel.

"Daniel Mercer has crossed a line," he begins. "He's violated the Guild's code and weaponized black-market alliances to build something far more dangerous than we anticipated."

Behind him, a projected satellite image flares to life, a remote mountain facility surrounded by forest. Multiple buildings. Guard towers. Defensive turrets. Motion sensors.

"This compound was once a military research site. Decommissioned. Forgotten. Daniel's repurposed it. Our intel confirms he's been using it to develop and house next-gen weapons designed for mass-scale targeting."

The room shifts. Tension builds.

He continues, voice steady. "Multiple Guild teams will be deployed to infiltrate the facility tonight. Each team will enter through different access points and complete specific objectives: disable security, retrieve data, clear hostile presence. But only one team is tasked with securing the prototype."

He looks directly at us. "Team Three — led by Jace Ravencourt — will infiltrate through the north tunnel. You'll navigate underground service corridors to reach the central lab. That's where we believe the prototype is stored. This tech cannot fall into the wrong hands."

A schematic appears behind him, detailing multiple floors of the facility, server rooms, surveillance nodes, and sealed labs with unknown contents.

"Expect armed resistance. Expect mercenaries. And expect traps. You will have no comms once inside. Teams are on isolated blackout protocols to reduce trace exposure."

His tone sharpens. "This is not a test. And it's not a rescue mission. It's a strike. Suit up. Full briefing in thirty. We move at 0200."

The hall slowly empties, voices dropping to whispers, boots echoing across marble as teams peel off toward their respective prep rooms.

I feel the others pause behind me — Jace, Luca, Tex, Noah — but I don't move.

Neither does Lucian. His eyes meet mine across the space, and for a moment, there's no commander. No mission. Just my dad.

The boys drift away, giving us the illusion of privacy. It's only then that Lucian walks toward me, the lights from the map still glowing behind him. He stops a few feet away.

"You stayed quiet," he says softly.

"I was listening."

Lucian nods, then exhales through his nose, not quite a sigh, but something close. "You've always listened too well for your own good."

We stand there in silence, the hum of electricity and fading footsteps the only sound.

Then, more quietly, "You look so much like her."

He's never said that to me before.

"Mama?"

Lucian nods once. "The way you set your jaw when you're determined. The way you walk into a room like you belong in the center of it and dare anyone to say otherwise."

My throat tightens unexpectedly. I want to ask him more — about her, about us, about what he sees when he looks at me — but I can't find the words fast enough.

So instead, I say, "You're sending me into a place built like a fortress. Against mercenaries. You sure you're not the reckless one?"

That earns the faintest tug at the corner of his mouth.

"If I could keep you off this mission," he says, "I would. But this team is the best we have. And you..." He trails off, eyes darkening. "You're not one to hide away, Gracie."

I nod.

But he doesn't stop there. "I need you to come back," he says, voice barely above a whisper. "No heroics. No sacrifices. No last-minute changes to the plan. Do you understand me?"

I do. But I also know this world doesn't offer guarantees — especially not to people like us.

So, I meet his eyes and say, "I'll come back. You'll just have to trust me."

He stares at me for a long moment.

"You're your mother's fire," he murmurs. "And my storm."

He pulls me into a hug then nods toward the exit.

"Go," he says. "Suit up. I'll see you on the other side."

THE LOCKER ROOM IS COLD. Not the kind of cold that bites, but the kind that wraps around you slowly, sterile, industrial, humming faintly with fluorescent lights overhead.

The door clicks shut behind me. I'm alone.

The boys have gone to their own lockers or are already waiting in the mission wing. This room is mine—gray walls, black benches, rows of matte steel lockers. A digital display on one wall counts down from thirty minutes. Our launch window.

For the first time all day, there's silence.

No briefing. No eyes on me. No decisions to make.

Just my heartbeat and the low buzz of fluorescent lights.

I peel off my jacket and drop it onto the bench. My shirt follows. One layer at a time, I shed everything soft, everything familiar. I've done this before — training drills, mock missions — but this is different.

Because this is real.

I open the locker Lucian assigned to me. Inside is the gear I've been fitted for: tactical bodysuit, armored vest, comms earpiece, utility belt, gloves, and a sheathed blade engraved with the Guild crest.

I dress in silence.

Gloves last.

I flex my fingers once, testing the fit. They feel tighter than they did in training. Or maybe that's just me, the pressure, the adrenaline threading through every nerve.

What scares me is how much I want to be ready. How much I want to prove I'm not just the girl Daniel tried to break. That I'm not running anymore. That I'm not hiding.

I secure the last strap of my vest and reach for my knife. The handle is smooth, warm from the lights. It slides into place at my side like it belongs there.

The second locker is heavier.

When I open it, it hisses slightly, a secure weapons case built into the base. My ID tag flashes green as the biometric scanner accepts my clearance. The lid pops up with a soft click.

Inside: two handguns. One compact SMG. Two extra magazines. And a box of ammo stamped with a faint Guild seal.

I sit on the bench and take my time. There's something steadying about the routine, something almost meditative.

Click. Magazine in.

Slide back. Chamber check. Safety on.

The first handgun is a Glock—light, efficient, modified with a grip that fits my hand perfectly. The second is heavier, closer range with more stopping power. I tuck them into their holsters: one under my arm, the other at the small of my back.

I've done this a hundred times in training.

But never like this.

Never with this kind of finality. Every click echoes louder than it should.

No fear. No hesitation. Just the knowledge that this gear, this loadout — it's not for drills or simulations.

It's for real targets. Real danger.

Real blood.

I stand and recheck the gear once more, fingers brushing over each knife sheath, mag pouch, and strap until I know it all by muscle memory. There's a rhythm to it now. A sharpness in my movements I didn't have even weeks ago.

You're your mother's fire, Lucian said. *And my storm.*

I'm starting to believe him.

I look at myself again in the mirror, guns strapped across my body, hair tied back, eyes steady.

I don't look like a girl pretending anymore.

I look ready for war.

38 HERE WE GO

The corridor hums with low energy as we file into the mission bay one by one, shadows slipping into formation. Final checks. Secured gear. Loaded weapons. The scent of gun oil and steel clings to the air.

We're minutes from launch.

Jace is beside me as I double-check my vest and pull my gloves tighter. His presence is quiet, steady — like it always is — but now it hums beneath the surface. A thread between us.

He waits until the others are a few steps ahead, then leans in close. "I need to talk to you."

"Not now."

He reaches for my hand but I pull away. "No, Jace. I can't do this with you."

He freezes. "Please, Isobel. I just need a moment."

I turn and stare. "What, Jace? You've been icy to me all morning, and now you want to talk?"

"I just..." He runs his hand through his hair, then steps up to me, reaching for my face.

"No, Jace." I smack his hand away.

His eyes harden. "You're choosing him."

I stare up into his eyes, like he can see everything inside me. "I said, not now."

He holds my gaze for a moment. Then he lifts his hand, pulling off his ring, holding it out to me.

"Take it." His jaw flexes.

"Your Guild ring?" I arch an eyebrow.

"Please, I just need to make sure you're safe."

"How will this keep me safe?" I stare at him.

"There's a tracker embedded in the metal. Noah would be able to track it if anything happens to you."

I stare down at the ring. It's icy silver, most likely white gold. Cold, elite. The dark blue sapphire glints with some brightness hidden in its depths. It represents Jace perfectly.

"Fine." I take the ring and tuck it into the inner lining of my vest, pulling the zipper to secure it. His eyes heat as it rests against my chest.

I turn before he can say anything else.

I fall into step with the team, my weapons balanced across my body, my heart steady in my chest, and Jace's gaze burning quietly at my side.

The transport hums beneath us, low and steady, like the breath of something alive. None of us speak. The air is too thick, with sweat, with silence, with everything we left unsaid.

Jace sits across from me, rifle resting in his lap, eyes locked forward. His jaw is tight. Focused. The kind of stillness that comes before impact.

Tex is next to me, shoulder to shoulder, warm and solid. He hasn't said a word since boarding. His leg bounces faintly, and I can see the fire in his eyes, the itch to move, to fight.

Noah's checking their comms, recalibrating the shared channel one last time. "Ping test: green across all units."

Luca flashes me a grin like it's a joke, but even his edges are sharp tonight.

The cabin lights shift from white to red. Five minutes.

The dropship starts its descent, tilting lower through the trees. I can feel the change in air pressure. My stomach flips, and my fingers clench around the harness at my hips.

Outside the window, nothing but darkness and fog. Our target lies buried beneath a mountain range that looks dead from above, no thermal signatures, no comms. But we know what's under it. A fortress. Mercenaries. Prototypes built to kill. And somewhere inside, the weapon Daniel's betting his war on.

Jace stands first.

"All right," he says, voice low. "This is it. We drop in silent, no chatter. Single-file through the north tunnel. Suppressors on. Tex, you take point. Luca, cover rear. Noah, you're second. Isobel, on me."

We all nod.

He meets my eyes for half a second longer than necessary, just long enough that I feel it in my chest, and then the bay doors slide open with a *hiss*. Wind howls through the chamber. A metal staircase drops down, swallowing itself into the dark earth below.

We move. One by one, boots hit steel. Then dirt. Then cold stone.

By the time I reach the bottom, the dropship is already gone, swallowed by fog, the sound of its retreat muffled by the trees.

Silence presses in.

Tex signals forward, rifle up, eyes alert.

We enter the tunnel.

It's carved from old rock, reinforced in parts with metal beams and rusted scaffolding. Moisture slicks the walls. Our footsteps echo, soft and careful. Every breath tastes like iron and dust.

Luca's voice whispers in my ear through the comms. "Tunnel forks in thirty. Stay left."

I move closer to Jace, just behind his right side. He glances back, just once, to check on me, and then we keep moving.

We're ghosts now. Five shadows beneath the world, slipping into the mouth of something we may not walk out of. But we don't stop. We move forward. The tunnel narrows before it opens into a junction chamber, stone giving way to steel.

We halt.

Noah moves ahead, crouching low, and pulls out a small device from his belt. The screen glows faintly green as he scans the doorway.

"Motion sensors. Infrared grid. Passive trip alerts," he mutters. "Nothing lethal, not here. They're watching movement."

"How long to loop the feed?" Jace asks.

"Forty seconds if I'm perfect. Sixty if I mess up and we all die."

"Don't mess up," Luca says dryly.

Noah flashes him a tight smile and starts working. Wires coil into the panel beside the door, fingers flying fast, and I watch his jaw tighten in focus.

Tex shifts behind us, watching the rear. His stance is loose, but I can tell he's ready to lunge at the first shadow.

I glance up. The tunnel's ceiling bristles with old tech, a collapsed ventilation system, security nodes blinking red. We're in.

Too far to turn back now.

"Got it," Noah breathes. "Looping begins, now."

The door hisses open. We move fast.

The chamber beyond is wide, part lab, part storage. Glass consoles. Abandoned terminals. Crates stamped with blacked-out logos. There's a faint hum in the air, like the walls are alive.

"Cameras up top," Jace murmurs. "Noah?"

"Still looped. But we've got thirty seconds. Tops."

We sweep the room.

Tex takes the right flank, disappearing behind a column of crates. Luca scales a short ladder to check the catwalk overhead. I stick close to Jace, my SMG drawn, scanning the far corners.

Nothing.

Too quiet.

Jace gestures to a sealed door on the far side. "That's our way in. Lab's through there."

Noah's already beside it, cracking the next lock.

"You okay?" Jace murmurs, low enough only I can hear.

I steady my breath. "Yeah."

He doesn't ask again.

The door opens with a sigh, revealing a long hallway bathed in artificial white light. Lab coats lie discarded on the floor. A coffee cup, long discarded, sits beside a crashed tablet.

It's like the whole place was abandoned in a heartbeat.

"Keep eyes up," Jace says. "If they knew we were coming, they'll wait till we're deep."

Tex swings back into place at the front. We move forward, tight formation, boots silent on the tile.

At the end of the hall, a reinforced door stands sealed with biometric sensors glowing red.

I step closer to read the sign etched above the door in thin block letters:

SECTOR 4 — PROTOTYPE STORAGE

Luca lets out a low whistle. "Looks like we found the right place."

Jace turns to Noah. "Can you get us in?"

"I can try," Noah mutters. "But I'll need time."

Jace scans the corners. "Then we cover him."

We form a perimeter around the door as Noah unpacks his tools again, cracking into the wall's access panel.

Tick. Tick. Tick.

Each second feels like a countdown. I flex my fingers around my weapon. We're here. This is it.

The door slides open with a sharp hiss. Cold air rushes out, metallic and sterile.

We step inside. The lights flicker overhead, dimmer than the hallway, tinged faintly blue. The room is massive, rectangular, lined with reinforced glass cases and dark crates, each one labeled in code.

Weapons meant for people like us, to kill people like us.

Noah's voice is a whisper through the comms. "I've never seen half this tech before."

"Don't touch anything unless I say," Jace warns.

We move through the aisles, splitting into a wide sweep. My boots click softly against the floor. Every surface reflects ghostly shadows, warped by glass and frost.

I pause in front of one case.

Inside is something long and sleek, like a rifle, but not. Its barrel is jagged, non-standard. There's no trigger. Only a pulse module.

This isn't normal weaponry.

This is black market innovation. This is Daniel's playground.

Beside me, Luca exhales low. "You feel that?"

I nod. It's not just the chill. It's the silence. Too deep. Too empty. Like we're walking through a memory. Not a live facility.

Jace calls out softly, "We sweep fast. Mark anything that looks active. Extraction team is ten minutes behind."

As the others move ahead, I pause, fingers resting on the side of one glass panel.

And I murmur, almost to myself, "This is too easy."

The words hang in the air.

Jace hears. He stops walking, turns halfway back toward me. His jaw tightens. "Say that again?"

"It's too clean," I whisper. "Too quiet. No guards. No heat signatures. No dead ends. It's like... he wanted us to get in."

The air shifts. Behind us, the door *slams* shut with a mechanical shriek. A loud clunk echoes through the chamber, magnetic locks slamming into place.

Tex curses. "Shit."

Lights above us snap red. A voice crackles to life over the comm system, deep, distorted by static. But the tone is unmistakable.

Calm. Cold. Familiar.

Daniel.

"Welcome to my house," he says.

I freeze.

"Did you think I wouldn't see you coming? That I wouldn't recognize my own blood walking through my front door?"

Jace raises his weapon, eyes scanning the corners. "Cover! Now!"

We scatter, behind crates, under cover, weapons up. But no guards pour in. No assault team.

Just his voice. Filling the chamber like a ghost.

"You always had her fire, Isobel," Daniel continues. "I almost snuffed it out, but you've spent too long learning from people who don't understand what true power *is*."

"Shut it down," Jace hisses to Noah.

"I'm trying," Noah growls, ripping into the wall's control panel. "He's overridden the primary circuit. We're locked in."

I clench my jaw. My grip tightens on my SMG.

"I should've killed you both the day I found her," Daniel says. "But you…" There's a soft, thoughtful pause. "You were a good experiment. Let's see how far you've come."

The lights *cut out.*

Darkness swallows the chamber.

Then— a faint, electric whirring. Something powering up. Multiple somethings.

Behind the glass, one of the crates *shifts*. And then another.

Inside them?

Movement.

Jace curses under his breath. "He's not sending guards."

He lifts his weapon as the first crate door *blasts open* and a humanoid form steps into the red-lit chamber.

"He's sending machines."

The first machine lunges from the shadows.

It's fast. Too fast.

Metal slams into the floor with a screech as the humanoid form bounds forward, tall, silver-sleek, no face. Just a glowing red eye at its center and clawed limbs that move with terrifying precision.

Jace fires.

Rounds punch into its shoulder, sparking on contact, but it doesn't stop. It *adjusts*, jerks sideways, and comes again.

"DOWN!" Jace roars.

I dive left as the bot smashes through a crate where I stood seconds before. Splinters explode across the floor.

Tex meets it head-on.

His fist crashes into the bot's side, then again — metal-on-metal, raw power — but the thing absorbs it, twists, and backhands him across the chamber.

"Tex!" I scream.

He hits the floor hard, rolling to recover. "Still alive," he grunts. "Bastard's got a hydraulic core."

More crates shatter open. Three. Five. Seven. Figures spill into the room, some humanoid, others animalistic, all fast and brutal. A storm of claws and metal limbs. Gleaming red sensors lock onto us, their prey.

Noah drops to one knee and fires a round into a jointed leg. It drops. Sparks fly. "Aim for the seams!" he shouts.

Jace spins beside me, unloading a mag into another one's torso, then switching to a sidearm in the same breath. "Go for the connectors. They're armoring the cores."

"Since when do prototypes move like this?" Luca yells, ducking a spinning blade that nearly takes off his head.

I bolt forward, sliding under a table as one of the smaller machines lurches past me. Its head swivels 180 degrees. It leaps. I twist, jam one of my daggers into its neck seam — *pop* — and wrench it free just before it collapses in a rain of sparks.

My chest heaves.

I look up.

The room is *chaos*.

Red lights pulse. Jace is shouting orders. Tex grabs one bot by the arm and *rips* it off with brute force. Noah hurls an EMP charge across the floor, and one machine collapses in a twitching heap.

Luca's knife slashes into exposed wiring, spraying black fluid. "I'm gonna need a damn upgrade after this!"

I duck behind cover, fire a burst of rounds into a creeping spiderlike drone. "You're doing fine!"

A massive bot — easily twice my size — thunders toward me. My SMG's empty. I throw it down, yank the pistol from my vest, and fire point-blank into its knee joint.

It *staggers*.

Jace is there in an instant, vaulting onto its back, planting a round directly into the control node. The bot collapses in a heap.

"You good?" he breathes, reaching for me.

"Still breathing."

We spin, backs to each other, scanning the room. The last machine twitches, half-melted by Noah's EMP, Luca finishing it with a clean strike.

And then...

Silence.

The red lights still flicker. The air tastes like ozone and metal.

I lower my weapon slowly, breath ragged.

We're alive. Barely.

39 FORGED IN BLOOD

The room is still ringing with the echo of my voice when we hear it.
Clap. Clap. Clap.

Slow. Measured. Mocking.

The sound carries, amplified by the steel walls, drawing all of our eyes upward.

There, on the second-floor catwalk, under the flickering red emergency lights... Daniel.

Alive. Whole. Smiling like a goddamn king.

He's in dark tactical gear, crisp and clean. His arms are folded over the railing. Behind him, two guards in heavy body armor stand motionless.

My mouth dries out.

Jace steps in front of me, shielding without touching. Tex lifts his weapon. Noah grabs his arm, whispering, "*Not yet.*"

Daniel's smirk widens.

"Well, well, there she is," he says, voice clearer now that it's no longer filtered through static. "My little survivor. My pretty, poisonous girl."

My spine stiffens.

Jace growls under his breath. "One more word and he dies."

"No," I whisper. "Not yet."

Daniel leans forward on the railing like he's settling in for a show. "Did you like my welcome party?" he asks. "Custom built. A lot of money. But you were always worth the investment, Izzy."

Tex snarls, "Say her name again and I'll rip your tongue out."

Daniel's gaze flicks toward him lazily. "The guard dog speaks."

Jace's voice is a blade. "You're going to regret coming out of your hole."

Daniel ignores him. His eyes — cold, calculating — stay on me.

"I watched you in that fight. You've grown teeth. Claws. But don't let them lie to you, sweetheart. You're still mine, where it counts. Still broken in the ways I made you."

I take a step forward. "You're right about one thing," I say. "You made me."

The boys tense. Jace's hand hovers near his weapon.

"But not into what you think," I go on. "You didn't make me weak. You made me *ready*. For people like you."

He laughs, but it's tight now, clipped. "You think you can take me on?"

"Without a doubt."

Behind me, I feel the others fall in beside me. Not in front. Not behind. Beside.

Daniel straightens, the smile slipping.

"I should've killed you when I had the chance," he mutters.

"You had plenty of chances," I say. "And now? You're out of time."

His guards step forward slightly, but he lifts a hand to stop them.

"You want to prove you're not afraid?" Daniel calls down. "Then come find me."

He presses something at his wrist.

A door on the far side of the chamber hisses open, access to the upper levels.

And then he turns and walks away.

Like we're not worth his time.

The moment the steel door hisses open, Jace is already moving. "Let's go."

Tex doesn't wait for a second order; he's on Daniel's trail like a predator unleashed. Luca mutters something sharp under his breath and pulls his blade tighter in his grip. Noah grabs his tablet and runs a quick scan ahead, already plotting the quickest route.

I'm right behind them.

The second we pass through the threshold, the air shifts, less lab, more fortress. Metal catwalks, concrete stairwells, fluorescent lighting buzzing overhead. We move fast, boots slamming against steel, weapons drawn.

"He's trying to draw us in," Jace says through clenched teeth as we climb the stairs. "Trying to break formation, make us reckless."

"It won't work," I bite out.

But my blood is pounding.

Because I want him.

Not just stopped. I want him at my feet.

"Don't let him get under your skin"—I turn to look at the guys— "you let your emotions take over, we get sloppy, then mistakes happen."

We hit the first landing, a long corridor with doors on either side, some open, some sealed shut. Red overhead lights pulse as the facility begins full lockdown. It doesn't matter.

We push forward.

Noah points down the hall. "Motion detected. Northeast wing. He's running."

Jace nods. "Cut him off from the right."

We split into a tactical V-formation, Luca and Noah peeling off to flank while Jace, Tex, and I charge straight through the middle.

Door after door blurs past me. I don't stop. I don't blink.

And then— A shadow darts across the far end of the hall.

Daniel.

He turns a corner.

Jace is already barking commands. "Tex, breach the side door. Isobel, with me!"

We pivot fast, crashing through an alternate hallway. The floors are slick with condensation. Pipes overhead groan like the building itself is trying to slow us down.

We don't stop. A stairwell looms ahead, narrow, steep. Daniel's boots clang above us.

"I've got visual!" Luca shouts through the comms. "He's heading toward the training grounds."

The door seals behind us with a *clang* of finality.

The night air is bitterly cold, slicing across sweat-slick skin. Floodlights mounted along the rooftop perimeter cast long, stark shadows over the training grounds, a concrete jungle of raised platforms, narrow pillars, blocks and walls of all sizes spread across the rooftop like a deadly playground.

Tex gives a sharp nod and slips to the left, vanishing into the concrete maze. Luca charges down the center with Noah on his flank, seamlessly fading into the shadows. Jace taps my arm once, and we break right.

"Stay alert," Jace mutters, sweeping his rifle left to right. "Watch for trip wires, traps, gas. Anything."

My fingers tighten around my pistol. My heart's still pounding from the sprint, but this— this is worse. This is the waiting.

"He knew we'd make it this far," Luca's voice filters through my earpiece. "He wants a show."

Tex lets out a low growl. "Let's not disappoint him."

A speaker above crackles to life again.

No words. Just music. A slow, crackling waltz, something old and broken, warped by static. It drifts through the grounds like a taunt.

Jace's voice is low. "He's playing with us."

"No," I whisper. "He's *stalling*."

A flicker of movement. I spin, gun raised—Nothing.

But the hairs on the back of my neck stay standing.

We walk further. Luca and Noah rejoin us. We don't speak.

My heart stops cold.

Daniel stands near the center, just beyond a towering stack of concrete blocks. His stance relaxed but ready. The lights paint his face in hard lines, making the grin on his lips look *inhuman*.

No armor. No weapons in hand.

Just a gun holstered at his side, and a sickening calm in his eyes.

He's waiting for us. Just looking at me.

"I gave you everything, Isobel. A home. Food. Structure. You think Lucian would've protected you the way I did? You think he even cared you existed?"

"Don't talk about him."

"Why not?" He holds his hands out. "We've got nothing but time. Where is your sperm donor, anyway? Hiding in the base as usual, letting everyone else do the work for him?"

Daniel looks around. "He stole the love of my life away from me, but I got her and more back, didn't I, baby?" Spit flies from his mouth like he's gone feral.

"I'm not sure you're capable of love."

"I was the one who shaped you. You were nothing when I got you. Weak. Fragile."

"I was *five*," I snap.

That calm smile twitches, falters for half a breath.

"You *beat* me," I say, the words sharp and sudden, like broken glass. "You starved me when I disobeyed. You *sold me* when you ran out of money. You made me bleed and then told me it was love."

His face hardens. "You were supposed to die. But your mother wouldn't stay compliant unless I had you as a bargaining chip. Nevertheless, you were strong enough to survive."

"I was a child." My voice rises. "And you, were a manipulative coward with a belt and a sick sense of power."

The silence that follows is electric.

"I loved you, you know," Daniel says after a long moment. "In my own way."

"No," I say, stepping forward. "You don't get to call it that."

He watches me carefully now. Measuring.

"You're not afraid of me anymore," he says.

"No."

"You should be."

"I'm not."

An evil grin spreads across Daniel's face. "Oh, Isobel." He lets out a sharp whistle.

From the shadows—they step forward.

Men. Armed. Silent. Clad in dark tactical gear. Dozens. Emerging from side corridors, maintenance hatches, behind stacked crates. *Surrounding us.*

Then Tex.

Two men drag him forward. There's a cut on his head. Blood running down the side of his face. Two men holding his arms tightly.

My stomach drops, my pulse quickening. Every sound dulls except the rush of blood in my ears.

My hands tighten into fists.

We're boxed in.

"Oh, look what I found," he says, a deranged laugh ringing through the air. "A little birdie told me this one's important to you."

I keep my face blank. *What bird?* I mentally shake off his words. He's toying with me. He always does. I won't give him my fear.

"You're so full of shit."

"Oh, Isobel." He tsks. "You are so beautiful, so strong and determined," he adds, voice almost tender. Then, low and gleeful, "Wonder if you'll still have that same look when you take me in your mouth. You looked so good on my cock."

Rage tears through me.

Jace raises his gun.

Daniel lifts his hand. "Ah-ah, I wouldn't do that if I were you." He holds a gun pointed at Tex.

I don't flinch. I don't look away from Daniel. "You're pathetic." I can't help but grit my teeth. "You had to rape an eighteen-year-old girl."

"Oh, but you wanted it." He looks at the guys, taunting them. "She barely fought me. She just laid there and took it like a good girl."

Tex fights against the two men holding him but he can't break free.

I raise my weapon, eyes locked on Daniel.

"I wonder if you suck better cock now." He licks his lips.

"You sick fuck! Keep running your mouth and see what happens," Tex yells at him.

One of the guys punches his ribs. Tex huffs a breath. Daniel laughs.

"You've trained this one well." Daniel glances at me then back to Tex.

I tear my eyes away from Tex. I can't let the panic show on my face.

"So, what do you want?" I call out to him, trying to stall for time.

"Oh, Isobel, I want you to be mine. Mommy's getting a bit old, and honestly, she's not so lively nowadays."

I hate my name in his mouth, it makes me grind my back teeth. Something in me goes still. The fear burns out, replaced by heat. My eyes move to Tex—bloodied, restrained, breathing through the pain— then the men holding him, at Daniel, standing like this is peak entertainment. All I can think about is tearing him apart right now, shooting him right in his stupid, smug face.

"I see the fire in your eyes." He taunts, grinning wide. "Let's see how strong you'll be."

A gunshot cracks through the night.

Loud. Final.

I'm frozen. My breath hitches. No.

No.

I watch Tex crumple, knees buckling, his body slamming against the concrete with a sickening thud.

Daniel's gun is still raised, smoke curling from the barrel.

He shot him.

He shot Tex.

A scream tears from my throat before I can think. "TEX!"

Gunfire erupts around me all at once.

Automatic rounds shredding through the night, splintering concrete, lighting the shadows with flashes of muzzle fire.

Shouts ring out. Orders. Panic. Chaos.

I don't care.

I'm already running.

I'm running from one block to another. Every instinct is screaming to take cover. But I won't leave him alone.

Someone yells my name. I don't stop.

A bullet clips the concrete beside me.

I flinch, duck, sprint.

The air reeks of smoke, blood, and gunpowder.

"Hold on, Tex, I'm coming—" My voice cracks, my throat thick with pain.

I drop behind a low concrete barrier for cover, my heart slamming against my ribs.

Tears blur my vision.

This wasn't supposed to happen.

He wasn't supposed to...

I peek out.

Daniel's gone.

His men are moving back through the concrete blocks but still engaged.

All I can see is Tex lying motionless in a growing pool of red.

I scream his name and launch toward him, slipping across the slick concrete as I reach his side. Blood pours from his torso, bright and fast and *wrong*.

"No—no, no, no—" I press down hard, hands already soaked.

His body arches with a groan.

"Reinforcements ETA: one minute!" Noah shouts from somewhere.

Tex coughs, blood flecking his lips. "Iz..."

"I'm here," I choke out. "You're okay. You're going to be okay." Tears roll down my cheeks.

His hand finds mine, gripping tight, *too tight*. Desperate. "Don't... cry for me."

"Shut up," I hiss. "You're not going anywhere."

An explosion rocks the far side of the training ground.

"I need a medical bag!" I scream.

"Coming!" Noah tears toward me, dodging gunfire, diving over a narrow pillar to slide into place beside us. "Iz... It's not going to help."

"Hand it over, Noah!"

"There's too much blood! That bullet hit something major."

"I don't care," I growl at him. "Help me!"

He shoves supplies in my hands. "He doesn't have long," he murmurs low.

Noah places a hand on Tex's shoulder, squeezing it.

Tex's grip loosens.

"Hey! Hey—stay awake!" I press harder, heart pounding so loud it drowns the battle.

Because in this moment, there's only the blood.

Only the fear.

Only *Tex*.

His grip slips.

"Don't you dare." My voice is barely a whisper, trembling as I lean over him, pressing both palms harder into the wound. "You're fine. You're going to be fine. We've gotten out of worse, remember?"

Tex's eyes are glassy. He coughs, blood bubbling at the corner of his mouth, and he tries to smile through it. His chest rises in shallow, broken pulls.

"This can't be happening," I choke, shaking my head like I can shake the truth away. "Fight, Tex, Fight!"

He reaches into his pocket, pulling something out. His hand finds mine. It's weak but still warm. He squeezes once. Pressing the rough object into my hands.

I know what it is without even looking at it.

"No, Tex. No."

"Take it, Iz." He coughs, the sound wet and wrong. "I'll be watching over you."

"You're not dying, Tex."

Tex takes my hands from his chest and holds them.

"Hey! What are you doing? You'll bleed—"

"Iz, just be with me."

"Tex," I choke on air. "Please, don't do this."

"It's okay." He closes his eyes for a moment, and when he opens them there's something more terrifying there. Acceptance. "You'll be okay."

My chest caves. "Please, you can't—*don't leave me.*"

"Don't be sad," he says. "Promise me."

Something in his eyes shatters me entirely.

"I-I promise." I sob.

"I'll always be with you." He pushes the words out as he squeezes my hands tight.

I can't speak. All the things I want to say. But there's not enough time.

"Don't forget me." He chuckles.

I hold onto the sound, trying to commit it to my memory. Because I know this will be the last time I hear it.

"As if I could ever forget you." I cough out a watery laugh, trying to give him a smile.

"She's calling for me." His blue eyes look past me. "She says I've kept her waiting."

I close my eyes, dropping my head, as my heart tears itself apart.

"Go to her... Go to Ellie. She needs you."

His eyes flutter open one last time, and somehow, he still manages a smile, crooked, familiar, *Tex.*

"Tex—"

"I love you."

I watch the light leave his eyes.

His chest deflates.

Hands falling away from mine.

It's *quiet.*

Like he took all the air with him.

I press my forehead to his and whisper, "I love you too."

FORGED IN BETRAYAL
- COMING IN 2026

Thank you so much for reading! If you liked Forged in Blood, please consider leaving a review! It would mean more than you know.

Reviews help indie authors find new readers and keep stories like Isobel's alive.

Even a few words—what you felt, a favorite moment, or just one word—makes a real difference.

Thank you again for taking the time with Isobel's story. I can't wait for you to read the next book in the series, Forged in Betrayal.

ACKNOWLEDGMENTS

There are so many people to thank for making this dream come true.

To my boyfriend — thank you for being my steady place, my loudest cheerleader, and the voice that always tells me, *"You can do this."* Your support made every late night and every rough draft feel like a little less of a storm. You are my anchor, my lifeline, and my rock. I love you endlessly.

To Jenn. My other brain cell. Thank you for reminding me that no matter how dark it gets, there is always someone worth holding on for. You always support me in anything and everything. You never fail to make me laugh or help me figure out a solution to a problem. I'm incredibly blessed to have someone like you in my life. My ride or die.

To D.M. Randall, thank you for being an amazing friend. Meeting you has truly been a blessing. Thank you for all of your help, encouragement, and advice. You have helped so tremendously. Isobel's story is infinitely better thanks to you. You have made me a better writer and reader. I cannot thank you enough for being an exceptional human being.

To my parents — thank you for supporting my dream. Thanks for holding up your side of the bet, Dad. Thanks, Mom, for sending me to writing camps as a kid.

To my brother, Jasper, Aunt Sandra, Grandma Thresa, and my Great Uncle. I love you all and thank you for loving me unconditionally.

To my editor, Sarah Ridding. Thank you for helping me and making my dreams come true. You gave me the confidence I needed from the start.

To the readers who picked up this book: thank you for giving Isobel's story a chance. I hope you love her and the boys as much as I do.

To the readers who cheered for this book when it was just a messy draft on a reading app: thank you for believing in me before I did.

To my Beta readers: Annelle, Comet, and Julie. Thank you for your kind words and feedback.

To my friends who cheered me on and encouraged me. Thank you for your support.

And finally, to the little girl I used to be: you made it. We made it.

With love,
Kitt Fiona

ABOUT THE AUTHOR

Kitt Fiona has been writing stories for as long as she can remember — from scribbling in notebooks to crafting full-length novels fueled by chocolate, snacks, and just enough chaos. A passionate storyteller at heart, Kitt finds magic in the details.

She's a collector of Pokémon cards and beautiful notebooks she's too afraid to write in, a designer and crocheter of custom Pokémon plushies (yes, she takes orders), and someone who just has too many hobbies. When she's not deep in her fictional worlds, you'll find her belting Ariana Grande, dancing to Sabrina Carpenter, or cuddled up with her three dogs: Honey, her emotional support sweetheart, Zeus, the lovable goofball who still thinks he's a lap dog, and Link, the sweetest cuddle bug who just wants to be loved. Possibly playing *Stardew Valley* or *Pokémon*.

Kitt also wants to thank her boyfriend of almost four years, who has supported her endlessly through every plot twist, creative obsession, and midnight brainstorming session. His love and encouragement have been her anchor — always cheering her on and embracing every one of her hobbies with a smile.

Now, with a heart full of stories and a keyboard full of characters still waiting their turn, Kitt is beyond thrilled to share her world with readers.

www.ingramcontent.com/pod-product-compliance
Lightning Source LLC
LaVergne TN
LVHW091702070526
838199LV00050B/2257